BY DAWN'S EARLY LIGHT

Echoes of Liberty, Book 1

JASON FUESTING

Ordered Operations

By Dawn's Early Light

ISBN: 9781090703064

Published by: Ordered Operations, Inc.

Cover Design: © 2019 Cedar Sanderson

Structural Editing: D Jason Fleming

Acknowledgments

Thanks, Cedar and Amanda (both of you), without the three of you, this would never have been finished. Thanks to the rest of the crazies and mad geniuses that helped me along the way. Finally, Elizabeth Bannon, that first story I started writing for you so long ago helped keep the dream alive.

Ice

———

Space was dangerous on a good day, a day when everyone knew what to do. Improvisation only adds to the danger and so far everything had been improvisation. Nobody on the *Fortune* had a choice, or rather the choice was unsettlingly clear: ice or asphyxiation.

"Nothing's ever easy," Eric mumbled to himself as he stared at the displays projected against the inside of his helmet. *Radar is green. Ish. Links to all team members, green. Main link back to the Fortune, green. Task status, then O2 checks.*

Eric blinked, trying to ease the eyestrain from the hours of watching his men through monochrome green light enhancement. A sparkling green haze, the leftovers from the last three hours, clouded the view around him.

Hours of boredom, stuck in a suit while we pry apart an ice comet.

Eric yawned as he checked the time display.

"Team one, status," he said.

"Anchors set, connected to the tether," came the reply.

Eric glanced to his right. Barely visible above a distant ridge of ice, team one's lead gave him a thumbs up.

Good, almost done.

He glanced at his millimeter wave display and its thousands of moving contacts. A frown creased his brow as he looked at the blinking overload indicator on the display. *We really need to find upgrades for these suits. How am I supposed to warn people if my gear can't track everything?*

"Team two," he started. Flickering red on the radar display stilled his tongue. "Indy, looks like we've got another wave of stuff incoming from eleven o'clock. Take cover. Looks small, but it's going at a good clip."

"Copy that," Indy responded.

Dozens of red dots amid the sea of blue contacts winked in and out of his display as his suit's computer strained against the number of simultaneous objects it could track. Each heartbeat brought them closer. *All going the same direction. Wait. Shit.* His display lit up with a cascade of yellows following a different vector.

Eric pressed against the ice as he blurted, "All teams take cover!"

Breathing hard, he glanced in team three's direction. A huge red contact lit up the radar display. *That's almost on top of--* A large shadow streaked through the haze, sending shards of ice and rock debris billowing in its wake. *Wow, that was close. That had to be what was causing those yellow returns.*

Cautiously, Eric pushed back from the ice and spoke, "Teams, sound off!"

"Team one clear, all we got was a light peppering. No damage."

Silence.

"Team two?" Eric asked.

Digitally distorted static erupted from his headset. Eric gritted his teeth for several moments before the transmission ended. Eric sighed and pounded the side of his helmet with a fist hard enough to fritz his low-light projection with each strike.

"Say again, team two," Eric said.

"Team two clear. We got peppered pretty hard but somehow nobody's hurt. Also, anchor set and tethered."

"Team three clear. Set and tethered."

About time, we're done here.

"Roger, Indy. Prep to return to the *Fortune*. I'd like to get out of here before something else happens," Eric replied. His eyes narrowed as he looked over the status of his team. "Sokolov?"

"What?" Richard Sokolov growled.

Eric sighed.

"Stow it, Dick. Getting some odd readings over here, check your O2. Think you might have a leak."

"Hold on. Nope, gauge says I'm just fi-- *blyad*!" Static.

"What's going on?" Eric demanded. Sokolov seldom fell back into his native tongue. The ice cloud obscured the man's last known position.

"Was looking at the gauge and it just dropped half through the yellow. *Yeblya lezha pribor*! Who the hell did we loot this shit from?"

"We didn't," Indy chimed in. "Your suit's original to the ship. Probably a hundred years old."

"Great. Just great," Sokolov groused.

"Cut it, you two," Eric grunted. "Sokolov, you reading a little under ten minutes left?"

"More or less."

"Looks like my monitor is accurate. We should be back long before you're sucking vac. You good?" Sokolov grumbled. "Everyone, get back to the cable and hook on," Eric ordered before switching channels. "Desi, Friedrich. Anchors are in, we should be good. Sokolov took a strike. He's okay, but his suit is leaking. Don't take your time reeling us in."

"I can only reel in so quickly. The cradle's only rated for a certain impact," Desi's exotic accent rolled across the radio. Eric knew next to nothing about her past, other than overhearing her mention where she grew up, Orleans.

A vibration through the line from the winch signaled their trip to safety had begun and Eric eyed the haze as it drifted past them. Shifts of three teams each had worked the last eighteen hours to cut this ice comet into four fragments. One by one, each fragment had been reeled in and secured in the bay below him.

Last one. We've been lucky. Too lucky. A bead of sweat trailed down the side of his neck, just where he couldn't do anything about it in the confines of the suit. A sudden chill down his spine sent Eric checking his millimeter wave warning display again. *Nothing big, nothing fast.*

Eric relaxed as the cable pulled them clear of the debris cloud toward a stretch of what appeared empty black to the naked eye amidst the surrounding star field. Magnified many-fold by the enhancement rig grafted into his helmet, the feeble illumination from the system's distant star reflected brilliantly off the edges of a pair of bent hull plates amidships. Four square meters of steel plating sealed the rent just inside the shadow cast by the ship. He stared at a stretch of darker steel peeking from the patch. That puncture had vented Environmental Control into the void. *What is that?* Eric looked closer and then averted his eyes from the frozen smear of blood left by the doomed technician who had almost been lucky. The *Fortune* had seen better days.

"*Mon chéri,*" Desi broke his reverie. "The captain ordered an orbit change once the cargo has been retrieved. Lt. Pascal will meet you in the bay."

"Roger that, Desi." *What now?*

His light amplification faded out as lights flickered on in the bay ahead. Eric and his team unhooked and kicked off the comet fragment, reorienting to land boots down. He absorbed most of the landing with bent legs and his boots jerked as the maglocks engaged. While his team of miscreants filed through the airlock, Eric watched the ice comet shard drift into the bay and strike the makeshift cradle the engineers had cobbled together.

Eric winced as vibrations from the bowing cradle shot up his legs. Cracks spidered across the fragment's surface. Smaller chunks and ice dust leapt from the fragment and bounced off the deck below. After a few unnerving seconds, both the cradle and the comet stilled.

"Guess the engineers earned their pay, eh, Friedrich?"

Eric glanced over his shoulder to find Lt. Pascal.

"I'd say so, sir. Wasn't sure if the cradle was going to collapse or if the fragment was going to shatter like the first one did."

Pascal nodded and sighed, "Yeah, what a pain in the ass."

Eric shifted his weight as he glanced about the hanger before asking, "So, LT, why are we staying out here and not going in with the others?"

"Sensors guys picked up an object nearby," Pascal replied. Eric felt vibrations through his boots and grabbed for the nearby stanchion as the *Fortune*'s acceleration pulled at him. "We're matching orbits and checking it out."

"Nothing out here but ice, sir. What's worth burning fuel when we're low as it is?"

The lieutenant smiled.

Eric asked, "What?"

"You're right, Friedrich. There's supposed to be nothing out here but ice. This thing, whatever it is, has too much mass to be just ice. At least that's what Simon told the captain."

"So an honest asteroid?"

"Not likely. Our sensors are still jacked up and the cloud isn't helping. Return's unusual for an asteroid or a comet fragment at this orbital. We'll find out shortly. Should be alongside in five or six minutes, so you've got time to change out tanks."

Eric shrugged and walked over to the stowage locker to do as suggested.

Weird, but whatever. Just want to hit my rack, but I guess that's not happening any time soon.

At least Lieutenant Pascal's estimate turned out to be accurate. Eric's clock had just ticked over six minutes when he noticed an irregular arc of black occluding the starscape behind it. Lack of light and reference points made judging scale difficult, but the shadow was easily larger than the *Fortune*, possibly by several times. The lieutenant glanced back at him and the others that had filtered in over the last few minutes.

"Okay, duty nav is telling me we've matched vectors. The plan is pretty simple, go over there and find out what's special about it. Radar doesn't show any fast moving debris nearby so random strikes aren't likely anymore, but be cautious anyway, we've already lost too many people. Keep your eyes open, and stay in contact. Friedrich, you're with me."

Eric nodded and one by one the men around him disengaged

their maglocks and pushed off toward the silent shadow overhead. Eric and the lieutenant were traversing the gap when the *Fortune*'s dorsal observation lights flickered to life. Only a quarter of the infrared spotlights had activated. Half of those flickered and failed, but the handful of that remained gave more than enough light to amplify. At first glance, Eric was inclined to dismiss the behemoth before them as just another dirty ice ball circling the outer reaches of a barren system, but an odd shadow lurked just below the surface.

Eric toggled his radio and said, "Hey, LT, you tracking that shadow? Our one o'clock?"

"Good eye," Lt. Pascal commented.

Eric beamed as they adjusted their approach to touch down where it seemed closest to the surface. Pascal unholstered a small pistol and fired a piton into the ice. Tethering to it, he motioned for Eric to do the same. "*Fortune*, how do you read?"

"Signal is loud and clear, Pascal," the *Fortune*'s communications officer replied.

"I've got my men covering elsewhere, but I believe we've found your artifact."

"Any ideas, lieutenant?" a rough voice cut into the channel.

"Nothing certain. Whatever it is, it's big and appears to be embedded in the ice, Captain."

"Continue your investigation, Pascal," Captain Fox replied.

"Aye, sir."

Over the next fifteen minutes, Pascal directed the others to join them as their own searches came up dry.

"*Fortune*, I believe we've located the thinnest part of the ice, but we'll need equipment to get through," Pascal transmitted.

Eric's heart beat a bit faster as he waited for the reply. *This thing is huge. What the hell is it?*

"Pascal, have your men return to the *Fortune*. We're sending Ensign Winters and a few others from engineering over. You're to remain to coordinate."

Lieutenant Pascal looked over at Eric, "Permission to keep Friedrich with me?"

Another pause.

"Granted, but he's your headache, Pascal," Captain Fox replied.

Eric rolled his eyes. The officers always acted like having him around was a chore, but they never passed up the opportunity to have him nearby.

Lieutenant Pascal glanced at him. "Before you ask, and I know you're going to, Winters spent a decade as an asteroid miner. Foreman by the time he quit, if I recall. If anyone can crack this quickly and safely, he can. There's a reason he led the planning effort for cracking that last one."

Moving shadows across the ice surface caught his eye and Eric looked up. Several vac sleds traversed one of the spotlights just forward of the aft cargo transit bay. According to his few acquaintances in maintenance, the sleds were difficult to work on and spent more time under repair than they did under operation.

"Lieutenant Pascal, Ensign Winters and engineering team on approach. I figured we could bring a few air tanks in addition to our gear so you two can top off."

"Roger that, Ensign. Good thinking," Pascal replied.

Thanks to the extra reaction mass, the sleds approached much faster than his team had and were spiked and tethered in half the time it had taken Eric's group to arrive. While his team unstrapped their equipment, Winters attached a corded black wand to his tablet and slowly waved it about while pacing a circle around Eric and Lt. Pascal

Eric's radio crackled as Ensign Winters addressed his crew. "Tori, Spinks, set the base up over here, tether it off at least ten meters. Azarov, Church, help them set up the inductance drill when they've got the base anchored. Everybody else back off, there's a hollow chamber underneath us. It might have atmosphere, so there's a chance we'll have some decompression when we breach it."

The team carefully assembled the base, anchored it, and then mounted a large bore drill piece.

"Captain, Pascal. Winters is activating the inductance drill."

"Carry on."

The flat bit descended to the surface and slowly rotated against it for several moments before water began to climb its sides and the bit began to descend. Eric noticed most of water slipped up the surface of the drill bit into a collar instead of puffing off into space. He shot an inquiring glance at Winters.

"Hydrophilic surface coating. Draws the liquid to a chamber so it can be reclaimed. The umbilical from the drill to the sled carries more than just electricity, Friedrich," Winters explained. The ensign's eyes darted back to the drill. "Careful, slow the bit!"

Before the operators could react, the slow stream of liquid water became a jet and then shards of ice and liquid water burst forth lightning quick in all directions.

"Shit! Kill the power!" Winters yelled over the shocked voices that filled the channel. Eric flung his hands up to shield his face. Ice pinged off his visor and pelted his suit. A shadow passed overhead and more ice pelted him from behind moments later.

The chaos on the channel squelched out, overridden by the ship's command channel. "Pascal, *Fortune*. Status?"

"We had a blow-out, Captain. Pocket had atmosphere. Temp and pressure were higher than Winters expected. One minute."

One by one, the team called out their status as the ice cloud dispersed. The drill was gone, so was the sled it had been secured to. A ragged hole slightly larger than the drill base remained where their equipment had been. Checking behind him, Eric spotted the battered sled and the drill. The drill had been blown off the ice by the decompression and uprooted its tethers on the way out. Held by the umbilical and the sled's anchor, instead of shooting straight out, it had followed an arc and imbedded itself in the ice behind them.

"*Fortune*, Pascal. No injuries to the crew, though we're patching two suit leaks. The drill and the sled it was attached to might be a loss though."

Captain Fox sighed over the radio. "At least the crew's safe. Carry on."

While the team gathered at the bore, Ensign Winters smirked and said, "Now you see why I got out of ice mining, Friedrich. Too fucking dangerous."

"Hey, that thing still had the price tags on it when we pulled it out of the crate. Do you think it's still under warranty?" Church asked. His question brought several chuckles.

"*Fortune*, Pascal. Looks like the blow-out opened up a chimney of some sort, too narrow to traverse. Bends out of sight about three meters in. We'll need some time to widen it."

"Pascal, *Fortune*. You've got three hours before we need to leave."

"Acknowledged, *Fortune*," Pascal replied.

Eric stared down at the darkened hole, imagining what might lay at the other side. *Nothing's been all that dangerous so far. Could be something valuable, maybe I can get a bonus for going above and beyond? Wait, or what if there's nothing down there? We could be back home three hours sooner if I do this. Either way, that works.*

"Sir," Eric said before Lieutenant Pascal could issue orders.

"Yes, Friedrich?"

"If I ditched my propulsion pack, I think I could fit."

"You sure?"

"Yes, sir. Looks like it would be tight, but I should be able to manage."

"*Fortune*, Pascal. Spacer Friedrich has volunteered to enter the chimney while we widen it. Any objections?" Pascal asked.

"Provided he knows the risks, none," the Captain replied.

"Roger, *Fortune*. I'll keep you updated. Friedrich, give me your pack. Winters, did you bring a SAR belt on one of those sleds?"

"Standard load includes a search and rescue belt, LT. Church, grab the one from your sled," Winters said.

"Friedrich, you familiar with what's on a SAR belt?" Pascal asked.

"Part of my cross-training, sir," Eric told him.

"Good. Well, no time like the present, off you go. Stay on the radio."

Eric nodded as he handed his pack over and slid into the shaft. He passed through several meters of jagged ice before the surface suddenly smoothed out at the curve. Continuing on, the ice smoothed into a clean sheen, like it had melted and refrozen dozens of times.

Eric paused when he came to a bend and pondered what that meant a moment before toggling his radio.

"Well, Lieutenant, the shaft continues at least another eight meters after the curve. It curves again, upwards. Uh, up relative to my face. Would be straight ahead if you haven't moved since I crawled down here, I think. It's weird, LT. Ice is real slick down here. Still frozen, but it looks almost like glass."

"Got that. How's the fit?"

"Well, not too bad actually. I suppose now is a bad time to point out I'm mildly claustrophobic?" Eric commented as he pulled himself through the narrow tube.

Pause. "No, now would not be a good time for that. What else?" Pascal replied with mild amusement.

"Past the curve it starts getting narrower. Sec, I'm going to see if I can squeeze through," Eric said, looking at a particularly narrow spot.

God I hate tight spaces.

Pushing further in meant he had to crane his head to the side to get his helmet to fit through. Using fingers and toes, he scooted against the ice hugging him from every direction. And then he stopped.

Fuck.

The top of his helmet hadn't hit anything. He couldn't get any traction with his fingers and his boots only slid across the ice behind him to similar effect. He was stuck.

You've got to be shitting me. No, calm down. Calm. Down. Nobody's getting stuck out here. Help is only like ten minutes away. Breathe in. Breathe out. Fuck me. Stop panicking, asshole.

"Panic kills," Eric whispered to himself repeatedly as beads of sweat trailed down his forehead. "Panic kills, asshole. Okay, what are we going to do? We're not stuck, life just hates us. Narrow tunnel, no traction. Make ourselves smaller? How? Right."

Eric exhaled, forcing every bit of air out of his lungs that he could and tried pushing off with his boots. He moved forward a few centimeters.

Fuck yeah. With the ice even tighter around him, he couldn't inhale completely. *Aw fuck. Keep going, keep going, asshole.* A few more centimeters, and even tighter than before. *Maybe I should turn back. Ah shit, how?* He toggled the oxygen saturation with a chin switch, breathed what little he could, and then pushed again.

He drifted into a much wider open space, a chasm filled with ice glass, stalactite-like spikes, and frost everywhere.

"Friedrich?" Concern colored Pascal's voice.

"I'm okay," Eric panted into his radio. "Almost didn't fit, but I'm through. Far side is, ah, interesting."

"How so?"

Eric panned his light across the chamber. "Chamber, bigger. Lots bigger. There's something in here, huge. Looks like maybe the ice melted away from it. Suit's detecting radiation, alpha and beta particles mostly. There's only one area I can really get to. It's coated with frost. Give me a second, I'll try to clear some off." Eric braced himself against the ceiling of the chamber and began brushing back frost to reveal their prize. "It's--this is a hull plate."

"Say again, Friedrich. Hull plate?"

"Yeah. It looks brand new. Different from most of the plating I've seen before, shinier but more dull at the same time if that makes sense? Uh, I've found something. Looks like it might be a hatch or an airlock of some sort. Design is different from ours, but similar. I'm going to see if I can't find a way in."

"Wait a second; let me confer with Captain Fox."

"Roger," Eric replied as he brushed away more of the hoarfrost.

"Captain says you're good, but be careful, we don't know whose ship this might have been. Keep an eye on your suit's displays, no telling what sent this ship to its grave."

"Uh, sir, I found something else. There's labeling by the hatch, and a set of ensigns to the right. I'm taking pictures, but my data link isn't working."

"Describe what you see, Spacer."

"Hatch is inset to the hull, maybe a few centimeters. Yellow and black hatching along the frame. Writing in English says this is 'Aft Airlock #2'. Series of numbers separated by dashes over that. One dash one hundred forty dash eleven dash letter 'Q'."

"Relaying to *Fortune*, continue."

"Appears to be five ensigns on the hull next to the airlock. From the top, alternating white and red horizontal stripes. Upper left quadrant is dark blue, white dots. Quite a number of them. Second ensign, a bit harder to describe. Uh, red lines to the center from the sides and corners. The red is framed thinly in white; rest of the ensign is blue. Third ensign, left and right third of the ensign is red. Inside band is white with some sort of red emblem centered. Fourth ensign, blue. Upper left-hand quadrant is the second ensign. There's a set of stars off to the right, and another single star below the inset second ensign. Uh, last ensign is identical, except it doesn't have that lone star from the previous."

"Roger that, standby." Eric spent the next few seconds examining the hatch when Lieutenant Pascal broke in. "Did you copy that?"

"Uh, no, sir. Squelch didn't even break."

"*Fortune* says that numbering system sounds like a Protectorate ship, but the ensigns aren't from any known colony of theirs. You can come back if you want and let us take over, Captain doesn't want to put you in any further danger."

Eric smiled. *Nah, this is too cool.* "Negative, LT. I'm good. Haven't seen anything remotely dangerous yet. There's no power to the airlock, but I think I've found a manual override."

"Copy, proceed."

Eric engaged his maglocks and bent over the door as he pulled the electric driver from the SAR belt. *Looks to be about fifteen millimeters.* Eric fit what he hoped was an appropriate hex bit to the driver and inserted the end into the female override fitting. He slowly depressed the trigger and the resulting torque nearly pulled the driver out of his hands. Eric paused to brace himself before pulling the trigger again. The bit slipped intermittently, ever slightly too small. A puff of cold gas announced the door's opening.

"LT, hatch is coming along. Should have access in about fifteen seconds."

"Roger that. You might lose us on radio when you get inside, so don't do anything stupid. Captain says those numbers you gave gives us an idea the size of the ship embedded in this ice ball. Nearest guess is three hundred meters. Those numbers, the first identifies the deck, larger numbers being toward the belly, the second, how far from the front of the ship you are while the third is how far from the centerline."

"Door's open LT. Airlock had gas in it, so I'm going to see about sealing it behind me. Might still be atmosphere further in."

"Copy, what's the airlock look like?"

"About what you'd expect. Mostly bare. Hand-holds, another door on the inside. Wait, there's a placard here. USS Gadsden. Ship's sigil is a yellow background, some kind of coiled rope-like creature. Below that, 'Don't Tread on Me.'"

"Heh. Sounds like a privateer or maybe military, maybe the Persians. I'm pretty sure Pershing hasn't sent anything this far out though. We'd've heard about that. Proceed, Friedrich. We're probably thirty minutes or so from being able to follow. Find the bridge if you can, should be amidships and towards the top. Captain's quarters shouldn't be far from that."

A visual search of the compartment before him revealed a matching override fitting identical to the one on the hull on the inside. "Sealing her up, LT. By the way, use a fifteen millimeter on the override bolt, it'll slip like it's the wrong size, but sixteen's too big."

"Odd. Good luck."

Eric keyed his radio one last time as the outer hatch closed, "Friedrich, out."

Turning to the inner door, he realized, like its outer brother, this one was unpowered. The override fitting on this door was also much larger. *No way I've got a bit that big.*

Eric frowned and was about to turn around when he spotted a recess next to the hatch's frame labeled "Auxiliary Entry Tool, 1 pc, NSN 1820-00-C17-6436." The recess held a canted metal bar a little over a half meter long with a perpendicular hexagonal head at one end. Eric pulled the bar out of the recess, inserted the head into the override fitting, and tested which direction it wanted to turn.

The fitting budged clockwise, the direction he had the least amount of travel.

"I always pick the wrong way first," Eric muttered as he pulled the head out. He dropped end of the bar almost to his knees before inserting it again. He heaved upwards and could hear the gears in the frame grind before giving way. *Of course they're stiff, they haven't seen maintenance in how long?*

Opening the inner door proved harder than he expected and doing so produced the huff of air he expected. Eric watched as the suit's sensor readout as the pressure in the room climbed. His headset crackled and hissed as his helmets external audio feeds detected air pressure. *Pressure at .2 bars. Ambient temperature, one degree Celsius. That's odd, I think? Shouldn't this place be frigid as hell? Negligible particulates. Carbon dioxide levels below the sensor's tolerance. Oxygen, too. Almost all nitrogen. Humidity bone dry. Air pressure's way too low.*

Cautiously, Eric stepped into the next compartment and surveyed the dark interior. The walls were lined with racks, each with a suit. Each suit bore the ship's yellow sigil on the breast. "Heh. Two-part airlock. Yeah, Pascal might be right, could be a privateer. Maybe not though, these look like service suits, not combat," Eric muttered to himself. He paused on his way to the hatch on the other side and stared at the thin glass display next to the door. Without power, the screen was black.

Whoever they were, they spent a lot of money on this ship. Hatch looks like an old design, too. Old, but effective.

Eric sighed. This one had another large override fitting. Eric noticed another entry bar in a similar recessed space on the other side of the hatch he'd opened.

Better leave one for Pascal.

Leaning through the opened hatch, he returned the first bar to its alcove and sealed it with the second bar from his side.

Using the second tool Eric cranked at the mechanism for the hatch leading further into the ship. The hatch resisted. He shoved. The resistance against him disappeared suddenly as the door cracked and the air pressure equalized. Eric nearly toppled over the raised section of the hatch, but caught himself.

Stupid. Of course this would be isolated from the rest of the ship. His air pressure gauge now read .98 bars. *Still cold and dry. If there was oxygen, it'd be safe enough to take off my helmet.*

Silence reigned in the hallway beyond and a few meters down the hall his flashlight illuminated a protrusion that ringed the passageway. Eric glanced back at the hatch he'd just come through. *Yeah, close this too. That rim looks like an emergency pressure door. No telling if it works without power or not. Not going to chance it.* He cranked down the last hatch and then proceeded to pan his light about as he wandered off down with the bar slung over his shoulder.

Pausing in the middle of an intersection with a side-passage, Eric noted it seemed every side passage had small plaque similar to the one over the airlock. *1-112-7-L*

Passageway.

He glanced back the way he came.

"If that was one-forty and this is one-twelve," he said to himself, doing the math in his head.

Yeah, almost two meters per number. Another hundred meters or so to go, though access up would probably be closer to the centerline.

Several passageways later, Eric caught himself humming a song and realized the constant silence bothered him. He paused momentarily by a poster depicting a man in a white uniform with a finger to his lips.

OPSEC? What the hell is OPSEC?

He shrugged and continued on. Passing through a sealed hatch he had to open with the access tool, Eric found himself in a much larger compartment the plaque called a quarterdeck. The flooring here was white tile, not pale blue sealed plastic. Stanchions connected with thick blue rope lined the walls. Something drifted through his peripheral vision startling him out of his internal monologue. He'd automatically hefted the bar back to swing before realizing the drifting form was a corpse curled into a fetal position.

Breathing heavy from the adrenaline surge, he reached out to the drifting form. His suit's Geiger counter began a slow click as he grabbed the corpse's oddly mottled green and brown uniform. What appeared to be an octagonal hat tumbled away off the corpse's head to drift across the quarterdeck aimlessly.

Not much above background radiation.

Eric rotated the body so he could get a better look. The corpse wore a white armband with large black, block letters centered on it proclaiming, "SF." Below that smaller lettering spelled out, "Security Forces." Eric squinted and froze. Two embroidered sections lined the tops of the uniform's slanted breast pockets. In dark stitching, one said, "US Marines", the other "Friedrich."

He'd seen death before, but his name on a corpse? That bothered him. He'd also seen the bodies of engineering crew when reactor containment had failed, having been on a working party that transferred them to be jettisoned. This corpse appeared the same but far more dessicated.

Shifting the corpse brought a black device that had been on a sling over the corpse's shoulder rolling towards him.

Looks like a projectile weapon, not energy.

Not wanting to disturb the corpse more than necessary, he examined the weapon and found a way to disconnect the weapon from the sling by pressing the button at the attachment points. Eric looked over the rifle.

Safe, fire, burst. Arrow on this switch is pointing to safe. Not much different from our gear at all. Forward of those engravings he found another set. *FN Manufacturing? Never heard of them. Either small enough we haven't looted anything from them yet, or really, really old.*

He pressed a button on the side to no effect followed by the button below it. A piece of the weapon rattled and drifted loose. Eric caught it. *Ah, there's the cartridges. That must be the magazine release. Good enough for me.*

Noticing what appeared to be a pistol in a holster at the corpse's hip, Eric reattached the larger weapon to the sling and carefully drew the smaller black weapon. Keeping his finger off the trigger, he examined the sleek metal weapon.

No selector, much larger bullet. Looks like a button in the palm, probably a mechanical safety. Wonder if that's a magazine release? Yep. Looks like thirteen cartridges. No clue what a M1911A3 is, but this feels serviceable.

He pressed back the slide slowly to reveal the top of a cartridge in the chamber. Eric looked up at the corpse as he let the slide return home.

"I know it's just nerves, but I'm taking this if you don't mind," he whispered and paused.

This is silly. Fuck that.

Eric laid a hand on the corpse's chest and whispered the same prayer uttered at every funeral he'd attended since the crew of the Fortune had adopted him, "Lord, receive this man into your waiting arms. He has been long from port and long from home. May he find rest and safe harbor wherever he has gone."

Prayer finished, Eric continued across the quarterdeck toward a large white hatch on the far side. He paused by a clearly ceremonial setting. The matting on the floor before him contained the ship's emblem. To either side stood rows of what might be large-bore penetrators as big around as his thigh. Colored cloth floated from the poles between the slugs. Central to the display, a stand stood at the end of the mat on the floor with several poles with colored cloth secured to them. Eric recognized several of the lengths of fabric as the ensigns by the airlock. Four of them were off to the side while the central shrine displayed the one with red and white stripes as the centerpiece. He glanced at the other four in the shrine.

POW-MIA, You are not forgotten. Must be some kind of memorial. US Navy. Not sure what that symbol is. Hmm. US Marine Corps. Nice red. USS Gadsden, ship's symbol again.

He glanced down below the hanging cloth and noticed a stand with a plaque that read, "USS Gadsden, SBBGN-X."

No clue what the BB-whatever means. Hey, is that wood? Wow, I haven't seen wood like that since I was a kid.

Eric gravitated to a display off to the side. The simple wooden stand, labeled "Chain of Command" held a number of picture frames, presumably ordered by seniority. Most of the top row was conspicuously empty.

Eric looked over the names for the slots pondering if this might have meant something. President of the United States, Vice-President, Secretary of Defense, Secretary of the Navy, all important sounding, but also all empty. The first frame in seniority to have a photo, a stern-faced older male, was labeled Chief of Naval Operations.

Admiral Mullin, huh? Yeah, not a privateer. Military warship. Eric skipped over to a photo of the commanding officer, Thomas Morneault. *Looks like he'd give Captain Fox a run for being a hard-ass. Both of them could probably chew through a bulkhead. Sounds like a name from Orleans. Desi might know.* The Gadsden's executive officer looked significantly less angry. *Well, Parsons is easier to pronounce, I guess I'd be happier too.* Eric shrugged at the last photo, Command Master Chief, and moved on. *What kind of name is Sweeting? That guy is just too happy.*

Eric opened the white hatch barring his way to the bridge, stepped through, and sealed it behind him. He ducked past several corpses in blue uniforms on the way up the ladder well, making sure he did not disturb the radiation scarred remains. He pulled himself up the ladderwell, shivering as he passed more bodies. He paused to adjust his suit's temperature upward.

Too many bodies around here, this place is a goddamn morgue.

After the first flight of steep stairs, he noticed the flooring was no longer a pale blue, but a darker blue with white flecks in it.

Heh, wonder what that means?

He continued up a number of flights before a plaque had caught his attention.

"05-75-1-C, Bridge," Eric said to himself as he fit the entry tool into the door's fitting. Eric paused, looking at the hatch on the opposite side. The plaque label, "CIC", meant little to him, but the hatch was conspicuously armored and someone had painted "Combat Information Center" on it. "Heh. Well, she's a warship for sure. I'll check the bridge first."

Aside from the half dozen corpses, the bridge was spotless, cramped, still as a crypt, and completely dark. Enough space had been left open between each of the work stations to allow the operators to get to their station and little else. Like the previous corpses, these new ones did not appear to have struggled. Eric started to poke about when a realization struck him. Five of the bodies were strapped into chairs. One sat in a chair half slewed around like he had been talking to the corpse behind him, the only corpse not secured to a chair. The ones in the seats had simple polished black boots, black belts with tarnished white buckles, possibly silver at one point, and the lettering on their coveralls was white. The odd corpse out wore what probably had been expensive looking shoes, a light brown belt with a brass buckle, and gold lettering on the name tapes.

Eric reached moved around the floating corpse, trying not to touch the stern-faced man. *US Navy. No clue what that silver insignia on the collar means. It's got wings, so maybe he's the pilot? Captain maybe? Gotta be captain.* Eric glanced down at the nametape as he checked the man's pockets. *Morneault. Yep, captain.*

"Sorry, Captain Morneault, just checking for keys. No disrespect intended." Eric fished a necklace made from linked silver metallic balls from around the corpse's neck. A set of keys and two stamped metal plates swung from the end of it. Eric read the stamped lettering on the tarnished plates. His brain refused to process the last line. *Morneault, Matthew, 210-42-3521, AB+, Christian, January 30, 1965.*

"Nineteen sixty-five? They had to be using a different calendar." Eric stuffed the chain in a belt-pouch and stepped off the bridge. *If I were the captain, where would I have my quarters?* He looked at the ladder up. *Nah, if the main airlocks are on the main level, why would I want to walk farther? Still need to be near the bridge though. No other doors on this level, let's try the next one down, shall we?*

He traced his path back down another deck and looked about at the doors near the ladderwell.

Ah, here we are, CO's stateroom.

Eric tried the door and found it locked. The key he'd taken from the Captain fit smoothly into the physical override for the electronic lock and Eric let himself in. The far wall had been covered by a large version of the red and white striped ensign with gold fringe. A simple bed filled another wall and a desk with shelves filled the other. Eric looked over the obvious computer workstation, and then pored over the small items on the desk. Finding a photo of a woman and a few children, he slowly shook his head.

I wonder if they knew what happened to their father.

His eyes were then drawn to a large poster on the wall alongside the bookshelf. The writing was warped, like someone had tried to write without lifting their pen, but readable.

"In Congress, July Fourth, Seventeen Seventy-Six," Eric chuckled to himself about the date before reading further aloud. "The unanimous Declaration of the thirteen united States of America. When in the course of human events it becomes necessary for one people to dissolve the political bands which have connected them with another, and to assume among the powers of the earth, the separate and equal station to which the Laws of Nature and of Nature's God entitle them, a decent respect to the opinions of mankind requires that they should declare the causes which impel them to the separation. Hmm. Earth, huh? Interesting."

Eric jerked, half bringing his improvised club to bear when his headset crackled, spitting only noise.

Pascal must've gotten in. I should go. He glanced at the next poster. *We the People of the United States, in Order to form a more perfect Union, establish Justice, insure domestic Tranquility, provide for the common defense, promote the general Welfare, and secure the Blessings of Liberty to ourselves and our Posterity, do ordain and establish this Constitution for the United States of America.*

Eric's radio crackled again. He could almost make out something intelligible.

Got to go.

As he turned about, he grabbed the computer tablet off the desk. His radio crackled again as he stepped out into the hall.

"…drich. Pasc… do… copy, over?"

"Pascal, this is Friedrich. I copy."

"…you broken… clear."

Eric sighed, cursed his radio, and began moving as fast as he could down to the quarterdeck where he transmitted again. "Pascal, Friedrich. Do you copy, over?"

"…rich, Pascal. Much clearer. What's… status?"

"Your signal's still breaking up, wait a second," Eric replied as he worked open the hatch back to the airlock he'd entered from. As he opened the door, his headset crackled again.

"Friedrich, Pascal, how copy, over?"

"Pascal, Friedrich, signal's clear. Mine?"

"Clear now. What's your status?"

"I found the bridge and the captain's quarters. You won't believe what's up here."

"What'd you find?"

"Well, first off, this isn't a privateer. It's a warship."

"Good, and?"

"The crew's all dead. Looks like radiation burns, but the only thing radioactive is the bodies. They're barely above background. That's not what's crazy though."

The lieutenant sighed, "What's crazy, Friedrich?"

"The captain's ident lists his birthday as nineteen sixty-five."

Pause. "Say again."

"You heard me. Nineteen sixty-five."

"That's not possible. That's--"

"I know. It's December third, 216 PE. That date has to be from before humanity came to the stars. Lieutenant, this ship's from Earth!"

"Hey, let's not get carried away. In fact, keep that to yourself until we can go talk to the captain and see what he says. I highly doubt this ship is five hundred years old, not when its design includes artificial grav. Grav plates have only been around for-- Hold on, command channel." Eric glanced back at the corpse whose pistol he'd taken as seconds ticked by. "Friedrich, get your ass down here, fast. *Fortune*'s leaving in five minutes, with or without us."

Eric nearly stumbled. "What?"

"You heard me. Beat feet, spacer. Captain thinks there's someone else out there and he's spooling up the drive."

Shit shit shit!

Eric disengaged his maglocks and launched himself down the passageway. Using the bar to correct his trajectory, Eric sailed most of the length of the corridor in a fraction of the time it had taken him to walk it. He nearly bounced off the wall at the end of the hallway, but engaged his maglocks to keep from flying off.

"Hurry up, this way," the lieutenant yelled. He stood on the inside of the airlock door. As Eric ducked through, Pascal worked the next door and waited for Friedrich to seal his door before opening the next. Working together, they managed to maintain the atmospheric integrity of the ship while moving quickly. Eric stopped to cycle the outside airlock shut, but Pascal pointed towards Eric's maneuvering pack and moved to cycle the airlock shut himself.

"We've got two minutes. We're good, Friedrich. Had them leave a sled for us," Pascal said as the airlock door slid shut.

Pascal pushed off, leaving Eric to follow him through the chimney several seconds behind.

Pascal cleared the jagged maw of the tunnel entrance and immediately spat, "Son of a bitch."

"What?" Eric asked. Pascal didn't need to answer, he saw for himself as he drifted free of the ice. The *Fortune* was moving away at speed. "Motherfucker. They left us!"

"I know, I know. Give me a second."

Eric saw a small flash out of the corner of his eye followed by an ephemeral line of violet motes that traced an almost perfect path to the *Fortune*.

Lieutenant Pascal's shoulders slumped and his helmet settled in the palm of his hand. "Fuck me."

"What was--," Eric started to ask.

"Railgun."

"Fuck."

Eric's headset blared static into his ears.

"Attention pirate vessel, this is Captain Hines of the PMV *Shrike*. By the authority granted to me by the Protectorate of Man, I order you to stand to and prepare to be boarded."

The *Fortune*'s engines flared, going to maximum burn. Flickering pinpricks of light along the hull caught Eric's eye as the *Fortune* began to veer into a sharp turn. The *Fortune*'s point defense turrets were spitting a hail of slugs toward the pirate hunter. Shock froze Eric's gut.

What do they hope to do, piss them off?

There was a brief flash as a rail slug slammed through the *Fortune*'s unarmored hull at over a hundred kilometers a second. Eric blinked as the ship he'd grown up on came apart in slow motion. Gasses escaped through ruptured plating as the ship bent in on itself and spewed a cloud of glowing dust and debris. Two engines guttered out, unbalancing forward thrust. The wreck began a lazy, twisting cartwheel. Several heartbeats later, a brilliant, blinding actinic flash replaced the blackness of space as the fusion containment dewars failed. It was horrible. It was beautiful.

Dumbstruck, Eric and Pascal could do little but watch.

"Any surviving pirate personnel activate your personal beacons if you have them or transmit in the clear. You will be afforded all legal protections set forth in the Charter by the Protectorate of Man until you can be tried for your crimes. You have fifteen minutes before we depart."

Decisions

Eric's mouth hung open in shock as the flash abated, leaving shadows of debris amidst an expanding, glowing orb of cooling gas. He blinked, failing to come to terms with the horror before him. Something tugged at his arm, drawing his attention. Lit by his helmet's internal displays, Lieutenant Pascal's serious visage demanded his attention.

Pascal tapped at a metal plate that formed the top of his visor. *What? Oh, the contact transducer!* Eric leaned forward, pressing an identical plate on his helmet to Pascal's.

"No radio, Friedrich. In fact, turn your unit off, contact only," Pascal ordered.

Eric nodded what little he could and shut down his helmet radio. "What are you thinking, sir?"

"What am I thinking?" Pascal's laugh was pinched and his eyes, ringed with red, were fully dilated. Beads of sweat threatened to pull away from the man's face. "What am I thinking, Friedrich? I'm thinking we're absolutely--," Pascal blinked and the audio connection hissed as he shook his head. Pascal's breathing steadied. "Sorry, sorry, Eric. Can't afford to lose it now. Look, neither of us are engineers, right?"

"No?"

"Right, so we're not likely to rig anything on this wreck, right?"

"Well, I guess not?"

"And how long do you think it will be before anyone comes looking for us?"

"Months, if ever?"

"Okay, so staying here, we die. The Protectorate will probably execute us for being pirates, so if we go with them, we die."

"What do we do then?" Eric asked, trying to keep his voice steady.

"Well, if we stay here, we die from hypothermia, anoxia, dehydration, or starvation. If we go with the *Shrike*, we face probable execution. Depending on which end of what law they determine we've broken, it could be a criminal execution, so firing squad, hanging, or torture. Though, it could be a civil execution, so something they think is 'humane.'"

"Humane? How is an execution humane?"

Pascal snorted, "You'd be surprised what people can fool themselves into thinking, Friedrich. Especially when someone they've come to trust helps them get there." Pascal paused as his eyes lost focus. He blinked and stared Eric in the eye. "I'm not the Captain, Eric. With the *Fortune* gone, I'm technically not even in charge anymore. So, freeze to death on this chunk of ice or take our chances with the Protectorate?"

"How likely are we to get executed?"

"Only slightly less likely than you are to die if I put my knife through your O2 line right now."

"Well, at least we'll be warm on the *Shrike*, right?" Eric asked with a strained laugh. *God, we are so fucked. So terribly, terribly fucked.*

Pascal gave him a sad grin. "I can't even promise that."

"Well, shit."

Pascal's eyes flicked to one of his helmet displays. "Look, we've got another few minutes, so think it over."

"Fuck it, LT. If we're going to die, I'd like to at least get another meal first. Skipped breakfast before we did that EVA. I'm starving." Eric gave a half-hearted smile.

"So we're taking our chances?"

Eric nodded.

"Are you sure? These people are not what you think they are." With Eric's questioning look Pascal continued, "It's hard to explain, Eric. You've always been a pirate, right? The average Protectorate citizen is afraid of being free like that. They'd deny that to their last breath though. They've begged their leaders make them slaves and then convinced themselves they're better off for it. They don't think like you or me. You are either a servant of the state or an obstacle to their perfect world."

"That doesn't make any sense."

"Eric, they've been at war with the Confederation off and on ever since the Confeds split. Anyone not under their control is a threat to their idea of a perfect society. Pirates like us have survived for this long because those two have been eyeballing each other and not us. The moment someone gets serious about cleaning up the Reach, we're done. Does this make sense? Our idea of right and wrong is a foreign concept to them."

"I guess, sir?"

"Enough of the 'sir' crap, Eric. If I'm going contact them, you have to understand what you're in for, and you have to know what the story is going to be."

"The story, uh, Pascal?"

"My name is-- Don't laugh; my parent's named me Blaise."

Eric snorted and said, "Ouch."

"Yeah, you have no idea. The story is going to be really simple, but you have to commit it to heart. You have to stick to it. Any slip and we're both dead. Got it?"

"Okay."

"First, the truth. Our life support systems were damaged and we were out here harvesting ice to replenish what we could. You were part of the work crew that was reeling in the ice."

"I was."

"You were. The best lie has just enough of the truth in it to be believable. If anyone asks why we ended up on this chunk of ice, it was bigger and we thought we could get more in a shorter amount of time. That's bullshit, but they'll buy it. Got that much?"

Eric nodded.

"Now the lie: you and I were part of that work crew and neither of us was in charge. I cannot stress this hard enough: you and I were not in charge." Eric couldn't miss the emphasis on the 'not'.

"I got it, but why?"

"Because they hold field executions for pirate officers, not trials."

"Oh," Eric gulped.

"Yeah, 'oh' is right. As far as they care, a midshipman like you is close enough to officer. So, what was that again?"

"Neither of us was in charge."

"Right. We're both forced conscripts, remember that."

"Okay."

"Not 'okay', Eric. You need to believe this is the truth because until we get to the other side, it is the truth. No slipping. You remember that disciplinary board right after we left port? The one for Banks?"

"Yeah, that asshole lied straight to the Captain's face. I saw him do it."

"And didn't blink an eye, like he was singing praises to the Almighty. We'll have to be even more convincing. They'll separate us when we get on the ship. Question us. Beat us. Even drug us. They'll do their best to keep you awake. They might not feed you, and your cell is going to be as cold or as hot as they can make it and then they'll swing the other direction to keep you off balance. It's all to get you turned around; make you despair. They'll lie. Expect them to tell you I turned on you. If they think you have family or friends, they'll use everything they can to get you to talk. Hold to the story, no matter what they say. Got that? No. Matter. What."

"I got it, Blaise. I got it."

Pascal's eyes wandered for a moment.

"What's that?" Pascal asked.

"What's what?" Eric craned his head down in his helmet.

"This," Pascal asked, pulling the black pistol from Eric's belt pouch.

"That? I found it on the *Gadsden*."

Pascal moved to toss the weapon.

"Wait!" Eric grabbed Pascal's wrist.

"What? We don't want them to know the ship is here, Eric. If we live, we can come back and take our time looking around. Maybe even try to get her free and working again. This is evidence."

"Well, shit," Eric frowned. "Still, don't just toss it off into space." Pascal raised an eyebrow. "If that ship's from Earth, then if you found the right collector it'd bring enough money to retire on, right? Besides that, it's a piece of history!"

Pascal nodded. "Fine, go put it somewhere in the airlock then. You bring back anything else?"

"Uh, yeah. This." Eric dug the tablet he'd taken from the captain's quarters out of another belt pouch.

"Heh. Might be able to pass it off as an antique, some old electronics looted forever ago. We do use a lot of outdated gear. Wait, give me your knife." Eric tugged his knife from its scabbard and handed it over. With a slow, determined motion Pascal scraped a small label off the back of the tablet and handed the knife back. "There, that looked like a manufacturer's label. Serial number, that kind of thing. Still it looks just like any other tablet anyone else has. If they open it, it'll be real hard to mistake electronics that old. Did you check to see if it worked?"

"No, I found it right as you radioed me."

"Well, if it doesn't work, play it off like it got damaged, okay? Radiation, sun spots, or some crap like that. Unless the guy talking to you is an electronics guy, he's probably not going to know the difference. Anything else?"

"Nope, that's it."

"Okay. When I make this transmission, there's no going back. Anything else you want to say or ask? We still have a few minutes."

After a few seconds of thinking, Eric shook his head. "Not off the top of my head. Sounds like this is our best chance, even if it is a shitty one."

"When I'm done on the radio, I'll want you to repeat everything back to me to make sure you've got it straight. You'll probably have a few minutes to stash that weapon. You can turn on your radio, don't transmit." Eric nodded and took the gun from Pascal. Pascal floated back a few feet and muttered to himself, eyes closed before making the sign of the cross. Eric's radio crackled as he made his way back through the ice chimney.

"PMV *Shrike*, PMV *Shrike*, come in." Silence. "PMV *Shrike*, do you copy, over?"

Eric cranked open the outer hatch as Pascal made another attempt. *That had better be distance lag, not them ignoring us.* Eric glanced about the airlock and spotted a recess occupied by emergency equipment. He slipped the handgun behind the air mask and slipped outside to close the hatch.

"Unknown radio source, identify yourself," came a reply after the fourth contact attempt.

"PMV *Shrike*, this is able crewman Terrance McNiel, survivor, along with able crewman Eric Friedrich. No injuries, oxygen enough for another hour or so."

"Confirmed, Crewman McNiel. We have triangulated your signal. Someone will be picking you up shortly."

Eric noted the time lag on his chronometer as he emerged from the chimney. Pascal motioned him over. Uncertainty gripped his guts as Pascal's helmet made contact with his.

"This is the story we're going to stick to, Eric. When I'm done, I want you to repeat it back to me."

Eric listened with mild amusement. *Stupid? I can play stupid. Hell, I'm pretty sure I am stupid. I feel dumber already.*

"Good," Pascal said when Eric had finished repeating the plan. "Stick to that and we might live long enough to be free men again. Eric?"

"Yeah?"

"Whatever happens, die with honor."

Intake

ERIC GLANCED AT PASCAL AGAIN AS THE APPROACHING MOTE IN THE monochrome green light amplification grew into a small, boxy shuttle. Pascal's eyes were closed and his lips moved slowly. *Praying.* Cocooned in the EVA suit, the man appeared calm, but the beads of sweat clinging to his face despite the climate controlled environment spoke otherwise. Pascal's eyes twitched as he prayed. *Why am I not as worked up about this as he is?*

Eric's stomach clenched as a spotlight on the shuttle snapped on. His helmet blended the white light into the monochrome. *Wish our tech worked that well.*

"Crewman McNiel, this is Intake Three. We are approaching from your ten o'clock. A hatch will open on our starboard side. You and your comrade are to discard any weapons and enter. Understood?"

Pascal's eyes snapped open. "Roger that, Intake Three. We are standing by for your arrival." Pascal's head swiveled in his helmet toward the approaching shuttle before he glanced at Eric. Using one of several hand signals taught to every crewman of the *Fortune*, Pascal asked how Eric was doing.

Eric managed a weak smile and replied with another hand signal, okay.

Pascal nodded as the shuttle slowed to a halt relative to their position. A hatch opened before them, spilling red light into the void.

"Crewman McNiel, Intake Three. Starboard hatch is open."

"Confirmed, Intake Three. Friedrich, let's get moving."

Eric pushed off of the Gadsden's icy grave, following Pascal. His heart beat faster as they approached. Glancing about as Pascal entered, Eric noted five other identical entry points. The hatch cycled shut the moment they crossed the threshold.

Good thing I'm not entirely claustrophobic.

Little wider than a passageway, Eric suspected the compartment ended just short of the shuttle's centerline. Small protrusions lined the armored walls to the front and back of the shuttle. Eric tried not to think of why the far corner's plating was noticeably darker than the rest, nor how several small circles of bubbled metal had gotten there.

Space for twelve here. Five other compartments. Assuming they're the same, then they can move seventy-two prisoners per shuttle.

Their radios crackled.

"Welcome aboard," a wan, accentless male voice announced. "We will be accelerating in thirty seconds and returning to the *Shrike*. You will find universal oxygen umbilicals placed every half meter along the fore and aft walls. Next to each umbilical you will find a stanchion to secure yourself for the duration of our transit."

Eric spotted small reflective bulbs in compartment ceiling's four corners as he moved to the nearest oxygen port. *Cameras.*

"Once secured, take no actions or movements unless ordered to. Failure to comply will be met with escalating force until compliance is gained."

Eric blinked and glanced at the camera before pulling the oxygen tube from its receptacle. He felt more than heard the connector's click as it locked into place in his suit's external feed. Engaging his maglocks, Eric suppressed a shudder and waited. Acceleration shoved him against the back wall.

"Shit!"

Within seconds, he found himself confused and blinking. His fingers suddenly felt cold, and his lips tingled on the edge of numbness. *Oxygen?* Light-headedness began to seep in as he checked his suit's environmental readout. *O2 normal.* Brow furrowed, Eric glanced over at Pascal to see the man shaking his head slowly, disoriented. His heartbeat slowed. Dimly he realized thinking took effort. Fatigue crept in. Eric shook his head. He stared at the oxygen line. A thought bubbled to the surface. *We've been drugged.* Thought fled as he fought to stay awake.

"You know what I think, Petra?" a male voice asked, panting.

Eric opened his eyes to a swirling cascade of blurred light.

"What's that?"

Woman.

His entire body stung with pins and needles, but he was awake. *What the hell happened?* Still in his suit, he was being carried between two people, his arms over their shoulders. His vision began to clear.

"I say after we get these two apes down to in-processing, we pay the boys in flight maintenance a visit. This fucker's heavy."

The vanishing blur revealed the swirling cascade's source. With his head down, a clear viscous liquid sloshed in a pool at the lowest point in his helmet, the front of his visor. *Great, I puked in my helmet.*

The woman snorted. "I'm okay with that. His friend isn't any lighter. Hey, zip it, I think the antidote the medics gave them is kicking in."

"They couldn't wake up earlier? Figures."

Eric blinked away the grogginess. His oxygen monitor proclaimed two minutes left in his tank with blinking red numbers. A door cycled open nearby as someone tapped on his helmet.

"Hey asshole, rise and shine."

Eric felt a shove from behind and fell forward. Disoriented, the floor rose faster than he could react. Blinded by flying fluid, Eric wrestled with his helmet seals and tore it off. He retched before collapsing on the metal grating. As he tried to clean his face with gloved hands, a speaker popped and crackled.

"Prisoner Eighty-Seven, stand to."

Eric blinked at the sudden female voice and looked about the circular chamber. A meter long segment of the metal wall before him slid aside. A box emerged from the darkness beyond. "Prisoner Eighty-Seven, deposit all clothing and equipment into the receptacle provided. You have thirty seconds to comply. Be aware, personal conduct will reflect on in-processing and subsequent case handling. Civility will be answered in kind."

Eric stumbled forward to the box. As he stripped off the suit, he glanced about. *Where are the cameras?* Grudgingly, he tossed the last of the outer suit into the box and began to turn about.

"Prisoner Eighty-Seven. All clothing is to be deposited into the receptacle."

"You've got to be shitting me."

"You have ten seconds to comply."

"How about you have ten seconds to kiss my ass? It's fucking cold in here."

"Compliance is mandatory."

"Fuck your compli--" Eric shrieked as every inch of exposed skin felt dipped in fire and a high-pitched, grating whine filled the room. Shocked by sudden agony, he pitched to the floor gasping. The whine and the burning sensation vanished.

"Compliance is mandatory. Deposit all clothing into the receptacle. Summary execution is authorized."

"Motherfucker," Eric gasped from the floor. "Fine, you want the rest?" Using the box, Eric pulled himself to his feet and unzipped the inner suit. He stepped out of the single piece garment and flung it into the box along with the waste disposal shorts he had been wearing. "There, you've got it all? What now, boss?" Eric asked as the box slid back into the darkness beyond the wall.

"Prisoner Eighty-Seven, retrieve the safety equipment provided in the receptacle and proceed to the yellow foot prints at the center of the compartment." A smaller box emerged from the hole.

Safety equipment? Eric eyed the slim blacked-out goggles and the small black set of nose plugs before grabbing them. The box retracted and the wall began to close as he turned for the center of the room. Eric stepped across the narrow gap between the grille and the slightly elevated center. He shrugged as he aligned himself with the widely spaced foot prints.

"Prisoner Eighty-Seven, don the safety equipment provided. Refusal to do so will not delay the decontamination process and will be seen as consent to begin without proper protection."

Eric frowned. "So, uh, can I ask why this is necessary or are you just a pre-recorded message?" he asked. Darkness descended as he pulled the goggles on and adjusted their fit.

"The decontamination process uses agents that may cause dramatic damage to certain types of soft tissue, specifically those found in the lungs and eyes. It is recommended that you refrain from breathing or moving during the process to minimize the potential for injury and/or death."

Eric snorted at the comment and pushed the plugs into his nostrils. Chilled, he rubbed his arms. "Thanks for the warning?"

"The Protectorate appreciates your compliance. Prisoner Eighty-Seven, phase one will proceed in ten seconds." No stranger to what might turn into a limited oxygen situation, Eric purposefully hyperventilated as the sounds of servos springing into motion filled the chamber. "Prisoner Eighty-Seven, hold your arms and hands out level. Good, now do not move. Proceeding with chemical decontamination."

Streams of cold liquid pelted him from several directions and then cut off. Eric blinked under his goggles. *That's not that bad.* The cold began to sting. *Shit.* Stinging became burning and burning became agony. Eric involuntarily ground his teeth. *Can't move,* he repeated to himself. Jets of cold liquid extinguished his agony.

"Chemical decontamination complete. Standby for photo decontamination."

What? Several points around him burst into brilliance. The goggles weren't blacked out. They were filtered like a welder's hood. The lights clicked off when the burning sensation approached unbearable. Servos whined about him. The pain began to fade, replaced by a searing chill.

"Decontamination complete. Prisoner Eighty-Seven, you may remove your safety equipment. Discard them in the box behind the open door."

Eric pulled the nose plugs out but stopped as he pulled the head-band off. His hair was gone, all of it, even his eyebrows. "What the fuck is this?"

"Destruction of the pilus and outer dermal layers is a byproduct of the decontamination process. Prisoner Eighty-Seven, proceed to the open door."

Scowling, Eric stalked across the grille to the doorway. The pair of helmeted and armed troopers in bulky body armor drew him up short on the far side. Although he could not see faces behind the reflective visors, Eric felt their glare as they flexed their hands on the grips of their weapons.

"Prisoner Eighty-Seven, over here," Eric heard the familiar female voice say, this time in person instead of through a speaker. Hyper-focused on the guards, he had completely missed the medical station to his right and the brunette next to it motioning to him. As he padded across the frigid metal floor, he became acutely aware of her curves and just how naked he was. She rolled her eyes and cleared her throat, "Not on your best day, profligate."

Somewhat deflated, Eric waited where she pointed. She rummaged through several drawers and placed various items onto a tray. *Not too different from Ship's Medical. She's a doctor?* One of the guards set a stool down next to him and motioned for him to sit.

"Prisoner Eighty-Seven, as part of in-processing you are to be given a thorough medical examination. This will include a blood draw and several immunizations. Are you allergic to anything?"

"No, Ma'am. My name is--" She cut him off shaking her head and motioned as if tapping something in the air before her.

"You are Prisoner Eighty-Seven. Prisoners do not have names. Now, have you recently been exposed to radiation sources outside of this ship?"

Just an ice ball. The Gadsden does not exist. "No, Ma'am." Another tap.

"Any non-visible implants?" Eric shook his head and she tapped the air again. "Have you otherwise taken any medications or other substances that may interact or interfere with medical procedures that may save your life should you require treatment? Dishonest answers may lead to undue suffering on your part."

"No, Ma'am."

"The last time you drank?" she asked.

"Ma'am?"

"Alcohol."

"Oh, last month. My eighteenth birthday party." He bit the inside of his lower lip. *Do not volunteer information!* Pascal had been very clear.

"Last time you partook in any narcotic or mind-altering substances?"

"Never."

"Are you currently or have you ever been a habitual user of alcohol or other addictive substances?"

"No, Ma'am."

"Are you aware of any sickness, congenital defect, or other factor that may or may not affect treatment during your stay aboard the *Shrike?*"

"I cleared my last medical exam without a snag," Eric answered after some consideration.

"Do you have any sexually transmitted diseases?" the doctor asked.

Eric blushed.

"Answer the question, Prisoner Eighty-Seven," she ordered.

"I'm a virgin, Ma'am." Eric caught the first break in the dry, reactionless clinical routine, the beginning of a smirk. The twitch of her lip roiled anger and embarrassment in his gut. His blush deepened.

The doctor nodded and pulled a black glove from a coat pocket. Eric noted silver circles on the finger tips and the palm as she pulled it snug. As she walked over a small blue light began blinking on the back of the glove.

She stood over him motionless for several seconds before he noticed her lips moving and it clicked. Not just implants, but expensive ones he'd only heard rumors about. She leaned forward and tilted his chin up with her ungloved hand. The doctor stared into each of his eyes for several seconds before shining a light mounted in the black glove's palm in them. Unnaturally straight, miniscule lines he glimpsed around woman's right pupil confirmed his suspicion. The doctor swiped a finger that trailed flaming pain across his forehead as she circled to his side. She did not seem to notice his grimace. Still mouthing words, she tilted his head away from her while squeezing his wrist with the gloved hand. She repeated the exam from the other side. Every touch seared his burnt skin. When she placed her gloved hand on his back, agony seized his breath in his throat.

"Cough." Eric blinked at the stars flying through his vision and complied. She moved her hand elsewhere and repeated the request. After several coughs, she moved in front of him.

"Open your mouth." Eric found a new appreciate for pain when she rested the gloved hand on his chest as she stared into his mouth. He'd begun to sweat from the pain and every dripping rivulet felt like a soldering iron. Her hand wandered about, pressing here and there, but he managed to keep quiet.

"When was your last meal?" she asked as she wrapped a fabric cuff around his left arm.

Eric grimaced as she cinched the cuff tight and then grit his teeth when the cuff's fabric dug into his skin as it inflated. Caught inside the expanding cuff, his arm throbbed with each heartbeat before the cuff began to deflate.

"Twelve hours? Sixteen? Something like that," he managed to reply as the pain faded.

"How much did you eat?" she asked, removing the cuff.

"Not much. Some tea, a few crackers."

"Last bowel movement? Urination?"

"When you're in the suit, that's what the shorts are for. Sorry,

By Dawn's Early Light

didn't look at the clock." Her eyes narrowed and she retrieved what appeared to be a plastic framed pistol with a narrow tip. The doctor fit a clear vial into a recess at the back of the device before pressing it against his upper forearm. He felt the tip of the object flex.

"You might feel some discomfort." Eric barely heard the click as a sharp pain lanced through his arm. The doctor held the gun up and pulled the vial of his blood from the back. She retrieved a different device that had several vials of clear liquid protruding from the side and touched it to his arm several times. Each contact left a stinging numbness.

"Stand up." She sounded irritated. "Over there by the counter. Keep your feet spread and place your hands on the counter."

Eric heard the door cycle as he bent over to reach the counter. The guards had left.

Out of the corner of his eye, he watched her pull off the black glove and retrieve two disposable gloves.

"Prisoner Eighty-Seven, the Protectorate affords many legal privileges to those accused of crimes, even to pirates such as you. Per policy, I am to inform you that the following procedures are standard for a complete physical of males your age of unknown origin and are in no way a punitive measure in and of themselves."

Eric heard the gloves snap and glanced over his shoulder to see the doctor applying a gel to a glove. *What the fuck?* Disgust soured his stomach as she spread his cheeks and smeared the chill gel between them.

"Should you wish, you may attempt to pursue the matter with your legal counsel," she said and applied pressure.

Stop. His body reflexively clamped down.

"You are free to do so when you are allowed to meet with them. However, should you decide to file a complaint, please be aware," she said. Her detachment etched gibbering warnings in his hind-brain. "We control everything on the *Shrike*. Everything, including you. No one will help you."

Eric grunted and gripped the counter top as the doctor grabbed his shoulder and she forced her fingers in. Eric closed his eyes and tried to block out her violation.

"Guards, we're done here. Issue him a blanket and take him to his cell," the woman said. She leaned in close to his ear and whispered, "No one will help you, pirate. Tell the interrogators what they want to know or the next time won't be nearly as pleasant."

Eric shuddered. He'd heard her first human emotion: satisfaction. The door opened. A guard stepped in, pointed at him, and then pointed through the open door.

Cellmates

ERIC SIGHED IN RELIEF AND APPREHENSION AS HIS ESCORTS DREW UP short of a door. He clutched the scratchy dark roll to his chest, trying to savor the little warmth it contained. Trekking through the silent cold halls of the *Shrike*'s detainment ward had convinced him the promise of warmth more than outweighed the price of pain from the prickly material scraping his skin.

One guard stepped to the side of the door. Eric felt the weight of a telling stare through the featureless visor as the man toggled a control on the door panel. Speakers on the panel crackled, and before he could tell what he was hearing, the lesson was plain: they can listen any time they choose.

"You'd probably like that, wouldn't you?" a gruff man demanded. Eric couldn't place the accent, but taunting tone set his teeth on edge. Exhaustion and misery sapped his usual anger response to that tone.

"Give. It. Back." The second man sounded more like a former crewmate from the *Fortune*, Sokolov, deep in timbre and accent. From the cold anger in the man's words, Eric's primitive animal brain whispered warnings. In the pause between the two men's words, Eric had heard a quiet, forlorn sobbing.

The guard at the door's helmet swiveled to the other escort who nodded and began to sling his rifle. The second guard pulled a thin cylinder off his belt. The man at the door motioned at Eric and tapped another control on the door pad. The door slid open with a hiss.

Several bare cots lined the far wall. A single prisoner with close cropped brown hair and clad in bright orange coveralls lay sprawled out atop a dark blanket. The man's head snapped toward the door and he half sat up as the guards shoved Eric through the doorway. Eric nearly dropped his blanket as he caught himself on a cot. The man in the coveralls gave a shark-like smile.

"Oh, fresh meat. Hello, meat." Booted footsteps came from behind Eric. "Oh, evening gents. I was just giving this back."

Eric stumbled as he was shouldered out of the way by the second guard.

Shark began to rise as the guard flicked his wrist. The collapsible baton clacked as it locked open. Half way out of his rack, Shark had little time to react before the baton caught him in the ribs. A second blow to the back of the head sent him to the deck. The guard stood silent over the motionless man. Shark stirred and tried to rise. The guard delivered a swift kick to injured ribs. Shark groaned and pushed up to one knee. Eric watched in mute horror as meaty thumps resounded through the room from repeated blows to Shark's ribcage. Shark slumped under the assault and rolled onto his back. Baton upraised, the guard paused, as Shark weakly raised his hands in surrender. The guard began to lower the baton. Shark grinned and lunged, throwing a fist into the guard's groin. The guard staggered back two steps. An electronic whine from behind sent Eric instinctively moving out of any potential line of fire. The guard with the baton surged forward and punted Shark in the jaw. The thin arc of blood painted itself across the ceiling and the wall. Something clattered as it bounced off the wall. Blood poured from his mouth as Shark giggled, spat several teeth on the floor, and began to rise again. With a sharp pop and a dazzling instant of light, Shark went rigid and toppled.

Eric glanced at the guard behind him who immediately swung

his point of aim toward Eric's movement. Raising his hands, Eric stumbled backwards and dropped onto the bunk behind him.

The first guard grabbed Shark's leg and hauled. Eric wasn't sure what bothered him more, the bubbling wheeze Shark made, or the fact he began to laugh again as they dragged him from the room. The guard with the energy rifle cautiously backed out of the room and the door closed. Eric found himself staring blankly at the floor.

What hell did I get myself into?

Motion drew his eyes from the trail of blood and shattered teeth. With a flurry of blond hair, a naked woman darted across the room, snatched the second blanket off Shark's bunk, and bolted back to the corner from which she came. In the moments before she disappeared under the blanket, Eric clearly saw two matching hand shaped bruises on her hips and several more bruises on her arms and shoulders.

Eric blinked and realized a man sat on a bunk between him and the woman.

Eric stared at him for several moments, considering everything that had just happened, and muttered, "What the fuck?"

"Welcome to hell, meat," the man replied.

"My name isn't meat. My name is--," Eric began. The red lighting replaced the white with an ominous clack of electric circuits swapping over.

"Save it for the interrogators, meat. No one cares, and if they do, they're not your friend. In fact, no one here is your friend so shut the fuck up and go to sleep before the guards come back wondering why we're making noise."

Taken aback, Eric sat motionless. The man shuffled under his own blanket. In the dim light, the woman's blanket shivered. Eric shrugged and tried to make himself comfortable despite the constant stinging, but the slightly too small, slightly too thin blanket conspired otherwise. Between the lumps in the mattress, the contortions necessary to keep under the sheet, the ever-present chill, and the intermittent sobbing, time passed at a crawl before sleep claimed him.

White light stabbing into his eyes dragged him from his sleep. Eric groaned as he stretched out. His hands brushed against metal. He opened his eyes and sat up. *Fuck.* Bleary eyed, Eric stared at the trail of dried blood, at the seven other racks in the room, the two other figures beginning to stir under their blankets, and the recess containing the cell's only toilet. *Fuck my life. Why couldn't this all have been a dream?* Sighing, he stood up, began to lurch to the toilet, and stopped short.

Every shipboard toilet he'd seen had a pressure indicator of some sort and this was no exception. Eric sighed. *Son of a bitch.* Blinking bright red, the indicator taunted him. Eric had seen what happened when someone ignored the warning. The memory of highly pressured blackwater fountaining against the ceiling and soaking everything for meters brought small chuckle. *Banks, you jack-ass.* The smile faded. *You were always worth a laugh.*

He considered doing his business anyway and simply not hitting the flush. Given how capricious the rules were so far, he expected that would be some sort of infraction. Giving his cellmates something to be angry about didn't appeal to him either. *Fine.*

The light blinked green when he started to return to his bunk, but returned to red when he paused. *Seriously?* Eric glanced about, searching for the cameras. *Dickheads. Probably laughing their asses off at this.* He returned to his rack and sat. *I'm surrounded by assholes.* The indicator blinked green. *Yeah, keep firing, assholes.*

The door hissed open and all eyes turned to the two guards stepping into the room. The lead guard pointed at the other man in the cell who sighed and followed them out. The door did not close behind them.

Eric stared at the door. His remaining companion stared back at him from under her blanket.

"They're fucking with us, right?" he asked.

She did not answer.

"So, uh, what do we do?"

No answer.

Eric sighed, padded over to the door, and peered outside. Several guards stood at the edges of the hall and several prisoners in varying states of dress were exiting their cells.

"Hey, what's going on?" Eric asked. Several prisoners shot concerned glances his way. The closest guard slowly swiveled his head toward Eric.

Eric yelped as he was yanked backwards into the cell.

"Shh!" The blonde was wide-eyed. "They'll beat us both!"

Eric focused on her face, trying to avoid the distracting features nearby. "Well, what's going on then?"

Fear played across her face and she stuttered several times before spitting out, "Showers," and fleeing for her bunk.

What's wrong with her?

She whimpered from under the blanket as Eric padded closer to her bunk. Squatting, he looked her in the eye and mustered as much an earnest tone as he could.

"Lady, I don't know what happened to you, but I know I didn't do it. Help me and I'll help you, okay?" She shook her head. Eric rocked back on his heels. "How about this, all I'm asking is for you to help me figure out the rules here. I'm not asking for anything else, okay?" She shook her head again. "Okay, well, I'm going to go take a shower. If you get your ass beat because of something I did, it's on you." Eric paused on his way out to glance back. She hadn't moved.

Eric stepped out into the hall and followed another prisoner past several closed cells to a much larger open doorway with six guards posted outside. Eric half expected the guards to swing into motion any moment at some infraction of the imaginary rules, and found himself releasing breath he hadn't known he was holding as he passed them.

The spattering of warm water called siren songs to the cold in his bones. When the wall of damp warm air hit him, he barely knew what to do. *Holy shit, warm! Finally!* Will power alone proved barely sufficient to keep him behind the person he was following. *No, if I get around this guy, I'll probably break some bullshit rule. Safer to take it slow, watch what everyone's doing.* Eric found himself in a room lined with lockers as two inmates finished stuffing their coveralls in their lockers. Not seeing anything else that seemed likely to bite him in the ass, Eric fell into step behind the pair.

He paused at the threshold when he saw two of the eight prisoners showering were female. Men and women served side by side on the *Fortune*, but unless crewmates were married, they lived in separate living spaces. Relationships were expected, but Captain Fox's law had been crystal clear: if something interfered with ship's operations, it was proscribed. Frowning, he forced himself to step into the steamy open space and keep his eyes off their curves.

As a whole, the inmates outwardly ignored his presence, but as he slipped under a cascade of heavenly warmth, he felt the attitude in the room shift. Despite the water, he shivered as the feeling threw drew a memory from his early days on the *Fortune* back to him. Even though there had been hell to pay later, he'd been jumped in the showers by a few of the lowest ranking apprentice crewmen. Being disrespectful, they'd said. More like they were the lowest rank on the boat and thought they could get away with bullying a kid half their age. Eric turned to keep his back to the wall.

Shower quick, get out before something happens.

To maintain an outward appearance of calm, he gathered soap in his hand from a wall dispenser. Like several of the other inmates, he made a point of studiously not watching the people around him while getting warm and clean as fast as possible. His skin began to ache as he warmed up. Time and cold had dulled the pain from his decontamination, but the slickness of his scalp reminded him precisely how little freedom he truly had.

Good, done, now to get out.

Eric froze as a soapy hand touched his chest. Eric opened his eyes to find a short black-haired woman with a disarming smile.

"Haven't seen you around. What's your name?" she whispered in his ear, pressing herself against him. Something in her tone set his teeth on edge.

"Quiet guy, hmm?" she purred. "Tell me your name, I can make it worth your time." The soft hand on his hip slid forward. "Doesn't feel like it would take long, hon. What do you say?" Eric grit his teeth as his stomach soured. This had to be some sort of set-up.

"Maybe you're into something else?" she asked.

"I'm into you leaving me the fuck alone," he rasped.

"You sure, hon?" she asked with a knowing smile.

"Very." Anger flashed across her features before she stalked off. Multiple eyes watched her stalk off, not just his. More than a few returned to him once she was gone. *Move.*

Eric made his way back to the locker room and dried off with a towel plucked from a rack before padding back to the central hallway. He stopped short of his cell.

Two guards stood by his door. One made it plain with a wave of a baton that Eric was to come with them. The other tossed him his blanket.

Fuck my life.

After passing through several security checkpoints and an obvious pressure door, his silent sentinels stopped outside a locked door. A few seconds later, the door hissed open and a diminutive man in blue coveralls carrying a clipboard stepped through.

"Prisoner Eighty-Seven?"

Eric nodded.

"Come with me."

As the man led him through what looked like an administrative space, Eric sighed in silent thanks for the warmer air. His new escort punched a code into a panel and motioned Eric through.

Eric stopped just inside the door as it cycled shut. The room was miniscule, hardly three meters on a side, and nigh featureless. Aside from two mirrored walls, a single small table occupied the center flanked by two cheap seats. *Hm. Well then.* Eric settled into one of the chairs and pulled the blanket tighter, resigning himself to wait for the next surprise.

The door's opening hiss snapped him from his sleep. A man carrying a briefcase in one hand and a cheap foam cup in the other hurriedly entered. Eric had not seen a suit in quite some time.

"*Guten morgen,*" the guy said and coughed as he sat his briefcase and the cup on the table. "Oh, I'm sorry, I meant good morning. Last client didn't speak English." The man chuckled and leaned forward, offering his hand. Eric stared. As he sat, the man opened his briefcase and began flipping through files. "I believe your case file says you are Prisoner Eighty-Seven?" Silence. "Look, I'm Tomas Holmes, the public defender. I'm legal counsel for your upcoming trial."

"Trial?"

"Yes, trial. Every accused in the Protectorate is entitled to a trial. Ah, yes, here's your file. Prisoner Eighty-Seven. One Eric Friedrich, I presume?"

Eric slowly sat forward. *How does he know my name?*

"Normally I would take that as a yes, but procedure mandates you answer verbally."

Lieutenant Pascal's warnings began to echo through his head. Eric chewed on his lower lip and answered, "Yeah, that's me."

"Good, good," the man mumbled to himself as he read through the file and absentmindedly sipped from his cup.

Coffee. Holy shit, that smells good.

Eric's stomach growled. His lawyer looked up, "I hate to say this to a client, but I'll be honest with you. This doesn't look very good for you, Eric. I suppose it could look a lot worse. The Protectorate's laws against piracy are extremely explicit, but we might have enough wiggle room to get a positive outcome, relatively speaking of course. I don't know about you, but I'd prefer thirty years in prison to being executed."

He'd been here a day and a half. The thought of spending thirty years in prison left a cold mass in his gut. Being an old man before seeing freedom again did not appeal. His stomach growled again. Tomas looked up from the paperwork and his head cocked to the side as he stared.

"Good God, man, are you all right?" Tomas asked.

"What?"

"You look absolutely thrashed. When was the last time you ate?"

"Two days ago, I think."

"Two days?" Tomas flipped through the file. "Eric, it says here that you were picked up outside of Protectorate space. Were you?"

"I don't really know where we were, sir. I wasn't a navigator."

"Call me Tom," Tomas said, grinning. "Here, take my coffee."

"What's so funny?" Eric asked, trying not to gulp down the hot drink.

"Well, like I said, the laws are very explicit. Where, how, and why you are apprehended matters quite a bit. So does your treatment post-apprehension. You look like a textbook case of prisoner mistreatment."

Eric sighed. "You don't say?"

"Listen, if you were outside Protectorate space, you're entitled to certain presumptions and a certain level of treatment. Under the Universal Code, you're entitled to humane treatment befitting your crimes. Breaking the Code carries some extremely stiff penalties, especially for law enforcement, and you will surely receive sympathy from the court."

The door hissed open.

"Time's up, counselor," the short man said. Eric bolted back the remaining coffee and sat the cup down.

Tomas commented while stuffing the last of his paperwork into his briefcase, "Do your best to keep your nose clean, Eric. I'll speak with the warden and try to get things straightened out." Tomas snatched up the empty cup and darted through the doorway.

The short man motioned for him. "This way, prisoner."

Clenching his jaw with frustration, Eric stood and followed the man back to the office door. "Prisoner Eighty-Seven," the man remarked as he swiped his security card, "You will be escorted back to your cell. Your next consultation is scheduled for tomorrow."

Eric followed the guards back towards his cell. He frowned when they did not stop, but continued past his cell and the showers. One of the lead guards badged through a side door and pointed inside. Eric nodded and complied.

The layout reminded him of where he'd met his lawyer, a simple cell with mirrored walls and a single table in the middle. A short man in coveralls waited in a chair on the far side of the table. Unlike the spacers' uniforms, this man's uniform did not have nametapes. Eric sat in the only open chair.

"Good evening, Eighty-seven," the man said as Eric cast a quizzical stare at the man.

"Evening?"

"Ship's clock says eighteen hundred hours, I'm sure that qualifies as evening where you come from, does it not?"

"Well, yeah? It's just that," Eric trailed off when he noticed the man smiling. Pascal's warning came to him: *All to keep you off guard, to make you despair.* Eric nodded. *All right, have it your way.*

"So, the results from your medical scan came back. I'm always delighted to work with Doctor Isaacs. She's very thorough, a consummate professional." Eric's eye twitched. "She's given you a clean bill of health and cleared you to proceed to the next stage in your detention." The man slid a sheet of paper and a pen across the desk to Eric.

"What's this?"

"Next of kin notification." As Eric looked at the empty form, a sinking pit formed in his gut. He had no family and everyone he cared about died with the *Fortune*. Eric pushed the paper back. "Surely you want someone notified of your detention?"

"Nope."

"Are you sure?" Eric nodded. "Being obstinate or no family?"

"Both?" Eric grinned and paused a moment. "Neither? Does it really matter? I'm not putting anything on that form."

"As is your right. Before we begin, I do have an administrative matter that needs resolved. We're having some issues classifying some of the items you surrendered on intake. Would you mind helping us ensure the inventory is correct?"

"Sure?"

The interrogator pulled a data tablet from under the table and tapped the screen a few times before sliding it across the table. "These items. What are they?"

Eric glanced at the pictures on screen. "The first few are safety equipment and multi-purpose tools."

"We'd figured as much. I'm much more interested in the last three."

"No clue. I'd guess some sort of machine parts."

"Some sort of machine parts? You don't know what they are?"

Eric shook his head. "Folks forget stuff in the belts on accident all the time. I'd imagine the guy who handed me the belt forgot they were in there. No idea what they are for though."

The man nodded and tapped at the tablet's screen. "So, admin's done, now the questions. Can you tell me where you were born?"

Eric blinked. He'd expected them to drill him about the *Fortune*. "Uh, no."

"No? Is that 'No, I can't tell you' or 'No I won't tell you?'"

"Can't. I have no idea where I was born."

"Ah, and your parents?"

"I don't really remember them."

"Well, Eric, let's put our cards on the table, shall we? We already know a bit about you, so lying or being evasive isn't going to help you. Your friend Terry's been pretty talkative."

Play along. "I'm sure he has."

"Oh? You two don't get along?"

Shit. "Meh, not really."

"Define 'not really.'"

"He's just some guy I've worked with before."

"And what kind of work would that be?"

"Whatever needed done. You know what it's like, right?"

"Let's pretend I don't."

"Well, it sucks being the low ranking guy on the ship. Scrub this, clean that, there's a work detail that someone needs to volunteer for and today that's you," Eric said, hoping his tone evinced some sympathy.

The man chuckled.

Eric asked, "Ah, you're familiar with being voluntold?"

"Unfortunately. I guess that's one thing we have in common."

"Well, I'm sure you've got more questions." Eric smiled to himself at the interrogator's sudden frown. *Gotcha.* Eric pondered making a game out of taking control of the conversation.

"Well, first, when did you join the pirates?"

Eric's stomach growled. "How about this, get me some food and I'll keep talking."

The man's frown deepened. "Answer a few questions and if you give me information we don't know, I'll consider rewarding you with some food."

"I'm not sure you're in a position to--" Eric's head snapped back from a fist he didn't see coming. Stars danced as he rubbed the bridge of his nose. "Or I could answer some questions. You said something about becoming a pirate?"

"Yes, yes I did. When did you join the pirates?"

"I didn't join the pirates, not the way you probably mean it." The interrogator gave Eric a deadpan stare. "Seriously."

The man tilted his head as if he were listening to something and motioned Eric to continue.

Eric continued, "I don't remember much detail, I was a kid. Something happened to my family. The pirates took me in."

The man leaned forward. "Tell me what you remember and if you're not bullshitting me, I'll fill in some blanks. I'm a nice guy like that."

"Well, where do you want me to start?"

"Work your way back from now. How many ships have you been on?"

"Well, just the one. The crew took me in, I remember that much."

"What was the ship's name?"

They're already dead, no harm talking about them. "The *Fortune*."

"And her captain?"

"Captain Fox."

"You say they took you in?"

"Yeah, like I said, the details are pretty much gone. I was too young to really remember it. They told me that they'd found a ship dead in space, that I was one of a handful of survivors."

"Did they ever tell you anything about that ship? Its name? Did they mention how it came to be 'dead in space'?"

"The name didn't seem too important to me at the time, sorry. As for how it got that way, they weren't quite sure either." Eric smirked. "I remember hearing the explanation when I was a kid and being really confused. They said something about small arms and being a kid, I thought they were talking about people with tiny arms, you know? Now? It was a mutiny or sabotage or something."

"They didn't tell you?"

"Well, I never really followed up on it."

"Why not? I would think something traumatic like that would be something you'd want to know more about. Closure."

"That's not how I meant it. I did ask, but I was a kid, you know? It was a lot to wrap my head around and past a certain point, I just accepted that it happened and there wasn't anything I could do about it. When I was older, I was told that when the *Fortune* showed up, we'd been adrift for days and had very little oxygen left."

"How exactly do you have multiple survivors and no one knows what happened?"

"If I remember right, two of the other survivors weren't much older than me and had been stuffed in a hiding spot when the shooting started. Beyond that, I guess you're right, it doesn't make a lot of sense, but that's what I know. Anyone else that could give you more information was on the Fortune when you guys destroyed her."

"Very well. Do you know what kinds of weapons were used in your supposed mutiny?"

"I think I remember hearing they found both energy and projectile weapons."

"Hmm. And your parents? Do you remember them at all?"

"Not really. I remember Dad being gone a lot. And always being serious. Mom," Eric trailed off.

"Yes?"

"Well," Eric frowned, uncomfortable, "It's just that I don't. I don't remember their faces. I can't remember their voices."

"And that bothers you?"

"A bit, yeah. It should, shouldn't it?"

The interrogator's features softened momentarily, "It would bother me, yes. You loved your parents then?"

"I guess. I mean, it sounds bad to say it like that, but I've been on my own for over half my life now and I can't really remember the half they were around for. I think if we'd had more time together, the answer would be yes."

"Well, since you're cooperating I'll be honest, Eric. Your parents were both officers in the Protectorate Navy. They had booked passage on a civilian transport that went missing. We never found the wreck. I would expect some investigator somewhere to be thankful for anything else you might be able to tell us about the *Vyzov* and its disappearance."

Eric rubbed his forehead. He'd expected everything Pascal had warned him about, but not this, not being thanked for shedding light on the past. Pascal's echoing warnings kept echoing in his head, transforming that feeling into distrust. This was too convenient.

"I don't know much more than that."

"Did they ever tell you where they found the *Vyzov*?"

"Yeah, but I don't remember." The interrogator frowned. "Hey, it was almost a decade ago."

"Well," his interrogator began, "We've established where you've been since the *Vyzov*'s disappearance. If you can help me expand on the what and why, I'll see about getting you some food from the galley, maybe even something to wear."

"Sounds like a decent idea to me."

"So, you've spent the last twelve years on the *Fortune*. What was it like? What did you do?"

Eric made a show of scratching his chin, stalling for time to think. "Well, it was what it was? I mean, I grew up in it, so it's what I came to expect. Captain Fox kept a tight ship."

"Tight ship? Clean or disciplined?"

"Both, really, but he was a stickler for discipline. Insisted that the ship came first. Makes sense when you think about it. Take care of the ship, the ship takes care of you."

"Interesting. How strict was discipline on the *Fortune*?"

"Depending on what you did, very."

"Say, if you got caught stealing from other crewmen?"

"Ten lashes."

"Lashes? As in they whipped you?"

Eric nodded.

"Interesting. Were you punished more harshly if you stole from ship's stores?"

"Not directly," Eric replied. Seeing the question coming, he continued, "There's more to it than that. Basically, at the end of every voyage, we split the profits. Stealing from the ship's stocks meant the voyage cost more, so less profits to go around. Folks looked at stealing from the ship like stealing from the whole crew. Officers tended to look the other way when someone got back at a thief. Stealing from the ship? You'd have to be an idiot."

"Did your captain not expel crewmembers?"

"Oh, he did, but someone had to make it clear they weren't a good fit. Addicts got the boot like that."

"So what about murder, rape?"

"Murderers earned summary execution. Rape was punished similarly."

"Interesting."

"You keep saying 'interesting.' Why is it so interesting?"

"By Protectorate standards it sounds like the *Fortune* was run in an almost civilized fashion. Most pirate vessels we've recovered tend towards more barbaric methods of control. You are aware of that, yes?"

Eric shrugged. "Not really. It's not that I never left the ship; I just didn't have much to do with other pirate crews."

"Speaking of leaving the ship, do you know where any the *Fortune*'s ports of call were?"

Shit.

"Not a clue. I wasn't a navigator."

"Not even a name?"

Eric shrugged. "Once you've seen one airless rock, you've seen them all. After a while, they all start looking the same."

"So the *Fortune* never traded at populated worlds or stations? You expect me to believe that?"

Eric shrugged.

"Eric, you're not helping yourself. Obstructing an investigation is a crime in the Protectorate, you know that, right?"

"No, I didn't know that, but you're still not going to like my answer."

"Why's that?"

"Because we rarely visited anywhere other than home."

"Where's home?"

"Not a navigator, no idea."

The interrogator's eye twitched and the man sighed. "Okay, what color star does home orbit?"

"Yellow."

"Is home a planet?"

"No."

"Moon, then?"

"Nope."

"What exactly is home?"

Eric paused. "An old mining station in an asteroid belt."

"Does home have a name?"

"Port Solace."

"How many people in Port Solace?"

"I don't think they ever did a census."

"Guess."

"A few hundred?"

"How many other ships ported there?"

"At least a dozen, maybe two."

"Same size as the *Fortune*?"

Eric snorted. "Nah, we were near the bottom of the pile for size."

"How many of them were warships?"

"Most?"

The interrogator glared at him. "We know multiple pirate groups take advantage of the Neutrality Accord, can you say for certain the *Fortune* has never visited any system protected by the accord?"

"I can't really say. Never heard of the Accords and I'm not a navigator."

"Ableton, Anchorage, Avalon, Baffin's Forge, Black Harbor, Caldera, Caledon, Cold Harbor, Corregidor, Dante, Erwin's Fall,

Grant, Jefferson, Jenkin's Station, Hope, Orleans, Pershing, Seraphim Prime, Teriador, Washington, and Whistler's Solace. Any of those mean anything to you?"

"One of my crewmates grew up on Orleans."

"Go on."

"Orleans is a Confederation planet. Same with Avalon and Pershing. Corregidor too, if I remember right."

"Jenkin's Station?"

"Name sounds vaguely familiar."

"It should."

"Why?"

The interrogator sat the tablet on the table and tilted it toward Eric. The display rotated as a black window opened. Seconds passed before white lettering appeared in the top left corner: Jenkin's Station. Eric assumed the white blur below the label hid details they didn't want him to know. The text vanished and the brilliant blues and greens of a planet seen from orbit filled the screen. The video panned up, showing an orbital station with dozens of ships either docked or otherwise in transit. It paused as the interrogator tapped the screen and skipped ahead. As the camera panned across one of the station's piers the interrogator paused the video and spread two fingers on the screen to zoom.

"Jenkin's Station is protected by the Accords. Which ship is in berth four on pier six?" The man asked.

Eric squinted and broke out in a cold sweat.

"Which ship?" the interrogator persisted.

Eric swallowed and answered, "That's the *Fortune*."

"Yes. Yes it is. When they took you aboard, who took care of you?"

"Excuse me?"

"When they rescued you from the wreck of the *Vyzov*, who took care of you?"

"Oh. Shit, sorry, change of subject threw me for a loop. One of the communications techs volunteered to take care of me."

"Their name?"

"Shannon. Shannon Eety."

"And this Mrs. Eety, she was a decent parent?"

"Miss Eety. I suppose you could say she was. I was a handful, considering what had happened. She couldn't have children of her own. Pretty sure that was why she volunteered."

The interrogator nodded. "Have you ever heard of a system or planet referred to as Haven?"

Eric snorted, "Haven? It's a myth."

"That's not what your companion said."

Eric shrugged. "I dunno what Terry told you, but it's bullshit."

"He seemed pretty convinced."`

"Terry's fond of convincing himself of a lot of things that aren't true. Haven is a myth, a child's tale. Think about it for a minute, if there was a truly free system independent of all this shit, who would want to leave? Why come back to this?" Eric chuckled. "If you're chasing Haven, I've got a starship to sell you."

"Fair enough. Let's forget about Haven. How about you tell me more of what you did for Captain Fox on the *Fortune*."

"I mopped. I pushed a broom. I helped out with whatever needed done, really. Move this over there, go get that thing over there. I stood around, minding my own business."

"That seems implausible. Every additional body onboard is more mass. Mass costs money, so why would Captain Fox keep unskilled labor around?"

Good point. The best lie has just enough truth in it to be convincing.

"Well for one, there's never a shortage of bullshit work to do and people who think they're too important to do it." That comment brought a hint of a wry grin from the interrogator. "Two, I have a knack for figuring things out. I'm pretty sure they had plans for me once I was educated enough."

"Really? Why would you believe that?"

"You don't need to understand a lot of math to move boxes. They taught me algebra, geometry, trigonometry, calculus."

"Calculus? Single variable or multi?"

"Single, but I wasn't done yet."

"Show me." The interrogator scribbled on a sheet of paper and slid it across the table. Eric held his hand out for the pen. "No, do it in your head."

"Fine. Well, first answer is pi." The interrogator nodded. "Second is," Eric paused for a minute as the problem was harder than it looked. "I hate anti-differentiation. Second answer is something like inverse hyperbolic tangent of x plus e to the x times whatever this squiggle is. I'm assuming that's a constant. As for the third, I think I saw something like it when I skipped ahead, but I haven't done that yet. What is it?"

"Fourier transform. Not bad, Eric. Any ideas what these plans Captain Fox had for you? We never see normal crewmen with this level of esoteric knowledge."

Shit, Eric, you fucking show-off, shut up!

"Not really. Electronics and comms? Engineer maybe? Cheaper to have an in-house specialist than to pay someone outside? Something higher than storekeeper?"

The interrogator smirked, "Yeah, storekeepers don't need that kind of math. Electronics might be plausible, but technicians get by with algebra. Calculus is a tool for engineers, designers, and the like. I'm curious what other education they gave you."

"Well, I did start on a few modules dealing with basic alternating and direct current circuits. I can tell you what a resistors, capacitors, and inductors are and how they function. I was a bit confused by the idea of non-linear resistivity though. At least in terms of what that meant to circuit design."

The interrogator nodded and entered something on the tablet. "Did you ever cover synthetic gravitons?" Eric shook his head. "No? Did they ever put you in charge of anything? Even small things like work details?"

Hah.

"Nope. Not once."

The interrogator looked him in the eye. "Are you sure? The level of education you've received is something we expect for highly technical ratings and officer candidates, not low level crewmen."

Eric shrugged. "I can't tell you what I don't know. I just know I wasn't in charge of anything. For all intents and purposes, I'm just some poor, oppressed sod."

The interrogator glanced back to his tablet and remarked, "Well, it looks like our time today is almost up. Last question, Eric. Your parents were respectable naval officers and you've clearly inherited much from them. Why did you never come back to the Protectorate?"

Eric shrugged. "I didn't know they were Protectorate officers. Why would I come back to a place I never knew I came from?"

"Fair enough. Someone will be along shortly with your food. We'll see more of each other later," the interrogator replied as he packed up.

"Uh, sir, one question before you toss me back to the wolves if I may?"

"Make it brief."

"What exactly are the rules down there? Nobody's told me shit and I've already seen one guy get beat nearly to death. I'd like to avoid that if I can."

"To be fair, the guards are given significant discretion as to the application of the rules, but unless things have changed since I worked detention, if you stay away from red lines, keep your mouth shut, and don't mess with other prisoners then you should be fine. I would say I'm sorry for you having to witness Mister Frost's lesson, but such displays are more persuasive to new prisoners than verbal warnings. Good day, Mister Friedrich."

Seeing little else to do but wait with the interrogator gone, Eric slumped forward and rested his chin on folded arms. *First rule of piracy: Always sleep when you have the chance, you never know when you won't be able to.* The clatter of a metal tray snapped him from his sleep.

"Eat. Guards will to take you back to your cell in five," the crewman delivering the meal said over his shoulder as he left.

Eric stared at the mystery meat in brown gravy on rice dish before cautiously trying a bite. *Wow, wish the food on the Fortune was this good.* The meat patty disappeared along with every other item on the tray save for the small roll of colored hard candies. Something bugged him about the multi-colored packaging. Maybe it was the cheerful lettering. *Charms. Hah.*

With a yawn, he realized for the first time in a while he wasn't cold. Standing to stretch, something orange in the seat across from him caught his eye. Curious, Eric picked up the cloth. *Better than nothing I guess.* He stepped into the cheap boxer style shorts and tied them off. The door hissed open behind him. On the way out he pocketed the candy. *Might be able to trade these for favors.*

Returning to his cell under guard, Eric made a point of looking for patterns in the layout. Nearing his cell block, Eric grew bored with the repetitive design.

Every boundary secured with deployable security bulkheads. Eight cells per block, two blocks separated by supporting infrastructure, common corridors connecting the support sections. One hundred twenty eight prisoners per wing. At least three wings, so three-hundred eighty four prisoners, assuming single level and three wings total.

What kind of warship carries brig space for this many people? How big is this ship? You could fit the whole crew of the Fortune in these three wings. Factor in space for food storage, propulsion, weapons, life support.

Eric strained to remember various considerations for ship design. The *Fortune's* executive officer, Commander Murphy, jokingly threatened to 'build my own damn ship and push off this garbage scow' multiple times a voyage. Eric vaguely remembered when Captain Fox asked what Murphy would build and why. Eric hadn't overheard the entire discussion that followed, but the parts he picked up had been informative given Murphy's past working in a shipyard.

The Shrike is easily twice the size of the Fortune in terms of volume. That's crazy. A random thought struck a glancing blow to his incredulity. *But the Gadsden, how big did Pascal say it was? Three hundred meters? Had to be bigger than that.*

Lights in the cell block flickered and died. Eric stumbled to a halt. The guards grabbed his arms from behind as the emergency lighting activated unevenly and pushed him forward at speed. On arrival, Eric found himself unceremoniously dumped into darkness beyond the doorway.

"Really getting sick of this place," Eric muttered out loud. The cell door whined as it closed and Eric froze. Even tertiary systems like the doors should not be running on minimal power.

"Svoboda?" Panic tinged the woman's voice when she asked, "Frost?"

"No, just me," Eric replied. *Svoboda must be the guy who told me to shut up.*

"What's going on?" she asked, relief in her voice.

"I'm not sure, something with the power." Several sharp vibrations kicked through the deck plates. "Or not."

"What was that?"

"These racks are bolted to the floor, right?"

"Yeah, why?"

"Get under yours."

"Why?"

"That was a rail salvo. We're shooting at someone, which means we're going to be maneuvering soon and probably pretty hard. That and there's no telling when they'll shut off artificial gravity to save power."

Whimpering carried across the darkness, but no further questions came. He padded his way across the room and knelt by the woman's rack.

"Here, take these," Eric said, handing her the candies he'd saved, and made his way back to his bed.

Eric stuffed his blanket under his rack to do the same when the door whined open and another shadow was thrown in with them. Without light to see by, Eric could only interpret the cacophony that followed as staggering followed by a quick trip to the floor.

"Fuck you, too!" their new companion bellowed. He sounded drunk. Another series of sharp vibrations shook the compartment and the drunk hooted. "Come on, buddies! Come and get 'em! Shoot straight for once, ya Navy pukes!"

Not Frost. Doesn't quite sound like Svoboda, either. Accent's wrong, more lilting than guttural. "Svoboda?"

"Who's asking?" the shadow slurred.

"The cellmate who didn't get his face caved in yesterday?"

"Oh, evenin', pup. Enjoyin' the fireworks?"

"You could say that."

"Nothing like getting shot at to make a man feel alive," Svoboda mumbled. Eric heard the results of what must have been an attempt to stand. "Fuck, I'm drunk and it's gettin' worse. Ya mind helpin' me to me rack, lad?"

"Sure. Keep talking so I can find you. It's a bit dark."

"Oh, ya want me to talk? I ain't sayin shit."

Eric snorted. "Dude, what the hell happened to you?"

"To me? I think they drunked me."

"Drunked?"

"I said drugged. I wouldn't talk then and I won't talk now!"

Eric nearly tripped over the man in the dark as the entire compartment seemed to shift violently. *There's the maneuvering I was talking about.*

"Every man should laugh in the face of death," Svoboda chuckled as Eric hauled him to his feet. The man mumbled, "Kate-lynn was a pretty young lass. She had a magnificent ass. Not rounded and pink, as you might possibly think. 'Twas grey with long ears and ate grass."

Eric snorted.

Svoboda grinned at Eric and mumbled, "Aye, that's the spirit, lad."

Eric got the man to his rack, all the while being harangued by limericks that would make most pirates blush. In the last moments before Eric fell asleep, Svoboda was still singing to himself, albeit haltingly and in an arguably more atonal fashion than earlier, if that were possible:

"Hark! When the night is falling

    Hear, Hear! The pipes are calling,

    Loudly and proudly calling, down through the glen.

    There where the hills are sleeping,

    Now feel the blood a-leaping,

    High as the spirits of the old Highland men."

. . .

Groaning brought Eric from his nap back to a now humid and incredibly stuffy dark cell. If his exhaustion was any clue, he'd been out for three hours, maybe four or five at most.

"Dear God, whatever I did last night I will never do again," Svoboda muttered. The man's accent had changed back to what it had been when Eric had first met him.

"You don't remember?" Eric asked to pass the time.

"Not a clue. My head's killing me."

"A few minutes after the lights got cut, they tossed you in here. You sounded impressively drunk for a prisoner with no access to booze."

"Tossed me in here? Back up a bit, yesterday's fuzzy."

"When we got up, the guards pulled you out. I got to see my lawyer."

Svoboda chuckled darkly.

"What's so funny?" Eric asked.

"Don't believe the lawyer shit for a minute. Keep going."

"Well, after the lawyer I spoke with an interrogator."

"You tell them anything?"

"I'm not sure."

"Not sure?"

"They kept jumping topics and it tripped me up. I tried not to tell them anything useful. Fuck them."

"That's the spirit. What next?"

"The lawyer and interrogator took maybe an hour? Two? On the way back, the lights went out and they rushed me in here. Few minutes later, they tossed you in."

"Did I say anything while I was drunk?"

"Oh yeah, you were babbling nonstop."

"What'd I say?" Svoboda sounded mortified.

"Well, you rattled off a ton of limericks. Most of them were really, really bad. Pretty sure you sang some equally horrible sounding song, too. Something about glens and highlands. You also told me they drugged you."

"Drugged? That explains everything. Bastards."

"How's that explain everything?" The weight pulling him down vanished. "Shit, there goes gravity."

"Won't be long now. Best be quiet and get to praying, son. "

Eric set his jaw. *Whatever you say, old man. I've been in enough space actions to know the only folks who see the end coming are all on the bridge. There's no point in worrying about it; if it happens I won't be around to regret not worrying.* Lying under his rack in the dark with minutes ticking to hours, Eric found his thoughts wandering. Calculus, starship design, orbital mechanics passed the time but could not keep his thoughts from returning to uncomfortable subjects.

With the *Fortune*'s destruction and his arrest, Eric slowly came to face the fact that he was adrift. *I have nothing. They're all dead. Shannon, Desi, Sokolov, the Captain, all of them. I haven't seen Pascal in how long? Days? Weeks? I know they're messing with the clock. Is my day even a full day? Is it longer? Does time even matter? Were my parents actually Protectorate Navy? Did Fox tell me the truth about finding me? Fuck. Maybe these assholes are right? What do I owe the pirates, really? Maybe I can get out of this.* Being locked in a dark cell that was steadily getting warmer with little more than looping dark thoughts irritated him.

"Fuck this. Being a prisoner sucks," Eric blurted, brushing sweat from his brow.

"You haven't seen half of it yet, boy," Svoboda remarked.

"How long do you think this will last?" the woman asked. She squeaked as unseen forces shoved everyone against the bottom of their bunks for several seconds.

"Until it's over," Svoboda answered. "That or we die. Either way, until it's over."

"Either one of you want to tell me why I got accosted in the shower? Some woman offered," Eric coughed, "Services in exchange for my name."

Svoboda chuckled, "That would be Kaylee. She does that to all the new people."

"Why?"

"Interrogators reward prisoners for any information they dig up on the others. Sometimes that reward is clothing. Sometimes it's whatever drug you might be addicted to."

"That's--"

"Ingenious?"

"I was going to go with depraved."

Svoboda laughed. "No, of all the messed up things here, at least that one makes sense. If you can get the prisoners to turn on each other, less work for you. I'll grant you, it can be immoral, but you want depraved, that's the fact the guards will cave your skull in if you're caught talking."

Eric sighed. "That, I've seen. How do you know all this?"

"Been here a while, boy. You can whisper, but more than that and guards come calling. I'd lay good money their microphone system only kicks in over a certain volume."

"And you're telling me that they reward people for breaking the rules?"

"As long as you're not caught, yes."

"None of this makes sense. Why?"

"Conflicting rules, latitude to enforce them? Keeps the prisoners off balance and allows them to decide which rule gives them what they want more."

"That's some sick shit."

"Welcome to the Protectorate."

"Why hasn't someone caved in our skulls for talking?"

"Whatever's going on, they've cut the power to anything non-essential. No lights, no air circulation. The mics probably don't draw much power, but all that network infrastructure they're attached to does. Or I could be wrong and they're just letting us think they're not listening. Might not want to blab about whatever you don't want them to know just in case. Beyond that, it seems the guards do what they want. Sometimes you'll get away with talking for a while, other times the slightest peep brings the truncheon."

"Wow." Eric paused in thought. "So when I got tossed in here and you told me to shut up, you were doing me a favor?"

"Suppose you could look at it that way."

"How else could I look at it?"

"Doing myself a favor is more like it. Less I know, the better. If I don't know anything about you, they can't torture or drug it out of me. Besides which, if you got executed because of something they pulled out of me, your blood's on my hands. I've got enough blood on my hands already without resorting to the ostensibly innocent. Giving you the benefit of the doubt, of course."

Flickering lights and the sound of fans spinning up jerked them from bored catatonia.

"Bout time," Eric remarked as he emerged from under his rack.

Svoboda looked over at him from the top of his own. "Was hoping whoever that was would get lucky and core us."

"Why would you want that?" the woman asked, horrified.

"Tired of being helpless and waiting for the knife, lady. I'd rather die with honor, knowing these Protectorate assholes got sent to hell with me than be put down like an animal." Svoboda coughed repeatedly and spat on the floor before continuing, "If the lights are back on, then the listening devices will be back soon, too, assuming they were ever shut off. Best we get back to shutting up and forget we ever talked."

Eric frowned but could not argue. While he welcomed the break in the monotony and crushing silence conversation brought, he had no desire to see more of the guards. The clack of an extending collapsible baton echoed in his mind and he shivered.

Svoboda rolled off his bunk. Standing straight, he rolled his shoulders and began a series of slow, deliberate stretches. He motioned to Eric.

"You could be here for months," the man whispered. "Doing nothing but sitting around, you'll waste away before you ever get off this ship. Let me show you a few things to keep you sharp. Maybe you'll learn, maybe not. Either way, it's something to do that isn't sitting around being bored."

Eager for anything that passed time, Eric nodded. Svoboda led him through a myriad of stretches, most of which focused on loosening major joints and muscle groups.

"What?" Eric quietly asked when the man paused some time later.

"You've been in a fight before, yes?"

"A few."

"And you won?" Svoboda sounded doubtful.

"Usually."

"Good, hit me."

"What?"

"You heard me. I'd like to see what you think you know. The guards won't care, they generally only show up for talking."

Eric shrugged. He leveled a haymaker at the man's head, and found himself flipping across the floor before he knew what had happened.

"Sloppy. Very sloppy. I thought you said you won those fights?"

"Mmph," Eric mumbled, picking himself up. "I did."

"Sad. Would you like to actually know how to fight, or are you content to win through dumb luck, brute force, and ignorance?"

"Well, dumb luck, brute force, and ignorance have been pretty effective so far," Eric said as he cracked a grin. At the man's deepening frown, Eric quietly followed up with, "Though, on the serious side, actual instruction wouldn't hurt."

Svoboda nodded. "Come back here. Stand the way you were, and do that again, but quarter speed."

Eric squared off, and before he could move Svoboda began critiquing him. His stance was wrong, his hips pointed the wrong way. His center of balance was off and would only get worse with the swing. Eric began his wind-up as prompted while the man continued. Eric telegraphed his intentions too early. The punch was infective, too slow, and failing to use his hips to full effect sapped the blow's strength. Instead of ducking or rearing back as Eric expected, Svoboda moved inside the swing while pivoting toward the punch and caught Eric's arm with both hands. Continuing the pivot, Svoboda sank to one knee while dragging Eric around in a wide circle. He let go just before Eric toppled.

Eric's stumbled forward. He turned to face Svoboda and

nodded. *Inertia, center of balance. I gave him my arm and begged him to throw me. No, I threw myself.*

"Okay, I see what you meant. How do I do better?"

"First, I teach you how to fall without hurting yourself."

Eric lost track of time while he learned the basics how to get thrown across a room filled with metal obstacles without injuring himself. He picked up the various ways to roll out of an impact quickly, but slapping the floor to break a fall eluded him for several attempts.

The door to their cell hissed open, and the pair froze, expecting the guards and their batons to make an appearance. Seconds passed before Eric glanced over at his cellmate who shrugged in reply. Eric padded to the doorway and glanced out. Several other prisoners were doing the same thing.

"Guards at the shower room. Guess it's shower time."

Svoboda nodded. "That's enough for now. I'll show you more later."

"So, uh, why are you showing me this to begin with?" Eric asked.

"Passing time, nothing more. Well, perhaps our roommate might factor in a bit. Frost is rather unpleasant to deal with. The thought of having a capable helping hand doesn't hurt. We can't depend on the guards to deal with him," Svoboda replied.

Eric rubbed at his aching muscles as he wandered down the hall to the showers. As before, every prisoner seemed to be studiously ignoring everyone else. Unnoticed scrapes and bruises sang under hot water and soap. He emerged from the showers a short time later without being accosted only to find a pair of guards waiting for him outside.

A brisk walk led to him sitting in yet another cheap, uncomfortable chair behind a desk, waiting.

"Good morning, Eric. I hope you weren't disturbed by last night's excitement?" the interrogator said as he entered with a satchel over his shoulder. *Same man from last session.*

"Nah," Eric replied, "Sitting in a dark room hoping the next loud noise isn't a rail slug tearing through the hull isn't a new thing for me."

"Such is naval service, long stretches of boredom punctuated by periods of terror," the man said as he dropped his satchel by his seat, pulled out the chair, and sat. "So, have you given any thought to what we went over yesterday?"

"Uh, to be honest, I'm still a little bleary-eyed. Bored stupid doesn't mean I slept well. What part of yesterday are you referring to?"

The man pulled his tablet out of the satchel as he commented, "Your parents and your loyalty to the Protectorate."

"Well, yeah, that had rattled around in my head a bit while I was going stir-crazy."

"And?"

"And what? I wasn't old enough to remember my parents or what they believed in. The only Protectorate I've known has been trying to kill me and folks I came to call friend for the last decade. Why would I have any loyalty to a people that have been trying to kill me my entire life?"

The interrogator blinked, mouth paused mid word. "Mr. Friedrich, perhaps we have not been clear. Under our laws a citizen such as yourself is afforded certain privileges not granted to non-citizens suspected of piracy. Such privileges are precisely that, privileges. Do you know the difference between rights and privileges?" It was Eric's turn to blink. "Privileges can be revoked, Mr. Friedrich. All I need to do is say the word and you get to find out how your Confed partner's life has been this last week. So, which is it? Carrot or stick?"

Eric opened his mouth to speak but the man kept talking.

"We had our computer forensics experts look over your data tablet."

Oh fuck.

"They were perplexed at its vintage. How did you come to be in possession of it?"

"Uh, picked it up from supply?" Eric stammered.

A vein on the man's temple throbbed as he rubbed the bridge of his nose before continuing. "Sorry, did I hear you correctly? Did you just tell me you picked it up from supply?"

Eric shrugged, "I don't know what you expect me to tell you, man. A lot of things worked that way on the *Fortune*. You didn't ask supply where shit came from, you just requested shit. Why is that hard to believe?"

"So Captain Fox's supply gets their hands on antique systems regularly? And issues them to their lowest ranking members?" The man shook his head and tapped at his tablet. "I can see issuing systems with faulty batteries, but I have a hard time believing you'd take a tablet out on a mission that can barely stay on long enough to finish booting.

"Son, I was going to try to use that tablet as a carrot. I was going to see if we could fix it for you. While religion is frowned upon in the Protectorate, religious texts are a privilege afforded to accomplished citizens in good standing." Eric stared at the man. "The battery lasted long enough for our tech to identify the open application. But, speaking of data forensics, we found some interesting data saved on your suit camera. You have some explaining to do, son."

"But--"

"Save it, I'm done giving you the opportunity to waste my time. No, you can cool your heels here by yourself. Enjoy missing breakfast."

Eric sat in dumb silence as the interrogator grabbed his satchel and stormed out of the room.

"Well shit," he commented to no one in particular.

Eric sat back and slipped into bored catatonia as minutes slipped by. He started at the sound of the door opening.

"Eric, what did you do?" Tomas asked as he entered. He sighed at the Eric's quizzical stare. "I was prepping for an appointment when I overheard Mr. Hettinger. He's pissed. What happened?"

"Well, I honestly don't know what his problem is. He came in and started laying down some guilt trip about how I should be loyal to the Protectorate."

"And?"

"And I told him I had every reason not to be."

"Oh dear. What words did you use? Exactly what words?"

"I think it was something like 'Why would I have any loyalty to a people that have been trying to kill me my entire life?'"

Tomas gave him a disbelieving look. "That's it?"

"Yeah."

"What's the context? What were you talking about? Be specific." Tomas sighed and wiped his brow after Eric's explanation. "Good, that doesn't qualify as a renunciation."

"Er, renunciation?" Eric asked.

"Under the Protectorate Code, citizens making disloyal statements can be stripped of their citizenship. What you said, while it comes terribly close, doesn't qualify."

"Tomas, can I ask you a question?"

"Sure, what's on your mind?"

"What would have happened if I had actually renounced my citizenship, even unknowingly?"

Tomas frowned. "You don't want to know."

"I do, tell me."

His lawyer shifted in his seat uncomfortably. "Depending on your crime, you would be subject to anything from increased interrogation methodology to immediate termination."

"What?!"

"Under the Admiralty Code, the Reasonable Doubt Doctrine only applies to citizens. So long as the judicial authority entertains a reasonable doubt as to whether or not you committed the crime in question, you are protected against summary punishment."

"I--wait, you're telling me they don't have to prove someone committed a crime to execute them?"

"The Admiralty Code is a bit more complicated than that, but the simple version is if they're a non-citizen, no."

"But," Eric sputtered several times before finding his words, "That hardly makes sense. On the *Fortune*, you were presumed innocent until proven guilty."

"An outmoded legal anachronism, useful for coddling sheep and placating the morally weak."

"Excuse me?"

"Look at it this way, Eric. The Protectorate Provost deals with criminals every day and it's a vast, vast organization. The Naval Provost, a tiny part compared to the rest, bears a disproportionately heavy load. On the civil side, we are the preeminent immigration, trade, and travel enforcement bureau." Tomas cleared his throat. "In their military capacity, they patrol common space lanes, patrol select extra-stellar zones, and provide interdiction services where needed. They also deal with pirates. Does that sound like something anyone can do on the cheap?"

Creeping horror fought to keep him from pondering the implications. Real justice didn't happen because real justice was expensive. *Smile. Act like this isn't sickening.* Eric offered, "Well, I guess not."

"Precisely. Average citizens complain about the fees lawyers charge, but even the most expensive fees vanish when you compare them to the cost of operating an interstellar warship. Operating a fleet of them? Unfathomable, but necessary. There's only so much currency to go around, and the Protectorate listens to its citizen's needs. They need security, but not at the expense of crushing poverty. As a result of popular demand, the Admiralty Code has evolved to limit costs. Can you imagine how many more lawyer billets the Naval Provost would have to staff if they accorded everyone the same privileges? Let's not even discuss the quaint idea of rights, here. How many more ships would they need if they had to transport every person who crossed their airlocks back to face trial? Those costs spiral, Eric. Larger ships mean more fuel, more food, more air. More lawyers, more fees. While I wouldn't mind a slice of that pie, it would be a financial black hole and in the end we would have neither security nor money."

Eric's skin crawled. "So, the guy picked up with me, he's been executed?"

"Oh, I have no idea," Tomas shrugged. "Probably."

Eric blinked. "I suppose that's what he meant, then."

"Who meant what?" Tomas asked.

"Mr. Hettinger. He told me that all he had to do was say the word and I'd find out how that guy's life has been the last week."

"That's preposterous. He's an interrogator, not an adjudicator."

"So, he was bullshitting me?"

"Not entirely. The adjudicator monitors all interrogations and can render judgment at any time."

Eric shivered. "The whole thing is unnerving. I say one wrong thing and I get a bullet in the face."

"Actually, no. If we still used bullets for that sort of thing, it would be to the back of the head. Fewer issues with unreliable penetration. Energy weapons don't share the same limitations or benefits of ballistics but just about any angle would work provided enough wattage. Besides which, energy costs money and airlocks are cheap." Eric stared at the man's sudden smile. "It's a joke, Eric. There are laws against dumping waste in space lanes.

"Though, seriously, your comrade might be fine. You said he was a Confed citizen? Well, diplomatic relations are a factor with executions. Depending on who he is there's a decent chance he's still drawing oxygen.

"Oh, I'm not sure when I'll see you next. My schedule is completely trashed thanks to the excitement earlier. I did file the paperwork like I said I would. The magistrate granted a preliminary injunction, but I don't expect much more than that until we return to Protectorate space. They'll pull your file once we're in range and double check any data before presenting it to a judicar. If you can keep your nose clean and not say or do anything stupid, you should be fine."

Tomas paused in the doorway.

"Eric, have you eaten today?"

"Not yet."

Tomas scowled as he left and Eric slouched in his chair. He had begun to drift back into a bored stupor when the door opened. The same attendant who'd brought him food earlier had brought another tray. When Eric finished the man escorted Eric back to his cell.

Winter

Days passed, but exactly how many escaped him. The night cycle seemed to always start and end sooner than it should. The sleeplessness bothered him, but hunger compounded his discomfort more. No matter what or how much he ate at the common cafeteria Svoboda had shown him, hunger continued to gnaw at him. Eric spent the majority of his wake periods sore and nigh exhausted.

With little else to do, the exercise routines Svoboda taught him filled his time. While no means an expert, by what felt like the sixth day Eric had managed to learn enough of what Svoboda had called the art of falling that the older man added a close-quarter hand-to-hand drill and quiet sparring to their routine. On what might have been the eighth day, things changed.

Lights flickering brought him out of deep sleep. Eric sat up, rubbing at his eyes and noticed the woman's bunk lay empty. *Odd, they haven't pulled anyone out in the middle of the night before. I should've heard it.* He stood and stretched for several moments before Svoboda groaned and made to get up. Sobbing carried from the hallway as the cell door cycled open. Eric turned to the door and found himself face to face with the muzzle of a guard's energy rifle.

"Woah," Eric uttered, raising his hands and backing away from the doorway as three more guards entered pointing their rifles at his mentor. Eric blinked in confusion. The muzzle pointed at him never wavered as the others pulled Svoboda from the cell and the guard backed through the doorway.

The woman toppled through the doorway from a shove and collapsed face down on the floor as the door cycled shut. Eric rushed to her side and hissed when he rolled her shaking frame over. Deep purple bruises circled her wrists and her neck. Swelling pressed her right eye shut and blood trickled from her nose and a multitude of cuts.

"Holy shit." Surprise vaporized as the situation clicked. She was wearing orange coveralls. *You only get clothes when you cooperate.* "What did you tell them?"

She lay limply in his arms, sobbing.

Anger tinged his words when he asked again, "What did you tell them?"

"Everything," she sobbed. Her cries grew louder when his hands tightened around her wrists.

"What?" Eric asked. "What do you mean everything?"

"I tried telling them I didn't know anything," she bawled.

"What is everything?" Eric snarled, clenching her wrists.

"You and Svoboda," she gasped between sobs. "They kept asking. I didn't want to tell them! Please don't hit me."

Disgust surged through him as the despair in her tone hit him, damping his anger. Eric sat back on his haunches and let go of her hands when she pulled away from him.

This is wrong. This is all wrong. Nothing makes sense.

His mental logjam loosened while his gut tightened at the thought of betrayal. Yet there were her injuries. He stared at her blankly. From her feeble attempts to stand or crawl he realized the interrogators must have done something to her legs.

Later. Sort this out later. Help her now.

She squeaked and began to wail when he moved over and picked her up.

"Quiet," he said, trying not to let his anger color his words as he carried her to her bunk. "I'm not going to hurt you." By the time he gently laid her on the mattress and covered her, she had quieted.

"Look, lady, I'm not going to lie. I'm pretty pissed off right now." She hid her face. "But I'm not sure I'm angry at you. They beat it out of you." Eric paused for a breath and the door hissed open. "Fuck, what now?"

"Ah, good morning, meat," Frost said as he sauntered in. "Ah, missed me while I was gone, Leah?" Frost smiled, showing a mouth full of pearly white teeth. The woman whimpered. "So good to be home again. What did I miss? Where's our friend?"

"Friend?"

"The guy from Proske, Svoboda."

"They just took him."

"Oh? Good," Frost said, and started to unzip his coveralls as he walked toward them. "Go mind your own business, meat. Leah and I have some catching up to do."

Eric scowled up at the man. *Not happening, asshole.*

"Scram, meat. Nothing personal, I don't share." Frost fixed him with an icy stare. Heartbeats passed and inside the blink of an eye, Frost grabbed Eric by the throat and lifted him to his feet. "Last chance. Go."

Eric blinked as color faded from the edges of his vision and his skin tingled. "Fuck you," he spat. Light exploded and stars shot across his vision as Frost's fist hammered against his face. Eric heard more than felt something pop with the first punch and by the fourth, brilliant crisscrossing stars blotted out the world before it all went black.

An incessant high pitched ringing clawed at Eric's ears. He was on his back. He couldn't see, something was in his eyes. He couldn't feel his face, couldn't feel much of anything. Most importantly, he couldn't breathe, something thick filled the back of his throat. He tried to swallow, but gagged instead. His stomach clenched and he rolled just in time as it emptied itself with surprising vigor. Panting, he pawed at his eyes and when he opened them his hands glistened with blood. Amid a puddle of his last meal and a startling amount of blood, two broken teeth glistened back at him.

He shook his head a few times, trying to clear it and the ringing resolved into a warbling cry. *Leah.*

"God, I love it when they fight," Frost sighed somewhere behind him.

The satisfaction in Frost's voice turned Eric's stomach and lit something dark deep in his soul. As Eric struggled to sit up, Frost slapped Leah to shut her up. Insensate, she put up little resistance as a naked Frost wrestled her face down. The world spun as Eric staggered to his feet.

"I knew you missed me," Frost sighed, either unaware or ignoring Eric's movement.

Moments later the man grunted when Eric's elbow crashed into the side of his head. Grabbing the rapist by the shoulders, Eric heaved, pulling Frost off Leah. The sight of her, bloody handprints across her hips, hair splayed out as she looked wide-eyed over her shoulder at him, pupils pinpricks from fear, etched itself into his memory.

White hot agony shot up Eric's leg. Air rushed from his lungs in a howl of pain as he toppled over from Frost's kick to his knee. Grabbing at the side of the bunk, he managed to get half way standing when Frost kicked him in the ribs. Something popped. Frost bounced his head off the bunk's frame with a fist.

"Fucking white knights," Frost spat, kicking him again. "Couldn't leave it alone, could you? Couldn't just walk away?" Hands grabbed him and the cell heaved and rolled as Frost tossed him against Svoboda's rack. Hands tugged at his legs and he dimly heard fabric ripping. "You wanted it, you're going to get it." Eric struggled to rise, but a hand grabbed the back of his head and pressed his face into the mattress. Stars swarmed as he fought to get air. Eric felt Frost press up against him as darkness enveloped him.

Noise boomed in his ears, resolving into a song he vaguely associated with his parents. Eric felt more than heard noise of a sizable starship drive. It was dark. He heard a click, and light spilled into the cramped room he was in. His father knelt, dropping several bottles of water and protein bars at his feet.

"Love, sixty seconds," Eric heard his mother say from outside the closet.

"I know," Father said, his features hardening. "Eric, you remember what we

talked about, right? No matter what you hear, stay quiet and do not come out of the closet. Do not open the stateroom door. If we don't come back, the fox will save you when he gets here."

"Thirty seconds."

"I heard you," Father growled in annoyance as he stood and pulled a magazine from the vest he wore. "Son, grow up strong. Live with honor, protect the weak, punish the wicked." The door closed and darkness hid Eric's confused face. He heard metallic clacking outside the closet the adult in him knew were the sounds of slides being racked and bolts riding home on full chambers.

"Eric, we love you," he heard Mother say right before the deck under him bucked and the sound of the drive stopped.

"God, forgive us," Father muttered.

The stateroom door opened, and as it cycled shut, he heard his parents yell, "Liberty or death!"

The sound of automatic gunfire jolted him awake. *Live with honor.* Blood coated the mattress before him. He was slumped against Svoboda's bunk. *Protect the weak.* He hurt. Every breath brought pinching agony. Pressed against the floor, his battered knee screamed. He couldn't feel his face and could taste only blood. Everything that wasn't numb echoed cries of pain. Frost had violated him in a way Doctor Isaacs couldn't. The world wavered, threatening to fade back to darkness again. *Punish the wicked.*

"Don't worry," Eric heard Frost say behind him. "I washed it off." *Punish the wicked.* Leah's mewling carried over Frost's grunts. *Punish.* Eric weakly rolled to a sitting position on the floor. *The.* The sight of Frost on top of Leah sent a shiver through him. With every thrust the anger flooding his vision beat a deeper crimson. *Wicked.* Eric's hands closed on the discarded set of orange coveralls on the floor next to him. Shifting to get his good leg under him, he wound the fabric around his hands.

Launching forward, Eric looped the fabric around Frost's neck before the man could react. Eric heaved back. Chaos followed, with grunts and limbs flailing as the pair rolled off onto the floor. The lancing agony from his injured knee only enraged him further. Despite Frost's flailing, Eric managed to stay on top. Frost tried to rise, but Eric inched his good knee up between the man's shoulder blades and leaned back, pulling with everything he had.

Eric closed his eyes, trying to muster whatever strength he could find to keep pulling. Seconds passed as Frost's struggles weakened. *Live with honor.* Eric heard a woman sob. *Protect the weak.* Frost had gone limp some time ago. *Punish the wicked.* Sometime after Frost had gone limp, the surge of adrenaline broke like a fever, leaving him weak and shaky.

"Eric," Leah said, "He's dead."

Eric opened his eyes. Frost's face, craned to the side, looked bloated, purple. The man's eyes were open, stained red from broken blood vessels, and unmoving. Eric slumped forward and unwound the bloody cloth from his fists. Panting, he dragged himself onto Svoboda's rack.

Fuck you, you piece of shit. Fuck you, and fuck this place. Eric blinked as realization dawned on him. *And screw the Protectorate shitheads who made this possible. No, the Fortune was more my home than the Protectorate ever could be.*

"What are you doing?" Leah asked as Eric took Frost's bloody coveralls.

I'm a pirate. We keep what we kill.

He opened his mouth to say just that when the door cycled open. Eric raised his hands weakly as a half dozen guards piled into the room.

"Nice of you to show up late to the party, assholes," he growled.

An energy rifle pulsed in response and the world dropped away beneath him.

Interrogation

HE WAS DIMLY AWARE OF A RHYTHMIC HUM, ONE SO DEEP IT WAS felt more than heard. His entire body ached, but he was warm, almost hot, and weightless. Thought moved languidly, like he the border between sleep and waking. Something was in his mouth and he couldn't move or open his eyes. Even though logic told him he should be panicking, Eric found himself oddly at peace.

Sometime later the hum changed, the low end dissipated leaving a higher pitched faint whine he couldn't hear before. A chill began to spread from the crown of his head. He still couldn't move. The line of cold inched downward followed by a progressive feeling of weight. A quick riot of sound surprised him before he realized it was liquid draining from his ears. When he could hear again, the whine had quieted to a nearly imperceptible level that echoed slightly.

Hollow? I'm in some sort of tube? Something rubbery pulled up against his armpits as the chill dragged past his chest. *Where the hell am I?*

Panic crept about at the edges as the line dropped further and paused even with the top of his toes. With a loud metallic whump, the last of the warm liquid vanished leaving him hanging limply from whatever the two rubbery supports were under his arms.

An unfamiliar voice echoed up from below, "I must protest, this is a grievous violation of medical ethics."

"Duly noted, Doctor. Stand aside."

That voice. Hettinger.

"My oath prevents me from allowing you to harm my patient, Major."

"Also noted and easily resolved. Once your people have finished, this man is no longer your patient."

"That's preposterous, do you even have anyone rated to provide care for someone in his state?"

"Doctor Barnes, perhaps you should speak with our Director, Doctor Isaacs. I believe her qualifications supersede your own."

Sharp pain from his side distracted Eric from the conversation and buzzing filled his ears. Gloved hands guided his body as they lowered him onto an unseen surface. Numerous sharp but fleeting stings kissed his arms and wrists. A familiar female voice pierced the receding buzz.

"Doctor Barnes, I assure you I am more than qualified to care for your patient. I ran a nano-med level facility before joining the Provost."

Doctor Barnes made a non-committal grunt. "This whole situation is still highly unusual."

"I apologize, Doctor. We had little choice, both then and now. The medical facility in the detention zone did not present the best option to treat his injuries."

"I never did find an adequate reason for his injuries in the file provided, Doctor."

"And you won't. State security takes precedence."

"Be that as it may, the injuries he presented with on admission leave little room for the imagination. Multiple blunt trauma to various points on the cranium and thorax, micro-fissures on both orbital bones, malnutrition, mild hypothermia, multiple broken ribs, two fractured pre-molars, a missing molar, massive trauma to the knee, nasal fracturing, concussion, epidural hematoma, defensive wounds on the hands and arms, rectal tearing indicative of forced penetration. His records were remarkably bare. What sort of mad house are you running?"

"The type you are not cleared for, Doctor. What is his status?"

"The nasal fracturing, fissures, damage to the ribs, blunt trauma, and tearing have been repaired. The concussion and the dental issues, corrected. He needs at least another two days in the tank for me to sign off on the hematoma and the rebuild of his knee. Treatment of the hematoma was unexpectedly problematic due to spontaneous spot bleeds."

"Expected."

"Expected how?"

"Minor side effect of exposure to certain substances."

"What substances would that be?"

"Again, you're not cleared to know, but I'm sure you could figure it out. Your file says you should be bright enough to, anyway."

"How is interfering with nano-reconstruction minor?"

"Cost-benefit analysis, Doctor Barnes. Nothing more. Do you have anything else we should be aware of?"

"Aside from a complaint to the Ethics board, no."

Light and melodic, Doctor Isaacs' laugh sent chills down Eric's spine. "Do what you feel you must, Doctor Barnes. Do what you must, as do we." Doctor Barnes grumbled and stomped off. "Major, you have your orders. Once he's been turned over, you'll have less than forty-eight hours to get what you can from our friend here before we are forced to present to the judicars. Do I need to stress the importance of what he needs to clarify?"

"No, Ma'am."

"Good. I have little enough time to waste it playing at niceties with the naïve. Do not needlessly interrupt me again. Get me that information, Drew. You have your orders."

"Yes, Ma'am."

Footsteps led away and a door cycled. Someone wheeled Eric's gurney into another room.

"Good, thank you, Rob. We'll finish up here."

"Anything else, Doctor Barnes?"

"Just the clean-up of the tank room."

"Roger that, Doctor."

"Doctor?"

New voice, female.

"Yes, nurse?"

"According to these readings, the paralytics are still active, but he's conscious. Likely has been for some time."

"Interesting. Anything else?"

"Everything else is inside parameters."

"Good, administer the counter-agent, slow dose."

"Are you sure, Doctor Barnes? Don't you want security here?"

"Nurse, we have enough chemical restraints in this room that if I can't deal with him, I doubt adding security personnel to the mix will help."

A hot sting on Eric's arm accompanied the chuffing whine of a pneumatic injector. Several seconds passed before the warmth in his arm spread. Eric's hand jerked as a sense of calm descended over him.

"Relax, you've been asleep for quite some time, several weeks. You may experience some nausea, and disorientation as the medications work out of your system. Lack of muscle coordination is very common. I've administered some anti-anxiety medication along with the counter-agent to help your transition. When you can, sit up and we can finish the exam." Something electronic chimed and Doctor Barnes sighed. "Nurse, Doctor Chekta is requesting additional assistance in ward two, low priority. Do you mind seeing what she needs, I can handle this."

"Not a problem, Doctor."

Eric struggled to sit up as the nurse left. He was naked, save a white sheet covering him from the waist down.

"Shit," he groaned, "Feels like I have a hundred kilos sitting on my chest."

"Paralytics, son. That's expected," Doctor Barnes replied. "Now, tell me your name."

Eric blinked and stared at the older man in the white coat as he fought back sudden nausea. "Eric Friedrich."

"Good. Citizenship status?"

"Protectorate, I think? I'm pretty sure."

"Date of birth?"

Eric gave the man a puzzled frown.

"Possibly nothing. Most people are fuzzy about some types of memory recall after the procedures you've been through. Will need a few more tests to make sure, but it should only last a few days, tops. Last thing you remember?"

"Before waking up in the tube?"

"Yes, before that."

"Energy rifle leveled at my face."

"That explains some of the damage, I suppose. Why the rifle?"

Eric grinned. "I killed a man." The doctor's hand slipped into his pocket. "It's alright, Doc. Frost had it coming."

"How exactly do you justify killing another human being?" Doctor Barnes asked. Eric could hear the quotes around justify.

"He tried to rape my cellmate. I think I stopped him? Doc, my head hurts. It's all disjointed." Dr. Barnes frowned and glanced at the tablet in his hand.

"Sip what's in the cup in front of you. It's mostly water, but the paracetamol should help."

Wobbly, Eric reached for the cup. The doctor waited a few minutes before continuing.

"Now, you think you stopped this Frost from raping your cellmate?"

The question broke open the floodgates and Eric shuddered as the memories fit into place. "No. I didn't. I mean, I remember what happened now. I tried to stop him, but I couldn't. He knocked me out." The doctor's eyebrows rose.

"Do you remember this man forcing himself on you?" Unsure, Eric nodded weakly and rubbed his head. "It sounds like you tried to do the right thing, Eric. There's nothing to be ashamed of."

"No, I don't remember that, Doc. I mean, I guess he could have--" Eric shuddered and gawped. He couldn't breathe. It was dark, someone was pressing his face against something lined with cloth, a mattress. He tugged with all his strength at the hand at the back of his head, but it wouldn't move.

Snapping of fingers shattered the illusion. "Eric? Back here, Eric. You tried to do the right thing, Eric. Do you hear me? The right thing. You'll need counseling, but time will help you come to terms."

"He did it anyway."

Doctor Barnes rubbed his forehead and looked at him gravely. "Son, you did more than what most would. You stood up. Fail or not, you tried to stop it."

"When I woke up the first time, he was raping her."

"Try not to think about--Wait, the first time? Her? You were kept in co-ed cells?" Shock, confusion, and horror warred across the older man's expression.

"Co-ed, yeah. He'd knock me out, I'd get back up. Knocked me out twice."

"I'm not judging, Eric, but why? What motivated you to keep getting back up?"

"I," Eric sighed as frustration and echoes of anger filtered through him, "I don't know." *Live with honor, protect the weak, and punish the wicked.* Eric shivered at the echo of his father's voice. "I wasn't raised to just stand by and let that kind of shit just happen, Doc. I just, I-I got so angry when I couldn't stop him."

The doctor nodded, tapping away at his tablet.

"So, murdering this man was an act of hate or vengeance?"

"No, not hate. Not even vengeance. Justice. What kind of person rapes another person? When I woke up the last time I figured either he died or I did."

"He died or you. Why you?"

"Because then I," Eric paused. "Then I would have died with honor."

The doctor visibly froze.

"Where did you say you were born?"

Eric puzzled over the doctor's reaction. "I didn't."

"Where were you born, then?"

"Protectorate space somewhere. I don't remember, honestly. Something happened to my parents and I was rescued by pirates. That's all I know."

"Pirates?"

Eric sighed, "Yes, pirates. I grew up on the ship you guys just destroyed. Or, I guess, destroyed a few weeks ago."

"I guess that explains it, then. Sorry, that turn of phrase reminded me of someone I knew when I was younger, that's all. Look, I have to turn you over to detention now that you've checked out. Drink this," the doctor said. Eric knocked back the offered cup's flavorless contents and watched the doctor jot more notes into his tablet.

"Doc, I don't feel too good," Eric said as his sight blurred a few minutes later and his stomach leaped into his throat.

Doctor Barnes nodded as he laid Eric back on the gurney, "Common side effect of the medication in that last cup. Your body might be healed, but your mind is not. I've given you something to help with that. As in all things, Eric, this too shall pass." The older man shook his head and tapped the tablet's screen. A door opened moments later.

"He's ready?"

"Yes, Mr. Hettinger, he's about as ready as he's going to get."

"Good. Thank you for your efforts, Doctor. We'll take it from here."

"One thing though, Mr. Hettinger."

"Yes?"

"You were there for my conversation with Doctor Isaacs, so you remember the exposure to substances bit?"

"Yes?" Impatience billowed from Hettinger's voice.

"I don't know what that substance was, so I have no idea if there are lasting effects. There's no way for me to tell you for certain that Mr. Friedrich won't have any further issues stemming from that brain injury."

"Issues like what? Worst case scenario."

"Worst case? Well, by regulation and standard of care policy, I can't guess."

Hettinger harrumphed. "And if you were a guessing man?"

"Stroke, hemorrhage, death. I can't say for certain, but given the areas we had spontaneous bleeds, I'd expect short term memory to be the most effected with the possibility of seizures. Rate of incidence may or may not coincide with stress level."

Hettinger growled and barked orders out the doorway. With guards entering the exam room, Doctor Barnes leaned over and pulled Eric to a sitting position. The older man whispered in Eric's ear as he did so.

The words meant nothing to him, but the doctor's serious cast stilled Eric's tongue as he was led from the room.

Nawgale huayheh? What does that mean?

Eric was still turning those two words over in his head when he noticed the guards were leading him through unfamiliar corridors. Crewmen in coveralls stared after him as they passed.

What, never seen a naked guy walking down the passageway before?

As they passed through a blast door at a security checkpoint, Eric realized how segmented the *Shrike*'s design was. Inside the detention areas, the hallways were bland, repetitive. Outside, where the medical facility had been, the halls were better lit and far more comfortable, less bland. By the time the guards stopped, he'd determined the cell blocks were nigh completely isolated from the rest of the ship. The average crewman on the *Shrike* had no clue what happened beyond the checkpoint's blast shield and probably never would.

"After you, Mr. Friedrich." Hettinger's interruption jerked Eric back to reality. The man was waving him through another identical door. Entering the chilly interrogation room, Eric noticed one difference from the others he'd been in, a door on the opposite side of the cramped room.

"Eric," Hettinger said and sighed. "I'm not going to pretend we're friends. I could remind you of your responsibility as the son of Protectorate naval officers, but I won't. I won't beat around the bush: tell us what we want to know and this will go a lot easier on you. That might seem like old hat, but the rules have changed." Eric heard the door behind him open and he observed a second man enter with his peripheral vision. Leaning casually against the wall just outside of arm's reach, this new interloper appeared wholly uninterested in what was going on. His broad features, short haircut, crisply ironed coveralls, and demeanor lent the man a seriousness of purpose similar to Hettinger, though the grin gave a subtle hint of menace. "I have been explicitly authorized to take the kid gloves off, Eric. Have you met Ted?"

Eric glanced over at the second man.

"No? Well, Ted's a specialist. You see, I'm an information person. Ted?"

Ted grinned as he drawled, "You might say I'm a bit more of a people person." It came out more as "Ewe moight say oima bit moave ah peepol pehson."

"Yes, a people person," Hettinger echoed. "So while I'm here to look for information, Ted is here to help you remember that information."

Ted snorted and pulled a pair of black gloves from a pocket as he eyed Eric. "Aye, motivation."

"Like the average Protectorate citizen, I don't care for hurting people, but Ted here is a bit more--"

"Ambivalent," Ted finished.

"Ah yes, thanks Ted. He's a bit more ambivalent on the topic. Ted, do you mind educating our friend here on the finer points of your job?"

"Awright, Mister Drew. See these gloves here?" Ted asked as he pulled them on. "If ya hit bare skin hard enough, it splits. Since we need you right and pretty for the trial, we can't have that. That's what these gloves are for. Helps to reduce friction."

"Now Eric, does Ted look serious?"

Eric nodded. His head snapped to the side. Pinpricks of light danced across the room and his eyes stung.

"When Mister Drew asks you a question, you answer," Ted said as he gripped Eric's chin and pointedly directed Eric's gaze back to Hettinger.

"Thanks, Ted. One more time, Eric. Does Ted look serious?"

Eric coughed before earnestly replying, "Yes, Ted looks pretty serious."

His head snapped to the side again. Eric tasted blood. He'd bitten his tongue.

"You'll have to excuse his eagerness to help you, Eric, but how can you say he looks serious? You didn't even look at him. Now, look at Ted and tell me if he looks serious. Don't make him hit you again. Also, don't call him pretty. He doesn't appreciate that."

Eric stared up at Ted's neutral expression. "Yeah, I'd say he's serious."

"Would you say he enjoys his job?" Hettinger asked.

"I would say--" Eric started to say yes, but caught a gleam in Ted's eyes and paused. *Now is not the time to be a smartass.* He considered Hettinger's earlier words. "I would say no?"

"Go on, I can hear there's more," Hettinger said with a smirk.

"He said he was ambivalent. That means he has mixed feelings about it."

"Good, see Ted? I told you Eric was a bright kid. Now, do you think Ted's mixed feelings means he won't do his job to the best of his ability?"

"No, I'm pretty sure he wants to do the best job possible."

"Do you hear that, Ted?"

"Aye, not every day you find someone who appreciates a job well done, Mister Drew."

"No, it isn't, Ted. No it isn't, especially amongst pirates." Ted flinched. "Oh, Ted, you didn't know?"

"No," the man growled as his expression darkened.

Hettinger caught the glimmer of fear that flitted across Eric's face. "Ted's family was killed by pirates, Eric. How did they kill your sister, Ted?"

"Rape." Ted's voice had gone almost as flat and emotionless as his eyes.

"Now, from what he's told us already, Ted, his ship was almost civilized. Right, Eric?"

"Yes, almost civilized," Eric stammered.

"Did you ever deal with pirates like that, Eric? The kind that would rape a young girl, barely fourteen, to death?"

"Just once. Captain Fox hated them."

"Just once? Why? Why just once and why did Fox hate them?"

"The *Fortune* had taken some damage and the main drive

hiccupped while we were transiting in-system. The engineers killed the reactors and couldn't get them back up. They were the only other ship in system. If Fox hadn't bargained with them, the *Fortune* would've been a cold tomb until we fell into a gravity well."

"And Fox hated their type?"

"He saw them as animals, less than human."

"There are ways of dealing with animals gone bad, Eric."

"Sure, you shoot them, but we couldn't."

"Why not?"

"The Compact."

Hettinger pulled out his tablet. "Go on."

"About the Compact? I asked Fox the same thing about why we didn't use them for target practice if they were such horrible people. He said the Pirate's Compact prevented him from doing so. From what I could tell, it's some old agreement amongst pirate groups that they would not prey on each other. Beyond that, I don't really know, Fox didn't talk about it at length."

"Interesting. I would expect someone in your position to be a bit more cognizant on the topic."

"That's the only time it came up. Maybe Fox's policy of no fighting in port was part of it? I don't know. It's possible."

"Many things are possible, Eric. Some are not. As we discussed before, the *Fortune* had docked at Jenkin's Station. While you were there, some two hundred containers of mixed machinery were sold by Fox to multiple buyers from the Confederation. These containers were last seen on the PCV *Nadezheny* en route to Bernard. What makes this interesting is that Fox also sold three cylinders of enriched uranium along with two experimental warp helixes stolen from a Protectorate research facility to a buyer we have been unable to identify. Given the distances between the sources and time frame involved, it is physically impossible for the Fortune to have obtained these goods on her own. Explain."

"I can't."

Stars filled his vision as his head bounced off the desk.

"Ted, our friend here has a medical condition that makes continued blows to the head problematic."

"Sorry, Mr. Drew."

"No, entirely my fault, I should have let you know. No harm done so far that I can tell. There's no shortage of other soft tissue, take your pick."

Ted wrenched Eric's chair back and glowered. Eric's grunted at the hammer blow to the leg. The burning sensation from sudden cramping sucked the air from his lungs as his leg convulsed. He would have toppled from the chair had Ted not grabbed him.

"The quadriceps femoris," Ted told him, "is the largest muscle group in your leg."

"As you can tell, Ted is a fan of proper education, Eric. Now, unless you want him to continue sharing his education with you, you might want to consider sharing yours with me."

Eric glanced between the two. "I can't tell you what I don't know. How many times do I have to tell you I'm a dumbass kid before reality sinks in?"

Hettinger raised a hand as Ted drew back. "Not this time, Ted. We'll pretend he's telling the truth for now. We've got time to come back to this later."

Eric suppressed a smirk.

Less than forty-eight hours and I'm home free, dick. I'm as good as out of here.

As the clock ticked away, Eric found himself buried under an endless avalanche of questions punctuated intermittently with bouts of pain and the inability to breathe. From generalities to specifics, the questions ranged wildly from the mundane to topics obviously important to the Protectorate. That they had access to petabytes of data, yet were grilling a relative nobody like him wasn't lost on him, either. The Protectorate wanted more and what they were looking for wasn't found in shipping manifests, banking transaction logs, or port listings. Try as he might, the only comment Eric could make based off the topics covered was that the Protectorate was intensely interested in the pirates operating in the reaches between the borders of Protectorate and Confed space. Not just Fox and the *Fortune.* All of them. Despite it all, Eric stuck to the story. The story was life.

As the questions, blows, and time came and went, his inability to figure out what they were after grated on him.

"So," Eric spoke up in during one of the few brief pauses. Ted had stepped out some time ago. "I've answered more questions in, well, however long I've been in here, than I probably have the rest of my life. Do you think you can clarify one thing for me?" Hettinger glared up at him from the tablet. "I get you're interested in the pirates, but I'm a nobody. You have to know that by now. I don't know anything you don't already know. Why grill me like this? It doesn't make any sense, it's a waste of time and money."

Hettinger's tablet chimed and he looked down. The man grimaced and reached for the coffee he'd brought in from his last break. Eric shivered. During every break Hettinger had taken, the temperature in the room plunged until the interrogators had returned. Eric had little doubt as to how close to hypothermia he had come during what little sleep he'd managed before Hettinger woke him at the end of the last break.

"That's a fairly astute observation, Eric. I'd punish you for asking, but it appears our time together has come to a close, so I'll humor you a bit. A large portion of intelligence gathering is not gathering new information but verifying what you already have. In that regard, you've been very valuable. On the new information front, you've given us much to think about. For what it's worth, the executive board of Turing Interstellar and the families we could contact send their thanks for your information concerning the *Vyzov*."

The door behind him cycled. Eric found himself face down against the table as strong hands pull his arms behind his back and fit a pair of manacles around his wrists. Ted stood him up and prodded him through the back door into a much larger chamber. Two of the walls in this room were glass. Several uniformed people stared around their computer monitors at him from behind the windows. A medical examination table and a myriad of surrounding medical devices dominated the center of the chamber.

Ted drug one of the ubiquitous simple metal chairs to the center of the room and pushed Eric into it. Another door opened and someone entered.

"Out. Everyone." The anger in Doctor Isaacs' voice was unmistakable. "I don't care if you have a top secret clearance, get out. You too, Theodore." Most of the observers got up to leave, but a handful stayed sitting.

"Ma'am?" Ted asked.

"This interrogation is Inner Party only, Ted. Unless any of you hiding an IP-Gamma clearance, lock your systems and get out. No? I have authorization to terminate any potential leaks, direct from the Secretariat and the First Citizen." The last statement sparked hurried movement to vacate. Seconds later he was alone and listening to Dr. Isaacs' footsteps approach from behind.

"Oh, Eric. Do you have any idea how much trouble you're in? How much trouble you've created for me?" She asked as she sat on the exam table in front of him. Her hair was frazzled. She looked like she hadn't slept in quite some time.

"No? Sorry? What do you mean by trouble?"

Dr. Isaacs pursed her lips with irritation. On any other woman, Eric would have thought this expression attractive. Instead, Eric broke out in a cold sweat.

"Eric, you can drop the innocent routine, I know better. You and I both know you're a pirate and, citizen or not, you know that earns you an execution. You also know by now that there's no way you're escaping what you've earned. You have my respect for sticking to your script as admirably as you have. I can't imagine that has been easy for you, but unfortunately the only decision left for you to make is how you choose to meet your end."

Eric shivered at the slow smile that blossomed at his discomforted fidgets.

"Now that we have a mutual understanding, let me outline your options. You can keep quiet and play stupid and your death will be a long time in coming. Trying to lie your way out of it will only make me more… creative." Eric stared at her. "Now, that would be the deal Hettinger would give you, but I'm not Hettinger.

"A little over a standard day ago, the *Shrike* transmitted your case information to the system capitol's Provost on arrival, standard procedure. Today, I'm working on something critical when the *Shrike*'s communications officer orders me to meet him at the comm center. Imagine my surprise when I get there to find him and the *Shrike*'s captain waiting for me with an encrypted message neither of them are cleared to read. The Council is ordering me off the *Shrike* because of you, you know? Can't have the Naval Provost suspecting I'm a bigger fish than I appear. All that time, all that work, probably wasted because it will be turned over to some incompetent."

"Sorry?"

She sighed. "After dismissing the captain and the commander, do you know what I found in that message?"

"Not a clue."

"A dx-level order from Central Intelligence demanding we debrief you specifically for the contents of the images from your suit camera." She pulled a small handheld out of her lab coat and thumbed the screen. "Specifically these five emblems. I have been ordered to obtain that information at any cost. They were quite explicit that I was to ensure that information does not fall into unauthorized hands. We purged the technician who saw those images an hour ago."

"Oh."

"I hold a certain level of appreciation for Hettinger's approach. It's direct, it's simple, and works well in most situations, so let's use that as a starting point. That said, I may be able to sweeten the deal if you give me enough. You wouldn't ever be a free man again, but the Provost may be persuaded to amend the current charges to something less lethal."

"Go on."

"Do you know what those five emblems are?"

"For sure? No."

"What do you suspect?"

"I-I," Eric stuttered, his mouth suddenly going dry. A deep burning sensation started in the muscles at the base of his skull, like he'd pulled them. "I believe they're from Earth."

"Where did you find them?" Eric stared as she came to stand in front of him. "I've checked the data forensics and the photo analysis myself. You were the one who took those pictures, but there are no timestamps on the images. I'm not buying the shared suit script, where did you see those emblems?"

They exchanged stares for several seconds before Doctor Isaacs shrugged out of her lab coat and settled onto his lap. This close, he could see the revulsion she was trying to hide in her eyes. The feeling was mutual, but the primitive parts of his brain didn't care. *Her eyes.* They were a hue of blue he couldn't place. Her pupils began to dilate. Eric's stomach lurched with nausea. Coherent thoughts snarled together as thought and emotion wrestled through his head. She shook her head and stood up.

She opened her mouth to speak, but Eric blurted the first thing that came to mind, "Ferram's Reach."

"That's where you saw the emblems?"

Eric squinted at her, confused and mentally dug for what made him say those words. The room seemed much brighter and he was sweating. He sputtered, "No, the star is a class B."

Doctor Isaacs tilted her head. "What? What's that have to do with this?"

"Your eyes, they're the same color as Ferram's Reach."

Doctor Isaacs blinked. *Blushing?* Her eyes focused elsewhere for a moment. Her face contorted, clearly angry, and she spat, "Plan B, Hettinger."

"Plan B?" Eric asked as a door cycled behind him. Boots approached with purpose and seconds later he was yanked from the chair. Ted grunted as he shoved and prodded Eric in the back with a sidearm toward the open doorway. Eric stumbled into the hall to find three Protectorate marines in armored suits waiting. *Vac suits-- Oh fuck no. No, no, no.*

Fear slowed his tongue, but the sudden lancing headache para-lyzed it. One of the marines grabbed him as he fell forward and another helped drag him down the passageway. Every step, every jolt felt like a hammer smashing his closed eyes against his brain.

An eternity later the marines came to a halt. The two marines in front of him parted enough to reveal a thick metallic hatch with a thick transparent window. The airlock was dark.

"What's going on?" a familiar voice shouted behind him.

"Quiet, you'll find out soon enough," Hettinger said as Ted turned Eric to face the newcomers.

"Eric!" Pascal blurted. At the sight of the marines, the man's eyes shot wide and he paled.

Eric's fear clawed at him, tearing into what little calm the anti-anxiety drugs still afforded him.

"Your friend here has information we need. If you want to live, I suggest you convince him to talk," Hettinger told Pascal as he keyed the airlock.

Lights inside snapped on while the door opened. Eric could see stars through the window of an identical door on the far side. Calm settled over Pascal's features as the marines stuffed him inside. Hettinger glanced between Eric and Pascal. The interrogator's face hardened at Pascal's silence. The two stared at each other for some time before Hettinger stepped to the airlock controls.

Pascal dropped his chin to his chest and began to speak.

"Lo, there do I see my father."

Hettinger punched a key and the airlock cycled shut.

"Lo, there do I see my mother, my sisters and my brothers." Pascal's voice drifted through the door's speakers. His voice shook, but he spoke with confidence.

"Lo, there do I see the line of my people, back to the beginning." Pascal locked eyes with Eric as Hettinger lifted a safety cover. Eric blinked away a tear.

"Lo, they do call to me. They bid me take my place amongst them. In the halls of Valhalla, where the brave may live. Forever." Hettinger smashed the emergency override. The lights inside shifted red and the outer doors snapped open moments later. The speakers howled as the maelstrom yanked Pascal into the black beyond.

Ice ran down Eric's spine and settled in his gut. Hettinger turned to regard him. The outer door closed and the red lighting blinked off. Footsteps.

"Progress?" Doctor Isaacs asked. Hettinger shook his head.

Behind him, the airlock's lighting swapped to white. "Both of you could have walked away from this, Eric. Continue, Drew."

Hettinger nodded. "Ted, take the cuffs, they're worth more than he is."

The airlock opened. Ted removed the handcuffs and shoved Eric inside. The hatch closed. Pushing through the migraine, Eric clawed himself up to the window.

Behind the glass, Doctor Isaacs looked bored.

"You have the rest of your life to decide," she said. "Where, Eric?"

She scowled. Moments later, he heard a resonant hum. Air pumps. *Oh shit, oh shit!* He sobbed involuntarily and tears shot from his eyes as agony lanced through his mouth from what felt like a hundred small hooked knives prying out his teeth by the roots. The air pressure in his ears adjusted with a deafening bang. He dropped to his knees, crying from the pain. *Stop! Stop, please stop!* Panic crashed over him.

Eric forced down the sobs, gutting the pain as he pulled himself back up to the window.

"A wreck. We found a wreck," he gawped.

"Where?" she asked, her voice sounded tinny and distant through the thinning, cold air.

Eric opened his mouth to reply and winced as fire flashed across his brain. When Eric opened his eyes he couldn't find the words. He couldn't find any words. They had vanished like smoke in a sudden breeze. He blinked, and stared blankly at the woman in the lab coat on the other side of the glass. Slowly thoughts came to him.

What's going on? Where am I? Who are you?

The woman frowned. "Goodbye, Eric."

The lighting flashed red and gravity vanished. He felt more than heard a metallic thump behind him. Eric clawed in vain for purchase on the door in front of him as what remained of the atmosphere pulled at him. His skin tingled for a moment before ratcheting to a stinging burn as he drifted free of the outer door.

"Whatever you do, don't hold your breath," a voice whispered from a disintegrating tendril of memory. Fighting against himself, Eric opened his mouth and the escaping gas imparted a slow spin.

The ship he'd been on rotated out of view, replaced by a field of endless stars. In the distance he beheld a pale blue orb, a planet. As his eyesight clouded and darkness leeched in, Eric marveled at the greens and blues, the whites of the clouds and high peaks, the shimmering lights nestled on the night sight of the planet. *Beautiful.* As the last of the color drained from his vision, he distantly felt something touch his shoulder.

Adjudication

BLINDING LIGHT. ERIC RECOILED, BLINKING THE TEARS OUT OF HIS eyes. Penlight. Man. Coat. Doctor. Bright. Too bright.

"Back with us?" the man asked. Receiving no answer, he continued, "Do you know your name?" The man paused and sighed. "No? I thought as much. Do you remember me at all?"

Eric pursed his lips.

"No? I suppose that's expected as well." The man harrumphed and began to speak slowly. Eric struggled to keep up. "I'm Doctor Barnes. Eight hours ago you were exposed to vacuum. You lost consciousness. The process leading up to that moment aggravated a brain injury from your past. Do you understand?"

Eric nodded weakly.

"We've done what we can for you, but there will be lasting effects. Short-term weakness and nausea are normal. Whatever you've lost memory-wise should come back on its own in due time. Expect that to take months or potentially longer. Every person is different. There is a chance, however small, considering the locations and severity of the brain injury that some memories may not come back.

"Before we brought you back, we administered a few medications, anti-anxiety mostly, that should help you transition. You may feel quite groggy for the next few hours. Combined with the after effects of the injury, you may not feel quite like yourself. While some level of nausea is expected, seek medical attention for any sudden migraines, vomiting. Also, avoid narcotics and alcohol for at least the next month and anything that raises your blood pressure for as long as possible. Any questions?"

Eric numbly shook his head and the doctor helped him to his feet. Someone in pale blue motioned to him to follow. Eric shuffled after them to an adjoining room where two men waited. He found himself fidgeting with the zipper on the orange coveralls he wore as the nurse spoke with the men. The woman in blue told him the men were here to take him somewhere.

As Eric nodded and tried to thank the nurse, one of the two men fit him with handcuffs. Moving as quickly as his teetering gait could manage, Eric barely kept up with the two men. They stopped by an elevator.

Eric looked up and noticed a sign overhead, placed to be seen by those exiting the elevator. Pointing the way they had come, an arrow proclaimed the way to ship's medical. Below that an arrow pointed the same way for "Detention Block Access, Restricted Area." Eric mulled those words over as they waited. In dribs and drabs small details came back to him. A thought coalesced when he looked down at his orange coveralls.

I'm a prisoner. Wait, why aren't we going to the prison?

"Guys, where are we going?" he asked.

One of his escorts looked over at him, "The nurse wasn't kidding, Felix, this guy must've taken one huge hit to the head. He doesn't remember shit."

"Buddy," the second one said, "We're taking you up to Judicial. Your trial is today."

"Oh."

Footsteps approached and he saw a woman in black with a black duffle bag over one shoulder and a smaller metallic case in one hand.

Do I know her? I feel I should know her.

His escorts snapped to attention and saluted the new arrival.

"Carry on, marines," the woman said and nodded to them as she dropped her duffle to wait with them.

I know that voice. He stared at the black coat over black coveralls as his escorts showed him in and hit a button. *White. White coat, she should be wearing a white coat. Doctor... Doctor...*

Eric's mouth spoke on its own accord, "Doctor who?"

The woman looked over at him. Several emotions played across her face before settling into something friendlier than the rest. She cleared her throat before saying, "Isaacs. Doctor Isaacs."

"I know you from somewhere." Her expression didn't change as he looked at her face. "Your eyes. Did you know they're the same color as," he trailed off, looking for the words.

"Ferram's Reach?" she offered as everyone shuffled in.

"Yeah, that's it, Thanks, sorry, I--the doctor told me I'm going to have issues with my memory for a while. How'd you know I was going to say that?"

"Somebody I knew told me that before. They were just trying to get on my good side." She cleared her throat again.

"Oh. That's shitty," Eric sympathized. "Still, they were right. Have you ever been there?"

Coldly, she replied, "No, that's a good distance outside of Protectorate space. Have you?"

Eric frowned. He shrugged as he said, "I'm not sure. I think so? I had to at some point, I guess. I can't remember much about it other than the star was this gorgeous blue. No, I have been there. I remember I could watch it for hours. The shifting corona gave the color so much depth. I think all the blues reminded me of some-where. Home, I think. I can't remember home either."

Her lips curved downward ever so slightly and a chime announced the elevator's arrival.

"That's sad. Did your doctor say how long it would take to get your memory back?" she asked as crewmen filed out of the elevator.

"He said it could take years, if it comes back at all. There's so much I can't remember. I can remember remembering, but not, uh, the remembering directly. I think." They shuffled aboard the elevator. "I know they think I did something bad," he nodded to his escorts, "I can't remember what it was, but I'm pretty sure they kill people for it around here." Eric nearly missed the softening of her features before a mask of indifference smothered everything. Two people in light blue coveralls stepped into the elevator as the doors started to close.

"Well, I'm sure you'll have plenty of time to work on getting your memory back," she told him.

"I hope so," Eric said as the elevator stopped and the late arrivals stepped out. Her duffle bag caught his attention and his head throbbed. Snippets of garbled memory babbled at him. He rubbed at the bridge of his nose and shook his head.

"What?" she asked.

"You got fired? Yeah. Something I did got you fired. I'm so sorry."

She shifted uncomfortably. "That's not exactly how it happened. Don't worry about it, my next assignment is a lot closer to what I cut my teeth on. Should be a lot more fulfilling."

"Oh, what's that?"

"Iterative design." The elevator dinged and the doors opened. The marines parted for her as she hefted her bags. Doctor Isaacs glanced back before the doors closed. "For what it's worth, Eric, it was nothing personal."

As his escorts visibly relaxed they shared glances then looked at him for several long seconds as the elevator rose.

"Wow," the marine on the left breathed.

"What?" Eric asked.

"Been on the *Shrike* since it left Engleston last year, buddy. That woman was the commanding officer for detention and interrogation."

The other marine nodded and continued, "Stone-cold killer, like 'strap her own family down and pry off finger-nails.' This is the first I think anybody's seen her act like a normal person." The first marine nodded.

They rode the rest of the trip in silence. When they stepped out into a passageway crowded with security and manacled prisoners

Eric was still trying to figure out what was nothing personal. The marines walked him over to a collection of security personnel.

"Handing you off to the bailiffs," the marine told him as his comrade talked to security. Eric winced as his head started pounding.

Two bailiffs came over and the more overweight of the two asked, "Prisoner Eighty-Seven?"

Eric gave them a confused look.

"Eric Friedrich?"

"Oh, yeah, sorry. Just got out of medical--"

"Don't care," the other one cut him off.

Jerks.

"Hey, we have eighty-seven here, which court?" the impatient one said aloud.

"Thanks. Jeb, courtroom three."

As they led him away, his headache worsened and Eric realized something about the lighting aggravated it. Eyes mostly closed, he followed them into courtroom three.

"Sit here until you're called," impatient one told him. After Eric sat, the bailiff looped a chain around his handcuffs. Eric sighed and closed his eyes.

Maybe a short nap would help? I should have almost an hour left.

"Do you understand the nature of the charges brought against you?"

Eric jerked awake and blearily looked up. He was shackled to a chair in what looked like a small auditorium. A low railing separated his seating area from a single table that sat before a raised platform. Several seconds passed before he realized this was a court room.

The hell? What happened?

Eric looked about before remembering his arrival. Heart beating fiercely, he focused on calming himself. Two men sat at the low table, a man in a suit and another in orange coveralls. The man in coveralls stood.

"I do," he replied to the man in black behind the bench on the platform.

"Your plea has been considered and we have reviewed your case. Under the authority entrusted to me as Judicar, I pronounce you guilty. The sentence for trafficking in the quantity and type of goods you were found with is death, to be carried out immediately. Bailiff, next prisoner."

The man slumped and began to blubber as he was led away from the table and through an archway to the judicar's left. No one in the courtroom seemed to react to the pulse of an energy rifle seconds later.

Someone grabbed his shoulder and hauled him to his feet. Stunned disbelief kept his mouth shut as he was led to the table and forcefully put into the seat.

"Prisoner Eighty-Seven, one Eric Friedrich?" the judicar asked.

Eric swallowed and awkwardly stood. "Yes, your honor."

"You stand before the court accused of piracy. The Naval provost has chosen to drop the charge of murder in the first degree. Do you understand the charges brought against you?"

Wait, piracy?

The man next to him cleared his throat and stood.

"The Public Defender has further motions for consideration?" the judicar asked.

"I do, your honor. The Naval Provost moves for a continuance," the lawyer replied.

The man's cheap suit tugged at a memory. Eric briefly smelled coffee before a vague recollection surfaced. *Tomas, his public defender.* Eric squinted at the judicar and then at his lawyer. *Wait, why is my lawyer making motions for the Provost?* The judicar nodded and Eric noticed the corpulent man shimmered momentarily when he moved.

"On what grounds, councilor?"

"Exigent circumstances, your honor. The accused has been inaccessible for the bulk of his incarceration, making a proper debrief impossible."

The judicar frowned and looked down at the bench, "According to your records, you had open access to him for almost three weeks total, is that correct?"

"Yes, your honor."

"And in that time you were unable to obtain sufficient evidence of this man's guilt?"

"Not entirely."

"Councilor, either the accused is guilty or he is not. Either you have evidence to the same or you do not. I am awfully curious why I should allow you to waste more of the Public's treasury. Motion denied. Anything else?"

"The Naval Provost moves for extra-judicial isolation, securitatem publicam."

A sudden stream of blue light illuminated the judicar's shocked face as a robed figure materialized next to the bench. The figure flickered for several moments before color bled through.

Holograms.

"The Senior Judiciary grants the motion," the new figure pronounced and vanished as fast as it appeared.

The judicar frowned. "I see you briefed the Senior Judiciary, Councilor. Well played. Eric Friedrich, for the charges of piracy this court finds you not guilty. Under orders of the Senior Judiciary, you are to be remanded to the Navy who will transport you to where you are to be held in exile until such a time as the threat you present to the public has passed. All items inventoried at the time of your arrest are to be returned to you in their original form. Bailiff, next prisoner."

Eric turned to Tomas, confused.

"What?" the lawyer said.

"I thought you said you were my legal counsel?"

"Not your counsel, Eric. The counsel. Words mean things. Enjoy your exile, pirate." Tomas smiled.

"Fuck you," Eric spat as the bailiff dragged him toward the archway where two marines waited. *Goddamnit, it figures. Pascal was right. Lies all the way down. All of it.*

"Mr. Friedrich, we have a tight schedule if we're to transfer you to the *Relentless* before it departs. Please follow me."

Quarantine

As his marine escort promised, the schedule had little margin for delay. At the out-processing center, Eric listened to his escorts wheedle the administrative clerks multiple times as their deadline neared. When a hurried clerk finally presented a case containing his suit, the man tripped over his words apologizing for the absence of suit's undergarment.

At his escort's impatient glance, Eric assured the clerk that he understood policies on bio hazardous material. His inspection period, brief as it was, confirmed that every item listed on the intake sheet save the shorts was inside the case. *Pretty sure that's everything I had on me.* By the time he'd finished informing the clerk their inventory seemed correct, his escort had the door open and was waving him on.

Minutes later, Eric stood by himself at the end of a painted line on one of the *Shrike*'s shuttle decks. Looking over the bay, lines like the one he stood on had been painted in five other areas. Groups of people waited at the end of each line, most in prisoner orange. Less than a minute had passed before another pair of marines dropped off a burly gentleman similarly clad in orange.

Eric opened his mouth to speak, but the man shook his head.

Eric flinched at the sudden whine of an energy rifle discharge and looked over his shoulder. Prisoners backed away from a prone man on the opposite side of the bay. Steam and smoke rose from the dead prisoner as his coveralls smoldered.

Eric's eyes rose to the darkness above. He had thought the darkness beyond the harsh lighting hid only ceiling, but squinting, he could barely make out a catwalk that ran the length of the bay. Three figures paced back and forth above them. A fourth still had his rifle aimed at the other group.

"That's why, son," his companion whispered. "They're still listening."

Eric did not utter a single word for the thirty minutes it took for them to board the small transport that took them off-ship.

"Welcome aboard the *Relentless*, citizens," a man in dark blue coveralls greeted them as they debarked after less than an hour of cramped flight. "If you will follow me, I will show you to your staterooms."

Eric shared a glance with his burly companion before hefting his case of belongings and doing as bidden.

"Before we get far, I need to inform you that conversations with ship's company beyond those strictly necessary are forbidden," their escort noted.

"Define 'strictly necessary', uh, spacer?" Eric asked as they crossed the noisy hanger.

"Petty Officer, actually."

"Oh, sorry, didn't mean to demote you."

"No worries. Most prisoners aren't subject to this rule. You two, on the other hand, have been flagged for quarantine during our transit. Now, I haven't been briefed on the specifics," the petty officer told them. "And I do not want to know them," he stressed. "However, both of you know something considered controlled information and the quarantine is to prevent you from talking to others not cleared for that information. Provided you conduct yourselves accordingly, the main benefit for you is much better quarters than the rest."

"Better quarters?"

"Yeah, much better. This is a warship. We're not equipped for extensive prisoner transport and we normally don't do it. The Provost usually handles all of that. Between that and where we're holding you, I would imagine whatever it is you know, and please don't tell me, is pretty important."

"Okay, that's twice now you've said you don't need or want to know, why?"

"I'd prefer to stay on this ship when we get to where you're going. Whoever you tell, if they're not cleared, will likely get a one-way ticket to the surface with you or a quick execution."

"Wow. I bet that fucks with morale."

The man gave him a half-hearted smile. "Not really, you'll be isolated for most of the trip."

"So, you said much better? How 'much better' are we talking? I've spent most of my life aboard ship, and there's not exactly a lot of variety when it comes to living quarters."

The petty officer's eyes narrowed for a moment. When he answered, Eric could hear an underlying coldness that had not been there before, "Officer's staterooms. Two of you, one stateroom."

"Hoo, boy!" Eric's companion said with a grin.

Their escort remained tight lipped as they traversed several decks. Some ten minutes later they drew up short outside a locked door.

"Well, here's your accommodations. Food will be delivered from the Officer's Galley during scheduled meal times. Reading material has been provided, though you will not have network access. We expect to arrive at our destination inside the month," the petty officer informed them as he swiped a security card.

Eric followed his partner in and looked over his shoulder when the door hadn't closed immediately.

"Your accent," the petty officer said. "It's not from Engleston, is it?"

"Can't say I've ever been there."

"Former Navy? Provost?"

"Not based off what they charged me with. This does look pretty comfy though. Would you like one yourself?"

"Fuck you, pirate," the petty officer spat.

"Run along, little man," Eric dismissed the man as he triggered the door.

Eric turned, dropping his case by the nearest rack, and looked up to see his companion regarding him warily.

"Pirate?" the man asked.

"That's what I was charged with," Eric replied. He held his hands up when his companion's expression darkened. "Hey, they execute people for piracy, remember? They found me not guilty."

"Then why'd they charge you in the first place? The Provost doesn't usually lose their cases."

"Couldn't tell you, don't remember. Some doctor told me I have some sort of brain injury that interferes with memory."

The man chewed on his lip for a moment and slowly nodded. "Until three months ago, I was a machinist first class on the *Bystro*. She's a cargo hauler out of Unity. If you wake up one morning and remember you were a pirate, keep it to yourself."

"Fair enough," Eric left a pregnant pause at the end as he regarded the man questioningly.

"Jeff. Jeff Simmons. Yours?"

"Eric Friedrich. And if I do ever get my memory back, I'll do as you say. Until then, you think we can actually talk? I mean, I'm pretty sure that guy wasn't supposed to ask any questions. Also pretty sure if this is a navy vessel, they're probably not likely to be wired for sound like the *Shrike* was. That, and whatever it is we both know about, I'd imagine there aren't too many people cleared to know, so who would they get to do the listening?"

"Avoid anything related to your charges, just in case."

Eric nodded and sat on his rack. *Woah, it's a real bed. I could get used to this.* "So, what were you charged with?"

"I wasn't."

Eric coughed. "Say again?"

"I wasn't."

"How's that work?"

"The way they put it, I didn't commit a crime. I was just in the wrong place at the wrong time. My sentence is considered administrative, not criminal. Those bastards had the balls to tell me they were going out of their way keeping me alive."

"Wow."

Jeff grunted and settled onto his bed. "Oh, this shit is soft! Not hard as deck plates like the prison cots."

"Was just thinking that. So, wrong place, wrong time?"

"We had a drive malfunction a few days outside of Unity. Surprisingly, we got dumped into normal space instead of spread across the black as highly energetic dust. We spent a few days trying to patch the drive up enough to limp her home when our sensors picked up something nearby. Captain was curious, so we used the in-system drive to catch up to it. Damn fool."

"So what was it?"

"Well, it's hard to describe. It was clearly man made, but there wasn't anything wrong with it other than it didn't have any power as far as we could tell. You could fit most of it in this room, actually. Big dish transmitter on one side. Either way, Captain had us pick it up."

"And?"

"And what? That's what I don't get. Electronics and that on it were ridiculously primitive. Weird thing though, it had this gold plated copper disk on it with these odd markings. The disk was mildly radioactive. Heard one of the tech guys say something about electroplated uranium. We got back to port, Provost scooped us all the next day."

"How'd that go?"

Jeff grunted, "Poorly. I was eating a bowl of greasy noodles at one of the starport mobiles. Next thing I knew I had weapons pointed at me, folks yelling at me to get down, folks yelling at me to put my hands up, folks yelling don't move."

"Wow. And they didn't shoot you?"

"Oh yeah, they shot me. It was a total clusterfuck," Jeff grimaced, flexing his left hand. "I lost most of my left hand when I tried to put my hands up. Bystanders caught stray shots and I'm pretty sure the mobile was on fire when someone finally hit me with a stun."

"Holy shit."

"Yeah. They weren't happy about replacing it. My company had hired a lawyer I heard from a few times before we left system. That was maybe three weeks ago. The hand still feels funny. Tech said that's normal for a rapid replacement and should go away in a few weeks. Looks weird as hell without the scars."

"Well, my memory is really foggy. I was on the *Shrike* for a while, I think quite a bit longer than you. I didn't even know we stopped somewhere."

Jeff snorted, "Stop? The *Shrike* barely slowed down. The provost pilots were bitching about it. She popped in, announced her visit was time restricted, and any business that couldn't be conducted in six hours would wait until the next provost patrol came through. I got the impression that what we'd found was the only thing that delayed them those six hours. Whatever that thing was, someone thinks it's important."

"Sounds like it. Any idea what's so important about it?"

Jeff eyed the compartment and leaned in. "It was old. Real old. You know what a RTG is?"

"R-T-What?"

"Radioisotope generator."

"Can't say I remember those."

"Most folks wouldn't. They're rare as an Nthcom droid today, but they were used as emergency power back in the day. I grew up working in a ship boneyard, tearing apart old ships, going through wrecks, that kind thing. When your job has you taking ancient hulls and pulling everything useful out of them, you see all sorts of things. Radioactives make heat as they decay. RTGs convert that heat to electricity. Our electronics shop chief was a buddy of mine, we pulled one of the thing's tiny RTGs apart. He ran the numbers on what juice it still had left and what we figured it was supposed to supply new. Nearest he could figure it was between five hundred and maybe seven hundred years old."

Eric gave Jeff a confused look.

"Only one place sending that kind of tech out, that long ago, son. Earth. If you're in here with me, you know something about

Earth, too. Might be locked away in that broken head of yours, but you know something they don't want out. I can't tell you if you're better off remembering or forgetting it, but you'd best figure that out right quick."

"Not following, Jeff."

"Well, you don't remember now, right? Well, maybe they're tossing you away for good, but can you be sure they aren't stuffing you in a hole so they can get you back when you remember?"

"Good point. You have any clue where they're sending us?"

"Not a single one, sorry."

Eric shrugged. He looked around in his container of belongings and pulled out the tablet. Curious, he pressed the power button. The screen went from pitch black to a slightly lighter black for a few seconds before swapping to text on a white background. He had just enough time to read the highlighted section before the screen flashed and went black.

The Lord is my shepherd; I shall not want. He maketh me to lie down in green pastures: he leadeth me beside the still waters. He restoreth my soul: he leadeth me in the paths of righteousness for his name's sake. Eric frowned and hit the power button again. Again the device reset suddenly. *Yea, though I walk through the valley of the shadow of death, I will fear no evil: for thou art with me; thy rod and thy staff they comfort me. Thou preparest a table before me in the presence of mine enemies: thou anointest my head with oil; my cup runneth over.* Another reset, this time scanning lower on the screen. *Blessed be the Lord my strength, which teacheth my hands to war, and my fingers to fight: My goodness, and my fortress; my high tower, and my deliverer; my shield, and he in whom I trust; who subdueth my people under me.*

The tablet screen went black again and Eric sighed.

"Something wrong, Eric?"

"Meh, something's up with my tablet. Keeps shutting off right after I turn it on."

"Have you tried a hard reset?"

"No? I don't remember how."

"Oh, most models, you just hold the power button down for a bit."

"I thought you said you were a machinist?" Eric asked, holding the power button down.

"Cargo haulers don't have a lot of crew. We cross-trained."

The screen lit up momentarily, flickered, and went black again without going to the text. Seconds passed. *Maybe I broke it for good?* The screen flickered, white text streaming from bottom to top momentarily before freezing. *Initializing cryptographic API. Keyring loaded. RAMDISK driver loaded. What's all this?* The screen blanked and a large circular logo hovered amid a deep blue background. A second later, a box filled with text popped up in the center of the screen. *Department of Defense Computer System? Usage constitutes consent for monitoring? What the shit is this?* He tapped the red x at the box's upper right and it closed to reveal logo that filled most of the screen. *Department of the Navy. United States of America.* Neither label on the logo meant anything to him.

"That help?" Jeff asked.

"Nah, not really. I just realized I don't remember my login either."

Jeff snorted. "You've got shitty luck, man."

A speaker in the overhead crackled. "Tattoo, tattoo, lights out in five minutes."

"Well, guess it's bed time. See you in the morning."

"Sounds that way," Eric replied as he turned off the tablet. After returning it to his case, Eric laid back and stared at the ceiling. Time ticked by as he listened for the sound of boots outside his door that never came.

"Reveille, reveille. All hands heave out and trice up. Now man the translation watch," the overhead speaker droned.

Eric sat up in his rack, rubbed his eyes, and looked across the room at Jeff's snoring form.

"Hey, jackass, wake up."

"Fuck off! Shit, can't a guy finish a dream with tits in it just once?"

Eric rolled his eyes. "They're stationing observers for translation, Jeff."

"Oh?"

"Yeah, we've been in FTL for over a few weeks, right?"

"Something like that. Will be nice to get out of here. The food's been nice, but the monotony, not so much," Jeff commented, rolling out of bed.

"So, tits, huh?" Eric asked as he stretched.

"Oh yeah, great ones too. She looked like this one dancer at the club outside of Marxport. Dark eyes, dark hair, boobs the size of melons, and those legs. Yeah."

"Woah there, Jeff. You need a cold shower? I'm starting to feel a little uncomfortable over here."

Jeff snorted as he ducked into their small bathroom.

"You're safe," Jeff said through the open door over him using the toilet, "You're not my type. I don't imagine I'll be seeing anything that nice again." Eric heard genuine regret in the man's words. The toilet flushed. "Hah, just in time. Line safety just engaged. We should be popping into real space any minute now."

Eric sighed as he traded spaces with his roommate. "I'm still pissing anyway."

"Better do it quick then. Transition shift can do weird things to people. Don't be like the one guy we had in engineering on the *Bystro*."

"Oh?" Eric asked. He vaguely knew he wasn't unfamiliar with FTL transitions, but this sounded like a funny story wanting to be told.

"Yeah, lost his balance with his junk in his hand. Hit his head on the piping. Huge mess. Still holding it when we found him. Poor sap never lived it down."

Eric was still laughing when his stomach jumped into his throat and the floor fell away. His sinuses burnt, as if they'd been pressurized suddenly. The *Relentless* had transitioned back into real space and had done so extremely close to a gravity well. Eric devolved into sneezing coughs.

"You alright in there? That was pretty rough. These Navy folks must be made of sterner stuff."

"Yeah, that or they're crazy." Eric replied when his sinuses stopped trying to kill him. The line safety indicator blinked back to green and Eric flushed.

"Flight quarters, flight quarters. Flight crew to your flight quarters stations," the overhead speaker rattled.

Someone knocked on their door. As they both turned, the door opened, revealing several armed guards and two naval armsmen who tossed a pair of packages into the room.

"Foul weather clothes, put them on," the woman who opened the door told them, "You're off my ship in twenty minutes."

Eric traded glances with Jeff.

"What are you waiting for?" One of the armed guards barked, "We can drop you off without them if you want."

They stepped forward and opened the boxes.

Solitude

DAY 0

BUNDLED IN A PARKA, THE WALK DOWN TO THE FLIGHT DECK WAS stifling. Another crewman in blue coveralls and a white vest stuffed something in Eric's hands as they crossed onto the flight deck.

"What's this?" he yelled above the engine noise.

"Oxygen mask. You'll need it below until you can get to lower ground," Eric barely heard through his ear protection.

"Lower ground?"

"Crew chief will explain. Get moving."

Another flight deck crewmember in a gold vest trotted over and led him over to a small idling troop transport. The woman helped him aboard where the she settled him into a seat and hurriedly showed him how to secure his harness.

Eric watched out the open side hatches as two crewman with in purple vests drug a long fueling hose away and flight crew in green led other parka-clad figures toward him. One by one, the crew chief and the woman in the gold vest got the new arrivals on the transport and into a seat. Eric noted based on body shape, at least two of parka-wearing people were women. With the last of the seven new arrivals seated, the crew chief leaned back and pounded on the back of the pilot's seat. The pilot nodded and nudged the throttle off idle.

Four armed and camouflaged troopers climbed in both sides of the transport, took the last seats, and pulled the hatches shut as the engine whine spooled up to a full throated growl.

The transport lifted from the deck and slowly swiveled toward an enormous armored door that opened to the blackness of space. Crossing into the black, the engine noise vanished leaving them in an eerie silence. One of his companions coughed to break the quiet. Eric was still lost in the beauty of the planet beyond the cockpit when the crew chief spoke up several minutes later.

"We just got word that our primary LZ is too dangerous for us to attempt a drop, but the weather pattern looks like it will open up a small window at a secondary point, so we're going to be dropping you a fair bit higher than planned."

"How high is high?" one of his new male companions asked.

"Just short of six thousand meters," the crew chief answered. "If the weather guessers are right, you should have anywhere between fifteen minutes to an hour to find shelter. While I cannot stress enough the importance of getting off the mountain as fast as you can, getting caught without shelter up there will be fatal. Keep your masks on, find shelter, and wait the storm out. It should break overnight. Any questions?"

"Six thousand meters? Are you kidding me?" the man said, "High altitude pulmonary edema ring any bells with you? Are you trying to kill us?"

"Look, buddy, I like it about as much as you do. I don't make the flight plans, an' I don't fly 'em either," the chief retorted, "I just make sure this shit-show stays in one piece. If you want, you can get out now. No? Good. Next question."

"How long can we expect our O2 to last?" a familiar voice asked. I know that voice. Eric leaned forward but couldn't see the man's face. Svoboda?

"We're dropping our spare case of cans. It's all we can do."

"That doesn't answer the question, Chief," the familiar man groused.

"No, it doesn't. Next question."

"Nearest settlement?" Eric asked.

"Down slope. Anything else?"

"Food? Water?" the familiar man asked.

"We're dropping two cases of supplies with you. That should last you to the bottom if you're not slow about it. As for new water, you'll be surrounded by snow. Get creative. I hear heat works. Try not to eat it frozen if you want to live long, you'll cool off faster than you think."

"Topographic map?" one of his companions nearest the left hatch asked. "Compass? Rope?"

"No, no, and no. Planet is under information quarantine. If you don't have it on you, you don't get to bring it with. We didn't plan to drop you there, otherwise you might've gotten one or both of the last two."

"Fuck me," the guy by the left hatch sighed.

"Weapons?" the woman seated to his right asked. The man Eric thought might be Svoboda and the two troopers next to him chuckled. His memory was still fuzzy, though, so he wasn't terribly sure.

The crew chief shook his head and smiled. "These guys have orders to shoot anything that presents a danger to this flight. That would make an awfully short trip for you. Nothing further? Good, this is the mark forty-two individual atmospheric mask."

———

Behind him, Eric knew the others were trying to open the crates dropped with them. He reflexively shielded his eyes against the transport's down draft despite the mask he wore. A face appeared in the doorway above. The face furtively glanced back into the aircraft. Moments later a black case tumbled from the doorway. Eric jumped out of its path as it augured into the knee-deep snow. The engines above roared and he hazarded another glance skyward in time watch it pirouette and thunder into the angry clouds above.

Eric watched the clouds billow long after the transport had vanished into them, reveling in the eerie windswept silence. His eyes fell to the black case at his feet. Using his weight, he dragged the case out of the divot it had made. As he knelt beside the case fumbling at the latches Eric heard boots crunching toward him. He looked up, but behind the mask and the parka, the man barely looked human.

"Guess those bastards aren't completely soulless," his visitor said.

Eric squinted through his mask's lenses. *I know you from somewhere. Who are you?*

"Looks like a vehicle survival kit. Let me help you get that open, Eric."

"Do I know you?" Eric asked as he opened the last latch.

"Know me? You feeling okay?"

"No, I--I'm feeling okay, I guess. Headache started when we got off the shuttle, but I'm fine. Doctors on the *Shrike* said I had some kind of brain injury." Eric surveyed the case's contents. Several foam cut-outs were empty, but the majority held what appeared to be useful items.

"Oh. That's not good. Really not good," the man said as he stood and clambered over to the cliff's edge. "We need to get you off this mountain, fast."

"I don't see that happening," Eric sighed, pulling his arms in close. The cold was beginning to seep in where it could. His fingertips were already beginning to burn despite the thick gloves.

"I don't either, Eric." The man shook his head and leaned over the cliff's end. "Not without some drastic measures. Come with me."

Eric wallowed through the snow after the man. One of the crates had been opened, it looked as if an argument was taking place. Muffled by the masks, the voices were too faint to hear, but the body language was clear.

The man leading him stripped off his mask and barked, "Excuse me!" Everyone else stopped and turned. He waved them closer as he fit his mask back on.

"Folks, I'm going to make this quick," the man said to them once the crowd was close. "I grew up on a world that makes this mountain look like a hill. Unless anyone has more relevant experience, I suggest you listen. Objections?" The crowd glanced at each other uncomfortably. "No? Good. First of all, if you think we're fucked, you're right." He forestalled grumbling with an upraised hand.

"That said, we can get off the mountain before the storm hits. It's possible. Maybe not probable, but it's possible. The more we argue, the more oxygen we burn through, and the less probable getting off this rock gets. Are we clear?"

Most of the crowd nodded.

"Good. If you want to live, we have a very small window of opportunity and very limited choices. No one is going to like any of those choices."

"What choices are those?" one of the larger figures asked.

Jeff? Yeah, Jeff.

"Well, in case anyone hasn't noticed, we're above the frost line by good margin. No trees, only lichen, moss, and maybe some scrub under the snow. Unless there's a cave near here that means there will be no shelter. We can't say here."

"Well, no shit, buddy," another man in the crowd growled.

"The problem is, the air up here is way too thin. Without these masks, we wouldn't get enough oxygen. These masks are supposed to supplement not replace external oxygen, so those tanks will empty far faster up here than down the mountain. Right now, they're capped for max-output. We can up the cap, but then we'll only run out faster. The only solution is to get down as fast as possible, hopefully to an altitude where they're not necessary. Otherwise we get to experience firsthand what hypoxia feels like. First reduced judgement, then euphoria followed by death."

"Well, let's get walking," the same man said.

"There isn't enough time. Even if there's a cave nearby for shelter, at our current consumption rate we won't have enough oxygen to wait around, much less get down the mountain."

"Okay? So what's your plan, Svoboda?" one of the women asked.

Svoboda? Eric's brow knit. Memories lurked just beyond his reach clouded with further confusion as half-formed memories were seemingly pulled from his grasp.

"We jump."

"What?!" several spouted as the entire group recoiled.

"Fuck that," Eric reflexively spat, his stomach gone cold. Several of the others emphatically nodded.

"Look, how many of you are getting headaches right now as we speak?"

Several raised hands.

"Doc, and I'm not sure what your experience is, but you sounded like a doctor up there. What are the early signs of high altitude sickness?"

One of the figures looked at the rest slowly before his shoulders slumped, "Headache, nausea, fatigue, rapid pulse, swelling of the hands, feet, and face."

"My friend here," Svoboda shook Eric's shoulder, "Already has a brain injury the Provost gave him on the *Shrike*. Would it be fair to expect he'd be more likely to suffer cerebral edema, even with the supplemental oxygen, Doc?"

"It would."

"Any idea how long he'd survive untreated if that's what's causing his headache?"

The doctor looked at his companions. "Twenty-four hours, if he's lucky."

Svoboda pulled his mask up and spat on the ground. The spit bounced off the snow, frozen.

"Folks, it's somewhere around thirty below. It won't be long before the cold starts in on us. Between the cold and the lack of oxygen, we'll get tired, prone to panic, and worse yet, stupid. The faster we get down, the more likely we are all to live. Does anyone have a better option?"

"What's wrong with walking? Or sledding down?" Jeff asked.

"With slopes that steep? We don't have the right gear. No snow shoes, no climbing gear. Walking is too slow and we'd probably fall anyway. Also, storm coming and no shelter. Say we get lucky, then maybe we get a quarter of the way down before the cold and thin air get us. Sledding or sliding might work, but in the end stopping is still a problem. Beyond that, we don't really have anything to make sleds out of," Svoboda told the man. "Look, I'm not happy about jumping either. It's dangerous as hell and the only doctor around here is with us."

"Won't we cause an avalanche?" one of the women asked.

"Anything likely to fall would have been shook lose by the transport. I looked over the edge already. It's pretty steep but starts to level out near the cloud bank below us. If we're lucky, and I'm not saying we are, we'll shave at least a few hundred meters off the trip down. That by itself might be enough for some of us to survive."

"What if someone gets hurt?" Jeff asked.

"Well, this is a huge assumption, but if there are trees on this planet, I'm presuming the tree line won't be too far past those clouds. We'll send some folks to get something to make a stretcher or sled of some sort. We'll have to make do, just like we would if someone got hurt trying to hike down. Landing in the snow won't be the hard part, stopping will. In the end, we either spend the next twenty-four hours, if that, slowly freezing to death or we jump. If things go poorly, we're dead a lot faster and hopefully a bit less painfully. If things go well, we get to the tree line and we all survive."

"You people are fucking crazy," the woman who'd stayed silent so far commented.

"I didn't say it was particularly sane, lady. I just said it's our best chance of survival."

"Not mine," the man next to her said. "He's going to get everyone killed. Let's get going, Shelle. Anyone else coming with us?"

The group didn't move. As the two turned to walk away, Svoboda piped up, "You might want to stay long enough for us to divvy up the supplies." The pair froze in their tracks.

Under Svoboda's guidance, the group emptied out the two supply crates as equally as possible amongst themselves. Every person got four meal packs, including water, and an extra canister of oxygen. He also gave the two the spare compass from the black case, an ice axe, and a length of rope after telling them to tie it between them. Those that stayed used a few more minutes to pull apart the crates and making improvised panels to slide down on.

Eric stood at the edge of the cliff face, shivering in the cold and staring at the clouds below while clutching the metal case containing the last of his belongings. *Shame the tanks on my old suit are empty.*

"Okay, before we go, remember this: Do not land straight on your feet. Keep your legs bent, knees and ankles together, and your arms and hands on your chest if you don't have a case you're holding onto. Do your best to keep hold of whatever you have. We will need it down there. When it starts to level out, use everything you can to slow yourself down. Be aware the snow will try to pull it out of your hands."

"Let's hurry the fuck up before I either freeze or get second thoughts," Jeff blurted.

"Fair enough," Svoboda said. "See you down slope."

Jeff nodded and stepped off into thin air. One by one, the rest jumped until only Eric and Svoboda remained.

"Eric," the man said, clapping him on the back, "My clan has a saying that might help you. Audentes Fortuna Iuvat."

"What's that mean?" Eric asked.

"Fortune favors the bold," Svoboda said and shoved Eric over the side.

Eric's stomach flew straight to the back of his throat which opened of its own accord. Multiple seconds of uncontrolled screaming that sounded vaguely like "Shit! Shit! Shit!" fogged the inside of his mask. Stars shot through his vision from the back of his head bouncing off the steep snow embankment. Somewhere along the slide, the adrenaline surge burnt through the fear, leaving him wide-eyed and blinking through the slowly clearing lenses at the rocks they had missed from above surging up through the mist at him. His brain switched gears from "shit" and elevated directly to "fuck."

The first several rocks whizzed past him as he dragged his heels in a vain attempt to steer. Eric grunted as his luck ran out and he glanced off one of the stone sentinels. Feeling vanished from his left arm. He fumbled for the case, barely holding on to it. His eyes widened as the cloud cover thinned below. There was no tree line, just another cliff.

"Motherfucker."

Time and thought seemed to lurch to a halt. *I'm dead. This is it.* The headache he'd been fighting off surged, and as he blinked, he saw another image overlaid over the empty clouds below, a planet hanging in the blackness of space. He couldn't breathe. *It's okay. Let go.* Pain flared, forcing tears from his eyes. Memory snapped back into place as he cleared the cliff face and gravity's pull seemingly vanished. *They pushed me out of an airlock. They tried to kill me!*

Wind whistling past brought him back to reality. He looked down. *Oh shit!* Everything went dark.

Eric blinked. Everything hurt.

Why is my face freezing?

He tried to move but his limbs felt like they were gripped in a vice. Slowly his vision sharpened and he realized he wasn't wearing his mask. He looked up at the small circle of light above him. His mask was embedded in the snow between him and the light.

Got to get out of here. I am not dying alone in some snow drift somewhere. Fuck that.

He still couldn't feel his left arm, but he could move it, if barely. He shook snow out from under coat that had found its way there when he'd hit. Eric lost track of time as he struggled to free himself. As the light dimmed above, the weight in his gut receded as he realized he'd make it. With a delirious heave, Eric drug himself from the hole he'd punched into the snow on impact and flopped onto his back to find it was snowing.

Absentmindedly, he slid the mask over his face as he laid there panting. His skin began to tingle as the trapped warmth of his breath thawed his cheeks. *I'm alive.* He smirked. *I'm alive!* It started as a giggle, but quickly progressed to deep belly laughter. Eric pulled himself up into a sitting position. *Trees down there. We made it to the tree line. We made it.*

"Fuck you, I'm alive! Alive, you hear me? Alive!" Eric cackled as he reconnected the oxygen line to his mask and started shaking more snow out of every crevice.

"Hey, who's out there?" he heard a muffled voice ask. Eric looked in the voice's direction and initially saw nothing. *What's that?* He crawled forward, finding another hole in the snow a short distance away.

"Hello?" Eric said as he peered down. "Are you okay?"

"I'm a bit stuck? Cold, too." Eric recognized her immediately.

"Give me a second, I'll get you out of there, Leah," Eric told her as he surveyed the hole. "Can you reach up here?" He leaned in, trying to keep from collapsing the tunnel, but she was just out of reach.

"Hold on." Eric looked around again, spotting his case where he left it. *I could empty that out, use it like a big scoop.* Movement caught his eye as he started to rise. With the falling snow, it was hard to tell, but the figure appeared to be wearing the parka they'd all been wearing.

"Hey, you!" he yelled. The figure stopped. "Yeah, come here, I need some help!"

The figure clambered through the snow towards him.

"You hurt?" the figure asked.

"Nah, Jeff. Leah's stuck down that hole. It's not real solid, though. Don't want to cave it in."

Jeff nodded slowly. "What are you thinking?"

"Well, I was thinking I could empty my case over there and use it like a scoop, but it might be faster if you could hold on to me while I crawl in after her."

"That could work."

With Jeff holding his ankles, Eric creeped forward into the tunnel entrance and wrapped his gloves around Leah's.

"Pull!" Eric yelled over his shoulder. His left arm burned and his fingers spasmed under her weight, but he managed to keep his grip with some effort until she was on the surface.

"Holy shit, what have you guys been eating?" Jeff asked, out of breath. Inches away from her face, Eric saw a very unamused pair of eyes looking at Jeff behind her mask. Her eyes locked with his momentarily and darted away as she snatched her hands back.

"Where's everybody else?" she asked as she pushed herself up and stood.

"Dunno," Jeff replied. "I finally had the energy to move around just a bit ago. You two are the only ones I've seen."

"Well, we should probably search for them," Eric said. The two nodded. "Jeff, you want to go back that way, following the cliff? I'll go this way. Figure we go five or ten minutes and come back?"

"That works," Jeff agreed. "Make some noise, keep our eyes and ears open in case they're buried in the snow too?"

Eric nodded. When he looked over at Leah to see what she was thinking, she looked away. *What's her problem?*

"Before we go, check your masks like the crew chief showed us on the way down. Let's make sure everything's working right. I don't want anyone wandering off and freezing to death," Eric told the pair. He covered the intakes on his mask and sucked air in. As expected, the mask clung harder to his face as he breathed in. *No unexpected sucking noises or strange burning smells, and the seal's still good.* "Mine's good."

"Mine, too," Jeff echoed.

"I'm not sure," Leah said. Eric moved to look at her mask. She raised her hands. "No, it's okay. I'm just shaken up."

"Oxygen?" Eric asked.

"Should have a few hours left," Jeff said.

"Me, too," Leah added.

"Okay, we're set. Meet you back here in, say, fifteen minutes or so," Eric said. Jeff nodded, and started to move out. Eric took a few steps, watching Leah out of the corner of his lenses. She hesitated, glancing between the two of them. *Make up your mind, woman.* Eric shrugged and pushed on.

"Wait," she called. Eric looked over his shoulder to see her struggling to catch up.

"We've got people missing, Leah, and that storm's still coming. This cold isn't helping. I can barely feel my hands or my feet."

"I know, I know," she panted apologetically. "Me, too."

The pair trudged on for several minutes without speaking to each other before Eric stopped to catch his breath.

"I'm not sure anyone's out this way, Leah. They should've heard us, or we should've heard them."

"Yeah, I'm thinking--"

"What?"

"Over there, Eric, something red."

Eric followed her outstretched hand to a small rise topped by scrub ahead of them. One of the snow-covered branches glistened red. The wind picked up and the limb bobbed out of view. He glanced upward. *Oh.*

"Leah, wait here."

"What?"

"I don't think you want to see this," Eric said, stepping toward the rise. He heard her follow him a few steps and stop. Eric made his way up the rise and hesitated before he could see over the brush. More blood spots on the snow.

"Is it Svoboda?" Leah asked.

"I don't know," Eric called back.

"It's that bad?"

"No, I don't see anything yet, I'm not sure I want to."

"You don't have to, Eric."

He looked back at her. "Yeah, I do, Leah. Whoever it is, I owe it to them. Would you want to be left out here, lost? Abandoned?"

She looked at her boots. "No."

Eric sucked his breath in to steady himself, and pushed forward the last few steps. He held a hand up to forestall Leah. Clinically, he knew the bloody ruin in front of him was one of his group, the parka was a give-away, but the scene's totality refused to register. Limbs were twisted at unnatural angles, blood spattered.

Rock. He hit rock.

"It's one of us," he told her mechanically, "Still not sure who though. Wait there."

Stiffly, he pushed through the brush and knelt by the corpse. It was staring skyward, but the mask's lenses were thoroughly spider-webbed. Eric reached out and stopped just short of touching the mask. *No.* Eric rocked back on his haunches, putting his chin to his chest as best he could with the mask.

"Lord, receive this man into your waiting arms. He has been long from port and long from home. May he find rest and safe harbor wherever he has gone," Eric whispered to the whistling wind and leaned forward.

Gently, he pulled at the mask's chin, prying it upward. He felt the seal slip, blood ran out from under the mask. The corpse gurgled and wiggled slightly. Eric jerked back, ripping the mask off by accident.

Oh fuck! Fuck, what do I do? Svoboda? I can't tell!

The man's features were nearly lost in the mass of caked blood and his nose had been broken, flattened by the impact that had smashed the mask.

The man's eyes flickered open and focused on him momentarily. He gurgled again and spat a froth of broken teeth and blood. Eric realized the grunts that followed weren't random, he was trying to speak. Eric leaned forward and then stared at the man in horror.

Barely intelligible, the man begged, "Kill. Me."

"How?" he managed. "I don't have anything to do it with."

A tear slid from the man's eye.

"Fuck. Fuck me. Fuck me running. Buddy, what do you expect me to do? Strangle you? I don't have a knife."

A sob behind him startled him. Eric looked over his shoulder. Leah stood at the edge of the brush, a knife in her shaking hands.

"Take it," she sobbed.

"Leah--" he started.

"Take it!" she snapped at him, shaking harder. Eric eyed the knife and cautiously reached for it. She nearly dropped the knife when his gloves touched it. Once it was in his hands, Leah turned and ran back the way she'd come. *Fuck, why me?* Eric turned to his fallen comrade. At the sight of the knife, the man weakly smiled.

"Thank. You," he coughed, nearly gagging on blood as Eric pulled open the parka.

"You'd do it if I were the one dying, right?"

The man gulped, nodding weakly. Eric fought to keep his emotions down as he lifted the man's chin. *Damnit, damnit, dammit.*

"Be at peace, brother," Eric sighed as he closed his eyes and pushed the knife in. The man gurgled, jerked for a few seconds, and went still. Eric opened his eyes some time later. Life had left the man's eyes, leaving them disturbingly empty, vacant, like glass made to look like eyes. Eric tugged the knife free and looked skyward. *Lord, what have I done?* A myriad of thoughts and feelings whirled through his mind mirroring the snow drifting down from the clouds. Guilt. Horror. Sadness. Lost in his thoughts, Eric jerked when something touched his shoulder.

"Eric?" Leah asked.

Locked inside his head, Eric didn't answer.

"Eric?" She shook his shoulder. "I think I see the others, Eric. We have to get moving."

Eric blinked. *Others. Moving.*

"Right. You're right, we have to get moving," Eric forced himself to say as he looked at the body before him. He wiped the blade off in the snow and forced himself to his feet. Several shapes in parkas were wallowing through the snow from the direction they'd left Jeff.

"Are you okay?" Leah asked.

Eric glared at her through the mask, fighting back sudden anger. "Would you be? I just killed a man, Leah. No. No, I'm not okay. I'm very not okay."

She backed away a few steps, hands up. "I'm sorry, Eric. I-I don't know what to say."

Eric shook his head, and looked over her shoulder. One of the approaching group was carrying someone else on their back. *This just isn't going to get any easier, is it?* He sighed, "Go see what happened to the rest, Leah. I need a few minutes to myself."

Leah nodded, and trudged off. Eric glanced down as he turned to the body, realizing just how he'd been holding the knife. *Shit, she probably thought she was next. Idiot. You're fucking this up.* Eric glanced at his mask's oxygen indicator. *Forty minutes left at current settings. Got to get off this mountain.*

A glint off metal in the snow next to the body caught his attention. *I really shouldn't do this, but we're out of choices.* Eric knelt and pulled the dented oxygen canister from the snow. He paused again, considering the still form. *I didn't even ask your name. I hope wherever you are, you understand.*

Eric leaned in and rifled through the man's pockets. After pocketing what he found, Eric stood and stumbled his way to the approaching group.

"Eric, Leah told us what happened," Svoboda said from Jeff's back.

"Not really wanting to talk about it, old man," Eric cut him off.

"Fair enough. Let's get to the tree line, then. There's a few tricks I can show everyone that should make moving in this mess a bit faster. You should at least thank Doc for picking up your case. You left it back where you met Jeff."

"Oh, sorry. Thanks, Doc."

"No problem, you mind carrying it? Two cases are a bit much."

"Yeah, give it here. Seriously, sorry, I'm not normally this forgetful," Eric said, realizing Doc was also lugging the black survival case the air crew had dropped.

"Don't worry," Doc replied, handing over the case. "We've all had a lot on our minds."

As the group moved down the mountain, Eric held the knife out, hilt first, to Leah.

"Keep it, I'll find another," She told him. A few steps later, she handed him the sheath.

"Stop here. Put me down," Svoboda told them shortly after they crossed into the trees.

"Won't argue with that," Jeff huffed, slipping Svoboda to the snow. "What's the plan, boss?"

"First, take this hatchet. Second, we're going to need at least eight pieces of wood for each of you guys still walking. We don't need huge hunks of wood, just branches between a quarter and a half meter in length," Svoboda told them and then paused. The man glanced at the trees around them and then made a small circle with his thumb and forefinger. "Actually, just bring back whatever you can find about that thickness. We can make it work."

"Anything else?" Jeff asked.

"Yeah, don't get too far apart from each other. We don't know what kind of predators are out here, and there's only so many weapons to go around."

"Predators?" Leah asked.

"Yeah. Watch the snow. We've passed tracks of a number of different animals since we left the cliff. Not sure what all's here, but if I had to guess I'd say rabbits, deer, and there's at least one set that looked like a large cat of some sort."

"Large cat?" Leah asked, glancing about.

"Relax, they weren't that fresh. If it's anything like the cats from back home, it was probably looking for shelter and won't bother us. Get going, no telling how much time we have left before this storm really gets started or how bad it will get when it does," Svoboda told her.

As group began to set out, Svoboda glanced over to Eric. "Mind staying here, Eric?"

Eric nodded, resting his hand on the knife. "Sure? Wouldn't I be more useful gathering with the rest of them?"

"I'm not exactly mobile and don't really want to find out if I'm wrong about predators the hard way," Svoboda said. "I'm obviously injured. If they're going to try to drag any of us off, it'll be me."

Eric looked about, casting his glance back the way they came and along the mounds of snow.

"If they're cats, you're looking in the wrong place, son. Look up. The smaller ones will be in the trees more often than not in normal weather. Remember that, since we'll be here a while," Svoboda told him. "Now, help me get propped up against this tree. My back is killing me.

Eric got his arms under Svoboda's and drug him over to the nearest tree.

"Much better," the man sighed. "Clipped a few rocks on the way down. Doc did a quick look over as best he could. He's pretty sure nothing's broken, just bruised and sprained to hell and back. Haven't felt this beat up in at least a decade."

"What were you doing then?"

"Jumping out of perfectly good starships."

"You're kidding, right?"

Svoboda grinned. "Son, the shit I did when I was your age, you wouldn't believe."

Eric regarded him doubtfully.

"Have you ever done ship to ship boarding?" Svoboda asked. "I'm not talking through a docking clamp, here. Both ships still under power a few clicks from each other with just you, your suit, and nothing but faith in God and your calculations between you and a long stay in the black?"

"Why the hell would you do that?"

Svoboda grinned. "The things you do for God and Country, lad."

Eric shook his head, keeping a wary eye on the countryside.

"Speaking of things you do for God and Country, you sure you don't want to talk about what happened earlier?"

Eric glanced at the older man warily for a moment before softly saying, "I'm not sure that's the best idea."

"Why might that be?"

Eric sighed. He opened his mouth to speak, but words didn't come.

"Eric, you know it's all right, don't you?"

"How can it be alright? I just murdered a man."

Svoboda chewed on his lip for a moment. "You gave the man a harsh mercy, lad. Leah told me what he looked like. There's no medical care here. You had no choice."

"I don't know that. We. We don't know that."

"No, not for certain but the odds aren't in anyone's favor. Still, that's beside the point. The fact is, he was a dead man but his body hadn't caught up to it yet. You ended his suffering. It was not murder."

"It feels like it."

"It always does the first time."

Eric stared at Svoboda. "The first time? How many men have you killed?"

Svoboda's face sank, "I've done exactly what you did for other people, and it doesn't get easier. They didn't do anything to justify killing them. You have a good heart, son. That's why that bothers you. A good heart, a warrior's spirit, but not enough experience to know what to do with them."

"What's that supposed to mean?"

Svoboda shook his head with a wistful smirk. "Where I grew up, what you did is not asked for lightly. By our standards, you're no longer a child, Eric. What you did took heart and courage to face what needed done regardless of the personal cost. I know you don't feel proud, none of us ever do."

"But why me?"

"Why anyone? Would you rather save yourself the pain you feel now, knowing that he'd still be lying there waiting for the inevitable?"

"That'd be horrible."

"And that's exactly why you're not a child anymore. Adults understand life is pain and sometimes you choose pain for yourself to spare others. I'm sorry that the first lessons in that are as harsh as they have been for you."

"Lessons? Plural?"

Svoboda cocked his head to the side before realization dawned on him, "Right, brain injury, memory. You'll remember sooner or later. When you do, if you need someone to talk to, I'm here. Until then, anything else bother you beside the act itself?"

"I didn't ask the guy his name."

"Go on."

"I just," Eric frowned, "I don't know. Someone should remember him, that's all."

"And what if he wasn't a good person?"

"So what? He was someone's son. Maybe someone's husband, someone's dad. It just bothers me to know I took his life and don't know who he was," Eric said, pausing a moment to ponder what was really going on in his head. "I'm just being silly I guess."

"No, you're not. Remember that regret, Eric. It doesn't matter why you're doing it, killing should never be easy, even when it's for the best of reasons. When it starts to get easy, that's when you should worry about what that says about you. You hear?"

"Yeah, I guess."

"Good. One more thing, since the others should be back soon. Keep that knife on you and ready at all times."

"Why?"

"I'm not going to say I'm an expert on Protectorate exile worlds, Eric. It's something we knew of, but not through first-hand knowledge. The Protectorate dumps people on them and usually leaves them to their own ends. As such, exile worlds tend to be lawless planets. I don't know if that's the case here or not, but stay on your toes in case it is. Don't trust a single person we meet until they've proven they can be trusted. Perhaps not even then, since we're all here for one reason or another."

"You've mentioned 'we' a few times now, Svoboda. Who is we? You're clearly not referring to the Protectorate."

Svoboda started to speak, but stopped. Eric heard snow crunching seconds later and looked. The others were returning.

"If it comes to it, there will be time enough for that story later, Eric."

"This is what we could gather quickly," Jeff said as they laid out wood of varying sizes and thicknesses out in front of Svoboda. At Svoboda's direction, they used rope from the black case to modify the boots they'd been given. The man explained that the mesh of sticks would spread their weight out over a larger area, making it easier to travel. Using the remaining longer poles, they fashioned a primitive travois to move Svoboda with.

"Okay, swap canisters if you need to. Let's get moving," Svoboda said. "Snow's coming down harder, so be careful where you step. Keep an eye out for anything that might look like shelter. Looks like it'll be getting dark soon, we need a place to bed down for the night."

Onward and downward they trudged with Jeff dragging Svoboda and the cases on the travois. With the improvised snow shoes, making progress started off easier, but as the trees and brush steadily thickened, their pace slowed again.

"Careful, drop off up ahead," Leah called back. "Hard to see, circle wide."

"Stay clear of the edge, no telling how much weight it'll hold," Svoboda warned.

Several minutes later the group found a route around the drop.

As they came down the slope Svoboda remarked, "That looks like a shallow cave. Let's check it out. Wind is primarily coming from upslope, this might be our best chance."

On investigation the drop-off turned out to be a sizable rock overhang. Jeff eagerly set Svoboda down. At the man's direction, Jeff and Doc went to gather fallen wood where they could while Eric and Leah did their best to clear out an area to build a fire. Later, Svoboda walked them through how to properly stack the wood their comrades had gathered, pointing out the necessity of ensuring air flow to get a decent start.

"How are we planning to light this?" Eric asked. "The wood's kinda wet."

"No problem," Svoboda grinned. "Use this. Scrape your knife against it. Get the sparks onto the needles I had Leah gather from the back of the cave."

Eric knelt over their small mound of kindling and deliberately drew his knife across the small metal block Svoboda had given him. The bright sparks left after images where they'd flown. The needles lit by the third swipe, and, properly encouraged by blowing, were then pushed into place. A short time later, they had a sizable fire.

"Oh thank God," Jeff sighed, pulling his boots off. "I'm cold enough someone could use me as a thermal sink."

Eric made to do the same, but Svoboda shook his head. "No, at least half the group needs to be ready in case something happens. Any less than that and we're playing games with chance. That's you, me, and Doc right now. Doc, check the others out now that we can get out of most of these clothes without freezing. Me and Eric will keep an eye out."

Eric eyed Svoboda curiously. The man staggered to his feet.

"It's alright, Doc," Svoboda said as he motioned for Eric to lend him a shoulder, "I know, stay off my feet. I'm only walking over to that tree over there."

"You okay?" Eric asked, helping the man over to the promised tree.

"Yeah. Tired of being babied. I'm hurt, not broken. If you don't mind, I'd like to take a piss?"

"Oh, yeah, sorry."

Svoboda laughed. "Keep your eyes out there and away from the fire. Keep your low light vision as good as possible. We're far enough away, anyone looking at the fire is likely to miss us."

"Paranoid much?"

"It's only paranoia if they're not actually out to get you." Mirth flavored the old man's words. "Okay, done. I'll admit, usually when I used to do nature hikes like this, we were a wee bit better armed."

"How much better armed?"

"Oh, rifle and a few hundred rounds a piece. Two to six grenades each. Light mortar, couple kilos of explosives, and a light machinegun for the squad."

"For a nature hike?"

In a very serious tone, Svoboda informed Eric, "Bears are scary."

Eric snorted, and the pair devolved into snickering.

"Seriously though, ursines can be pretty inconvenient. Nothing compared to a highland wolverine though. That's what the radio was for." Svoboda laughed at Eric's puzzled look. "Air support, son."

"Well, I guess I can see why our load-out would be disappointing if you're used to having all that," Eric offered.

"It's not all bad. I've had to make do with similar before. At least this time I'm not dodging search parties and aircraft. That said, just about anything can be used as a weapon if you're motivated enough."

"Right."

"Seriously, Eric. If I wasn't beat up, I could probably kill you with half the shit in my pockets. I'd break a sweat doing the same with the other half."

Eric shook his head. "How would you kill me with a field ration?"

Incredulous, Svoboda replied, "Have you eaten one before?"

"Point taken."

"Mental exercise if you get bored. Pick a random item, figure out how you'd kill someone with it. Admittedly the easiest path is simply to beat someone to death with whatever it is, but be creative.

Similarly, ask yourself how you'd defend where you're at if you got attacked right then. Never hurts to have a plan."

"Seriously, what did you do for a living?" Eric asked, half grinning.

"Would you believe door-to-door salesman?"

"Not a chance in hell. It's just I can't see your average soldier doing half of what you talk about."

"And there's your problem, average," Svoboda grumped.

"Doc wants to see the two of you," Jeff grumped as he came up to them.

Svoboda nodded. "Keep your eyes out and away from the fire, Jeff. Just watch for movement. Still got that hatchet?"

Jeff nodded.

"Good man. Let's get back to the fire, Eric."

As they neared the edge of the firelight, they passed Leah on her way to join Jeff. *She looks pissed.* Svoboda groaned as Eric eased him to the rock.

"Take 'em off," Doc said. "Pants, too."

Eric shucked his boots, but hesitated with the heavy pants.

"You don't have anything I haven't seen hundreds of before. Off with 'em. We'll check arms and chest next."

Somewhat embarrassed, Eric slipped off the pants and let the doctor poke and prod at him. He tried to afford Svoboda some privacy by averting his eyes, but couldn't miss the mass of bruising that was one of the man's calves while Eric warmed himself. *Thank God for the fire.* Lower extremities checked, they swapped bottoms for tops. Doc hissed, looking at Eric's arm.

"You still have feeling?" Doc asked as he poked and tugged on it. "Does that hurt?"

"Not a lot, no. Aches more than anything, real sore, that's all. Didn't have any feeling at first. It's been a bit stiff, too."

Doc grit his teeth.

"How bad are we, Doc?" Svoboda asked, putting his shirt and parka back on.

"Really wish I had some real equipment. Any sort of imaging would be great."

"And I wish we had armor and air support. We're not getting that either, so what can you tell me?"

"Well, your legs are banged up and you bled a little. His arm's the same way. Not broken any way I can tell, but they look like they ought to be based on bruising."

"And the other two?"

"Jeff's probably been hurt more lugging your ass around than he got in the fall. Leah? Well, examining her was, what, interesting? Something happened to her, Svoboda, and I'm not talking on our trip down the side of the mountain. She wouldn't let me touch her, but I didn't see anything that stood out other than her attitude."

"Yeah, I know what happened to her," the old man said. "I should've warned you, sorry Doc. Just be happy she gave the knife to Eric here. Not sure if she'd've used it if you forced the issue."

"Same here. You don't threaten cornered animals," Doc replied.

"Exactly. I'm serious here when I'm apologizing. It's a breach of leadership and unacceptable."

Doc nodded. "Shit happens. We all appreciate what you're doing. Slip ups happen."

"True enough. I try not to slip up in ways that get people killed, though. So what about our oxygen?"

"We're all down to our last tanks. I actually have had my mask on bypass feed the last half hour to test how we're doing. I'm comfortable making the suggestion that masks are optional from here down, barring some sort of distress or anything else that requires increased oxygen."

"Okay. That works. The masks do help with the cold a bit. We'll have to make sure Jeff and the others know. Anything else, Doc?"

"Other than remembering to keep moving to avoid freezing and checking for frostbite, that's it."

"Okay. So we don't really have a good idea how long night lasts here," Svoboda said.

An idea came to Eric, but he decided against saying anything.

"What?" Svoboda asked, noticing the change in Eric's demeanor.

"Well, I was just thinking. We might not know how long the day

141

is, but we know how fast it got dark. There ought to be some way to extrapolate from that."

"I was getting there, Eric."

"Oh, sorry."

"No problem. Well, I was going to say that based on prior experience amongst a few other things, we're looking at a nine or ten hour night cycle at the very least. I'm going to ask folks to sleep in shifts. Anyone not asleep is out where Jeff and Leah are. Sound like an idea?"

Doc nodded.

"Okay, I'm going to ask Eric to stack our firewood into two piles. Jeff and Leah have first watch unless they've got valid objections. When the fire dies down, they need to wake you and Eric up, and add the next pile to the fire. When that burns down, someone gets me up. Figure we'll look at heading out at full daylight if the storm had passed by then. If not, we'll get more wood and look about.

"I'll relay this to the others, but if you have to get up, go no further than that tree. That way whoever's up has an idea where friends are supposed to be and where we're not. Also, the magic number tonight is seven."

"Magic number?" Doc asked.

"Yeah, if you see something move, freeze. You say a number, the other person has to reply with something that adds up to the magic number. As long as you don't move, you're hard to spot and you can get away with saying something short like a number without giving away your position. I say three, what's the response?"

"Four," Eric said.

"Right. Same with two and five, etc."

"What if the guy doesn't answer?" Doc asked Svoboda.

Svoboda replied, "Well, normally I'd say you kill him."

Doc grimaced at Svoboda's words.

Svoboda shrugged and added, "But we don't know if anyone we run into here is hostile or not. Since we're not seeing lights, I doubt anyone with good intentions will be out after dark, so if possible, disable them, we can ask questions later. If they use a weapon, kill them."

"Fair enough," Eric said.

"If something happens, whoever is on watch is to make as much noise as possible to make sure everyone else is awake. Depending on the threat, we all attack, fall back to here where it's harder to come at us from more than one angle, or scatter. I'll make that call if at all possible. If we have to scatter, get back up the mountain. Try to meet up at the huge rock we passed about a half kilometer up. Got it?"

Doc and Eric nodded.

Exhausted, Eric laid out by the fire once he'd stacked the wood as instructed. Despite the mask, sleep took him almost immediately.

***

Day 1

"Rise and shine." Jeff's voice dragged him out of deep sleep.

"Oh, fuck off," Eric groaned, stirring stiffly from where he lay. His head throbbed just short of unbearably.

"Sounds like a good idea to me," Jeff laughed as he added wood to the fire.

Eric swapped in his last canister for his mask, put it on, and woke Doc. The pair took their place at the tree outside, watching the snow fall in eerie silence.

"So, what'd you do to get sentenced to this shithole?" Doc asked.

"Well, my memory's still shot. I was charged with piracy though."

"Oh," Doc said. His tone shifted, sounding suspicious. "Piracy?"

"They found me innocent."

"Ah, fair enough. How's that headache you had earlier?"

"Pretty much gone," Eric lied. "Hurt for a bit though. Could've used a less exciting way to get down here, but I think I'm doing a lot better. You know, everyone really hates pirates. When I tell people about the charges, they act like I puked on their shoes."

"Why wouldn't they? Pirates are all rapists and thieves. Human scum, really. Destroying the foundations of civilization."

143

"Pretty sure I'm not a rapist. Killed a rapist though." Eric felt vaguely offended. Despite the holes in his memory, his gut told him the charges were true.

"They did find you innocent."

Eric shrugged. "What about you?"

"General practitioner on Unity for the last few years. A nobody, really, but one of my clients was evidently inner party. The charges were excessively vague. Endangering an inner-party member through medical negligence and a few others that sounded like the same shit rephrased to sound worse. They never told me who it was, just that I wouldn't be allowed to practice on Unity anymore. I may have told the judicar exactly what I thought of his uninformed opinion and just where he and the unnamed party member could go. Couldn't keep my mouth shut, so here I am."

"And people say pirates are criminals. I'm thinking if I were a pirate, there'd be a little bit of professional jealousy on my part. The Protectorate takes everything you are and you thank them for it."

"It's not like that, really."

"It's not? Odd, I'm pretty sure if it wasn't, you wouldn't be standing here with me under a tree freezing our asses off and watching snow fall in the dark."

"The system exists the way it does for a reason. Yeah, imperfections exist, but if I'd kept my mouth shut, I wouldn't be here."

Eric shrugged. "How do you explain Leah or Jeff?"

"Haven't really talked to either about how they got here."

"I know I knew how Leah got here, I just don't remember. Jeff? Wrong place, wrong time. Ship he was on found something old that the Protectorate wanted kept secret. He doesn't even know what it was, but here he is."

"He's a loyal citizen, he'll be okay."

"Really? He could've died. Still can, in fact, just like you or me. What happens when the rations run out? Hell, look at how broken Leah is. That's what your justice system does to good people."

"Your? Like it's not yours either?"

"Let's just say I can understand why folks would prefer piracy to living under the Protectorate banner."

Doc shook his head and said nothing until the fire began to gutter from burning down several hours later. "Time's up, go wake him up. I'm going back to sleep."

Eric nodded and made his way back to the fire.

"Hey," Eric said, resting a hand on Svoboda's shoulder. The next thing Eric knew, he was on one knee wincing in pain with his arm twisted up behind him.

"Shit, sorry," Svoboda mumbled through his mask, letting him go.

"It's all right," Eric replied, rubbing his arm. Eric stood and pulled the man to his feet. Svoboda shook his head and accepted Eric's proffered shoulder.

Once out at the tree, the old man nodded to him. "Get some rest."

Eric turned to go, but saw Svoboda fingering a black cylinder. "What's that?"

"A surprise for anyone sneaking up on us. Anything can be a weapon, remember?"

"Right. Well, see you in the morning."

Eric checked his oxygen levels again before laying back down. Svoboda had been right, the mask was drawing much less from the tank at this lower altitude and his headache had faded significantly.

Eric stirred and opened his eyes. It was barely light out beyond the outcropping and the fire hadn't died down much. *Fuck, why am I awake?* He shook his head, trying to clear it, but that only brought a surge of nausea and made the headache worse. Eric sat up, hoping that would help. It didn't. He got to his feet and stumbled out from under the overhang. Svoboda was not under the tree.

"Shouldn't you be asleep?"

Eric spun. Somehow he'd missed the old man sitting under a different tree.

"Can't sleep. Was going to water a tree."

"Plenty to choose from."

Eric nodded and staggered off into the trees. He dimly noted it had stopped snowing as he unbuttoned the thick pants. Eric felt slightly better after relieving himself. *Maybe it's the cold air?* He checked the readout on his tank and decided to walk a bit further to stretch his legs. Fifty meters further on the trees ended in an escarpment that dropped another hundred meters or so. A wooded white valley rimmed with equally white mountains stretched out before him. Eric leaned against a stump and watched the trees sway in the distance. A lone bird circled overhead, highlighted against the darker cloud bottoms by a ray of sunlight.

"Beautiful, huh?"

Eric winced and jumped.

"Shit, Svoboda, you have to stop sneaking up on me."

"Didn't think I was being terribly quiet this time around. You feeling alright?"

Eric shrugged. "Good enough for now I guess. If it doesn't get any better, I'll talk to Doc. Not sure what he can do about it though."

Svoboda nodded. "You didn't answer my first question."

"Oh, yeah. It is. I mean, it's not what I'm used to, but I can see folks liking it."

"Stay on a planet long enough, you'll learn to appreciate mornings like this. Cold, quiet, like you're the only person awake. We're not though."

"Why do you say that?"

Svoboda pointed. "Those trees? Too regular. That's an orchard. The open space near them, probably a lake or a field. That lumpy looking area is probably a farm field. Hard to see with all the snow, but half behind those tall trees is a sizable building. Look for the smoke. Someone's got a fire going already."

Eric squinted, following the finger as Svoboda talked. "I don't know how I missed that."

"Me neither. We get down there, we'll have to give you another good looking over." Svoboda froze.

"Hands up," Eric heard off to his right. His heart kicked into high gear as he lurched off the stump. "Ain't said nothing about moving! Keep still or I shoot." A man in ragged furs stood fifteen meters away on the edge of the escarpment holding an odd wooden contraption.

Where the fuck did this clown come from? And what the hell is that?

"My friend here isn't feeling well," Svoboda told the man as two more men hauled themselves atop the drop several meters behind the first. They fanned out, drawing long blades.

Okay, not so funny anymore. Damn.

"Nobody cares, meat," the man with the contraption told them. Eric twitched as his headache hitched higher. His heart pounded in his ears. "Empty your pockets and I might let ya go."

"Careful," Svoboda muttered under his breath as he tossed the contents of his pockets onto the snow. "Crossbows might be primitive but they'll kill you all the same. You think you can take either of those two?"

"I can try," Eric whispered as he did the same.

"Not good enough. Get ready to run. Try to lead them away from camp. He's going to shoot us no matter what we do anyway."

"How do you know?"

"It's what I'd do," Svoboda said, his works tinged with resignation, finality.

"Oi, enough yawpin!" the crossbowman barked, brandishing his weapon. "What's that in your hand? I said toss it!"

"Relax, friend," Svoboda said in a very disarming tone. "It's just a pen--" he pointed one end at the man and slapped the back with his other palm. The cylinder made a loud pop and something bright streaked the short distance between them leaving a trail of smoke before striking the man in the gap of his furs just under the throat. The man staggered back a half step, reflexively pulling the trigger on his crossbow. As the bolt sailed harmlessly overhead, the smoking dot lodged in the man's chest erupted into blinding light. "--flare."

The crossbowman shrieked and flailed about. His fellow bandits darted forward. Eric scowled, drawing his knife.

"Run, you idiot," Svoboda growled.

"Fuck you, I'm not leaving--" Eric flinched at an extremely loud boom from behind them. Something angrily buzzed past his ear.

The lead bandit's face disappeared in a cloud of pink mist. "What the shit?"

The third bandit skidded to a halt and turned to run. Eric flinched at a second thunderous boom followed immediately by another angry buzz past his ear. The back of the third man's hat flew apart. He dropped bonelessly to the ground a short walk from the now prone and gurgling crossbowman.

"Hands up," Svoboda said to Eric, "Out of luck now."

Eric dropped the knife. His heart thrummed against his chest as he slowly turned.

"On the plus side, whoever this guy is, if he wanted us dead, we'd be there by now."

Eric muttered, "Yeah, I kinda picked up on that, thanks."

Some twenty meters down the way, snow fell away as a limb detached itself from a tree. One second, it had been a misshapen tree and the next the lump against the tree shifted and became a snow-covered person. Eric had never seen anything like it.

I walked right past him without even seeing he was there.

"Holy shit," Eric blurted.

Svoboda snorted.

The figure approached slowly and deliberately, keeping his rifle leveled at them. Eric noted everything the man wore had been painted or dyed white over brown, including the wrapping around the rifle. Even standing up, little suggested a man stood underneath it all other than the legs. Eric could only place where a face would be based on how he held the rifle.

"Who do I have the honor of thanking?" Svoboda asked when the figure when it slowed.

"Hadrian MacGregor."

"Oh, a son of the crowned lion?"

"Aye, who be you to know?"

"Byron Mackinnon."

Byron? Eric frowned, eying the man standing next to him. *What exactly is going on here?*

"Oh? A Mackinnon? Out here? Ya don't say? Was hoping I wouldn't see kin out here. Sorry ya found us."

"Bryon?" Eric snickered nervously.

"Yeah? Got a problem with my name?" Svoboda asked.

"You have any pen flares left?"

"Maybe."

"In that case, no. Not a single problem. It's a great name," Eric mustered.

The rifleman and Svoboda chuckled.

"Ye might want to put your friend out before anything useful he has on him burns up with him," Hadrian told Svoboda. "Eh, he's still twitchin' a bit. Use this, and put him out of his misery."

Svoboda accepted the proffered weapon and staggered over to the burning man.

"Crows feast on your eyes," Svoboda told the man, cocking back the hammer on the revolver. A sharp report ended the man's mewling. "Mind helping?" he asked Eric as he kicked snow onto the smoldering corpse. Once the corpse had been extinguished, Svoboda tossed the revolver back to Hadrian.

"So, MacGregor, how's this going to work?" Svoboda asked the rifleman. Something about Svoboda's stance caught Eric's eye, the way he had one hand half behind his back. Then he saw the knife hilt drop from Svoboda's sleeve into his palm.

"Well, in better days, I'd welcome you with open arms, but these are not better days," Hadrian began. Svoboda's fingers caressed the hilt.

"Aye, and?"

"Well, these days I work for the man who owns this planet." Svoboda's fingers straightened slightly, allowing the knife to slip lower, exposing the blade.

"And your kin? Have ye forgotten home?"

Eric's eyes drifted over to Hadrian. Depending on what the man said, this could get very messy, very fast.

Hadrian chuckled. "Nay, I ain't forgotten home. My brothers died before I got here. They couldna kill me, by hook or by crook, so here I be. I owe my allegiance and my soul to home, but I owe my life to the Turings. What is a lone lion to do?" The rifleman's stance shifted to one more vaguely threatening. "I ain't forgotten my oath, if that's what ye mean. I'm no turncoat. Do ye doubt it?"

"Would you blame me if I killed you for being one?"

"I'd do you the favor and do it myself if that day ever came. That day is not today, may the sun rise forever over the highlands."

Byron warily asked, "Who were your brothers?"

Hadrian's shoulders wilted ever so slightly as he replied, "First SF."

"Eric? Svoboda?" Leah's voice echoed through the trees from the direction of camp. When the rifleman turned his head in her direction Svoboda glanced back at Eric and shook his head slowly.

"Lots of men in the first special forces division, Hadrian. Who were they, specifically?" Svoboda asked, icily calm.

"Operational Detachment Echo, team six."

"First sergeant?"

"William McCulloch."

"What was his daughter's name?"

Damn, Svoboda, how much more do you need from this guy? What are you going to ask next? Her favorite color?

"Colleen."

"Her favorite color?"

Eric resisted the urge to rest his face in his palm. Seriously? *What's next? Her favorite show?*

"She always wore green." Svoboda slid the knife back up his sleeve.

"I was McCulloch's first sergeant before he transferred to Echo, Hadrian."

Hadrian laughed, "You're that Byron?"

"I am. Your unit's loss was unexpected. Welcome back from the cold."

"Welcome back from the cold? Wish it were so. You're stuck here with me, with us, on this godforsaken planet."

"Leah, looks like we've found some friends, or at least not enemies. Get everyone to gather their stuff," Byron hollered in her direction. "So, how does this go, Hadrian?"

"My word gets you a meeting, but Turing calls the shots. He decides who stays and who goes."

"When you say he owns the planet, is he some sort of overseer?" Eric asked.

Hadrian laughed. "Overseer? He'd shoot you himself for making the suggestion. He takes some getting used to, but in the end, he's trapped like the rest of us. Tis his story to share, not mine. I don't work for petty tyrants if that's what you were thinking."

"I wasn't thinking that," Eric started. "It's just you said he owns the planet and it is being used as dumping grounds for the Protectorate."

Hadrian nodded. "It is. Like I said, it's his story to tell, but he's a bit prickly over the details. Be polite and you shouldn't have any problems."

Leah came trotting through the trees and nearly tripped when she noticed the camouflaged rifleman.

"It's okay," Svoboda reassured her. "If things go well, we'll have a place to stay. If they don't, hopefully we'll be able to top off and head out." Hadrian nodded. Leah cautiously joined the group, eying Hadrian the whole time.

"I won't bite, lass. Never seen a ghillie before?" Hadrian asked.

"A what?" Leah asked with narrowed eyes and a frown. She stepped closer to Svoboda.

"A ghillie." Hadrian pulled back his hood. Clear, piercing blue eyes shone from under layers of earth and gray face paint. Frost tinged the man's dirty blond beard. "Tis the suit I'm wearing. With a good ghillie, a man can disappear in plain sight. They're a beast in the summer, but in the winter, their warm nature is a blessing."

"Oh, no. I've never seen one," she commented.

Jeff emerged from the trees farther down the escarpment on the other side of the cooling bandits. He slowed his pace when he saw Hadrian, but kept coming until he nearly tripped over the three bandits.

"Uh, Svoboda?" Jeff asked.

"Yes?"

"You know there are three bodies over here?"

"Yep."

Jeff glanced between Svoboda and Hadrian.

"Waiting on Doc, Jeff. Figured I'd let everyone know at the same time so I didn't repeat myself. What's taking him so long?"

"Oh, the gun shots woke us up. When we didn't see you or Eric, we grabbed what we could and split up in different directions. If we didn't hear anything bad, the idea was to head this way to see what happened. Leah's idea. She volunteered to head down here first, just in case."

Svoboda gave Leah an appraising look. Her face flushed and she shook her head.

"It was your idea, Svoboda. I remembered one of the stories you told Eric while we were still on the *Shrike*."

"Leah, it might have been my story, but it was your decision. If this had gone bad, you would've been the only reason why anyone got away."

"Come on, Doc," Jeff hollered. "You're holding things up."

Moments later, Doc emerged at the edge of the escarpment behind where Hadrian had taken his shots from. He slowed a short distance away and scooped something from the snow before coming to a shocked halt.

"Relax, Doc," Leah said. "He's a friend."

"Oh. I guess these are yours then?" Doc said, offering two shiny brass casings to Hadrian.

"Sloppy brass security, Hadrian," Svoboda ribbed. "Captivity is making you soft."

"Soft? No, that's the liquor." Hadrian grinned and took the casings from Doc. "Aye, those be mine. Thank you."

"Oh, this world can't be all that bad if you can find booze here," Jeff chuckled.

Hadrian's expression darkened, "There's a wee bit more to it than that."

"There always is," Svoboda said. "Look folks, I'm pretty sure we've all figured out Hadrian here is not an enemy. The three corpses behind me, however, were. The bandits tried to rob Eric and me. I got one, Hadrian finished the other two. Once you're done picking over their remains for anything that looks remotely useful, we're going to follow Hadrian back to where he's staying. Any questions?"

"What's useful?" Jeff asked.

Doc looked sickened by the thought.

"Anything that's not got a hole or too much blood on it," Hadrian replied.

Eric glanced between the others. When nothing further was said, he trotted over to the cooling corpses, Jeff right behind him. Eric took the bowman's beaten up crossbow and the only two bolts while Jeff pocketed various small items. The bowman's shoes were ratty, as were the rest of his clothes. The only other item Eric found worth taking was a cloth-wrapped packet of meat jerky. The strong woody scent made his stomach rumble.

"Oh, care to share some?" Hadrian asked when Eric had unbundled it. Hadrian popped a small piece in his mouth. "Ah, nothing like hickory smoked deer jerky. Could use some more seasoning, but it's passable."

All eyes turned to Eric, who shrugged and handed out pieces to the rest of the group. *Could be worse, at least I got a piece.* At Svoboda's insistence, the travois had been left behind. Doc frowned, but did not push the issue.

Hiking down the mountain with Hadrian at the lead, the group did their best to keep up even with the thinning snow cover. Despite his injuries, the idea of having a place to go seemed to buoy Svoboda. The decision to leave the travois turned out to be wise. More than a few times, Hadrian deviated from what appeared to be an established path, leading them down narrow breaches in the undergrowth. Deer trails, Hadrian had called them, and insisted following them cut their travel time down significantly.

Most of his life Eric had been spent on ship or in densely packed cities. Kilometers of unpopulated forest, hillside, and mountains were a completely baffling sight. On several occasions, he'd asked Svoboda or Hadrian about tracks he spotted or why the trees stopped suddenly where they did.

Shortly before noon, Eric found himself walking alongside a tall wall whose thick, grey stones appeared so closely fit, he doubted he could fit a sheet of paper between them. After a short distance the group paused as Hadrian unlocked a wrought iron gate and let them inside.

"Now remember, polite," Hadrian reminded them as the house came into view. The house proper seemed enormous, with massive white columns that bordered an even larger porch sheltered beneath a long, wide balcony, which in turn lay under the main roof of the house. Large windows dotted the walls at regular intervals. Most were dark, though light shined through several on the second floor. Smoke drifted from the larger of several chimneys.

"Wow," Leah muttered.

"Yeah." Hadrian smiled. "It's an old design put together by one of the Turing family quite a few generations ago. Not sure how far back."

"I forgot how imposing some of the older architecture can be," Svoboda muttered as they climbed a set of steps onto the porch.

"Yep. Knock the snow off, and come on in. Actually, take those sticks off your boots, and leave the crossbow out here, too," Hadrian paused by the front door told the group. While they were slipping off their improvised snow-shoes, the door opened a crack.

"Oh, it's you Hadrian," a woman's voice said from inside. "Thought I heard clomping about on the porch. You're back early."

"Yep, found some lost lambs up in the mountains that Turing will want to meet."

"Oh? Think he'll ask them to stay?"

"No telling with him some days, Anne. You know that."

"True. He's where he always is this time of day. I'd better get back to working on dinner. Good luck."

"Thanks," Hadrian replied, eyeing the group. "Ready? Good. Follow me." Hadrian opened the door and let them inside.

Eric's eyes had trouble settling any one place in specific as the room on the other side of the door seemed far too large to be just one room. The sheer volume of polished and stained wood before him slowed him a step.

Before them, twin stair cases snaked up either wall to an overlooking second floor. Sizable landscape paintings and ornate friezes adorned the walls. Two smaller chandeliers hung to either side of their significantly larger cousin in the center of the room. Small lights flickered amongst the hanging glass shards, aided in lighting the room by other wall-mounted bulbs. As well-kept as the room seemed at first glance Eric noticed holes punched in the walls in several spots that had been hastily and improperly patched.

Traversing through the double doors between the stairs, Eric spotted similar signs of improperly repaired damage along the far hallway in the hardwood flooring and the walls. Hadrian paused at a door and when they caught up, he knocked.

"Enter," a voice on the other side told them.

Hadrian raised a hand.

"Wait for my signal," he told them before stepping into the room. He left the door open a crack.

"Back already?" Eric heard through the door. He presumed it was Turing.

"Aye." Hadrian's voice was much louder that Turing's. He hadn't walked far.

"That was terribly quick. Heard some gunfire earlier today, was that you?"

"It was. Ran into some cast-offs that went feral."

Turing sighed. "I really wish they'd stop dropping the dregs of humanity off on my planet."

"Speaking of which, sir."

"Yes?"

"The aircraft we heard yesterday did drop another batch."

"Oh?"

"Found them not to far from the mountain lodge."

"Ah. Did they find the lodge?"

"No, sir."

"Good. Where are they now?"

"Well, I spoke with them. They seemed like good people."

"So you brought them here?" Turing asked. His annoyance was unmistakable.

"I believe at least one of them has skills we need, sir."

"Oh?"

"One of them appears to be a medical professional of some sort, an actual doctor."

"From your tone, there's more. What is it?"

"Well, I know one of them."

"Surely you jest. While it may be quite small in the bigger picture, humanity's corner of the galaxy is a rather large place by human standards."

"Well, not directly know, no. Do you remember me talking about my first sergeant? One of them was McCulloch's first sergeant. I've heard stories."

"Well then. Perhaps it is a small world after all. Did you show them the kitchens?"

"Not yet, sir. I figured you would want to meet them and figure it out sooner rather than later."

"Oh. So I suppose they're out in the hall then?"

"Aye."

"I'm almost at a decent stopping point. Would you mind helping them get lunch in the kitchen? I'll interview them individually after they've had a chance to eat and rest a bit."

Hadrian backed out of the room, closing the door as he did.

"That went better than I expected," he told them. "Come with me. We'll find a place for your gear, first. No need to be wearing all that in here."

"I'll say," Jeff agreed. "Might be a bit drafty in here, but it's getting awfully hot in this getup."

Hadrian led them to a smaller room where they doffed their heavy clothes before continuing on to the kitchen. On entering, they spotted a middle aged woman with short brown hair tending several stoves.

"Anne, Turing wants to feed these folks. Said he'd pull them aside for individual interviews."

The woman's face lit up.

"Oh, good. I was hoping we'd have guests," she replied. "I'm sorry, but I'm working on dinner right now. All I can offer is some sandwiches and tea, is that okay?"

The group glanced back and forth at each other.

"I'm sure that will be fine, Ma'am," Svoboda responded.

By the end of the resulting shuffle, they'd been led to yet another room with a sizable wooden table. Despite their simplicity, the meat and cheese in the sandwiches hit Eric's palate like a gourmet meal. Deliciously bitter but tamed with honey, the hot tea warmed his chilled bones. Not long had passed before Eric found himself yawning and slumping his cushioned chair.

"Tired?" Leah asked him from across the table.

"Yeah, a bit," he replied. "Once I started to relax, all this tired just landed on me."

Sitting in the chair beside Leah, Svoboda nodded. "And that's why the perfect time to attack would be right now. Wait until the enemy has a chance to relax after a big event and they'll struggle to respond. Basic biology."

Leah gave Svoboda sideways glance.

"No, it's true," Doc noted. "Part of the adrenaline response. Once the event is passed and adrenaline begins to decline, there's a refractory period. If something happens before you're recharged, you've got some issues."

Everyone sat in uncomfortable silence for a second and jumped when someone knocked on the door. Hadrian peeked into the room.

"Byron, if you're ready, Turing would like to speak with you now."

Eric watched Svoboda leave. *Byron Mackinnon. That's still so weird. I'm used to thinking of him as Svoboda.* A cloud of savory scents wafted through the door when Anne poked her head in.

"Does anyone want another sandwich? More tea?" Anne asked.

"If you don't mind, I could go for more of both," Eric told her.

"I'll take some tea," Leah asked.

"Actually, I'm kind of exhausted, is there some place I might be able to nod off until this Turing guy wants to talk to me?" Jeff asked.

Doc murmured the same.

"Oh, sure. Let me get their food, I'll show you to the lounge while your friends finish up," Anne told them. True to her word, she appeared shortly with another plate for Eric, poured them both tea, and showed the other two out.

"So, how are you doing?" Leah asked, clearly uncomfortable with the lasting silence.

"Okay I guess, other than the headache."

"Same one from yesterday?"

"Yeah. It's not nearly as bad. In fact, if I don't think about it, I barely notice. I'm exhausted, but a lot hungrier than I thought. You?"

Leah sipped her tea. Her smile did not reach her eyes. "Same here. More cold than anything, really."

"You sure you're holding up okay?"

"I'm fine," she said, but Eric heard more in her voice.

"Leah," Eric started, reaching across the table to touch her hand.

"Don't touch me," she snapped as she snatched her hand back right before he could touch it. She scowled at him and continued, "Don't play hurt mister 'I'm just trying to help.' I saw what you did to Frost. Don't think for one minute I don't know what you're capable of."

Eric rocked back in his chair, words frozen in his mouth. From the doorway, Anne cleared her throat.

"Miss Anne, do you have some place I can be alone for a bit?" Leah asked.

"Of course, dear," Anne said with a congenial smile. The look she gave Eric as she turned to leave confused him further. Her features seemed conciliatory, but he felt little but judgement. *Fuck me.* He sipped his tea, trying to not let the sudden weight of everything drag at him. When Anne returned, he'd already finished his sandwich, bolted down the rest of the tea she'd left, and had just begun looking about the room from his chair.

"Eric?" Anne asked. "What's this thing with Frost Leah was talking about?"

"I really wish I could tell you," Eric said with a sigh. Before Anne's frown could translate into words, he continued, "Something happened on the ship we were both on. I don't remember much of anything. Doctors said something about a traumatic brain injury interfering with my memory."

"Oh. Is it permanent?"

"I was told it could be days, months, or even years before I get my memory back, if I get it back at all."

"Well, I guess that clarifies things a bit."

"Not for me it doesn't. I look at her, and I see fear. Why? I can't remember. I get snippets and vague feelings about a lot of stuff. It took me a bit to remember her name, but I don't remember anything else about her, or most of our time on the *Shrike* for that matter. I remember being on my ship, then things get progressively fuzzier going forwards or back. I know something bad happened to the *Fortune* and I know something bad happened on the *Shrike*, but beyond that? All I have is a swarm of tiny random details begging to be put together. That bugs the hell out of me."

Anne nodded in sympathy. "I can see how that would be confusing."

"It is. Very. Part of me is sad about this."

"And the other part?"

"I-I'm tired of getting kicked for things I didn't do. Or, well, things I don't remember doing. Part of me wants to get really angry about it all."

"Most people would, past a certain point," Anne said, sitting down in the chair Leah vacated. "But I'll tell you this, Eric. As confused as you might be, I think Leah's just as bad off."

"How do you figure?"

"She broke down in the hall. I couldn't follow a lot of what she said, but she is hurting about something. Something big, but beyond that I couldn't tell. Give her some time to rest, time to figure things out."

Eric sighed and looked out the window.

"Things will get better. Time heals all wounds." Anne patted his hand and stood up. "Would you like to join your friends?"

"I kinda want to be by myself, but at the same time, I don't know. I'm kinda afraid to be by myself, too. Does that make sense?"

Anne smiled, but Eric saw the masked sadness behind her eyes.

"It does, dear. Tell you what, come with me to the lounge and if it doesn't work out for you, I'll find a room you can lie down in. How's that sound?"

Eric nodded. The lounge turned out to be much closer than he'd expected, merely just across the hall. Jeff and Doc were sprawled out snoring on two of the many sleek couches that interrupted otherwise full-wall bookshelves. Anne closed the door behind him.

Curious, Eric scanned the shelves as he made his way to a couch at the far side. Some held large spherical objects clearly intended to represent a planet. No single one looked similar to another, much as he never saw a book title repeated. Some of the books were large and hardbound, but most were much smaller paperbacks. He paused at one section whose topics caught his eye.

Algebra, trigonometry, calculus, physics and real world applications, inorganic chemistry, organic chemistry, biology, genetics, micro miniature circuit design, applied nanoscale compositions. There's no way this guy has read all this. One book slowed him down. *Security is a Myth: Application of Intelligence Techniques to Information Security by Edgar Allen Turing. Same Turing as the guy running this place? Couldn't be.*

Eric gravitated to the broad window at the end of the room. It was snowing again outside, though not nearly as heavy as it was on the mountainside earlier. Watching the flakes spin and fall in the wind called to him, soothed him. Focused on the chaotic patterns outside, he was barely aware of sitting down on the couch integrated into the window sill.

"Eric?" He jerked, brought back to reality by Anne's voice. "Oh, sorry, I didn't mean to startle you."

"It's okay. You need something?" he asked.

"Turing wants to speak with you."

Eric yawned.

"How long have I been sitting here?"

"A bit more than an hour," Anne said, smiling at his sudden discomfiture. "You're tired, it's beautiful out there, and you don't have to be out in it. Don't worry. Now, if you'll come with me?"

The muscles in his legs and back burned as he rose to follow her.

Silent, she led him down the hall and let him through the door the group had stood outside much earlier.

"Ah. Come, come," the man at the far side of the room said at the sound of the closing door. Turing was facing a large mottled white square between him and the window. From the doorway, Eric could make out only thick brown hair above a long dark overcoat.

Eric cautiously made his way through the various tables and couches to the far side where Turing stood near the window. Save for more tables scattered about the center of the room and a wide open space at the far end, the room had been laid out similarly to the lounge. *These books are almost all a lot older than the other library.* Cluttered like the rest with what looked like random items, Eric glanced at the last of the tables as he passed. Tucked under a mostly blue sphere, he spotted an extremely primitive looking pistol of very large bore. His eyes drifted over as he passed another table. He read one label before he walked too far from the blue and green sphere: Australia. Eric looked up and realized the white square was a painting canvas on an easel.

"Eric, I presume?" Turing asked, still focused on the painting in front of him.

"That would be me, yes."

"Glad to make your acquaintance. My name is Edward Allen Turing. Seeing as we already have an Edward and an Allen here, Turing might cut down any potential confusion, especially since I'm the only surviving family member on this planet."

Eric mentally stumbled over the situation he'd found himself in. *This sounds so formal. I've never done formal. Well, time to make it up as I go along.*

"In that case, pleased to make your acquaintance as well, Mr. Turing."

"Good, good. Tell me, what do you think of this painting?"

Eric stepped forward from where he'd stopped to get a better look. He glanced up at the window and found himself nodding. It was the mountain he'd just come down.

"So?"

"Well," Eric started, pausing to buy time. "Nobody has ever really asked my opinion on art before."

"Just tell me what you think. Is it too bright? Too dark? Does it make you feel anything? Does it look like what's out that window?"

Eric leaned closer.

"Well, I don't know much about painting, but it does look like you've put a lot of work into it. It looks fairly close to the mountain, but something seems missing though. Not sure what. Overall, it feels kind of sad? Angry? Well, dark. Like emotion dark, not lighting dark."

"Yes, that's what I was thinking. I was considering adding some trees up here at the tree line. Maybe some clouds, too, to lighten the mood a little. Try to balance out that darkness with something lighter, happier."

"So, happy trees?"

Turing finally turned his attention from the painting to Eric.

"I suppose you could say that. Finding proper balance is one of the joys of painting. Well, one of the joys of life, really."

Eric found himself nodding in agreement.

"Though, to be fair," Turing continued, "This brings us to the question at hand, which is not really one of joy. What do I do with you and your friends?" Turing gave him a long, considering look. "I'm still trying to decide. What would you do in my shoes, Eric?"

"Uh, excuse me?"

"What would you do? It's not a hard question."

"I'm sorry, I didn't expect to be asked that. There are a lot of variables."

Turing flashed a rakish smile. "Yes, so many variables. What did you expect me to ask?"

"I'm not really sure. Probably whatever came to mind that would address whatever concerns you had."

"Such as?"

"What kind of person I am, what I might bring to the table, what my opinions about the other people in my group? It would make sense that you'd want to make sure I could fit in and be useful."

"Very true, those would be questions I might ask myself. Why wouldn't I ask you them?"

Eric frowned. *This has to be some sort of trap.* Eric considered Turing's line of questioning for a moment.

"Well, I don't really know what your point of view is."

"Why is that important?"

"It," Eric paused in brief confusion. "It would be very important. How this place runs, what problems you face, all of those things make up motives, worries, concerns. If I knew them, I'd know how you would judge my answers, what questions you would ask."

"Partially irrelevant. Those reasons apply much better to my first question, but only tangentially here. I asked why I would not ask those questions, not how I'd interpret your answers. So, why would I not ask those questions, from my point of view? Be honest."

Eric sighed. *This is going poorly.* "From your point of view, how would know you could trust what was said? I suppose I would have less reason to lie about others in my group, but how could you be sure? As for my skills or anything valuable, well, we've been dropped off in the middle of nowhere. As far as I know, this is the only place around. We'd probably starve if we couldn't stay, so I suppose you couldn't trust me to honestly evaluate my skillset either."

"Very good. So if you weren't sure what you could trust, how would you approach it?"

"Uh, well, I guess I'd not ask anything I knew I couldn't trust at all. It'd be a waste of time."

"And what would you ask?"

"I'd ask about things they'd have less reason to lie about, like the rest of the group, and cross-reference their answers with what the others had to say. There ought to be a pattern there."

"Excellent. So, what do you think of your friend, Dennis?"

"Who?"

"Oh, pardon me, I believe your group referred to him as Doc."

"Oh, Doc. Well, he seems decent, I guess," Eric started. At

Turing's quizzical expression, he continued, "He hasn't been harsh or otherwise acted like a jackass. He's helped us quite a bit."

Turing nodded. "Go on. Anything else?"

"Well, when Hadrian saved me and Svoboda--"

"You mean Byron Mackinnon?"

"Yeah, sorry. I'm not used to thinking of him by that name yet."

"Understandable. We'll get to that. When Hadrian shot the mongrels, dot dot dot?"

"Doc didn't react very well to seeing their bodies. I'm not sure if he doesn't have the stomach for blood or dead bodies, or if he doesn't care for violence in general."

"And you? Do you disdain violence as well, Mr. Friedrich?"

Eric thought for a few seconds. "I suppose you could say I'm ambivalent on the topic."

Turing nodded again. "What are your thoughts on Jeff then?"

"He can be gruff, but he's a good person. He more or less carried Byron by himself half way down the mountain and didn't complain once. He told me he was a machinist on a transport ship before he got sent here."

"Have you seen or heard him say anything to make you believe that is true?"

"No, but he hasn't given me any reason to doubt him so far."

"Did he tell you what ship he was on?"

"Yeah, the *Bystro*."

"Interesting, he didn't tell anyone else. I wonder why that would be."

"I don't know. We were roommates on the *Relentless* on the way here, quarantined together. He mentioned it when we talked the first time."

Turing frowned. "Quarantined? Biological?"

"Information."

Turing's eyes lit up over sudden wide smile. "A data quarantine? Oh, that is interesting. What do you know they don't want out?"

"I actually don't know. I--"

"I know, traumatic brain injury. It's an interesting cover story, but let's pretend I believe you, go on."

Eric frowned. No small amount of heat found its way into his words when he said, "I was going to say that based off of what Jeff was exiled for, it had to be something Earth-related."

"What did Jeff know?"

"His ship came across something from Earth."

"Something?"

"Well, it sounded like a satellite or something similar. A probe maybe? But old. Very old. Old Earth old."

"Interesting. Do you know what happened to the rest of his ship's crew?"

"No. He made it sound like they were all arrested. I think the only reason why he's alive is because he didn't know much about the thing."

"You're very likely correct. That's a shame. Captain Higgins was a very dependable captain. I see a question on your face."

"Why this huge effort to keep information about Earth quiet?"

"Because they're fools. Unusually efficient fools most of the time, but fools."

"I'm not following."

"Eric, you know my family owns this planet?" Turing asked and paused a moment before he continued. "Owned might be more proper, I suppose. How expensive do you think a planet is? To purchase that is."

"Uh, probably more expensive than I can tell you off the top of my head. Are we charging by mass or volume? I mean, mineral rich planets would be worth more I'd think. Well, I guess beautiful places have value, too, but who has the money to buy a world just because it's beautiful?"

"Precisely. Who would have the money to buy a place because it was beautiful? The better question is who would have enough money to buy a planet because they thought it could be made beautiful?"

"That sounds terribly expensive, making a planet beautiful."

Turing laughed. "About as expensive as buying the place would have been if we'd paid cash."

"Wait, if you didn't pay cash, how did you own the planet?"

"If family legend is accurate, the Protectorate gave it to us for services rendered. I can't speak for the accuracy of that statement. Nonetheless, we have a planet."

"Services rendered? What did your family do that was worth a planet?"

"That much has been buried. I have a few qualified guesses, but they're irrelevant to the discussion. The greater point being, with such influence and wealth my family has had access to far more information than anyone stepping foot on this planet today is ever likely to have had."

"That sounds fairly presumptuous."

"As inner party and members of the Secretariat, my ancestors have known some of the Protectorate's darkest secrets, Eric. Be that as it may, I never learned why knowledge about Earth was as protected as it is. If my ancestors did they never passed that knowledge down. Now, that said, the Protectorate is still full of fools. Try as they might, they can't be everywhere at all times. Sooner or later someone will slip up and they'll have a mess they can't clean up by carting off and/or shooting a large group of people."

"That might very well be true." Eric paused to consider his words carefully. "But that doesn't address what I was getting at. You're presuming you're right. What if they're not all fools? What if they actually have good reason to hide knowledge of Earth?"

"If they're not fools, then there must be something spectacularly dangerous about humanity's forgotten homeworld. Look around you. For the two generations prior to mine, my family has collected every Earth artifact they could. Do you see anything dangerous?"

Eric looked at the shelves and tables, at the variety of objects lying about.

"Does this globe look dangerous?" Turing asked as he walked over to the sphere. "This is what Earth looks like. Well, if it were ink printed on paper wrapped over a ball shaped to mimic its topography, perhaps, but you get my point."

"Not really, no. What about the pistol?"

"The flintlock?" Turing said, picking up the pistol. "Physically speaking, this is one of the most dangerous old Earth artifacts I have. Otherwise? Information is usually far more dangerous than a gun. Pulling a trigger might kill one or more people depending on diameter, projectile type, and muzzle velocity, but the right information can pull a million triggers."

Turing glanced down at the pistol and then tossed it at Eric. "Keep it, it's yours. Handmade by a silversmith in a place called Boston. I have several others, most by the same man."

"Silversmith?" Eric asked, turning the heavy pistol over in his hand.

Turing shook his head, smiling. "Before industrial processes were common, most everything was made by hand. Quite primitive actually, but the totality of it is quite impressive when you consider the limitations of the time. Real artisans, real skill. Smiths were metal workers. Silversmiths, well, dealt with silver primarily, though you're a sharp kid, I'm sure you figured it out before I said it."

"Are you sure it's actually Old Earth?"

"Oh, I have no doubt the provenance of some of my collection is false in some way. The most we could verify was that they came from Earth. Their stories? Not so much. If I recall correctly, dating of the wood in the handle places that pistol some nine hundred years old. By their calendar at the time, the late 1700s. The maker's mark is on the silver cap at the bottom of the grip."

Eric turned it over to find a stylized *PR. 1700s, huh? Maybe the dates on the Gadsden were accurate after all.*

"Does it work?"

Turing nodded. "Most collectors would frown, but those types are fools as well given the age and importance of the artifacts. Some of the older artifacts we recovered were in such poor condition, we had to take efforts to restore and preserve them. It wasn't cheap, but you can't really tell aside from the fact they look suspiciously newer than they should. Everything is functional."

"I-I don't know what to say, Turing. Thanks?"

Turing smiled, "You're welcome. Maybe once we can reliably manufacture gunpowder you'll be able to use it, relive a bit of the past as it were. Our most recent efforts have had some unfortunate complications. Explosive, even. Now, what was I saying? Oh, yes, the right information can pull a million triggers. I've pored over every book in this room. I haven't found anything that valuable. If there's an artifact that explains their caution, I don't have it."

"Well, I will admit it is a bit weird."

"Yes, quite odd. Did you know they removed it from the star charts?"

"What? That doesn't make any sense. Anyone with the right tools could rediscover it and put it back on the map."

"Correct, but who has the right tools? Or maybe the better question is who decides who gets the right tools?"

"That's--"

"Insidious?"

"Actually, yeah, that's what I was going to say. What if someone stumbles across Earth by accident?"

"I've pondered that myself for quite some time, actually. Given that I've never heard of someone doing precisely that, even with my family's connections, I must assume either it hasn't happened yet or, if it has, they didn't return. Thus, the likelihood is that Earth lies somewhere remote, away from normal routes. Then again, one cannot rule out the possibility that perhaps the fools aren't so foolish after all."

Haven.

"What if they didn't want to return?"

Turing froze for a second. "That's a possibility. Though, it stands to reason that someone coming across Earth would likely want others to know of their discovery at some point. Even if the planet was somehow devoid of human life, there's only so much you can exploit using manpower small enough you can control information flow."

"I suppose that's true."

"Now, where were we?" Turing tapped his lips, pondering out loud, "Information, artifacts, my planet, fools."

"We were talking about Jeff."

"Yes, so we were. Any other thoughts on the man?"

"Not really. He seems like a decent enough person, dependable. That's about it."

"Good enough, what about Byron Mackinnon?"

"Byron? Still weird, him being Byron not Svoboda. Well, I know I've known him for longer than anyone else other than Leah. I'm really spotty on details, though."

"Well, again, pretending I believe your amnesia, what can you say about him?"

"I'm pretty sure he's the only reason I lived to see my farce of a trial. He's also the only reason why I'm sitting here. If I trusted him much more, I'm pretty sure I'd march to the gates of Hell with that man if he asked."

"That's a terribly positive recommendation for someone who doesn't have much of a memory."

Eric shrugged. "You didn't try to get off that mountain. You didn't see or do what I had to do. He understood. He helped. Beyond that, I guess it's just a gut feeling. So far my gut has matched my memory when it comes back."

"Okay. So, it's safe to say you look up to the man."

"Yes."

"What do you know about his past?"

"Verifiably? Nothing. I know he and Hadrian share some sort of background. Military and he's not some run-of-the-mill soldier."

Turing chuckled. "No, he's definitely not run-of-the-mill by even the Protectorate's most foolish standard of measure. This brings us to Leah. What do you know about her?"

"She's beautiful?"

Turing snorted. "She is, but that's beside the point. Understandable, given your age, but beside the point. What do you know about her?"

"Well, I know her from the *Shrike*, but."

"But what?"

"Well, there's gaps. Big gaps. I know she was in the same cell as Byron and me."

"Anything else?"

"On the *Shrike*? No. The harder I try to remember, the less I can, if that makes any sense."

"Possibly. How about outside the *Shrike*?"

"We were dropped off at the top of the mountain together--"

"How many of you were there?"

"Eight."

"There's five of you here now, what happened to the other three?"

"You know about us jumping?" Turing nodded. "Two of them elected to try to walk out. Haven't seen them since. The third wasn't as lucky as the rest of us on that jump. He died." Eric's stomach knotted.

"That's an interesting way to put it."

"How's it interesting? He hit rock. I found him and he begged me to kill him." Eric scowled as he tried to keep his flaring temper under control.

"Calm down, Eric. I'm not trying to get a rise out of you. It's interesting merely because of the way you summarized it. There's a variety of reasons for how one chooses their wording. I was inclined after talking with your friends to believe you rather regretted that incident. I merely wanted to verify, not set you off. Back to Leah, what about her can you tell me since then?"

"She's been on edge. One minute she's trying to talk to me, trying to help me. The next, she's yelling at me like I've hurt her. I don't know what her problem is," Eric sighed.

"We'll get to that if you want, later. Continue."

"Well, I think she's braver than she thinks she is."

"What makes you say that?"

"When I put the guy out his misery, she gave me her knife to do it with. She didn't have to do that. When we met Hadrian, she came up with a good plan on her own and got folks to follow it. Thing is, she's also, I don't know, maybe it's body language, but she's really tried to downplay what she's done. I think if she'd stop flip-flopping on me, I'd trust her. I don't know what she did before she got picked up by the Provost or anything like that. I just get the impression she's decent people."

Turing sighed. "Yeah, she'll be a tough nut to crack. Other than you, I spoke with her the longest. I'm somewhat regretting I didn't take more psychology classes or the like, but the soft sciences always bored me to tears. I'd like to think you're not far off on your assessment. I came to similar conclusions once I managed to get past her combativeness."

"Well, us coming to similar conclusions is a good thing, right?"

"Better than you'd know yet, Eric. Better than you know. Now, that's the first part of my line of questioning--"

"I thought--"

"You thought wrong. I'll be honest with you here, Eric. Out of your whole group, so far you are the weakest link. Everyone else has useful skills but you. Even Leah is more capable. She was a lawyer, you know? Did gardening as a hobby?"

Eric responded in a near whisper, "No, I didn't know that."

"You might want to ask yourself why I'm still asking questions, and when that answer comes to you, it might help you understand why you need to answer those questions."

He's going to send me back out while everyone else stays. Goddamnit.

Eric sighed and asked, "What do you want to know?"

"What did you do before the Provost arrested you?"

"I was on a ship. It's fuzzy, but I know I was charged with piracy, so I'm assuming that ship was pirate."

"Ah yes, that fuzzy feeling again."

"Gut feeling, again." Eric scowled.

"Fair enough. Go on."

"Well, that's the thing, I don't really remember much. I know I knew the ship's captain. I know the crew liked me for the most part. I vaguely remember telling the interrogator on the *Shrike* that I thought they were training me to be a tech or an engineer. I didn't tell him I thought officer was more likely."

"Good thing you didn't. Still, that's an interesting leap. Nothing to officer candidate and back to nothing? That doesn't sound very likely."

Eric grit his teeth.

"If you're going to lie, at least make it believable," Turing continued.

Eric shivered as an icy chill drifted through him, dragging everything but his anger into the depths with it on departure. Jaw set, Eric enunciated each word slowly, "I am not lying."

"If you're not lying, you're the victim of some of the most unlikely circumstances. The odds simply aren't in your favor. It's are far more likely you think me stupid. In which case, perhaps you've mistaken the stupid person in this conversation."

Eric's eye twitched. *Don't do it, don't do it. Fuck that, this asshole deserves to get hit. No, No, I can't do that. I'll fuck over everyone.* He fought to keep himself still, knowing the moment he moved, he would not be able to stop himself.

"Again, let's pretend I believe you. I'll even pretend you were on a pirate ship if that makes you feel any better. What was the name of this ship?"

The words drifted emotionlessly from Eric's lips, "The *Fortune.*"

Turing went very still.

"How long were you on this ship?"

"Since I was a kid."

"And you're how old?"

"Eighteen."

"Does the name *Vyzov* ring any bells?"

Eric's headache flared suddenly. The sudden pain damped his anger. He rubbed the bridge of his nose while nausea boiled in his gut.

"Oh, this is weird," he sighed. He'd broken out in a sweat.

"Yes?"

"I, I don't know how to describe this. I don't remember, but I remember remembering? I remember telling the interrogator on the *Shrike* something about the *Vyzov*. The words sound like gibberish, all I can hear is the name."

Turing's brow knit and his visage darkened as Eric finished. He swept himself off the table he'd been sitting at and went to one of the bookshelves with an inlaid cabinet. Another wave of pain knit Eric's brow and he closed his eyes. He heard glass being moved. A few seconds later, footsteps.

"Drink this, it will help," Turing told him.

Sniffing the amber liquid burnt his nostrils.

"What is it?"

"What do you think it is? Drink it."

"I'm not sure alcohol helps with a headache. Pretty sure it's a bad idea in my case."

"Of course it is. It's a spectacularly bad idea if you think someone has brain trauma. I don't believe that's the case. I mean, I do suspect you have brain trauma, but I suspect something else as well. Worst case scenario, you're already dead, so it doesn't matter what you drink. Best case, we find out I'm right. If I'm wrong, at least you had something proper to drink on the way out."

Eric gave Turing a puzzled look and made no move to drink.

"Every time you remember something new, you get a jarring headache like someone's pounding a chisel through your skull?"

Eric nodded.

"Does the stinging come first, or the memory? How much time between them?"

"The stinging and almost immediately."

"What you're remembering that causes these headaches is always contextually linked to something being discussed?"

"Yes."

"Any left side or right side weakness, tingling, or other oddness?"

"No?"

"Granted, I'm a much better engineer than a doctor, but you don't show the primary symptoms of stroke. Sudden stinging headaches and the like are symptoms of aneurysms or other cerebral hemorrhages. If you have a brain bleed at all, there's nothing we can do for you here and you're already dead. If you've had these sudden headaches when you were perfectly calm since you landed here, that makes my hypothesis more likely. Drink."

Doubt slowed his hand, but he knocked back the tumbler. *Sweet, subtly woody.* Eric gasped moments later when every inch of his digestive tract from his mouth to his stomach lit into a steady burn.

"Good lad."

"What is it?" Eric coughed as he tried to hold back tears.

"Whiskey. What's it taste like?"

"It tastes like regret."

"Hmm." Eric looked up to see Turing tilt back his glass and swallow. "No, that's not regret, lad. That's fine whiskey. If you want regret, I've got a few bottles you might want to try, provided you're still around later. Evidently, the Irish were good at both whiskey and regret. If we ever get out of here, I need to find more."

Eric managed a weak grin.

"Another? We'll find out faster."

"Sure? Why not."

Eric still coughed when he sat the glass down, but his throat seemed to burn less.

"Okay, so tell me what you remember about the *Vyzov*."

Eric rubbed his forehead, pushing himself to remember. "I remember the interrogator telling me that the executive board of Turing Interstellar and the families they could contact sent thanks for my information concerning the *Vyzov*."

"Oh really? The executive board of Turing Interstellar? My, my."

Eric shook his head, but the swimming only got worse. "Wait, that Turing? Your family owned the *Vyzov*?"

"Owned the *Vyzov*? Before my family was exiled Turing Interstellar had no executive board. We," Turing stressed, "were Turing Interstellar. The *Vyzov* was supposed to be a new class of luxury liner. Stronger, lighter materials, less fuel usage, faster travel, more cargo space. There aren't many that can afford that style of travel, so other accommodations were made in the design so we could manage a profit off every run, passengers or not. Father knew the winds were changing on Unity, shifting away from us. He told me as much while I was still at the University. The loss of the *Vyzov* was the last straw. I remember seeing the beginning of the spin in the media. I got a visit by a courier with a sealed note telling me to pack my bags and run. I did. I was the only one that got away."

"Wait? You got away? If you got away, why are you sitting here?"

"I said I got away, not that they didn't eventually catch me. It took them five years despite their surveillance state."

"How'd you manage that?"

"Very carefully."

"No, seriously. I heard from Svob--Byron that the way things were on the *Shrike*, the whole Protectorate is set up that way. Cameras, microphones, everything. Is that true?"

"Depends on where you are, but yes."

"So how'd you manage to go five years in that without getting caught? I mean, I'd imagine they have all that hooked up to computers."

"They do." A slow grin crept across Turing's face.

"I dunno, image recognition and the like, that should have caught you within moments of you walking in front of a camera?"

"Who said it didn't?"

Eric blinked.

"How the hell does that work?" he asked.

"Pattern matching, facial recognition, they're known algorithms. You can skirt an algorithm in two ways. One of which is changing the pattern observed. Camouflage, makeup, disguises. Can you guess the other?"

Eric's pursed his lips together, thinking. He sipped his drink before realizing Turing had poured him another.

"Alter the algorithm itself?"

Turing's grin blossomed into a full smile.

"Precisely."

"Wow. How'd you do that?"

"Story for another time, Eric. So, think of something you couldn't remember that bothered you. I'd avoid anything dealing with Leah for right now. I'm not trying to scar you."

"Uhm, okay?" Eric muttered. *Something that bothered me. Not Leah.* A chill settled on his skin. He was weightless again, hanging in mid-air over the snowy slope. The memory blinked. The blackness of space surrounded him. He couldn't breathe, but he was oddly okay with it. Eric's eye twitched. *I accepted it.* "Got it. Next?"

"What led up to that?"

"They threw me in an airlock."

"They?"

"Uh, Doctor Isaacs. She was the director of interrogation. She sna--", Eric trailed off, wincing.

"What? What is it, Eric?"

"I, just, wait. Headache," Eric groaned, grabbing his head. "Sudden."

"Good, keep focusing, she what?"

"She snapped. They threw me in an airlock but--" Eric trailed off again, this time with a look of horror.

Turing snapped his fingers several times.

Eric took a long pull from his drink and sorrowful words tumbled from his mouth. "They threw my friend out first."

"Oh, dear."

Eric scowled, slamming his empty glass on the table, "That bitch killed my friend trying to get me to talk!"

"I'm sorry, Eric, but you might want to calm down."

"Why?" Eric growled.

"Well, for one, there's no one here you can justifiably be angry at. Two, if I was wrong, you're accelerating the process by raising your blood pressure. Pressure makes the brain bleed worse."

Eric froze for a second and leaned back in his chair as he wrestled with his anger. He ran his hand through his short hair a few times. "Okay, you're right. Man, my hair feels weird. Like, fuzzy or something."

Turing smirked. "You've never drank before?"

"Nah, not really. Maybe a sip or two. It usually tasted like I was drinking from a bottle of cleaning chemicals."

"Ah, well, I'll apologize for any after effects. Now, tell me about the ship you grew up on. You should find it remarkably easier to remember now."

Eric looked quizzically at Turing. "Yeah, it is. Why can I remember this now?"

"More on that later, continue while you can."

Eric frowned. *I don't like the sound of that.*

"I grew up on the *Fortune*. She was a heavily modified cargo hauler, a bit short of seventy thousand tons, but more of that was engine than you'd think. She carried two dorsal mounted two-hundred-fifty-six megajoule rail guns, an assortment of point defense weapons, and a few other surprises, odds and ends mostly. Total crew complement, less than six hundred."

"Only two rails? And two-fifties? That's rather light for naval engagements."

"Not when you're hitting merchants and making off with the goods before someone serious shows up."

"Is that what happened? Someone serious showed up?"

Eric's eyes glossed over as hundreds of images flickered past him. "Yeah, kinda. Fox had bought some information. We got there a week before the convoy was supposed to show up and waited in an asteroid field. Their escort was a pair of destroyers, not a frigate."

"So that's how the Protectorate got ahold of you?"

"Nope. We were going to play it quiet, let them pass. One of the destroyers detected us somehow. They opened fire, winged us. We got the hell out of there, barely."

"Well, if they didn't catch you there, how did they?"

"We did a standard escape and evasion sequence, dropping into deadspace, changing directions, that kind of thing. Our last deadspace shuffle, back-up life support shit the bed, couldn't handle the strain. That destroyer had put a shot straight through main life support, through and through. I'm not sure what happened exactly, but we scooted to the nearest system and laid up in the Kuiper belt collecting ice comet fragments. I'm pretty sure they were melting them down, filtering the water, and separating a good chunk of it into hydrogen for the fuel and oxygen. That was where we found it."

"It? What did you find?"

"I probably shouldn't tell you." Eric paused, lost in thought for a moment. The memories of his fallen shipmates haunted him. "We found a ship."

"A ship? That doesn't sound--"

"Stuck in a comet fragment long enough that the ice had reformed over it."

"Interesting. Go on."

"I was the only one to really walk around on her. It was a warship of some kind, bigger than the *Fortune*."

"Early Protectorate?"

Eric shook his head and glanced down at this pistol in his hand. "No. I didn't recognize the ensign the first time. Does 'The United States of America' ring any bells?"

"Ring any bells? That flintlock was made there." Turing smiled. He leaned back, and spun the globe of Earth around. Pointing to a territory in the upper hemisphere, he continued, "That is the United States. That ship is why you're here. Pity, the charlatans would never appreciate the history inside her hull. Shame they've burnt her like they do all the rest."

Eric snorted and slurred, "They'd have to find her first."

Turing's gaze slid over to him. It started as a chuckle, but seconds later Turing was laughing. "You managed to keep possibly the largest Earth artifact ever discovered a secret? Really?"

"Not entirely." Turing's laugh halted.

"While we were picking through the fragments, the *Shrike* was moving into position. They ambushed us while we paced the comet this ship, the *Gadsden*, was trapped in."

"You just made it sound like they didn't know it was there."

"As far as I know, they don't. The *Shrike* had to have been on silent running for a while to get that close to us. It still took them a good while to get a transport out to pick us up. I'm pretty sure they thought we were scouting out another comet fragment. That's the impression I gave them anyway. I don't know about my friend, but that was the story we agreed to. Tell them we were unimportant nobodies, the *Fortune* was picking up ice on the way home. It wasn't until they pulled images from my suit camera and started looking at the tablet I picked up--"

"Tablet? No, that can wait, continue."

"Well, we'd been on the *Shrike* a while before they started asking questions about the pictures. Something happened." Eric paused to rub the bridge of his nose. His head pounded. He motioned for another drink. "More. I'm only getting flashes and the headache is coming back."

After a few more gulps of amber Irish, Eric opened his mouth to speak, but a torrent of images and feelings froze his words.

"Eric? Are you still with me? What are you seeing?"

The worry in Turing's words shook him free.

Eric looked down at his clenched hands, expecting them to be clenched around a set of orange coveralls. He blinked slowly, caressing the pistol in his lap.

"I killed a man, Turing." Sorrow and cold anger frosted his statement.

"Did he deserve it?"

"He tried to--no, he did. He raped Leah. I tried to stop him. I couldn't." Eric's stomach churned at the words unspoken, the totality of what had actually happened.

"So you killed him instead?"

Eric nodded slowly and sipped at his drink.

"And you regret this, why?" Turing asked, genuinely confused. "It seems to me the man deserved his fate. You did the right thing by almost every moral compass I can think of, even most of those in the Protectorate."

"I. Enjoyed. It," Eric choked out.

"That," Turing said with a nod, "Can be problematic. Have you talked to Byron or Hadrian about this? They have a little more experience on the matter than I do."

"A little."

"Good. Kill anyone else?"

"Just the guy who didn't make it past the jump. I didn't enjoy that."

"Well, I would love to offer you some words of comfort, but none come to mind. All I can say is that your enjoyment is not the problem you should be looking at. Worry about why you enjoyed it, that will tell you if enjoying it was a bad thing or not."

"How can you say it like that?"

"It's rather quite simple to me, but I try not to talk about things I don't know much about. Talk to Byron, he'll be able to help you. I will point out that it speaks to your character that you're concerned about it in the first place. Fellows of proper moral character and courage always worry they are becoming monsters when they are forced to act like one," Turing told him. "Now, I'm sorry for that recollection, but I have a topic or two I want to cover before the whiskey wears off. What did you do on the *Fortune?*"

"Anything that needed done, really. I wasn't lying when I told the interrogator that. Fox liked to joke that it was cheaper to get them young and raise them to your own standards. He did say to me one day that he knew he was getting older and wanted more choices on his successor."

"Cheaper indeed," Turing responded with a grin. "A successor? So, then he actually was making an officer out of you?"

"I suppose. Before we got caught, I was in charge of a number of work details. They were also teaching me a lot of calculus, physics, that kind of thing."

"Ah, what was the last you remember of those two?"

"We'd just started on differential equations."

Turing smiled.

"Physics-wise, we'd only done basic kinematics. Had just gotten into electromagnetics."

"Ah, a decent start to a good education. I trust you enjoyed the math?"

"For the most part. It all seemed to just make sense."

Turing's smile widened. "Math is the only universal symbology, Eric, and physics is the language of the universe. Learn them both and they will serve you well. I suppose that concludes this interview. You should join your friends, I need to think a little while."

"Actually, I have a question if you don't mind," Eric spoke tentatively.

"Go right ahead."

"What's wrong with me? Why did the alcohol help?"

"Oh, that. I was correct, you don't have a brain bleed, or rather if you have one it's small enough that amplifying it by thinning your blood with alcohol has minimal effect. In either case, you'll be fine in short order. No, what you do have is far more interesting. Your problem is that someone did not want you to remember what we've just discussed."

"I'm not sure I follow."

"Your symptoms are consistent with a certain class of nanites

I've worked with. Most nanites designed to affect neurological systems have a significant number of safety features. You're lucky whoever dosed you did not have time to dial it in completely to specific memories. That, and they didn't disable the safeties."

"What would that have done?"

"Killed you. The alcohol affects how the nanites interact with brain tissue. It also alters the brain's sensitivity to how that class of nanites work. The safeties dial them back to prevent damage and, without them, the nanites you consumed would likely have had," Turing paused. He tapped his lips a few times before continuing. "Unpredictable but invariably and eventually fatal side effects."

"Invariably and eventually? That doesn't sound fast."

"Oh, no, it wouldn't be. You'd be a vegetable by now or worse. Death would come much later. Untargeted, the nanites tend to have the strongest response to memories closest to the time of exposure. It seems the most likely time would have been either right before or right after the incident when you killed that man."

"Well, I spent the next three weeks in a nanite tank," Eric offered.

"Three weeks? Impressive fortitude, surviving what put you in there for that long. But still that's not the likely vector. If they had three weeks, the nanites would have been targeted. It only takes half an hour at most with the right equipment. When you woke up, did you have memory issues?"

"Not really, no. Not like this. It was more like waking up after sleeping way too long."

"When they threw you out of the airlock?"

"That was when it started, yeah."

"So, whoever gave you something to drink or injected you with anything between you leaving the tank and you getting spaced. Though, focus on the tank side of that limit, the nanites take a while to get into position and synchronize. It seems someone on the *Shrike* suspected you knew something very important and they did not want your questioners to discover it. Very, very interesting."

"Who would want that?"

"That is the question, Eric. That is the question. Clearly not a loyal citizen of the Protectorate. This class of nanites was tightly controlled, too. They'd have to be very well connected to have them. So it's definitely not something casual. On the plus side, if whomever did this left the safeties on, it's entirely likely that this episode will render them inactive. Perhaps. I suppose I can try to find a more permanent solution if that's not the case. Either way, give me some time to think. Oh, and tell Hadrian I want to talk to him if you see him, would you?"

Eric pushed himself up to stand. The world swayed devilishly under his feet and he dropped back into his chair.

"Oh, never mind, I'll get him myself," Turing said with a puckish grin. "Sit, you'll be fine. Just remember not to drink so much next time."

Eric slumped back in his chair as the world swayed around him, unaware of Turing's departure. Nor did he notice the door opening again. His struggle to focus on the flintlock pistol in his lap all but drowned out the approaching footsteps.

"Turing said," Hadrian started, stalling in midsentence. "Wow, you're piss-drunk."

Nausea kept Eric's movements slow, deliberate. Eric looked up at Hadrian as the man sniffed at the tumbler Turing had poured him.

"Oh, the good stuff? Why can't I ever get the good stuff, Eric?"

"I'm not sure I follow?"

Holding out a hand, Hadrian smiled. "Come on, Turing has something to say to your group. You should be there."

"I thought he said he needed time to think?" Eric mumbled as he pulled himself up and nearly toppled over immediately.

"Turing always says that," Hadrian replied, catching Eric. He slung one of Eric's arms over his shoulders. "Always wants more time to think, but makes snap decisions. Whew, how many of those did you have?"

"I lost count. Five? Six?"

"Six, since you went in? Not bad, lad."

Under Hadrian's guidance, Eric bobbed and weaved across the room and out to the main entrance where his group had clustered between the stairs.

"Ah, there's Eric," Turing said as they approached. "Please, disregard his inebriated state, part of a diagnostic test."

Byron and Doc exchanged quick, concerned glances.

"But, as I was saying, I've come to a decision concerning your group. It was not easy. Some of you, such as yourself, Leah, have skills we will need in the coming months. Some, skills that we desperately need now. After conferring with Eric, I've decided that all of you are welcome here." Leah and Jeff smiled. "However, there are conditions."

"What would those be, exactly?" Byron drawled.

"Let's get the least pleasant out of the way first. Everyone who stays here needs to understand that they do so by my sufferance. While I am not an autocrat, the fact remains that I own this planet. It is what it is, no more, no less. Second, each of you will be assigned tasks based on either your expertise or your ability to learn. None of it will be easy. Every bit of it will be vitally important. Third, I expect everyone to exercise the utmost of their abilities to further the group, as if their survival depends on it. I will not lie to you. It does.

"What you see here may appear luxurious compared to what awaits beyond the wall, but this is only because of my father's forethought. What we have will not last. In fact, without everyone's cooperation, we will not make it through next winter. In exchange for your loyalty and your efforts, you will have room and board, and a solemn promise from me. I will always, always do my utter best to be as fair as possible. Though it may appear to be so at times, I will not be arbitrary. Every person accepted into this household is equally important and will be treated as respectfully as they treat others. Questions?"

"Yeah," Doc said. "What sort of diagnostic test involves getting an adolescent staggering drunk?"

"The kind that isolates a potential brain hemorrhage at elevation or determines other neurological activity is at play."

"Hemorrhage? I think I would've noticed. Drinking at this altitude would probably kill him if he had one."

"No probably about it, Doctor. The amount of alcohol ingested would have killed him about twenty minutes ago. I was betting on a different diagnosis."

"And that would be?"

"Something protected by doctor-patient privilege. If you want to know, I'd suggest asking him when he's sober. It's not my secret to tell."

"How many people are here?" Jeff interrupted Doc's fuming.

"Counting your group, twenty-two."

"Where are they? I've only seen three people here," Leah asked.

"We have several other residences on the property. Most everyone is helping finish the construction of another currently, seeing as we're somewhat cramped and I see that only getting worse."

"What kind of provisions have been made already?" Byron asked.

"Well, we have just under a year's worth of food left, provided we can't grow more. Cerberus Station conducts supply drops randomly in good weather, but they're nowhere near enough to sustain the population currently here. As far as tools go, we had a very primitive machine shop, but our machinist died a few months back before he could make it functional or teach anyone. I'm hoping Jeff can help with that."

"Cerberus Station?" Byron again.

"Yes, the Protectorate's orbital watchdog. The public face of it is, no doubt, that they help distribute provisions to those exiled below. The truth is, they're here to make sure we stay under lock and key."

"How does that work, exactly?"

"In concert with a constellation of defense satellites, they interdict any unauthorized traffic to this planet. They also conduct routine surveillance and, if necessary, direct action." Byron's inquisitive look prompted Turing on, "In short, any hint of advanced technology warrants either orbital or drone strikes. You may come across some evidence of those strikes in the future."

"Wait," Eric interrupted, "I've got a tablet, is that going to get their attention?"

"Unless it has a transmitter, it shouldn't. Most tablet sized devices are terribly short range, so you wouldn't have to worry unless one of the surveillance drones is directly overhead anyway. I am highly curious how you managed to keep it in the first place. Most prisoners are dropped here with only the barest essentials, but we can talk later. Next question?"

Doc cleared his throat. "Medical supplies? Facilities? You said no advanced tech."

"Sadly, yes, no advanced tech, so no nano labs, robot controlled surgery, or the like. Everything is manual. We have a physician's assistant who is in charge of our medical needs right now. We do our best to recover Cerberus's drops to augment our existing supplies, but for details, you'd have to talk to Leroy. I may have the depth and knowledge equivalency to qualify as a medical doctor, but I never saw the need to sacrifice that much time."

"Wait? You're not a doctor?" Doc asked, shocked.

"Not a medical one, no. You know the residency rules, and all the other regulatory hoops. I could pass any test you want to give, but I had better things to do than satisfy self-important bureaucrats to get a signed sheet of paper."

"You're practicing medicine without a license," Doc began to fume. "Endangering a patient's well-being, that's unethical."

"Please, Doctor. You forget yourself. On this planet, I am the licensing authority and the ethics board. If Eric had a hemorrhage anywhere in his skull, there's nothing any of us could have done to help him. If anything, I think getting drunk would be a preferable way to go out than the alternatives."

Doc grit his teeth.

"What kind of doctor are you, then?" Leah asked.

"I hold doctorates in both computer science and engineering; master's degrees in physics, mathematics, and electrical engineering; bachelor's degrees in biology, political science; and a minor in art history."

Eric snorted. Turing raised an eyebrow.

"Art history? Really?" Eric said.

"What?" Doc growled. "That's not remotely possible. You don't look a day over thirty."

"I am, but not by much. My family ensured I had the very best schooling available to me and unlike many of my generation, I took advantage of that."

"Let's say this doesn't work out, would we be free to go?" Byron asked.

"If you so choose, yes. All I would ask is that anyone wanting to leave come see me so we can work out details. I'm not one to keep the unwilling here, but I do have the responsibility of trying to keep this place running as smoothly as possible for everyone else. Essentially, all I'd ask is that you finish any major projects before moving on."

"What sort of tasks?" Byron continued.

"Yeah," Jeff said. "You said you wanted me to work on some kind of machine shop?"

"Well, firstly, I've put a few people in charge of managing the ongoing projects. Hadrian is in charge of the hunters and physical security here. Leroy is head of our medical staff at the moment. Denise is our civil engineer, she's in charge of infrastructure. Right now, I'm expecting you to be working with her, Jeff, though not necessarily for her. Ideally, if you can get some sort of manufacturing setup created, you'll be your own department. I'm currently looking for someone to head up our agricultural interests, and that looks like it will be you, Leah."

"Me?" Leah squeaked. "I was a lawyer! All I've done is some basic gardening!"

"True. Be that as it may, your credentials on the topic are still better than the rest of ours. Most of us hold doctorates or master's degrees in hard sciences, not agronomy. We've made a few ham-fisted attempts over the last few years to get something working, but yields have been less than stellar and all we've managed is to forestall the inevitable. As weak as it sounds, I'm hoping you'll help us reach our goal of yield parity. Barring someone better coming along, it seems you might be our best hope. I know it's a lot to ask, but you will have a lot of leeway and plenty of outside experience to lean on."

"I, I don't know what to say," Leah said, her face flushed noticeably.

Turing nodded, "As for you, Doc, I'd like you to work with Leroy and double check his work. I'm not fond of shuffling leadership immediately, but if you prove up to the task, we'll see."

Doc slowly nodded.

"Byron, I'd like to stick you under Hadrian for the time being. He's had a lot of positive things to say about you. I'd like to see if they're all true. If they are, then you and I have no small amount of talking to do."

"What about me?" Eric asked.

"That's what has been bugging me most of the day, actually. My first impression, mind you, was that you had little potential for anything other than manual labor. Thankfully, I was wrong." Turing glanced over to Hadrian. "Yes, I said it. Mark it on the calendar, Hadrian."

Grinning, Hadrian said, "Already done, sir."

"You do have a lot of potential, but right now, I'm not sure how best to tap that potential. Unfortunately, we have too many projects and not enough hands to work them, so it looks like the bulk of your time will be manual labor, potential or not. That said, I do intend on following up with you. I would like to see some sort of schooling done so you can be more than a set of useful hands. Until I figure out something more permanent, I'll assign your tasks myself. Does anyone have any other questions?"

Eric nodded. "Uh, one last one if you don't mind? Does anyone ever get off this rock?"

Turing sighed and shook his head. "Cerberus does send retrieval teams down infrequently. We never see those people again, so I would believe it safe to assume they're pumped for information and disposed of. The effective answer to your question is no. Barring a surprise visit from above, we'll all grow old and grey here. Possibly our children as well, if there are any. There haven't been, yet."

"How do they find people? You said they sent retrieval teams," Byron noted.

"That's one of Leroy's projects. I have my suspicions it's tagging of some sort, but without an actual lab, I can't confirm. If it's injectable, it would be terribly short range. There are other concerns, but nothing worth worrying about at this time. Anyone else?"

Byron raised his hand.

"Yes?" Turing asked.

"What's the local time scale compared to galactic standard time?"

"Good thing you asked," Turing replied. "Solitude's gravity is ninety-five percent galactic standard. The Solitude day is a few minutes past twenty-four standard hours, and a year here is four-hundred and eighty standard days. Due to axial tilt and precession, seasons here are almost exactly four standard months long. Anything else?"

Turing looked everyone in the eyes in turn.

"Well, then before we wrap this up, Hadrian, I need you to select five people for a mission tomorrow. I'd like you to start off for the west cabin and retrieve a list of supplies."

Hadrian nodded. "I'll have the list for you inside the hour."

"Good. Friends, welcome to Solitude."

Contours

DAY 2

"Up and at 'em, Eric."

The room was dark.

Why is Byron in my room? Wait, where is my room? Where am I? What the hell happened?

"Ugh," Eric grumbled. "Good lord, my head feels like…"

"You were hit by truck? Maybe a train carrying trucks? Perhaps a ship carrying trains filled with trucks?"

"What?"

"Never mind, you got to get up, son."

"Why?"

Byron sighed. "Because you turn into a combative jackass when you're drunk and someone tells you that you need to drink water to avoid a hangover. As much as you deserve the hangover, I'm thinking you'd be even less sociable."

"What time is it?"

"About an hour before dawn."

"Ugh. Fuck me," Eric grunted.

"Nope, sorry, not my type. Facial hair is a major turn-off."

Eric stared at the shadow he assumed was Byron, nonplussed.

"Do I have to go get a bucket of snow and dump it on you?" Bryon asked.

"I'm getting up, dammit."

"Good. Hadrian wants us downstairs in a half an hour."

"Byron? Where's the bathroom?"

Byron sighed again. "Close your eyes, hit the lights here by the door. Basic clothes, toiletries, and the like are in the locker. Your case is in the bottom. Bathroom's across the hall to the left. Oh, and be careful of the bucket by your head. By the smell, you puked in it sometime overnight."

Eric groaned and pushed himself in a sitting position as the door closed. Byron's advice did little to prepare him for the light that stabbed him in the eyes as he rooted out clothes and stumbled across the hall.

"Pay up," Byron told Hadrian twenty-five minutes later when Eric came drifting down the stairs. Hadrian sighed and handed Byron something as Eric reached the bottom.

"So, what am I awake for, again?" Eric asked as he adjusted the leather belt on his slightly-too-big jeans.

"We're going on a nature hike," Hadrian said.

"Nature hike? No thanks. Bears are scary," Eric mumbled automatically. Byron chuckled.

"Today's your first day of land navigation," Byron said with a smirk. He handed Eric a tiny metal box. "There's your compass, Lieutenant."

Eric squinted at the compass in his hand as he rubbed an eye with the other.

"Land navigation?" he asked.

"Part of your training," Hadrian told him. "Turing wants you useful and I needed bodies for the trip. Win/win for us."

"Shit," Eric commented.

Hadrian grinned and scratched at his beard. "We've got an hour or so before I plan on leaving. Byron, get him kitted up, take him outside, and see if you can't give him some basics before then."

Byron nodded. "You heard the man, Eric. Follow me."

Byron pressed on a panel on the side of the staircase and the wall slid back.

"The hell? Hidden staircase?" Eric asked.

"Yeah, this place is full of surprises. Turns out Turing's great-grand-whatever was a paranoid bastard. When the provost sent folks down here to confiscate any unapproved technology, they missed a fair amount of stuff. This storeroom level included," Byron told him on the way down. The stairs ended in small landing with a door in one corner and a window with a large gap below it. A skinny, dark-skinned man sat on the other side of the window sipping coffee from a slate grey mug. The cubby the man sat in was barely large enough to qualify as a closet.

"Eric, Rick. Rick, Eric. Rick's their supply guy. Also the armorer and one of the hunters. Met him last night when most of the folks got back. Eric was passed out by the time you guys got back, Rick."

"Oh, this is the guy Turing tried to give alcohol poisoning to?"

"Yeah, that's me."

"Nice to meet you, Eric." Rick said as he struggled to his feet and shook Eric's hand through the gap under the window. He continued dryly, "What can supply do for you two this fine morning?"

"There's only twenty people here and they have a supply section?" Eric mused.

Rick shrugged sheepishly.

"I'd tell you that Turing is pretty exacting in his desire to keep track of things and ensure efficiency, but that'd only be part of the truth," Rick told them. "Hunting accident tore my knee up right at the beginning of Fall. I'm not worth much for most of the jobs that need done, so this is the best I can do."

"No shame in that, Rick," Byron said with a nod, "Accidents happen and you're still contributing. We're heading out to the west lodge. Six people total, the rest will be following along shortly. I can't speak for the rest, but Eric and I have our own cold weather gear. Snow shoes would be nice. Food, backpacks, weapons, ammunition, a map. Not sure what the standard load is for you guys."

Rick nodded along as Byron went through the list. "Yeah,

Hadrian dropped off a note earlier. Let me double-check what he's cleared you guys for." Rick rifled through a stack of paper on the tabletop between them. "Ah, yeah. One second, I'll get stuff out for you."

"Byron?" Hadrian said from the top of the stairs. "Hey, something just came up. We'll be here an extra hour, get Rick to issue you a small load and go see if Eric can shoot."

"Catch that?" Byron asked Rick, who nodded in reply. "What do you have?"

"Well, we've got a wide assortment of projectiles in various sizes. What are you looking for? We have a few bolt actions and select fire weapons, but most of what I have are semi only."

Byron scratched his chin, deep in thought. "Way out to the west lodge, mostly open terrain?"

"Not really. There's a few spots like that, but it's mostly forest or dense scrub."

"Semi-auto rifle and pistol then."

"We've got a variety of sizes. Less ammo on hand as you get bigger."

"Hadrian mentioned you guys can't make new cartridges yet, so small or intermediate for the rifle, then. You've shot pistol, Eric?"

"Yeah. Fair amount."

"Preference?"

"I liked the ten mil better than the nine."

Rick smiled. As he disappeared back into the storeroom he called over his shoulder, "I've got something for you then. Really old design you don't see around anymore. Most of the hunters prefer it to the ten millimeter."

When he returned, Rick dropped two brown backpacks on the counter followed by several boxes of supplies. Byron guided Eric through splitting the bulk of the smaller items into two identical groups and how to pack them. The older man was adamant that everything in the second pack be placed identically as the first in case one of them needed to get something out of the other's pack in a hurry. While Eric finished up the second pack, Byron left and returned with their cold weather gear.

"Done? Good, put these on. Going to be hot, but we have to adjust the straps to what we're going to be wearing," Bryon told Eric as he tossed a parka.

Parka donned, Eric slung the pack over one shoulder and then the other. *Pack's a bit heavy.* He clipped the pack's integral belt together and cinched it tightly against the thick parka. *Hm. That helped the weight a lot, but this is going to be like wearing a furnace if we don't get outside soon.*

Rick asked, "You guys ready for the guns?"

Byron nodded. Eric's jaw dropped as the supply specialist set a rifle and pistol on the desk.

"What?" Byron asked.

"Those are old Earth," Eric stammered.

"Not really. They're reproductions from old schematics with minor design changes. Turing's father had a more than a few designs updated because he liked their look and ergonomics better. From what I understand, Nathan went to great expense to recreate a more than few things from the past."

Eric hefted the rifle and looked it over, tilting it this way and that while looking it over. *Empty, no magazine, on safe.*

"They're not much different than what I'm used to," Byron said and turned to say something to Eric. Byron's words stumbled to a halt in his mouth as he watched Eric absentmindedly snake a magazine from the counter and insert it into the magazine well.

"What?" Eric asked, keeping the weapon pointed at the floor as he racked the charging handle.

"I," Byron started and paused. "You're obviously familiar with the weapon."

"Not really, no. I handled one just like it before, but the design isn't far from what we used on the *Fortune*," Eric said, checking the safety again. *And almost identical to the one on the Gadsden.* "Actually, I'm not sure how this particular sling works. We normally used three pointers."

"Oh, that? Easy," Byron told him, stepping forward. As he explained, he pointed at various parts, "It's a modified three point in single-point mode. This clip here can be attached here for a single point or there for three. Worry about it later, just stick it on your pack for now."

"My pack? How?"

Byron mimicked putting the butt of the rifle into a stirrup at the pack's waist belt. "Right, now the barrel comes up under your armpit. That black strip on your shoulder? Yeah, goes around the barrel and through that clip. If you need the rifle, grab the pistol grip with your left, pull the retaining strap with your right, and it'll come right up."

"Oh, thanks." Rifle secured, Eric retrieved the pistol.

"Handled one like that before?"

"Yeah, not too long ago actually. Damn near identical, though what's the machining at the end of the barrel?" Eric asked as he inserted a magazine and racked the slide.

"Attachment point for a suppressor. I thought you guys used suppressors?"

"You guys?"

"Uh, freelance property recovery specialists, such as yourself? Turing told me. No judgement from me. We all do what we need to do to survive."

Eric blinked. *Freelance prop-oh, pirates.* As he slid the pistol into the holster at his waist he commented, "Oh, well, yeah, but ours were integral to the barrel, not screwed on."

Byron turned to Rick and asked, "You have any suppressors for that?"

"Some, yeah. You want one?"

"Now that I think of it, yeah. Suppressors to both, if you wouldn't mind." When Rick returned with two black cylinders, Byron asked another question, "You wouldn't happen to have subsonic loads for any of these?"

Rick nodded. "Short supply though, compared to the rest."

"Hollow points?"

Another nod. "Short supply."

"You guys have a range around here?"

"Backyard."

"Thanks," Byron said as handed Eric two spare magazines for

each weapon. Following Byron, Eric found himself the subject of a few curious stares from unfamiliar people. Curious as they might have been, no one said anything.

The pair emerged onto the back porch to find a long flat area that ended in several sizable dirt mounds at varying distances behind the house. A short distance in front of each mound stood a wooden framework. Eric noticed a simple box sitting on a bench against the back wall as he and Byron walked towards the back steps.

"Think there are targets in there?" Eric asked.

"Worth looking," Byron replied. Eric's hunch proved correct.

A few minutes later he stood facing a set of targets about ninety meters distant with Byron next to him.

"You've got three magazines for the rifle, so let's test your zero first. Put the suppressor on and take the left target," the old soldier said.

"Okay." Eric slid the suppressor onto the barrel and twisted as Byron had shown him. His bruised arm ached as he brought the rifle up. As he peered through the iron sights, Eric found the white paper targets easy to lose track of with the snowy background. Gently pulling on the trigger, Eric braced himself for the recoil. The rifle bucked against his shoulder with a sudden bark.

"Hit, left of center, twelve centimeters. Two centimeters high"

Eric glanced over. Byron was holding a set of binoculars to his eyes. Eric frowned and steadied himself. *Pull.*

"Hit, left of center, thirteen centimeters, one centimeter high. One more time if you would?"

Scowling, Eric wound the sling around his off arm and drew a bead on the target again. *Pull.*

"Hit, left of center, eleven centimeters, even. Adjust your windage, you're off."

Eric frowned as flipped the selector to safe and looked at the rifle.

"I'm not familiar with this style of irons, do you know how to adjust them?"

"Dial on the rear sight. Instructions are on it. Adjust fire to the right, say six or seven clicks. Shoot when you're ready, don't wait for me."

Bah, I should've seen that. I'm blind. Eric adjusted the dial six clicks in the direction indicated on the sight. Wrapping the sling around his arm again, he took up his shooting stance and squeezed off three shots over as many seconds.

"All hits, looks on average high one centimeter. You're still left by two. Adjust the front sight down one click, rear sight right by one and resume fire, just two this time and don't rush it."

Adjustments made, Eric leveled the rifle at the target and pulled the trigger.

"Bullseye, both shots more or less. Give me five at the center of the next target over."

As requested, Eric shifted and dropped five shots into the neighboring target.

"Not bad, all clustered pretty tight. Curious how you'd do at long range shooting. How much training have you had at this?"

"Just what Fox thought was necessary. He insisted everyone on the ship be proficient with most of what was in the armory in case we got boarded. We did monthly qualifications while we were out. I've been shooting rifle a little less than a year."

Byron harrumphed. "Empty the rest of that magazine, same target. Don't want to be wasteful, but I need a better picture of your skill than five shots."

Eric nodded and brought the rifle back up. Clearing his mind, he thumbed the selector to fire and calmed his breathing. *Pull.* Eric's thoughts drifted as he sent rounds downrange and he lost himself into the process. Desi's hand rested on his shoulder as she walked him through using a rifle. He could still smell her perfume over the burnt gunpowder when the bolt slid home on an empty chamber.

"You're a good shot with a rifle, I'll give you that. Groups are pretty tight for someone with only a year's worth of monthly quals. Either you've got natural talent or whoever your instructor was knew what they were doing."

"Both," Eric replied, stowing his rifle against his chest as he'd been shown.

I miss you guys, Desi.

"Well, let's get the pistol out of the way," Byron said and led Eric over to a much closer target stand. "Same drill, suppressor, five shots to verify zero, followed by the rest of the magazine."

Eric drew the pistol and screwed the cylinder onto the end. He had to shift his arm around the bulk of the rifle securely slung to his chest to get proper aim. Focused, he was barely aware of squeezing the trigger when the pistol jumped in his hand. More shove than an upward jerk, the recoil was less than he expected. Steadying himself, Eric worked at keeping his hits near center of mass. When the slide locked back, he glanced over at Byron.

"Not too bad," the old soldier commented. "You're a lot better with the rifle. Looks like you're anticipating the recoil and jerking the trigger a little. Nothing practice wouldn't fix. You ever do shotgun?"

"Yep."

"We'll have to follow up on that, assuming they have any. Go get your targets, Hadrian will probably want to see them."

Hadrian met them as they approached the back door. Eric beamed at Hadrian's approving nod.

"Not bad, Eric. The hunters might have use for you," Hadrian said. He looked to Byron and asked, "We ready to leave?"

"Just want to get a few fresh magazines first, but yeah," Byron replied. Hadrian motioned for them to follow.

"I had Terry get a few from supply," Hadrian commented over his shoulder as they rounded the house.

"Turing said something about a cabin and supplies. What is it we're doing, exactly? " Eric asked.

"The west cabin is up near the throat of this valley. It's a four day hike to it. We check the place out first, see if anyone has moved in, if they've taken anything, if there's anything going on around it. After that, we grab supplies off the list Turing gave me and fill any extra space we have left with whatever else seems likely to be useful. Figure it will be five to seven days back, even with most of it being down-slope. West cabin is one of the last few cabins we haven't drawn down the stores on."

"So, bringing back a lot?" Eric asked as they rounded last corner. Three people in thick coats colored with mottled browns and greens leaned on the porch railing near the front door. The clothing hid their genders, but the facial hair gave them away. Like so many of the new people Eric had met recently, their faces were half hidden behind protective goggles, beards, and clothing.

"Yeah, as much as we can carry and then some. We'll improvise something when we get there," Hadrian told him. As they approached, the three men pushed off the railing.

"Mornin', boss," the tall, lanky one said.

"Morning, Trev," Hadrian said as he nodded. "Eric, Byron, these guys are Doctors Travis Green, Trevor Meric and Terrence Hale."

"Call me Terry," Terrence corrected. Strands of white in Terry's full beard betrayed his age. "Only my mother called me Terrence."

"Doctors?" Eric asked as the group fit on their snowshoes.

"Well, Ph.D. not medical doctor. Structural engineering, terrestrial mostly. I was working on expanding into orbital station design when I ended up here." Terry said. He added with an easy grin, "Mostly, I'm a carpenter now."

"Sc.D. here. Astronautics. I helped design a few high profile spacecraft that landed me a teaching job at the University," Trevor commented. "Provost scooped me during their investigation of Turing's disappearing act."

"Just particle physics," Travis said with a shrug. "Not terribly useful out here, so I help with the carpentry."

"Let's head out," Hadrian said. Eric noticed the axe strapped to Terry's pack and all three men carried smaller axes on their belts. Only Travis had a firearm, a revolver on his hip.

"You have a degree, Hadrian?" Eric asked. "Seems everyone here does so far."

"Sure. Applied physics, specializing in ballistics and high energy applications." Hadrian replied. Byron snorted. Hadrian added, "Though, it's mostly OJT."

"OJT?"

"On the job training." Hadrian said. A few seconds later, he asked, "Hey, Terry, you figure eighteen years is enough to claim a degree?"

"I've seen you shoot. I'd say so."

The group paused at the stone wall while Hadrian inspected the area surrounding the gate. Hadrian waved Eric over as he unslung his rifle.

"People," Hadrian said, pointing at tracks just outside the gate. "No one uses this gate but hunters. We're the only ones with the key. None of my men have passed through here since the storm. How many people do you think?"

"Two or three?" Eric offered after a few seconds of studying the impressions in the snow.

"Anything else?"

Eric squinted and scratched his chin for a few more seconds as he racked his brain trying to coax more out. "Probably not made by people freshly off the *Relentless*."

"How do you know that?" Hadrian inquired.

"We were issued cold-weather gear. Sure, most of it was old and poorly cared for, but the boots were in relatively good shape. If they were wearing issued boots, you'd see tread in the tracks, right?"

"Not bad, Eric. Best I can figure, four people. You're probably right about the boot tread." Hadrian scowled and shook his head as he stared at the tracks.

"What?"

Hadrian looked back at the rest of the group. "Keep your weapons handy, folks. We're not the only people around."

A quick pull opened the retaining strap holding the rifle to his pack. Byron gave them a thumbs-up as he adjusted his sling. Trevor and Terry tugged their long hatchets free of their belts while Travis tugged out his revolver and thumbed back the hammer.

Hadrian walked up to the gate as he dug out the key. He froze.

"Cover," he blurted and hopped behind the wall. Confused, Eric did the same as the rest of the group rushed up to take similar positions against the wall. Seconds later a faint but growing rumble crossed the valley.

Hadrian scowled and slowly leaned around to peek through the gate, weapon at the ready.

"Transport, not drone. We're good," he said. "More folks from the *Relentless* getting dropped off."

"Think the folks being dropped off will be useful?" Travis asked Hadrian.

"They'd better be or we'll all be dead by next winter," Hadrian replied.

"Drones?" Eric asked as Hadrian retrieved his key and unlocked the gate.

"Cerberus Station runs a fleet of drones. They do fly-bys every now and then. Doesn't matter if they're doing surveillance or not, it's a good idea to stay out of sight. They're armed."

"With what?" Eric asked as the group filed through to the far side.

"Guided missiles and bombs at the least. Haven't torn one open to be sure that's all, but I have seen them attack ground targets."

With Hadrian at the lead and Byron bringing up the rear, they marched on. Intermittently interrupted by the growl of descending transports, Eric passed the time by striking up conversations. Byron spent a good portion of the morning educating Eric on the life of an infantryman. Hadrian spent the early afternoon teaching Eric about a hunter's perspective of the land while teaching him to use the compass and different types of maps to get around.

As the sun began its downward arc, Eric found himself exhausted and battling to put one foot in front of the other. Shortly before dusk an extremely weary, foot sore Eric slumped onto his bedroll near the campfire. Rest the first night did not come easy, nor did it the following night or the next. Conversations after the first day became infrequent as Eric struggled to stay standing, much less keep up.

Before noon on the fourth day, his spirits soared as they emerged into a clearing at the base of a rise. Atop the frozen hillside stood a squat log cabin. Propelled by a burst of hope, Eric caught up to Hadrian half way up the rise.

"Slow down, son," Hadrian told him as he started to outpace

the soldier.

"Slow down? We're almost there!" Eric snorted. He came up short a few moments later, and shouldered his rifle. "Front door is open, Hadrian."

"Top pane of the window there in the second floor is cracked, too. Any tracks?" Hadrian asked, farther behind.

"No," Eric replied as he got to the top of the hill. The door was open a few centimeters, but not enough to see inside the dark interior. "No tracks up here. Either they're still in there or they were gone before the snow."

Hadrian nodded and the team cautiously approached the doorway. Byron took up a position to the right of the door, Hadrian the other. Everyone else fell in to either side. Eric kept his rifle pointed at the doorway as everyone twisted boots out of snowshoes and shrugged off heavy packs. Hadrian's hands moved quickly. *On my signal, you kick the door open, step back, cover the middle. I sweep right, Byron sweeps left. You follow us in and keep up.* Eric and Byron nodded. Hadrian leaned forward and rapped his hand against the door.

"Knock, knock. Anyone home?"

Silence. Eric's heart pounded in his ears as he fidgeted with his rifle. *I've never done this.*

"Travis, you guys watch the door," Hadrian whispered over his shoulder as he glanced back at Eric. At Hadrian's nod Eric stepped forward, raised his leg, and planted his boot squarely in the middle of the door. By the time his foot had reached the ground, Byron had already scuttled between him and the doorframe at a crouch. Hadrian was on the old soldier's heels.

"Clear left!" Byron called out as Eric started forward through the door.

"Clear right!" Hadrian echoed. The cabin's ground floor was all a single room. A set of stairs climbed the far right wall and followed the corner up out of sight. Hadrian was backing up, rifle pointed up to the second floor. Byron had followed the left wall all the way around and glanced back at him from near the steps.

"You waiting for an invitation? Move!" Byron barked and pointed up the stairs.

Eric rushed around the circular table occupying the middle of the room on his way to the stairs. Imitating Hadrian, he spun around as he passed into the open area, pointing his rifle up and walking backwards. The stairs led up to a walkway with two doors. Eric's back foot struck the bottom step.

Keeping his rifle up and moving between the two doors, Eric made his way up the stairs as fast as he could. As he approached the first door, a hand on his shoulder nudged him forward past the door. A few steps later, the hand patted him on the shoulder. He stopped, front site zeroed on the other door. The door crashed open behind him.

"Clear!" Byron called from behind him. The hand nudged him forward and pulled him to a stop short of the door.

"I got the door," Hadrian said, slipping around him. "Your turn."

Something yowled as the door crashed open. Eric swung through the doorway rifle first. *Movement.* Eric jerked, tried to center the blur in his sights, and squeezed the trigger. Nothing happened. *Shit!*

Laughter erupted behind him and he froze, cold sweat dripping down his face. Then the smell hit him. Eric gagged on overpowering ammonia and stumbled to the door. Intermittent gagging interrupted Hadrian's laughter.

"Clear," Hadrian choked out. "Holy shit, Eric, you almost smoked that pussy."

"What the fuck? That's some nasty shit in there," Eric gasped.

"You spooked the ever loving shit out of a cat, Eric," Byron called from outside the room, snickering.

"He ain't going anywhere. Door's closed," Travis yelled from downstairs.

Hadrian clapped him on the shoulder, still snickering.

"Next time," Hadrian told him, "Identify your target before engaging. Helps if you hit the safety, too. Newbie."

"Forgot the safety? Oh, that's going to be hard to live down," Byron snorted.

"Fuck you guys," Eric muttered with a smile as they came down the stairs.

"McCulloch did the same thing his first raid. You'll be fine if you can learn from it," Byron said, wiping tears from his eyes.

"Yep. There's an outhouse out back, he'll probably need it. I'm going to look around, figure how much damage that damn cat did upstairs."

Eric opened his mouth to argue but his gut clenched, forestalling anything he could have said. The shakes started as they cleared the front door. By the time he stepped into the outhouse and closed the door behind him, he could barely hold his rifle. He stared at the hole in the bare wood seat. His rifle rattled as he tried to prop it up.

"You alright in there?" Byron asked.

"Yeah? I think so," Eric replied. He frowned at the wooden hole while trying to undo his pants.

"Shakes?"

"Yeah," Eric said. He grimaced at the cold as he sat down. "Holy fuck, this is cold."

"Hah, yeah, I'd imagine it is," Byron chuckled. "Shakes are normal after the adrenaline. You'll be dog-ass tired for a bit after, too. We'll make a decent soldier out of you yet, seeing as you didn't fuck it up too hard. That's what counts. Give it a bit, you'll be fine. Oh, and next time kick near the door knob. You waste less force and it tears your leg up less."

Eric emerged a few minutes later.

"Ah, didn't fall asleep on the shitter. Was getting worried you fell in or something. Pretty sure they don't have a coast guard around here and I sure as hell wasn't going to dive in after you."

"Very funny," Eric responded.

"Let's take a walk, let you burn off what little adrenaline you might still have floating around."

Rounding the cabin, the pair found Terry eyeballing a few nearby trees with Travis and Trevor trailing behind him.

"Ah, the brave hunter returns," Trevor said with a smirk. "Hadrian wants us to drop a few trees to improvise a few sleds, feel like lending a shoulder?"

"Give him a bit," Byron said. "We're walking the perimeter. If he's still up for it, I'll send him down your way."

"Alright," Trevor acknowledged. The man nodded and turned back to the trees.

Eric and Byron continued their walk around cabin. At the opposite corner Eric paused and held up a fist. *Movement.* Rifle up, he crept forward toward the trees. Something brown moved again, some forty meters into the wood line. Remembering Hadrian's admonishment about identifying his target, Eric slinked for a better angle through the evergreens. Just as he came to a halt, the elk lifted its head, silently regarding him for several seconds before turning its attention back to the underbrush at its feet.

Eric relaxed and began to drop his aim when something enormous and gray snarled as it streaked out of the brush. The beast nearly bowled over the elk by leaping onto its rump. The click from his safety disengaging was inaudible above the elk's trumpeting cry of surprise and pain as its attacker pulled the elk to the ground. A hand on his shoulder stayed his shot.

"Leave be," Byron whispered. "Your rifle won't manage to do anything but piss it off."

"The fuck is it?" Eric asked, his mouth dry.

"About a hundred and ninety kilos of hate and discontent, Eric. Let's get back to the cabin before it decides to find out if we taste better than elk."

Trevor and Terry had turned, staring in their direction. Byron pointed to the cabin.

"What was that racket?" Hadrian asked as the four stepped inside.

"A reminder of home," Byron commented as he shut the door behind them.

"Highland wolverine?" Hadrian asked.

"Yep."

Hadrian grunted. "They've never come this far into the valley. They usually stay farther up in the pass. We'll need to cull them before they threaten the game here."

"What's a highland wolverine? " Eric asked, eying Hadrian. The creature's lightning ambush replayed in his head.

"Hundred and ninety kilos--"

"Of hate and discontent," Eric finished Hadrian's sentence. "I know, Byron said that much."

Hadrian grinned. "Oh. Well, one part scavenger, one part predator, eight parts angry with a liberal seasoning of psychosis and anger management issues. Turing's grandfather wanted to be able to hunt dangerous game, so he imported a few of them back in the day off their reputation alone."

Eric frowned and looked out one of the ground floor windows. "How long do you figure we're stuck in here?"

"Full grown elk?" Byron pondered out loud as he searched the cabinets. "Give him five or ten minutes to eat enough to make him fat and happy. Or, at least, as happy as highland wolverines get. He'll probably stumble off to enjoy his food coma somewhere else. What's normally in these cabinets, Hadrian?"

"Canned food, some bottled water, that kind of thing."

"Looks like someone cleared out most of the canned food. Left everything else though,"

"Figures," Hadrian said from the table as he inspected his rifle.

"We found a few trees that will do, Hadrian," Terry spoke up a few minutes later.

"Good, how long till you can get the sleds together?"

"Once we get back out there? Maybe an hour. We going to try to get started back tonight?"

Hadrian shook his head, "Trek back is going to be rough; we need to get some decent rest in after that hike. How's your leg holding up, Byron?"

"Marched further on worse."

"How are you holding up, Eric?"

"Haven't had the headache since Turing got me hammered. My arm's still a bit sore, but I'm good I think."

"That all?" Hadrian asked. "Don't play it tough, if you're hurt, I need to know."

"Tired as hell and my feet are killing me, but I'm pretty sure I'll survive," Eric replied.

"You've been changing your socks?" Hadrian asked.

Eric nodded in reply.

Hadrian glanced toward Terry and Trevor and asked, "Any complaints from you two?"

"Just happy to have a chance to stretch my legs," Terry replied.

"Yep, nothing like hard labor and a run-in with a wolverine to make you appreciate life." Trevor said with a smirk.

Hadrian snorted and said, "Well, I'd say you two could take the rooms upstairs tonight, but you really don't want the last one, even with the open window. Everything in there's a loss."

"I wouldn't sleep in there, even in a vac suit," Eric muttered. Nothing outside had moved other than a few blackbirds. Hadrian's comment about importing wolverines earlier tugged at him. "I thought the Protectorate only recently started trading with the Confederacy."

"Popular history is seldom as true as we want it to be," Byron commented from the door as Terry and Trevor stepped out.

Hadrian nodded, "That, and praise be that Caledon has never been part of the Confederacy."

"Isn't the Confederacy a good thing?" Eric asked.

Hadrian snorted. "Aye, if the only thing you judge on is if the Protectorate's iron fist pulls the strings. Don't get me wrong, some Confed systems are decent enough, but it's a military alliance only. For every system trying to get ahead, there's two trying to hold them back, and a third trying to undo what little progress the first made."

Eric scratched his head, puzzled. "That doesn't sound like any of the Confed systems we've been to."

"Oh, which ones have you visited, lad?" Hadrian asked.

"Orleans, for one," Eric said.

Byron coughed. "Son, the Orleanians are one of the biggest parts of the problem. Last Confed system to slip their shackles and, by their politics, you'd think they miss them. They've always put style before substance. The people as a whole tend to be brave enough, but their leaders are all cowards and sycophants. If they didn't surrender before the assault forces landed, the Protectorate would control the planet inside a month, tops. A determined naval blockade would probably get them to fold first."

Hadrian shook his head, "Give the frogs a little credit, Byron. They'd still be fighting after a month."

"Oh, we gave them plenty of credit, Hadrian. Planetary government collapse in a month. Short of the legionnaires, their military would be ineffective within two weeks after that. Even with the legion bolstering them, organized irregulars would falter around the six month mark, given Protectorate assimilation protocols. Individual actors would last up to a year or so. That was our assessment last year."

Byron give the two an innocent grin while they stared at him.

"Our assessment?" Hadrian finally asked.

"That might be overstating it a bit. I was brought in to validate the field team's conclusions."

"Guess that makes sense," Hadrian muttered.

"Makes sense? Huh?" Eric asked Hadrian.

"McCulloch said Byron left SF for a bigger assignment. Talking like that, the only thing that makes sense is Central Intelligence."

Byron smiled. "We scare the things that go bump in the night. Overwatch calls, back in ten."

"Hey, come over here and help me real quick," Hadrian called over his shoulder as he walked over to long couch under the stairs. With Eric's help, they pulled the heavy couch away from the wall. Hadrian leaned against the couch, studying the wall.

Eric watched the hunter for several seconds, trying to figure out what he was up to. "What are we doing, Hadrian?"

"Oh, trying to remember how this works," Hadrian grumped, scratching his chin. He looked up. "Oh, right. Eric, those two lamp fixtures half way up the stairs? They go up."

Puzzled, Eric made his way up the stairs. Gripping the decorative brass fixtures, he pushed upward.

"You fucking with me again? What am I doing, exactly?" Eric asked.

"Not putting enough muscle into it."

"This isn't as easy as it looks," Eric said, scowling down at Hadrian. He set his feet and shoved with his legs. The fixtures remained stationary for several seconds before he felt something grind behind them. With a clack, the fixtures jumped upward several centimeters.

"There ya go, lad," Hadrian said from below. Eric leaned over the railing to see a section of floor slide shift and slide into the wall revealing stone steps that disappeared into darkness below.

"What the hell?" Eric asked, coming down the stairs.

"Concealed basement. The cabin was built over a cave," Hadrian said as he started down into the dark. Eric paused at the edge of the darkness at the bottom of the steps.

"Hey, I can't see shit."

"Aye, motion sensors would normally activate the lights. Sec, found the switch."

Sudden light reflected off the arched ceiling revealing a sizable metal door at the end of the concrete lined hall. Hadrian spun the large wheel on the door and pushed it open. Lights inside the doorway snapped on revealing rows of shelves and pallets containing a multitude of labeled boxes and crates.

"Why'd this work and the outside stuff didn't?" Eric asked.

"Turing's father said the drones regularly EMPed structures at one point," Hadrian said, looking over the shelves inside.

"How would he know?"

Hadrian shrugged. "No clue, but he was pretty certain of it when I got here. I was a trigger puller, not a tech guy. I can only assume something in the design protected some circuits more than others."

Eric eyed the door to the bunker as he walked through. "This door, solid steel?"

"Might be, but my guess is layered ceramic composite cased in steel. Doesn't feel heavy enough to be solid steel. Okay, so we're prioritizing food, but there's a few things I'm looking to bring back too. Go check the far side, look for ammo cans. Pick up four of the 6.8 and two of the 12.7. Make sure it's the black label."

"Roger that," Eric nodded and started walking through the rows of shelves. As promised, neat stacks of green metal cases of varying sizes lined the back wall. *6.8mm, check. 12.7mm, check.* "Hey, what's the 'L' behind the numbers on some of these mean?"

"Linked. We don't want those. Not yet anyway."

"Okay," Eric replied, and started moving cans up near the door. On his last trip to the back wall, he eyed the fat steel cylinders in the corner. Each was connected to a metal box mounted on the wall by a thickly insulated hose. "What's in these big metal cylinders?"

"Nothing, they're empty. They were going to be a backup for something else but never got filled."

"Well, what would have been in them?"

"Cryogenic storage. Where's the last of those cans?" Hadrian sounded annoyed.

"These fuckers are heavy," Eric commented as he dropped the last two cans by the door several seconds later. The frustration he'd been holding in check for months loosened his tongue. "You know, Hadrian, I just don't get this place."

"How so?"

"For a place with no tech, there sure is a lot of tech around here."

"Oh, that."

"Nah, not just that. It's everything. None of this shit makes sense. Nothing's made sense since the *Fortune* got hit. I, I just don't know what the fuck to think, Hadrian. I watched everyone I know die and it's been a non-stop stream of lies and fucked up bullshit from the moment I stepped foot on that fucking Protectorate shuttle. It's just too fucking much."

Hadrian regarded him silently for several moments before he whispered, "Specter Six."

"What?"

"First Special Forces, Operational Detachment Echo, Team Six. My team. I'm the only one left, Eric."

"Okay? What's the got to do with all this bullshit?"

"The PMV *Iscariot* had been conducting surveillance on Jenkin's Station and hampering movement into the Protectorate for two years prior. Our orders were fairly straightforward, really. Board her without notice, eliminate the crew, recover all usable intelligence, scuttle the ship in a fashion that indicated a reactor failure commensurate with the type of merchant vessel she claimed to be.

"When we set up on her hull, everything seemed to be going to plan. They hadn't noticed our approach so we set up our go-to-hell charges and prepped for entry. I remember the look on the bridge tech's face when I slapped the charge on the view plate he'd been staring out." Hadrian chuckled darkly. "Something to be said about striking terror into the hearts of your enemies, lad. Charge decompressed the bridge. Bridge crew went out with the air; we came in through the hole. Shit went sideways shortly thereafter."

"We were told to expect a token marine force, maybe a dozen grunts in all, half of them in their racks, and maybe four dozen spacers to run the boat, most of them intel weenies or techs. We weren't really worried about the spacers; they can't fight worth a damn. The marines though, those guys can fight. All in all, we expected around a half dozen marines to be breathing down our necks in short order. Two full squads jumped us. Me and Sergeant Cameron were the only two who made it back to the bridge in one piece. Cameron was dragging MacPherson, our medic, behind the consoles when I triggered the go-to-hell charges. Nothing happened. Last thing I saw was a pair of marines coming in the hole we blew earlier. We were trapped like rats." Hadrian's gaze snapped up from the floor and locked with Eric's. His voice trembled when he spoke again, "The whole team was at my wedding, Eric. MacPherson was my best man. Cameron, Dun, and Wallace were groomsmen. I convinced Val to let Holly be a bridesmaid."

Eric reassured himself the crate behind him hadn't moved. Nerveless, he dropped onto the crate as the soldier's stoicism melted away like fog parting in the wind. Hadrian trembled and clenched his jaw as tears welled. Eric wasn't sure if grief or anger lay behind the sudden mood shift.

"You talk about losing everyone you know? And lies? That's the only thing the rat bastards have to offer. They put Mac down like a fucking dog instead of treating his wounds. Those assholes had me for eight months. Do you know what it's like, spending eight months in hell? Do you know what it's like, seeing pictures taken from your front yard, from inside your house, and being told they had people watching your family, being told that if you didn't cooperate, the next pictures would be your family's bodies? You think you know hurt? Fuck you. You don't know shit. Suck it the fuck up and soldier on."

"That's enough, Sergeant Major," Byron barked as he entered the bunker.

The growling rebuke coiled in Byron's tone struck a chord in Eric that jerked him to his feet. Memories of Chief Wilkin's bitter disappointment at every failure, no matter how small and inconsequential, flooded over Eric as he bored holes in the wall across from him with his eyes. Hadrian reacted identically.

Byron paused in front of Hadrian. He stared the man in the eye for several seconds before placing a conciliatory hand on Hadrian's shoulder.

"Now's not the time or place. Go help your men get those trees down, Hadrian."

Eric listened to the anger in Hadrian's footsteps as they faded off. Byron slowly swiveled and came to stand in front of him.

Byron's features softened as he spoke, "At ease. Think of this as one of many lessons you need to take to heart, Eric. No matter how hard you think you've had it, someone else has probably had it worse. Far worse."

Eric glanced at the doorway, a dozen emotions fighting for his attention.

"I didn't know, Byron," Eric said quietly.

"That's the point of the lesson. Look. While we're all stuck here, we're on the same team. Most of the Teams, you know where everyone else has been, so shit like that doesn't happen often. There's no reason you should have known about his unit, no reason you should know about how many friends, how many family the Protectorate has taken from him or me. Do you have it rough? Yeah, a lot worse than most civilians will ever see. If they knew, a lot of civilians would envy the fact you've been able to keep your shit together and keep moving forward."

"Why? I mean, we were on the *Shrike* for maybe a two or three months and I didn't have to deal with anything like Hadrian did. Hell, Leah had it worse than me, too. Why would anyone envy me?"

Byron nodded solemnly. "Because they don't know any better, Eric. Because they haven't learned what we've had to learn the hard way, what you need to make sure you take to heart."

"What's that?"

"Life is going spend every moment trying to kill you. You can either roll over and die, or you fight through every ambush and push on. Shut up, accept responsibility for your faults, learn from everything you can, and don't let life win."

"So shut up, watch, and learn," Eric said to himself softly.

Byron nodded.

"Do you think I should go apologize?" Eric asked.

Byron's eyes flicked toward the door. "Leave it be."

Something in the old man's gaze nagged at him, a distant sadness.

Puzzled, Eric asked, "What?"

"Nothing you need to know, Eric. Just something that needs done, but can't be done now. Remember this, Eric, for when you find yourself in Hadrian's shoes. One day someone will need this lesson and you'll be the only one there to give it."

Eric nodded earnestly and Byron offered him a squat can. "Go upstairs, eat, and sack out. It'll be dark soon. We'll be moving out early if I'm reading Hadrian right."

He took the can and made his way out of the bunker. Someone had dragged their packs in next to the couch by the front door. Eric pulled his pack around as he sat and dug through a pouch to pull out a set of hiking utensils. Weary, he pulled the tab on the can's lid and peeled it back. *Fish? Meh.* He stuck his fork in the shredded meat and stuffed some in his mouth.

"Better than nothing, I guess," he said to himself. The pattering of little feet on the stairs caught his attention, and moments later a slate grey cat perched on his knees. "You have to have been someone's pet."

The cat meowed pitifully. Darker than its body, the cat's tail waved about as it kneaded his leg, purring.

"Ow, shit, stop, stupid cat," Eric blurted, and swiped the cat off his lap. He sighed and shoveled another fork of meat into his mouth. Purring even louder, the cat hopped up onto the couch next to him, crowding the can.

"Cat, really? My fish, not yours."

Soulful blue eyes stared back at him.

"Fuck off, cat," he growled after the sixth attempted fork interception. The cat meowed. Eric looked at what was left in the can. "Fine, you want what's left? Here, have it. Eating around you is worse than eating in prison."

Eric sat the can on the floor. The cat head butted his knee and hopped down. The purring continued unabated when the door opened and Hadrian stepped in.

"First you try to kill it, now you're trying to tame it?" Hadrian asked.

Eric smirked. He was considering apologizing for earlier despite Byron's advice when Hadrian paused by the steps down to the bunker and regarded him silently.

"Byron suggested I rack out since it'll be dark soon. What watch am I standing?" Eric asked to break the silence.

"I'll have him get you up."

"You sure?"

"Yeah. The next few days are going to be hell."

Day 12

Eric staggered up the last few steps up to the porch. Every muscle fought him as fatigue threatened to veto every movement. Shaking under the strain, he managed to get the front door open and staggered several paces inside before he shrugged off his backpack. Last of his energy spent, he half-collapsed, half sat onto the over-packed ruck and weakly unzipped his coat.

"Fuck that," he wheezed as Anne came down the stairs, a look of concern on her face. A shadow in the doorway announced Byron's arrival.

"You're all back?" Anne said with a smile as Byron slowly

shucked his pack.

"The others will be a second," Byron told her, taking a slug from his canteen.

"Oh, I'll go get some tea."

"Water first," Byron told her.

"Yes. Water. A lot of water," Eric managed. Byron gave him a long, considering look.

"Not a bad showing, Eric. Well, for someone who's never humped a ruck before."

"Humped a ruck? I just lugged almost sixty kilos half way down this godforsaken valley. I'm pretty sure I'm dying."

Byron cracked a grin as Anne brought in a tray of tall glasses of clear water. "Nah, you're not that lucky."

"Oh god, this water is good," Eric gasped after emptying half the glass. "Next person to ask me if I want to go on a nature hike gets punched. In the throat."

Byron chuckled.

"In the throat, eh?" Hadrian asked as he walked in and closed the door behind him. "I guess combatives might be a good thing to move to now that you won't get too lost out there. Nature hike, anyone?"

Eric rolled his eyes. "Why is it I'm this damn tired and you two look like you could go jog all the way to that cabin and back again?"

"Would you believe superpowers or deals with unholy entities?" Byron offered with a wry grin.

"That last one I just might. Shit, I'll be lucky if I can stand back up," Eric managed to answer.

"Dropped the sleds around back like you said," Terry commented as the rest of the team joined the gathering.

"We'll have lunch ready within the hour," Anne told them.

"Oh," all of the men sighed in exhausted anticipation.

"But you'll damn well be showered before you sit at my table," Anne added.

"Yes, ma'am," they replied in unison.

With some help from Byron, Eric lurched to his feet.

"What are we doing with the packs?" he asked Hadrian.

"They'll keep just fine until we eat."

Eric grunted as he climbed the stairs. Every movement hurt, from the muscles used to raise his feet, his strained back, or sore feet, but he eventually found himself closing the door to his room.

Undressing in his room proved another hurdle. Eric's stomach growled angrily at the thought of missing a real meal and having to eat another pre-packaged field ration. He couldn't safely sit, exhaustion would surely drag him under, but his aching back protested any idea of bending over to undo his boots.

"Fuck me," he muttered. *I wonder if I could get away with just standing under the shower with my boots on.* Eric snorted and ignored singing agony to reach for his boots. Minutes later, towel around his waist, he shuffled into the sink room to the sound of water spraying from multiple shower heads from the showers around the corner. A low moan echoed through the tiled chamber. Eric paused at the entrance to the showers.

"You need some personal time, Byron?"

"Nah. I'm too old for this shit," Byron replied with a weak chuckle.

Eric hung his towel and pulled on the knob for the nearest shower head. He echoed Byron's earlier moan as he ducked into a stream.

"Oh, god. Hot water, where have you been? I missed you so much," Eric sighed. Byron snorted.

"Hey, you going to eat or keep standing there wasting hot water?"

Eric whipped his head around to see Hadrian leaning into the now-foggy shower room in fresh clothes. Water dripped from other shower heads, but only his sprayed steaming water. Other than Hadrian, he was alone. *Shit. Did I fall asleep?* Eric tugged the knob and quenched the flow of water.

"Yeah, I'll be right down."

By time he fumbled clothes on and stumbled into the dining room, only hunger kept sleep at bay, and until the smell of chicken hit him, it was losing. His stomach growled. Several heads turned toward him at the table while the rest continued eating.

"Nice of you to join us," Hadrian said with knowing grin from the far end and went back to talking with Jeff.

"Over here, Eric," Leah said as she smiled and waved. "I saved you a seat."

"And some food. Were it not for her stalwart defense of that platter, you'd be sorely disappointed," Byron told Eric as he made his way to the empty seat next to Leah.

What's different about her? That smile. Has to be.

Leah tugged his seat back as he approached.

"Thank you, Eric," she said. "How did you know I liked cats?"

Byron began choking. His face going red, he pounded his chest with one hand. *Roll with it,* Eric interpreted the hand signal the old man made with his other hand while all eyes were on his face.

"I'm okay," Byron muttered. "You evidently can't breathe chicken."

"No, you can't," Eric told Byron. He looked over to Leah as he sat and said, "Oh, I honestly wasn't entirely sure. I figured he seemed fairly friendly and if there were issues with mice, he'd probably be able to help."

"She," Leah corrected him

Eric shrugged and stabbed a piece of breaded chicken off a platter with a fork. "She. Shows how much I know about cats."

"Her name is Muffin," Leah said with a glowing smile.

Eric scooped out the remainder of a bowl of mashed potatoes onto his plate, followed by several large spoons of corn.

"Muffin, huh?" he asked as he emptied one of the gravy boats onto his potatoes.

"She's actually a decent mouser. Caught one already."

"No shit?" Eric mumbled around a mouthful of potatoes. "Wow, this is, this is phenomenal."

"I helped Anne make them," Leah beamed. "We didn't have a lot of spices, but they're as close to my mother's recipe as I could manage."

Eric mixed some of his corn into his gravy and said, "Your mother is a saint. Remind me to thank her if we ever get off this rock. How's the planting stuff going?"

Leah deflated. "Oh, it's not. The new guy's in charge now."

"New guy?" Eric asked.

"Yeah, he showed up day before yesterday. One of the hunters came across him. Turing put him in charge. I can't say it was a bad decision though, he's a much better choice. I'm still in charge of small projects though like the herb garden."

Doc's voice carried from the hall, "You're lucky it's still not infected. I don't have nearly enough antibiotics to go around."

Leah nodded her head toward the door. "That should be him."

Eric turned his head to the door as it opened. Doc led a man with bandages wrapping his head into the room. Eric's fork clattered off his plate.

Wide eyed, Eric stammered, "What the shit? Pascal?"

"Eric?" Blaise said.

"I saw you die," Eric said and stumbled to his feet.

"Pretty sure I saw them toss you in the black after me," Blaise mumbled through Eric's embrace. "Ouch, watch the bandages?"

"Shit, sorry," Eric apologized and backed up a step. "What happened to you?"

"This? Gunshot."

"Motherfucker," Hadrian whispered behind him. Eric heard a chair grind as it slid across the floor behind him. Hadrian icily demanded, "Explain."

"Me and a dozen folks got dropped off in the evening, I guess, west of here? Got waylaid. They lined everyone up after they rifled through our shit and put a bullet in everyone's head."

"How many were there?"

"Four?"

Hadrian growled. Eric and Blaise watched the soldier stalk out of the room.

"Guess Fox was right, I do have a hard head for an officer," Blaise said with a slight smirk. "What's his problem?"

"Hadrian?" Eric asked. Blaise nodded. "He's in charge of security here."

"Oh, well, I guess that makes sense. Chief Wilkins was kind of a hard-ass, too. Someone tell me there's chicken left."

The silent crowd behind him let out the breath it had been holding, small talk started as he helped Blaise to an open chair.

"So, you're in charge of all the planting stuff?" Eric asked. "Why?"

Blaise bit his lip. "Bachelors in agronomy."

Eric laughed. "You're kidding?"

Blushing, the *Fortune*'s youngest officer told him, "Nope. Graduated summa cum laude and found out the hard way there wasn't much call for it on Pershing. Not if you wanted to make decent money anyway. Wandered a bit, ended up on the *Fortune*. What can I say? I was stupid when I was your age."

"I'm suddenly very sorry for all those jokes I made about officers having useless degrees in basket weaving."

Blaise chuckled for a few seconds before a serious cast erased his mirth. He raised his glass to Eric. "It's all good. To lost friends?"

Eric clinked his glass against Blaise's and Byron's joined theirs moments later.

"To lost friends, may we be worthy of their company again," Byron said and everyone drank. "Whiskey's better for this than tea, but I'll never pass up honoring my lads."

"So you know Eric, Blaise?" Leah asked several minutes later.

"Know? Since he was old enough to shave."

Eric rolled his eyes at Pascal's comment. Leah's next question evaporated at Hadrian's entrance. Anger rolled off the man in thick waves.

"Byron, Eric, meeting downstairs once you're done eating. Bring the rucks," Hadrian ordered. "Also, Rick, I'll need you open for business tomorrow early. No, scratch that, I'll get the keys from you."

"I," Eric started with a complaint on his lips, but suddenly thought better of it. He finished, "We'll be there."

Hadrian nodded curtly and left.

"You were going to ask?" Blaise said to Leah.

"Well, I was just curious how well you knew him, that's all."

"Oh? Well, he's a good kid. Never had any discipline issues, almost pathologically honest, always does the right thing."

Eric snorted. "How's your head doing?"

"Doc says it'll heal. He's worried about a possible fracture, but evidently there isn't much he can do about it here, so I'm supposed to take things light for a while. Spent yesterday going over plans for the spring with Turing."

"Yeah? He'd said something about the stuff they did before being inefficient."

Blaise nodded as he drank from his glass. "Grossly from the looks of it. No rotating crops, no testing soil pH levels, planting in wrong soil types, insufficient or too much sun for the crop, that kind of thing. Not that we can do much about pH levels, but it helps to have an idea for where to plant stuff if you can. I'm supposed to go over things with Denise and some Terry guy tomorrow."

"Sounds busy," Byron commented.

"Yeah, it will be. I don't see how we'll have the labor to do what needs done. I'm really thinking we'll have to start rationing food, no matter what Turing says."

"Is it that bad?" Eric asked. Leah and Blaise nodded simultaneously.

"Part of the problem is the lack of wood for any large scale project. They had a really basic mill set up on the far side of the property, but it got bombed a few months back."

"No shit?"

"Yeah, no shit. Lost a bunch of good people from what it sounds. That's actually one of Jeff's biggest projects, trying to get enough of a machine shop together to make rebuilding the mill possible. I tell you, this whole set up looks like we're trying to fly by pulling on our own bootlaces."

"I," Eric started, dragging it out to stall for time, "don't really know what to say? That doesn't sound good at all."

"It's not. Without that mill, I don't have any source for finished lumber. Granted I need more than just lumber, but without the lumber there's no new structures. Not even basic ones. A greenhouse would be terribly helpful here, but that's not happening any time soon. It gets more messed up when you consider labor. We're caught coming and going, really. Unless we start moving folks into the halls here, we can barely house new people, much less feed them, but in order to get anything done, we need more people. Not just more people, but people with the right skill sets. I'd kill to have Jorgen here. Between him and Jeff, we'd probably be able to build a damn ship and get off this rock in a week."

Eric nodded and tried not to think about the *Fortune*'s burly chief engineer as he drank the rest of his tea.

"So what do they have you doing, Leah?" Eric asked.

"Organizing some small scale stuff right now. Quality of life, I think was the term Turing used. Anne was complaining that we were running low on a lot of the common herbs and spices she has and I suggested putting together some herb boxes. We should be able to hang them under the windows to grow what we can year round. We could even prep vegetables before planting season is here to give them a head start. I don't know what I'll be doing beyond that though."

Byron shrugged when Eric looked over at him and stuffed the last food into his face as he stood. Eric wolfed down the last of his potatoes and followed Byron out the door to the front hall.

Hefting the ruck onto his back, Eric grunted under the strain.

"Did you guys really hike around like this every day when you were younger?" he asked as the pair made their way down the concealed staircase.

"Oh, I don't know about every day, but it sure felt like it. You get used to it, eventually," Byron replied as they reached the bottom of the stairs to find the door to the supply room open.

On the other side, Eric whistled at the stacks of boxes, crates, and shelving. *Pretty sure this room is about the same size as the whole floor upstairs. Wait, is that--why do they have spools of heavy duty electrical line?*

"Over here," Hadrian's voice carried from around a set of shelves. "Drop your rucks there by the door."

Freed from his burden, Eric made his way toward the shelves with an eye on the tangle of cabling and piping hanging from the ceiling. *That's an awfully impressive amount of fiber optics.* One particular cable caught his attention, a power line that led from the light next to the door around the shelves ahead.

Created by removing two short rows of shelving, the space on the other side had been converted to a small office nestled in clutter. Filing cabinets lined the back wall to either side of a large junction box. Hadrian and a black-haired, grim-faced man with a goatee were leaning over a large desk in the center of the space studying a sizable unfolded map.

"What are we looking at?" Byron asked.

"Map of the valley," the grim-faced man said without looking up.

"Byron, Eric, Julien. Julien, Byron and Eric," Hadrian introduced them.

Julien grunted.

Hadrian pointed to various spots on the map as he talked. "This is the manor, the stone wall and the like. Lake over here, largest stream runs through here. These dozen squares are the hunting cabins. The one we just came back from is this one here. Questions on the map before I go further?"

"What's that just inside the wall on the stream?" Eric asked as he scanned the confusing lines. *I hate topography maps.*

"Ruins of the mill and the old machine shop," Julien answered.

"What do the circles around the cabins mean? The ones with X's off to the side?" Byron asked.

"X's denote cabins whose supply bunkers have been tapped out. Circles are occupied cabins."

"Occupied?" Eric and Byron asked at the same time.

"Guests, Turing calls them. Anywhere else, we'd call them squatters," Hadrian groused. "We're more or less on friendly terms with most of them. Thankfully we emptied the supply bunkers below the occupied ones before the current residents showed up. Most of them are sponging off the food we left behind at Turing's insistence."

Eric gave Hadrian a curious look.

"Don't ask me. His logic was that folks would break into the places looking for supplies. If we left enough food for folks to live on for a bit, they'd be less likely to trash the place. Granted, showing up a bit later and letting them know Turing owns the place has made things a bit easier."

"So, friendlies?" Byron asked.

"I'd watch yourself around most of them, but they're friendly enough as pommies go," Julien commented. Eric looked at Julien, puzzled.

"Protectorate citizens," Byron explained. "Protectorate of Man, POM. Pommie?"

Haven't heard that one before.

"Now, aside from the room we're in, there's only one other place on the planet that has any guns. The house over on this mountainside here is the only one with any sort of weaponry left in the bunker. Given nobody gets dropped here with firearms that has to be their source."

"What was in it?" Byron asked.

"Would be faster for you to read," Julien said and dug several sheets of paperwork out from under the map.

Byron frowned as he skimmed and said, "I've seen Confed rifle companies equipped worse than this. I'm not kidding. Rifles, light machineguns, heavy machineguns, grenade launchers, ammo. Two hundred kilos of advex, twenty kilometers of--" Byron interrupted his list with a slow whistle.

"What?" Eric asked, glancing at the list over Byron's arm. *That's a lot of guns.*

"That's just the armory inventory. I'm still going over the rest of it," Hadrian said.

Byron looked up at Hadrian, incredulous. "What was Turing's father thinking? This reads like someone used a Build-Your-Own-Insurgency shopping list. Hell, the only thing you're missing is a medusa--" Byron laughed. "Nope, you guys have one of those, too. Hadrian, why in God's creation would you leave something like that sitting just sitting around?"

"What's a medusa?" Eric asked.

Hadrian ignored Eric. "It's not as bad as it sounds."

"Not as-- do you have something rated anti-tank around here I don't know about?" Byron demanded.

"Well, yes, but that's irrelevant," Hadrian replied.

"How is that irrelevant?" Byron retorted.

"When I showed Turing the manifest he insisted it was 'just spare parts.' Spare parts for the base model, not a mobile variant. He also believed the EMP that shut down the vault door rendered them inoperable," Hadrian commented.

"What's a medusa?" Eric asked again, irritated.

Julien scowled at Eric before growling, "Medusa; Modular area denial system, autonomous." Eric shrugged. "Hadrian, I thought you said this kid had promise?"

Hadrian sighed. "Enough. Eric, Byron will fill you in. Julien, he's a boot. He'll shape up or he'll get shipped out. "

"I'll keep a bag handy," Julien grumped.

"So let's pretend the medusa isn't a problem and the four of us aren't the only ones defending this place," Byron started. "When was the last time anyone was up that way?"

"I was there right before winter set in, so about four months ago. Place was clean, no sign anything human lived in the area."

"Okay, well, you've obviously got a plan, what is it?"

Hadrian glanced at the map with a frown. "Sneak and peek. We don't know what's going on there or how many people might be involved. Julien, you're about as subtle as a sledgehammer so you're staying to defend home. Byron, I'm pretty sure you're out of practice for this kind of thing, and besides which, I'm the most familiar with the terrain so it looks like I'm going." Julien and Byron nodded. "Byron, I'm going to need you to work with Julien on this."

"Can we use the twenty mike?" Julien asked.

"What am I doing?" Eric asked.

"Use whatever you can come up with an effective plan for, Julien, and Eric," Hadrian paused. "You're going to be underfoot no matter where I put you." Hadrian motioned for Byron to follow him and they stepped around the shelves. Ignoring Julien's stare, Eric eyed the junction box and the power cabling on the wall until the pair returned.

"Eric, be down here two hours before sunrise," Hadrian told him. "Any questions?"

Hadrian tossed something at Eric. "Here's a watch. Sunrise is at five thirty. Rest while you can, then."

Eric yawned deeply as he put the watch on. Curiosity got the better of him on the way up the stairs.

"Byron?"

"Yes?"

"Why would someone keep spare parts for something they didn't already have?"

"Eh?"

"Hadrian said the medusa unit at this cabin was spare parts. I mean, if they're extra parts, that implies they've already got one, right?"

Byron chuckled. "I'm happy I wasn't the only one who caught that. That's one possibility of several."

"What are the other possibilities? I still don't know what a medusa actually is. An acronym doesn't really help," Eric commented. The pair closed the secret door to supply behind them and then continued up to the second floor.

"The term medusa covers an entire ecosystem of equipment, Eric. It's relatively new tech, something the Protectorate only started fielding in the last decade. I'm surprised Turing has one; well, at least one. They're hideously expensive.

"If you categorized the equipment in a medusa system, you'd have sensors, agents, and the controller itself. The controllers are usually pretty beefy processing platforms. Might have integral comms, might not. Like everything else in the system, it's all modular. Sensors can be everything from security cameras, helmet cams, seismic detectors, thermal cams, motion detectors, millimeter wave radar, you name it. If it can produce some sort of data feed that can be relayed to the controller, it can be used as a sensor. The controller takes those inputs and builds an understanding of the area it's deployed in from them, and uses the standing orders and rules of engagement it's been given to issue commands to the agents."

"So the controller is some kind of command and control system for these agents? When you say it builds an understanding, you mean like you and me looking at a map and figuring out what we need to do?"

"You could say that, yes," Byron said.

"Let me guess, the agents are modular too? Anything that can be wired to receive commands can be an agent, like, say, these drones we keep hearing about?" Byron nodded. "Wait, we're not just talking vehicles are we? Like, triggered explosives? Literally anything with the right hardware?"

"Yep."

"Why not mount the controller in a vehicle like one of the drones? Or like a tank or something with a ridiculous amount of armor or firepower? Wouldn't that make it harder to disable?"

"Later models are."

"Oh. That sounds less pleasant," Eric commented as the pair paused outside his room.

"Yeah, it's not. Thankfully they're pretty rare, and there are some flaws. Anything else you noticed?"

"We were sitting on top of the generator for this place."

Byron cocked his head. "Why do you say that?"

"There's no external power connection. Supply ceiling is crawling with some serious power cabling that all leads over to the wall we were sitting by and then down through the floor. I don't know what it's running on, haven't seen or smelled anything like gas. You didn't notice the faint buzzing or constant vibration?"

Byron frowned. "No."

"Oh, well, maybe I'm imagining things," Eric said and yawned again.

Byron seemed at a loss for words for several seconds. "Or maybe you'd be better at the intelligence game than I thought. Get some rest, Eric. You look like you're about to fall over."

"Later," Eric mumbled and stepped into his dimly lit room.

Thankful the heavy curtain was already closed against the noonday sun, Eric wobbled directly to the edge of the bed and half collapsed, half sat. He slowly regarded his pillow before looking down at the boots taunting him. *Why do you have to be all the way down there?* He fought his laces to free his feet and sighed as his head hit his pillow. *I'll get my clothes off in a--*

"Wake up, meat."

Eric snapped awake, already lunging. His fist found nothing but air. Breathing hard, he glanced about, certain something was watching him. Aside from odd shadows cast by the moonlight from the curtain, everything seemed where it should. He waited, listening. Nothing moved.

He fiddled with his watch, trying to figure out which button triggered the backlight. *One o'clock? I should go back to sleep.* Eric nestled back into his pillow and closed his eyes but sleep refused to come. *How can I be exhausted but not sleepy? Guess I might as well get dressed.*

"Oh, holy shit," Eric groaned when he tried to get out of bed. Every movement only made another muscle group scream in rage. Gritting his teeth, he pushed through the pain and staggered to his feet. *Yeah, a hot shower should help with this.*

Sensitive to every ache, Eric set about his morning routine. Having showered and shaved, Eric slipped into a fresh set of clothes and made his way down to the kitchen. *I wonder if there were any leftovers? That chicken was phenomenal. Hmm, what's this?* The light in the kitchen was on and a tea pot sat on a running burner.

"Up late, or perhaps up early?"

Eric jumped at Turing's voice and spun to find the side pantry open. Turing was facing away from him eying a shelf.

"Up early. You?"

"Ah, up late myself. Anne should be about soon to start the bread. Would you like some tea?"

"Sure, I guess."

"Any particular kind? We have quite an assortment."

"I'm not really a tea drinker."

Turing glanced over his shoulder with a curious look. "Why ever not?"

"Most of the tea that passed through the *Fortune*'s holds, we sold. Some folks at Port Solace would pay serious money for it. There were more folks at Port Wander who'd pay though."

"Ah, that makes perfect sense. I'd pay a significant amount of money for fresh tea about now. Most of these have been stored for a while, but even with nitrogen, you can't keep it forever. Bit of a bother, really. Well, the water's almost done, I'll pick something tasty. Care to join me?"

"I've got time, what do you have in mind?"

"I'd like to see that tablet of yours if you don't mind. Meet me in the study?"

Eric nodded and went to retrieve the tablet from his room. When he stepped into the study, Turing was setting down the tea pot, two cups steaming on the table in front of him.

"So, you said some customers would pay a high price for their tea? What kind? What sort of money is serious money to you?" Turing asked as he motioned Eric to sit. Eric handed the tablet over and took a seat.

"Oh, well, the normal stuff, I wouldn't know. Most of that was just boring, but one particular score does come to mind. Fox had it under lock and key on the ship until we stopped at Jenkin's Station," Eric said.

"Terribly interesting for tea, unusual even. Why would he do that?"

"Because it sold for a bit over a million standard credits a kilo to a collector."

Turing choked on his tea. "A million a kilo? Seriously?"

Eric drew the explanation out, adding sugar to his tea. "It wasn't pilfered, believe it or not. We recovered it from a wreck out in the Reach. The casks were still sealed, old Earth."

"Casks? Plural?"

"Twenty-five of them. Ten kilos per cask."

"Good god, man, that's almost a quarter billion. Do you know who bought it?"

"No idea, I just remember my share of the profit."

"That's a shame. My father was very fond of good tea, especially rare tea. I wouldn't be surprised if he was the end buyer. Still, you must have made a goodly amount off that transaction."

"Yeah, I think my share of the sale was a bit more than one hundred thousand."

"One hundred thousand? And you were how old?"

"Sixteen."

"Not bad, I suppose, all things considered. What did you do with it?"

"Nothing. Not much call for money on the boat, so every penny I made was kept in Shavely's, only bank on Port Solace. Need something safe from prying hands? We'll secure anything for a cut."

Turing snorted and picked the tablet up off the table. "How droll. So a hundred thousand for one job? Did they all pay that well?"

Eric sighed, "No, I didn't have a normal cut either until the last few years. I think I was averaging about thirty thousand a year before that. Sixty after."

"Sixty thousand is damn good for someone your age, Eric. Granted, my situation may distort my perspective a bit, but I believe the average wage in the Protectorate is a bit more than half that, maybe two thirds, for skilled tradesmen. Does this Shavely's outfit offer compound interest?"

"I think they do, but it's not very much."

Turing chuckled.

"One doesn't need big numbers with compound interest, Eric. That type of oversight has destroyed many an economy. Sixty a year plus, say three percent a year for twelve? Being generous," Turing mumbled as he did the math in his head and sipped his tea. "That puts your account at somewhere around seven hundred thousand. Not bad for someone with your means. Not bad at all.

"Okay?"

"Well, put it in perspective, Eric. Normal people in the Protectorate retire with less saved."

A slow grin crossed Eric's face.

"Put that way, I sound like I'm rich. Well, by normal people's standards anyway."

"And so it seems. Shame all that is out of reach right now."

"True. It's fun to think about though. Me, rich," Eric said with a smirk.

"You were saying you recovered this tablet from the *Gadsden*?"

"Yeah, from the captain's cabin."

"US Navy, eh? Fascinating. Were you ever able to get past the login?"

"Technically? When I first messed with it, I'd hit the power button and the main app would pop up and then shut back off after a few seconds. I wasn't sure what was wrong, so I did a hard reset."

"To be honest, I'm amazed it works at all. If I had my old lab, I'd take it apart to see why."

"Oh?"

"Well, for one, it still has a charge. I barely recognize the ports on it, and you don't have a charger. It should be long dead. That's before we get to things like metallic whiskering and all the other fun elements that kill electronics over the long term. I'm sorry, I could go on, but I'm wasting time. We'll have to get into it somehow. So, do you have any experience with system cracking?"

"System cracking?"

"Bypassing security."

Eric shook his head.

"Well, first lesson then: most people tend to use very weak or trivial passwords. Mostly things that you'd normally find very easy to remember; birthdays, ident numbers, that sort of thing." Turing ran his fingers along the tablet's edges. "Interesting. This is removable." He pushed on the side of the tablet. With a click, a small card ejected part of the way from the side of the tablet. Turing pulled it out and gave it a look. "Your ghost ship captain was one Thomas Morneault?"

"Uh, yeah?" Curious, Eric leaned forward as Turing held it out. "Looks like an ident card."

"It is," Turing said and reinserted the card. He started laughing. "Bingo, one step closer."

Eric squinted at Turing and asked, "How?"

"If it works like some of our modern systems, at least conceptually anyway, the card has some identification keys on it, but requires a code to access the stored keys." Turing showed him the screen, which now asked for a PIN number instead of a password. "Well then, I have the chap's birthday from his ident, should we try it?"

"Go for it."

Turing tapped the screen a few times and shook his head. "Third of November, twenty-sixty-five, isn't it. Assuming I'm formatting it right, anyway."

Turing frowned. *Attempt failed then.*

"On the plus side, perhaps this Thomas wasn't as much of an idiot as I thought. This could take a while, provided the system doesn't flat wipe itself if we fail validation too many times."

"Wait, try January thirtieth, nineteen sixty-five."

Turing regarded him curiously for a second and tapped on the screen. Earnestly puzzled, Turing looked up over the tablet and said, "Where did that date come from? We're in."

"The captain had a set of old ident tags, stamped metal. That was the date on them."

Focused on the tablet, Turing didn't bother looking up as he spoke. "Probably the man's great-grandfather. Well, it appears that no matter how much things change, they stay the same. The layout isn't much different from the current operating systems." Turing bit his lip.

"What?"

"Well, the battery is terribly low, but it says it's charging. I haven't the faintest idea how. Ambient static charge maybe? No, I don't see how with a metal case like this. Well, unless--" Turing trailed off.

"Turing?" Eric asked after Turing sat motionless for a short time.

Turing blinked and looked up. "Yes? Oh, sorry, I lose myself in my thoughts. I'd very much like to take this apart now. Shame the data is likely more important than my curiosity. Let me disable the transmitter. There, should make what little infernal battery this thing has last a bit longer. Oh, it's almost time." Turing jumped out of his seat and retrieved his coat.

"Time for what?" Eric asked, glancing at the now-forgotten tablet.

"Take this and grab the binoculars," Turing said, nodding towards a black leather case amid the clutter as he handed Eric a coat. Curious, Eric did as requested and hurried after Turing

"So what are we looking for?" Eric asked once they were outside. Eyes glued to the starry heavens, Turing held out his hand and motioned. Eric pulled out a set of bulky, expensive looking binoculars from the case and handed them to Turing.

"What we're looking for," Turing commented as he hit a button and held them to his eyes, "should be overhead right now, bit to the west. Ah, there it is."

"I don't see anything."

"You won't for a few more seconds. It's still in the shadow."

In the darkness overhead a white star sprung into existence.

"What is it?"

"Cerberus."

"Can I see?" Eric asked and Turing handed him the binoculars. "Holy shit, Turing, what are these?" he asked, boggling at the information displayed in the periphery of the viewfinder as he scanned for the station.

"Expensive even by my standard," Turing replied with a chuckle. "Find her yet? Left thumb, button closest to you zooms out."

With a barely audible buzz, the image pulled back and Eric quickly located the station. "Oh, that's convenient."

"Hold the station in the center of the viewfinder. Apply slight pressure to the left pointer finger button, hold the station inside the brackets that appear until they blink. Then push the button the rest of the way."

"Whoa," Eric breathed when the image jumped. Instead of the tiny formless blob wobbling about before his eyes before, Cerberus Station filled the most of viewfinder in crisp detail.

"The display next to the compass at the top tell you the displacement offset. Keep that as close to zero and as steady as you can manage, the system can only compensate for so much. Tap the right ring finger button, does the read-out still display twelve hundred by five thirty by a hundred?"

"Yeah."

"Good, press the right pinky button."

"Uh, Turing, what's this data it's spitting out? Major and semi-major axis? Periapsis, apoapsis?"

"Nothing terribly important, just orbital data."

Eric looked over at Turing, leaving the question hanging.

"I'm keeping tabs on the station."

"Why? Planning an escape attempt?" Eric asked, somewhat hopefully.

Turing snorted and scoffed, "An escape attempt? If there were a way, we would have been gone long before your arrival. No, Eric, there's no way off this rock. The faster you get that through your head, the safer you'll be. The most dangerous thing in the world is false hope. Eric, do you know what it's like to see someone just give up on life? Do you know what it's like to see the light just disappear from your father's eyes and watch him waste away?"

Eric opened his mouth, but Turing heatedly cut him off, "No, you bloody don't. You have no bloody idea what that's like. I was the last one, the last hope Father had that even if they couldn't escape this place, then his line would go on. He didn't give up when they caught him. He didn't give up when they smashed this place and left him here. No, my father's hope died the day I walked through that door. It took his body another year to realize it.

"So, no, there won't be an escape attempt. There's no way off this sodding god-forsaken, worthless rock. I've made my peace with that. You should, too, before the truth crushes you."

"Shit man, I'm sorry," Eric sputtered.

Turing sighed. "It's okay, Eric." The heat in his voice vanished as he looked skyward. "I very much want off this planet, but I can't see how it's possible. Of all the things for those bumbling idiots to get right, creating an inescapable prison had to be one of them." Eric nodded and turned to go back inside when Turing emotionlessly breathed, "They're lucky."

"How do you figure, Turing?"

"If there was a way off of Solitude, I would start with the sycophant usurpers, my cousins and their parents. There would be no place they could flee to, no hole deep enough for any of them to hide."

Eric shifted his weight uncomfortably for several moments. "Well, I've got to get going. Have to meet Hadrian at supply in ten minutes."

Turing glanced back at him. "Oh yes, that business about the old house? I'm terribly curious how someone got into the vault. Between Hadrian and Byron though, I have faith the matter will be resolved. What's in that vault will be instrumental to our survival."

Eric let himself back inside. Despite the warmth inside, the Turing's sudden detachment chilled him the rest of the way down to supply. At the bottom of the stairs, the door into supply hung open.

Eric stopped at the doorway and knocked. "Hadrian?"

"In the office," Hadrian replied. "Come on back."

Eric rounded the corner to find the table crowded with a multitude of gear, full magazines, and two rifles.

"Just finished pulling all the supplies. Bags are half packed, you mind taking care of yours?" Hadrian asked. Eric nodded. As Eric stepped up to his pack, Hadrian commented, "We're not going to need nearly as much in the line of food. Hopefully we won't need the ammo, but I'm not taking any chances. Has Byron shown you anything related to demo?"

"Demo?"

Hadrian sighed. "Demolitions. Explosives. I'll take that as a no. Have you used basic explosives like hand grenades?"

"No." Eric caught the eye roll.

Without slowing his pack job, Hadrian began, "Okay, so, grenades are pretty straight forward: pull pin, throw grenade toward enemy, three to five seconds later boom. You follow?" Eric nodded affirmative. Hadrian leaned over and flipped open one of the hard plastic cases. "Take four."

Eric reached into the foam-lined case and gingerly pulled four ovoid grenades out of their slots.

"Okay, so, two of those in the back pouches on your pack, two in the rig hanging on the back of the chair next to you, right side pouch since you're left handed. See that spool of yellow and black wire next to you? Measure off about a hundred meters or so. Use the knife on the table, roll and weave it into the side of your pack like mine."

"Sure," Eric responded. As he played out the thick wire, he realized the wire had no metal core. Every half meter he found a mark with numbers that climbed as he pulled it out. *Well, that will make this easier to measure.* "What is this?"

"Detcord. If you like your fingers, don't set it on fire or touch anything electrical with it. Okay, last but not least for fun items you're carrying," Hadrian said, digging under his side of the table. "Put these on the outside of your pack. I'll carry the advex."

Eric took the two flat green plastic boxes Hadrian handed him. Curious, he turned them over and found matching embossed labels on both: Front toward enemy.

"Hadrian, I'm no expert here, but this seems like a lot of explosives."

"It is. I'd bring more if I could. P equals plenty, Eric. Always have P."

"Fair enough," Eric said and willed his hands steady as he gently cut the detcord. He liked having hands, after all. After a quick study of Hadrian's pack, Eric replicated the way the cord had been rolled and used the last meter to secure the roll to his pack. "What I was getting at, though, is you said this was supposed to be a sneak and peek. Aren't explosives the opposite of sneaky? And why do we have this huge stack of magazines sitting out? There's got to be at least a hundred of them."

"Eighty, actually. These mags on the table are spares for Byron and Julien," Hadrian said and sighed. "There's only going to be two of us, Eric. How many of them are there? Just four guys? Can we count on that? Explosives have always been a great force multiplier. If things go to shit, and you can almost always bet they will, then all the bang we're hiking in with might save our asses. That, and we might have to destroy the bunker. Can't do that with just a rifle."

Eric snorted. "No, that'd be pretty hard."

"What? I can see the look on your face, what is it?"

"Well, earlier you said Byron was out of practice so you wouldn't bring him, why bring me? I've never done this."

"Well, the simple truth is I need someone to watch my back, but I can't leave this place defenseless if shit goes sideways. Julien is a good soldier, but his idea of soldiering isn't quite what's needed. If we don't come back, Byron's the better choice for my job. You? Yeah, you're about as green as they get, but Byron says you have promise. You coming with me hits two birds with one stone. I keep home safe, and find out if Byron's right or not."

"Yeah, so don't fuck this up," Eric said solemnly.

"No. Never fuck anything up if you can help it. Perfection should always be your goal. Anyways, let's wrap up. I put six of the 6.8 and four of the 7.62 in the pouches on your pack. Since you're carrying the 6.8, you've got six mags for it in your chest rig. Do you know what size hat you wear?"

"Extra large."

"Figured your head was a few sizes too big," Hadrian said with a grin and tossed a camouflaged helmet on the table in front of Eric. "Normally we'd roll with boonies, but these are a bit warmer. Low light monocle is in the top flap of your ruck. Spare batteries are there, too. Last thing, we need to see if this ghillie cloak fits you."

Over the next half hour, Hadrian explained how most of the equipment worked while helping Eric get into and adjust his gear. As they left, Hadrian showed Eric how to add local foliage to the ghillie for better camouflage. By the time dawn arrived, the pair had cleared the wall by more than a kilometer.

Sometime shortly after noon, Hadrian stopped amid a cluster of trees.

"Rest here, check your socks, get some food in you. We're going to be here until nightfall," Hadrian whispered. Hadrian checked the immediate vicinity before settling in and doing precisely he'd instructed earlier. At Hadrian's insistence, the pair took turns keeping watch while the other napped. Thankfully, the material in the mottled white and brown ghillie helped keep him warm, despite the pine blocking the sun over him.

As the sun traveled farther along its downward arc, Eric became steadily more on edge. Shortly before dusk, Hadrian began going through his pack.

"Okay, so we're leaving the packs here," Hadrian whispered. "You're going to need to bring that detcord and the claymores though."

Eric stuffed a mine into each of the bulky stowage pockets on his chest rig and looped the detcord under an armpit and around his neck. Next came the night vision monocle which attached to an adapter on his helmet. After testing the monocle, Hadrian motioned for Eric to come over to him. The soldier had sketched out a rough map in the snow.

"Okay, so we're a bit over a kilometer away, here. The house is here. This flat space on the south side is the landing pad. The bunker is built into the hillside on the north, here. There's really only three decent points of egress off this rise. There's a trail that runs northeast from the house up past the bunker and another that runs southeast from the house through the landing pad. Trail by the bunker goes farther up the mountain, trail by the pad goes down. Third way out is our ingress point. Past the trees on the west side of the house, the rise continues for another klick before descending into open terrain. You copy?"

At Eric's nod, Hadrian continued, "First part of the plan will be pretty simple. Stay behind me and keep an eye out while I rig a light show. Once that's done, we'll swing wide to the south side. There's a small knoll on the edge of the field, right near where the trail starts to drop. I'm going to want you to position yourself about here on the 7.62 using that knoll as concealment from both the house and the trail. I'll rig another light show on that path while you're settling in. Once you've got overwatch, I'll scoot up the east side and set up another group of surprises on the other trail. We can fix just about anything other than you shooting me, so know where I'm at all times. Beyond that, do not fire unless I'm firing or I'm obviously compromised. Good?"

Another nod. "Okay, so once we've got the perimeter laid out, next task is to check the house. I won't lie, that's going to be a moth-erfucker if these chuckleheads have somehow set up in there. Still, if we get that far without getting spotted, I'll be happy as shit. Anyway, worst case scenario, I'll sweep around the north side, make entry through the back door. I'll want you to keep an eye on the south and east side windows. You should have decent line of sight into several of the rooms on the second floor. If shit goes to hell, you pop whoever is in there.

"Normally, we'd have radios. Can't hazard that shit with the drones around, so we're going to be boned for comms. If we're lucky, these clowns haven't found the night vision or figured out how to restore power to the place. If they don't have NVGs, we'll be able to use the IR designators for signaling. Don't point it skyward, just in case. That could suck. Anyway, we'll work out some quick blink codes before we scoot, we've got some time. Don't forget, night vision lets you see other folks in the dark. It does not make you invisible. Newbie mistake number one.

"Oh, and before I forget, the clackers for the explosives are short-range RF chirp, low power. It shouldn't attract a drone, but be damn ready to find cover if we get company anyway. I'll set the ID on the charges in order, so charge one will be the ones in the woods, two will be the claymores by the knoll, and three up by the bunker. Do me a favor and try not to hit them while I'm near. Getting almost blown up got old long a long time ago. Also, last chance to take a shit. Trust me, you'll thank me later."

Hadrian brushed the snow map away while Eric looked for a suitable place to dig a hole. After a brief bathroom interlude, Eric rushed to memorize Hadrian's impromptu blink code. Once Hadrian was satisfied the two pushed their packs under separate trees, tugged down their monocles, and pulled up the cowls on their ghillie cloaks.

Stalking away from the copse, Hadrian commented over his shoulder, "Oh, one more thing, remember the safety this time." The commando's toothy white grin stood out in the well-lit monochrome green night. Their already cautious pace slowed as they came up the rise to the woods west of the cabin.

"Cord," Hadrian whispered with an open hand out. As Eric handed over the detcord, Hadrian ordered, "Cover me."

Picking his steps carefully, Eric slinked forward to a nearby tree stump. Eric took a knee and deliberately swept the vicinity while

Hadrian bounded forward. Only the sound of the wind moved through the night's chill air. Eric could make out the outline of the cabin mostly concealed ahead of them. *That's a bit big for a cabin. Three levels?* Eric shrugged to himself, rubbed the back of his glove against his numb nose, and went back to scanning the area. *Nothing moving, no lights. If it weren't for that owl, this place would be dead.*

Hadrian slowed and slung his rifle over his back. Detcord in hand, he ducked under the boughs of one of the larger evergreens to Eric's left. Some thirty seconds later Hadrian emerged. Knocking snow over the cord, he made way to the next tree to his south whose lower branches were mostly bare. Eric watched the commando loop the cord around the trunk several times before moving on to the next.

Eric froze. *What was that, breaking glass?* Hadrian crouched lower and slunk to the next tree, staying in its shadow.

A drunken voice carried around the north side of the house, "I told you guys, this place is the motherlode."

Eric thumbed selector off safe as the crunching of boots in snow grew louder. *Too much crap in the way.* Eric frowned as a shadowed figure rounded the north corner. It lurched several steps, faced the building, and planted its feet. *What the?*

"You guys better not drink the rest of it before I'm done pissing."

Unable to see the figure clearly through the branches, Eric grit his teeth. *Really wishing this monocle had zoom. Do they have night vision or not? Fuck, can't tell.* The drunk weaved about for several seconds before veering back the way he came. Eric glanced back to where Hadrian had been standing to find only empty space. *Shit, where'd he go?* After some searching, he spotted the commando waving at him from the edge of the trees on the south side. *Shit, he's going to be pissed.* Eric abandoned the stump and tried to sneak as fast as he could.

"Watch your focus," Hadrian whispered to him when Eric caught up. "That's how folks sneak up on you. Doesn't look like they have any low light gear, so we should be good. Let's get you in position."

Eric tried not to stare as they cleared the tree line. Unlike the cabin he'd been to several days prior, this one was built more like Turing's manor. Easily several times the size of the west cabin, the house before him had a distinctly more modern feel to its design. *Fuck clearing that thing.* Eric glanced into the several large windows they passed. The interior was just as dark as the night outside. Nothing moved inside or peered back out at him. The pair paused at the southeast corner long enough for Hadrian to peek at the far side.

They made it half way across the open flight pad when the cloud cover parted. With sudden illumination careful plodding became a swift jog to the scrub ahead. Eric was still breathing hard when he handed over his claymores.

"Keep your eye on me once I'm out there, Eric. Use the illuminators like we talked about if you see something," Hadrian told him as they swapped rifles. The commando slinked off to the descending path off to the right as Eric deployed the bipod's legs.

Pushing his monocle up, he nestled into the brush behind the heavy rifle and tugged the lip of his ghillie over his raised monocle. Rolling half on his side to reach the pouches, Eric pulled two 7.62 magazines from his rig and set them next to the rifle. Snugging up to the rifle, Eric remembered one last thing. He pulled the remote detonator out, thumbed the power switch, and sat it next to the magazines. Prepared, Eric squeezed the pressure pad on the rifle's forward rail, activating the IR illuminator in a series of flashes. Moments later, Hadrian acknowledged Eric's message in the same fashion.

Damn, this scope kicks ass. Unlike his monocle, where anything distant presented as vague, blurry shapes and streaks of white noise, the scope made everything seem bathed in green daylight. Minute details like the wood grain on the front door to the house jumped out at him. He swept the length of the house and stopped just beyond, staring at the bunker entrance. *That's not good.*

The recessed entrance remained dark, but an immense tree lay lengthwise next to it. Above, the snow had been cleared away from a sizable fissure left by the tree's tumble to the ground. Light dimly illuminated the rim of the hole. *Back to Hadrian.* Eric spotted him coming up the east side, using the row of bushes as a screen from the house. Eric dialed back the scope's magnification in time to catch flickering in the light coming from the hole. He double tapped the illuminator as a figure emerged.

Fifty meters away, Hadrian froze. Eric lit up the man as he climbed out of the hole with the narrow beam. A few seconds later, the bright dot of an IR laser appeared on the side of the new arrival's head.

"I don't care what if you found that stash or not, David, either she's mine next, or you are," the figure shouted into the hole before continuing down the outside slope and following the path the drunk had earlier around the north side of the house.

Eric frowned as the man disappeared from view. As he shifted position, something snapped in the woods to the west. Slewing the rifle into the wind, he twisted the scope's magnification knob as the woods in front of him lit up.

"Fuck, Frank, that'd better not be you!" someone shouted amongst the trees, surprised. Partially concealed by trees, a person jerked their hand up to shield their eyes from the brightness.

Eye glued to the scope, Eric's right hand slowly snaked out and retrieved the detonator. In his scope the forest before him glared like someone had lit a spotlight. The naked eye saw only darkness. The light vanished. Straining to listen to snippets of faint conversation, Eric panned back and forth. Several figures moved through the trees, spread out in line abreast. *NVGs. Armed.* Eric thumbed the detonator to channel one.

Clad in mostly animal furs, an armed figure slowed, and then came to a halt, looking at the ground. *What's he looking at?* The figure bent over. Snow cascaded in neat lines away from the figure as he pulled a cord up from the snow. Eric squeezed the detonator.

With a sudden wallop followed by a torrent of angry buzzing, the forest disappeared behind a cloud of flying debris. *Holy shit!* As Eric blinked away the flash, echoes of the explosion bouncing off the surrounding mountains joined the pops and cracks of falling trees. Eerie stillness reigned scant moments before a pained moan broke the silence. Eric pulled the rifle to his shoulder as the wind shifted away from him.

"Frank! The fuck was that?" Eric heard someone yell from the bunker's direction. Movement, someone attempting a running stumble to the bunker, caught his eye. Before Eric could put the man in his crosshairs, a pair of muffled pops came from Hadrian's last known direction. The man he presumed was Frank tumbled into the snow. Hadrian advanced toward the fallen tree, weapon at the ready.

Another figure in furs scrabbled out of the hole above the bunker. Eric's rifle bucked against his shoulder, softer than expected. A patch of snow behind the figure sprayed into the air, brief sparks from the ricochet amplified into a burst of green-white. *Fuck.* A white dot appeared on the figure's chest as it brought its weapon up. Two soft pops and the figure staggered and fell back into the hole. The wind shifted again.

"Come on out!" Hadrian shouted, glancing between the hole and the north side of the house.

"Fuck you!" a male inside the bunker yelled back.

"Fuck me? Really? How about fuck you?" Hadrian said as he brought his arm back. His grenade bounced just short of the hole and arced inside. Earth and snow fountained from the hole, snuffing the illumination.

"You still there, buddy?" Hadrian shouted and lobbed another grenade into the hole as he finished. Eric winced at the report moments later. The pattering of debris tapered off. Save for a solitary wail from the woods to the west, the night was silent again.

Hadrian swung around the tree, and pushed up the hill, pausing just below the lip of the hole to glance back at Eric. The commando's hand hovered over another grenade momentarily before he shrugged, and inched forward. Peering over the edge, Hadrian stepped up, rifle aimed at the impromptu entrance.

With a deep blast, sudden light washed out the scope. Through his other eye, Eric saw Hadrian lit in brilliant white light from below in an instant of illumination. A second boom, firearm not explosive, followed and Hadrian staggered back before toppling backwards down the hill. *Oh shit!* A figure in ratty camouflage skipped to the top of the hole, and racked his shotgun as he cleared the rise.

Eric's rifle bucked. The figure jerked to a halt and lurched to face Eric. Eric squeezed the trigger again and his target fell bone-lessly back into the hole. Staring at the dark pattern spattered across the monochrome snow behind where the figure had stood, Eric grit his teeth. Hadrian writhed in the snow not far below. *Fuck.*

Eric repeated his new mantra and bit back the urge to yell at Hadrian. *Nobody knows where I'm at. Stay quiet.* Breathing approaching normal, Eric noticed the moaning from the woods had ceased. Nothing but the faint stirring wind competed with Hadrian's quieting groans.

Eric pulled his monocle down and peered toward the wood now that the snow and dust had settled. Shattered and whittled into nests of spikes by Hadrian's light show, shorn stumps poked through fallen foliage. Several of the thicker pines, thick gouges in their trunks and lower reaches stripped bare, leaned precariously against their upright neighbors. A squirrel scrabbled atop a shattered trunk and chattered angrily.

Unexpected movement as he scanned the area around the house brought his eye back to the bunker. *What?* Hadrian had sat up and retrieved his rifle. The commando shoved the monocle on his helmet up and angrily shook his head. He then deliberately dragged himself back up the slope leaving specks of darkness in the snow as he went. The man slithered to the lip of the hole and pointed his rifle inward. *What's he doing? Hell, what should I be doing?*

Several long seconds passed before Hadrian rolled on his side and gave a quick wave. Eric glanced at the woods and gathered the detonator along with his spare magazines. He rose from the hide and hustled across the landing field in a low trot.

Without taking his eye off the hole, Hadrian tapped the snow by him as Eric rounded the tree.

"Well, we're good and fucked now," the commando growled in a pained voice the moment Eric dropped to a knee. "There's at least three more in there. One female, possibly not hostile. Two males, definitely hostile. My NVGs got smoked by that asshole with the shotgun, can't see for shit. Spalling, probably. I'll be worse than useless inside where it's actually dark. We can't afford to wait these assholes out. You remember what was on the manifest. If any of the hostiles are familiar with explosives, we're just giving them time to leave surprises. I won't lie, this is a fantastically stupid idea but we're out of options. You ready to go say hi?"

The snowy air's chill settled into Eric's gut and his mouth went dry. Eric swallowed a few times before giving Hadrian a cautious nod, hoping he didn't show any outward fear.

"Good kid. Swap rifles," Hadrian told him. In the exchange Eric noticed dark liquid dripping from the commando's beard onto the ground and the front of the man's tattered camouflage.

Blood?

"Don't worry about me, you've got this. Treat this a bit like we did the cabin, but slow and quiet, not loud and fast. Watch your corners, keep an eye out for tripwires and traps. Shoot first, shoot straight."

Swapping in a fresh magazine, Eric sighed. *This is so fucked.* He lightly squeezed the two pressure pads on the foregrip, avoiding the third for the visible light. *Illuminator and laser, still work.* Chewing his lip, Eric closed his eyes and mouthed a soft prayer.

"Give 'em hell," Hadrian whispered as Eric stood.

Before moving, Eric considered the enormous divot before him. A pair of bodies lay sprawled half way down the hole, the two he and Hadrian had shot earlier. A metal wall lined the far side of the hole's depths. The remains of a cloth sheet stirred weakly over a narrow rent in the wall. Bits of plastic and glass mixed with twisted shards of metal, pieces of an electric lantern, lay strewn in front of the opening.

Each careful step sent an electric shiver through his feet on the way over the corpses in the gap. *Two hostiles.* Each breath filled his lungs with acrid tang, blood and burnt explosives. *Just like the cabin, but completely different. Shit, I'm going to get shot. There's no way I won't.* He paused at the tear in the wall and willed the whirlwind of thoughts and worries away. *None of that helps. I either know what I'm doing or I don't. Worry is going to get me killed sure as just standing here doing nothing.*

Eric pushed through the tatters of the cloth, every hair standing on end.

His heart beat insistently in his ears as he scanned the darkness. Several meters to his left, the passageway ended in the back of the bunker door. An access panel hung open on the inside, a rat's nest of wires dangling. A variety of crates lined both sides of the passageway with barely enough space between them for a forklift. Most of the crates bore signs of tampering. Lids had been pried off, corners smashed in, and contents scattered. Eric frowned as he crept through a field of scattered ration pack wrappers and sealed bandages that had been tossed on the floor. Ahead of him a sizable archway loomed.

No noise. Noise is death. Quiet, quiet, quiet. Wait, listen. Is that breathing? No, whimpering. That, that is breathing. Where?

Sparks of white flickered through the monochrome before him, the monocle emitted a barely audible high frequency whine. *Not enough light.* Eric squeezed the illuminator's pad as he slinked through the archway. He barely noticed the whine stopped as the enormity of the complex hit him.

He stood at the east wall of the complex. To his left, a maze of crates, broken into like those in the entryway, filled the space. No sound came from the scattered detritus clogging the maze. In the monocle, a weak, unsteady glow lit the southwest corner, casting wandering shadows from the far side of the maze. Visibly, however, the dark remained unbroken.

Ahead, the concrete dropped away. A thick diamond-patterned metal walkway covered the gap, leading to a large, open air elevator mounted into the wall. A sizable gantry spanned the space over the elevator. Eric counted five concrete levels below him, all densely stacked with crates, boxes, and equipment. *Great, clearing this is going to be hell. Fuck my life.*

Eric jerked, bringing his rifle to bear at sudden movement that vanished amongst the crates. He swallowed. Rifle pointed at the crates, he stepped sideways onto the grating and edged his way to the north wall.

"Shhh! Shut up!" Eric heard someone hoarsely whisper from the maze. "I thought I heard something."

Brilliant white light lit up the entryway far behind him. Eric pivoted without thinking, bringing the rifle to bear on a head poking out above the crates. His finger tightened. And then a burst of an earlier conversation with Hadrian over tactics shot through his head. *Patience. They don't know I'm here.* Eric's reticle stayed riveted to the man's face as the intruder searched the entrance area with his light. He took his finger off the trigger. *Soon.*

Eric glanced at the crates nearest to him. *Behind cover. Flank them.*

"Private, turn off that light. I told you don't use it until we know someone's there," a new voice snapped, a slight slur marring an accent remarkably similar to Byron's Svoboda identity.

"But, Sarge," the man with the light protested.

Eric recognized incipient panic in the man's voice while rounding another crate in the maze. He moved as fast as he could silently manage, stepping over and around empty wrappers, discarded cases, and general trash. The closer he got to the voices, the more trash and other items littered the floor, the more gaps in the crating. *They've taken crates out of here. They had to have. Got to be more of them, and not all here. More than the guys I blew up in the woods.*

"Don't but me, Private. Shut your hole and keep listening. Taylor, how's that charge coming along?"

"Trying to not blow us up, Sarge. I need light if you want this done faster," a third voice replied as Eric came to a corner.

Close. Last row. Eric risked a peek around the crate. The interlopers had cleared out a sizable area in the back corner of the maze. Trash littered the edges of the space with a row of sleeping bags arranged around the embers of a dying campfire.

The guy with the light, skinny and no older than eighteen, knelt at the edge of a set of crates looking out at the entrance. The rifle in his right hand shook visibly. A second man sat with a rifle in his lap and his back against the crates a row over from the first. He picked a pistol off the floor next to him, pulled back the slide as he eyed the chamber, and sat it back down.

"I didn't ask for complaints; I asked for status, Corporal."

"Got maybe a quarter of one row rigged. Gimme a minute and I'll have enough patched together to set the rest of this place off with it."

Right around the corner from me. Eric edged forward, holding his breath. The third man stood a handful of meters away, focused inserting plugs into small blocks inside the open crate before him. Wires dangled down from the crate in a mass that jiggled as the man worked, but the wires ended only in bare metal. *Not wireless, no detonator yet.* Eric palmed a grenade and began to tug it free.

"You think it's Caledonian commandos?" the kid whispered.

The sergeant grit his teeth. "Dostov, watch the doorway or I'll shoot you myself and save them the trouble. And no, it's not Caledonian commandos. Either we'd be dead by now or they would."

"Besides which, how would they get here?" their explosives expert quipped. "If they're here, they're just as fucked as we are."

One of the sleeping bags moved, a faint whimper came from within. The sergeant grimaced and checked his pistol again before scuttling over to the bag.

Pressing the muzzle against the fabric, the sergeant's whisper dripped anger, "I said be quiet, Confed whore. One more peep, you hear me?"

Eric stayed his hand. *No grenades. Protect the innocent. One of me, three of them, I need*--The label on the half open crate next to him caught his eye and Eric smiled. *That will do.* Keeping an eye on the three, Eric fished a slim cylinder with octagonal end-caps from the crate and inched back the way he came. *Grenade, distraction, delay one second. Just what I needed.*

Eric steadied himself, forcing his breathing to even out. He pulled the pin. *Loud and fast it is.* The grenade clinked as it bounced off the floor around the corner. A deafening bang strobed the makeshift living space with bright white light.

Time slowed to a crawl as he lurched around the corner, and the ringing in his ears faded to a barely audible drone. The explosives expert cringed in slow motion, and began to look up just as Eric slammed the stock of his rifle into the man's face. He tumbled languidly away, specks of blood arcing from his nose.

A flash lit the darkness to his right. Eric struggled vainly to turn. More flashes. And another, this one illuminated the kid as they both spun about. Brass cartridges cartwheeled away from the other kid's rifle while it kicked, spitting its deadly payload indiscriminately. The sergeant sat between them staring into space as Eric swung his reticle to the private's center of mass. The trigger felt like he was squeezing an iron plate. With no report, the rifle gently shoved back against his shoulder and a copper streak arced towards the panicking gunman. He pulled the trigger again. And again as he watched the kid's bolt cycling back and forth to kick out yet more brass. Sparks skipped across the floor. Wood boxes splintered as neat black holes appeared in them. The kid's spin turned into an uncontrolled fall and the rifle leapt from his hands.

The sergeant blinked and scrabbled to stand. Eric stepped forward, planted his boot, and kicked with the other. Time lurched back to normal speed as his boot connected to the sergeant's head, sending the man back to the floor. Eric kicked the sergeant's weapons away from him. Panting, he staggered back several steps, avoiding the convulsing sleeping bag.

"Stay on the ground! Stay on the ground!" he yelled, barely making out his own voice over the ringing in his ears. He jerked his weapon several times between the two men he hadn't shot before realizing the sergeant was clearly unconscious. Off to the side, the private laid at an awkward angle in a growing pool of blood. The young man's upper body twitched as he gurgled and he went still.

As the hammering in Eric's chest slowed, the corporal shuddered and began to sit up in a panic. Eric squeezed the pad his fore grip and his weapon light caught the corporal in a blinding beam. Eric hissed, "Stay on the ground."

The man recoiled and threw a hand up to shield his eyes from the beam.

"Ground it is, boss," he said.

"How many more of you are here?" Eric asked.

"We're it."

Eric's skin started to crawl. Something was looking at him. He brought his rifle up toward the entryway without thinking. Hadrian staggered under the intense beam from Eric's light, bringing his free hand up from the shotgun he carried. The man's beard glistened with blood.

"Fuck, son, that's bright. Mind pointing it somewhere else?" Hadrian muttered.

"Sorry," Eric replied as the commando gingerly moved toward him.

"Don't apologize. Good reactions keep you alive. Did I make some sort of noise?"

"No? Just felt like something was there."

Hadrian gave a pained smile. "That's a good sixth sense to have. So, what do we have here? Prisoners? Can't say I was expecting that."

"Shit," the corporal muttered.

"Someone rattle your cage?" Hadrian asked the man. "Spit it out."

"Dostov was right. Caledonian commandos."

"Oh, heard of us have you? Good. That will make what's coming easier."

"What? What's coming?" the corporal asked.

"Oh, you know, lad," Hadrian replied. Blood dripping down his beard gave his toothy grin an unnerving quality. "You know."

"No, no I really don't."

"I won't ruin the surprise," the commando told the man. "Eric?"

"Yeah?"

"Need you to go check the house and the back yard where our friends outside were." Hadrian pulled a small case out of a side pouch and held it out. If everything's clear, send up two greens. I'll take care of our two friends here."

"Three," Eric commented, taking the case.

"Three? No, I said two greens."

Eric nodded at the sleeping bag while he inserted a fresh magazine into his rifle. "And I meant three prisoners. Female's in there."

"Oh. Well, three then. Stay on your toes in case we missed something."

Eric nodded as he tucked the case into one of his pouches. "I'll be back."

"Oh, you boys made a right mess of this place. Turing is going to be so disappointed," Hadrian muttered as Eric rounded the corner to the hole. The cold that greeted him outside surprised him. *Was it that warm in there? How did I not notice? Meh, nerves. Wind must have shifted again.*

Snow crunched underfoot as he made his way toward the house. He found the front door still locked, though the paneling around the door and the door itself had been deeply scored. Eric looked closer. *Oh, that's not wood. Surface is, I think, but steel underneath. Nice.* He took his time checking the windows, partially not to miss anything, partially to give him time to listen and watch his surroundings. The back door fared similarly to the front, its wood exterior scuffed in places, but the steel underneath held. He peered into the dark interior through the last window. Inside, an empty glass sat on a coffee table. A blanket had been left draped over the edge of a couch. Except for the dust, the room looked as if someone had just gotten up to use the bathroom in the middle of the night. *If these doors aren't actually wood, I wonder what the windows are made out of? Would have to be as hard as the steel, otherwise someone would have broken them out to get in. Maybe just the ground floor? Hadrian expected me to be able to shoot through them, right?* He couldn't remember for sure, but Eric was fairly certain that had been part of the plan.

Eric turned toward the newly created clearing behind him and picked his way through the fallen limbs. Having circled the clearing several times, he paused to pull out Hadrian's case. Inside Eric discovered a simple break-action pistol and four sets of four flares. *Thank God they're labeled. Gotta love monochrome.*

Eric loaded the pistol with a green flare and pointed it skyward. *Might want to get line of sight back to the house, maybe they might answer with something?* After a quick walk gave him a view back down the valley, Eric launched the first green flare into the sky and reloaded. He watched the skies after launching the last, half expecting some sort of reply. Seconds ticked by. He started to turn back to the bunker when a streak of green arced up into night sky a good distance away. Eric nodded and plodded back to the bunker. He came up short on entering the makeshift living space.

Most of the trash had been swept to the outer corners. The campfire had been relit. A woman with disheveled hair sat wrapped in a blanket on one side of the fire, Hadrian and his shotgun on the other. Neither prisoner was visible. Warning them of his return, Eric coughed as he powered off and flipped up his monocle. While Hadrian continued to warm his hands on the fire like nothing happened, the woman startled at the sound. Despite being partially concealed in flickering shadows, Eric felt both anger and fear in her gaze.

Leah.

"Flares out?" Hadrian asked.

Eric grunted an affirmative, looking about for the prisoners.

"Answer?" Hadrian asked.

"One green," Eric said. The woman visibly relaxed at the sound of his voice.

"Good. Oh, Eric, this is Elizabeth. Elizabeth, Eric."

"Ma'am," Eric said, nodding to her. A shadow of a smile flickered across her face before she turned to look at the fire again.

Groaning, Hadrian lurched to his feet.

"Got a few things I want to check out. Keep an eye on her. Prisoners are over in the corner over there. They shouldn't bother you; they're a bit tied up at the moment," the commando commented with a wan grin.

"You feeling okay?" Eric asked.

Hadrian gave him a short stare and walked off. *Right. Not in front of the prisoners. What was I thinking?*

Eric sighed, and eased himself to the floor where Hadrian had been. *That's why he was sitting here.* Both prisoners were tucked around the row's edge, just barely inside the light and outside line of sight of anyone coming from the entryway.

"Wonder where he found the rope?" Eric mumbled to himself as he peeled off his gloves.

"He didn't," the woman replied. "I knew where it was."

Eric peered over the fire and saw her whole face for the first time as she locked gazes with him. She had been beautiful. Probably still was under the bruises and cuts. The ruddy splotches covering her face made his ache sympathetically.

"Elizabeth--"

"Liz. You don't have to apologize. I can see it on your lips. I don't want your pity."

Eric sighed. "Not pity, Liz. Empathy."

"Empathy, pity, what's the difference?" Elizabeth asked pointedly.

"The difference is I've been where you're sitting. It hurts."

"Been where I'm sitting?" Elizabeth spat. "What do you know about rape? What does any guy know about rape other than being the one doing it?"

Eric clenched his jaw. *Play nice.*

"Liz, I spent more than a few months in a prison cell on a provost cruiser. Before I got there, one of my cell mates had made it a habit to rape the woman in the cell. He didn't appreciate me objecting to his hobby. Put me in the infirmary for the better part of a month," Eric said. He breathed deeply before adding, "He raped me."

Elizabeth stared at him for several seconds before asking, "What happened to him?"

"He's not troubling anyone else anymore."

Elizabeth squinted at the fire. A few moments later she quietly asked, "How'd you do it?"

"I strangled him with his coveralls. Only weapon I had. No, I don't pity you, Liz. I know how it feels," Eric replied flatly. He picked one of the canteens sitting near the fire up and unscrewed the lid.

"And your cellmate?"

"Maybe you'll be able to ask her, if she's willing to talk about it," Eric said and sniffed the contents. "Might do her some good to have another woman around who understands. I saved her, Liz, and as far as I can tell, she's afraid of me."

Elizabeth waited until he'd finished drinking before asking,

"Afraid of you, in specific? Are you sure she's not jumpy around any man at this point?"

"That might be," Eric shrugged. He offered her the canteen.

Elizabeth sipped the canteen as she looked thoughtfully at the small fire.

"So, Eric. Who are you? What do you do?"

"What do I do?" Eric said with a small laugh. "What did I do before getting here might be a better question."

"Well?"

"I was an idiot. Still am, but I'm getting better."

Elizabeth grinned. "Oh? I hear admitting you have a problem is the first step to fixing it. Good on you. Any particular type of idiocy?"

"I was a pirate."

"Oh," she said solemnly.

"They rescued me from a wreck as a kid. I grew up on the ship. If it helps, the provost interrogator commented we were almost civilized by their standards."

Elizabeth rolled her eyes and half-heartedly asked, "Just a little raping, not a lot?"

"None. Rapists were executed. Murderers, too."

"How do you avoid murder as a pirate? Isn't that part of the job description?" she asked with a nervous laugh.

"You know what I meant," he said. Seeing continued confusion on her face, he added, "We avoided civilian casualties, as much as we could anyway. Armed folks were fair game, but shooting innocents, no. We were after stuff, not lives."

"You make piracy sound almost respectable."

He told her with a grin, "Well, evidently ninety-nine percent of pirates give the other one percent a bad name."

She returned his grin with more heart than her last laugh. Handing back the canteen she commented, "Still better than being one of those pommie bastards, I'll give you that. What'd you do on your ship?" Elizabeth looked over her shoulder, tracing Eric's stare to the prisoners. "Oh, right, OPSEC."

Eric blinked, remembering a field of stars and a drifting ice comet. "Sorry, I've never heard someone use that phrase before."

"Operational security. Don't say or do something that could endanger the mission."

"Were you military?" he asked her.

"When I was younger, yeah. Now? I've been off active duty for three years. Four?"

"Younger? You look my age?"

Elizabeth gave a surprised laugh. "Thanks, but I'm thirty-four. Former Lieutenant Commander Elizabeth Grace, Pershing Navy. Master pilot, journeyman navigator. At your service."

"Master pilot? What hulls?"

"Oh, Pershing doesn't use standard Confederate hull designations. I'm certified for most small craft, corvettes, all the way up to cruiser sizes as the Confederacy would deem them. Some days I wish I would have stuck around to see the *Sherman* from her berth."

"Standard designations? Must be nice living where you can afford standards. We used what we had and cobbled together the rest."

"I bet that resulted in interesting designs."

"You have no idea. What about the *Sherman*? For you to go all starry eyed as a pilot she sounds like one hell of a ship."

"Well, the provost already knew about her, so no point in keeping quiet about it. She's the largest ship in the Confederate Navy, or she will be when she leaves the yards. She'd probably handle like a pig to be honest. At that size anyway. Officially, we've told the rest of the Confederacy she's a heavy cruiser. That might be understating things a bit."

"Largest ship I've ever seen was a Haspian class freighter converted to a warship. How's the *Sherman* stack up to that?"

"No shit, a Haspian-based warship? Well, the *Sherman*'s a bit smaller, I'll grant you that. Mass-wise though, the *Sherman* would outclass that I'm willing to bet, since cargo ships aren't designed with armor and weapons in mind. The holds on a Haspian make her bigger without adding a lot of mass, when she's empty anyway. Where did you see a Haspian? And how--no what, what did they convert it to?"

"I think the term they used was mothership. They added basic point defense systems, installed new hold hatches, armored what needed hardening, and changed out the power plants. I think they fit eight corvettes in the bays by time they were done."

Elizabeth looked at him with obvious disbelief. "You're shitting me."

"Seriously. I remember Captain Fox saying anyone doing a sweep would see the engine noise of a Haspian and figure things were good. They'd miss the corvettes in the scatter until it was too late."

"I--wow. That's, that's so many things. Brilliant, I'll give you. Maybe--"

"Blasphemous?"

"Yeah, that, too."

"That was her name. The *Blasphemy*. Targeted Protectorate military convoys when they could."

"How'd they deal with return fire?"

Eric shrugged. "I asked the same question. All Fox said is that most of the ship was empty space. Evidently punching holes in paneling doesn't do you much good if you're not hitting something vital."

"No, no it doesn't. I'd imagine the fragmentation was more annoying than dangerous," She chortled. After they passed the canteen around again, Elizabeth gave Eric a serious look and asked, "How did they capture you?"

"We had a bad run. Got popped a few times, fried our life support. Spent a bit in deadspace patching it up. Well, patch failed on the way back. We were out of parts to fix it right, so we improvised. Pirate engineering, if you would. It leaked pretty bad, inside and outside. We stopped to harvest some ice comets in the outer reaches of this one system. That's where the Provost caught us. My ship tried to run for it, ditched everyone outside the ship, including myself."

"Wow, abandoned. That sucks. How'd it end?"

"Watched the *Fortune* take a slug straight to engineering. Now I'm no engineer but I know a dewar failure when I see it."

"Ouch."

Eric shrugged at her and emptied the rest of the canteen. "It is what it is, Liz. Nothing I can do to change it."

"Well, you grew up on her, right? The *Fortune*? Everyone you knew was on that ship."

Eric stared into the fire for a few moments fighting back ghosts of his past. "Yeah. Hurts, sometimes. Nothing I can do about that either but accept it and move on."

"No spacer likes to hear a story that goes like that. I'm sorry, Eric."

Eric shrugged again, chewing his lip as he stared into the fire. Changing the subject, he asked, "What about you?"

"Well, they got me on shore leave. Jenkin's Station."

Eric frowned. "How's that work?"

"Ship I was on ported at Jenkin's. I got off the boat to do some shopping and get real food. I was walking down a set of stairs then there was a flash of light and I woke up in a med bay. No clue how long I was out. It felt like forever, just questions and more questions. Then one day they handed me a bag with my clothes in it and shuffled me off to another ship and they dropped me here. That was two days ago? Maybe three? I don't know."

"What'd they ask about?"

"What didn't they ask about? They bounced around so many different topics. What did I know about current fleet strengths for the Confederacy as a whole and for pretty much every member state? Had I ever been to Caledon? What had I heard about pirate activity on the British border with the Reach? What about the Dead Stars border with the Confederacy? They spent days grilling me forever on Pershing, specifically orbital positions and hazards. Weeks probably."

"Why weeks?"

Elizabeth commented, "You've never been to Pershing, I take it."

"No, I've never been to any of Confed space for any length of time. Passing through the edge of a system, maybe a handful of times, but off the boat? Nope."

Elizabeth sighed. "Where to begin? Everything I know about pirates says a balanced education isn't a very high priority for you guys. I don't know how much history you were taught, but you know most of the Confed member states were at war with the Protectorate at one point, yes?"

"Kinda?" Eric said with a weak smile. "History never really interested me that much. Not until the last few months anyway."

"Well, unlike every other Confed state, we didn't need to kick the Protectorate off our world. They never took us. Every boot that they put on Pershing got rolled into a pile and burned like the trash they were," Elizabeth told him and accentuated her words by spitting into the fire. When Eric did not comment, she continued, "We mauled them. Badly. Still lost the naval engagement eventually, but so did they."

"Wait, you both lost? How's that work?"

Elizabeth flashed a fierce grin. "They disabled the last of our fleet. Left our boys adrift and made for Pershing without attempting to recover survivors. Orbital bombardment began almost immediately while their troop ships came in from the outer system. I guess they expected an easy, straight forward surface campaign. Their troop ships laid at low anchor to drop their cargo while the rest of the fleet joined in the fun.

"First phase was to take the capital region, so the bulk of the fleet was clustered in an arc about," Elizabeth stopped short. "Well, you probably can't translate arcs to distances in your head, but suffice it to say, they were all nice and densely packed.

"Pershing was doing orbital mining, pulling in larger asteroids from the middle belt at that point, and aside from a few scouting passes by small craft, the poms ignored the mining operations. The miners listened to pleas for help, pleas for mercy coming off the radios for hours. Most went mad listening to family and friends die before the last of the satellites and comm stations were destroyed.

"Well, one of the crews decided to do something about it. This crew had been up there prepping to adjust orbits for a handful of moonlets. They adjusted those orbits, all right. Using a solution from one of their eggheads, they used every rig they had and set off a chain of collisions while the bulk of the fleet was on the far side. Rocks of any size take a good long while to get pulled back down, even when you dump that kind of delta-V at them. Still, the funny thing is that the fools never looked up long enough to see what was coming until those moonlets were breaking apart under G and too close to dodge. Was like a giant interplanetary shotgun, tore their flock of buzzards to shit and back.

"All in all, those brave men destroyed dozens of capital ships. Counting escorts and small craft, that number rises to hundreds, if not thousands. Granted, we paid by not being able to make orbit for almost three hundred years, but that's not a bad trade if you ask me. No one else can claim to have stopped a numbered Protectorate fleet cold like that."

"The field has been our bigger, meaner brother ever since. Sherman's Field ain't as big as he used to be, but he's still there, ready and willing to end careless pilots."

"Wow," Eric coughed. "That had to have been impressive to see."

Elizabeth smiled. "Probably. It's a shame none of the video survived what followed."

"What? Why?"

"Between the Protectorate information warfare programs and the civil unrest that followed, we set ourselves back a few hundred years' worth of progress. We're stronger for it, though. Changed our culture," Elizabeth said with a smirk. "Most of the Confeds think we're backwards and paranoid because of that."

"Most of the Confeds are fools then. Though, I'll be honest, I'm not sure anyone else in the rest of the galaxy is much better."

Elizabeth sighed and shook her head. "No, I can't say they are."

"You know, with my interrogation they were awfully interested in a list of places. I remember Pershing was on that list. Jenkin's station, too. They had surveillance video from there."

"They had a list?"

"Yeah, Pershing, Jenkin's, and a ton of other places. They just rattled off this list of places and asked me if I knew anything about them. I didn't think anything of it at the time, you know? Hell, I didn't recognize most of the names in the first place."

"Do you remember any of them?"

"Uh," Eric stalled and scratched his head. "Caledon was on there."

Elizabeth nodded. "Makes sense. Pretty sure they've have been a knife in the Protectorate's kidneys since before Confederacy was clawed back, if I remember right. Good people, mostly. Do you remember any others?"

"Some place named Grant?"

Elizabeth's eyes narrowed as she leaned forward. "Go on."

"They didn't tell me anything, Liz."

"Oh, they told you plenty. You don't make lists without a reason. What's on the list tells you the reason if you're bright enough to figure it out. Next name, please."

"Grant? Uh, Jefferson?" Elizabeth's expression darkened as he continued. "Something with harbor in its name."

"Cold Harbor?" she asked quietly.

"Yeah, there was another one like that, too. Black Harbor."

Elizabeth flung the canteen into the darkness.

"What? What's wrong?" Eric asked. "What are those places?"

"Home," Elizabeth whispered fiercely. "Grant is the only other habitable planet in the Pershing system. Well, barely habitable, but we've been terraforming it. Jefferson is Grant's moon. Cold Harbor is the largest commercial station in the asteroid belt between Grant and Abrams. One of the largest shipyards in-system, too. Black Harbor is the largest military station orbiting Pershing."

Eric shifted his weight uncomfortably. "Oh. Well shit."

"They're targeting home, Eric. And I'm fucking stuck here. I've got friends who'd give their eye teeth to know what we do. But no, I'm stuck in this godforsaken hole. Goddammit," she growled, and rose to her feet, eyes shining with purpose.

I know that look.

She stalked toward the prisoners. Eric scrabbled to his feet when realized she'd palmed a jagged shard of wood on the way up. He raised his rifle.

"Liz, I can't let you do that. Put the weapon down," Eric ordered.

The blanket parted as Elizabeth whirled to face him.

"Or what?" she spat. "You'll shoot me?"

Eric thumbed his safety, ignoring the naked skin exposed by the blanket's unraveling.

"I don't want to, Liz, but God help me, I will. They're not worth defending, but honor is. I will not be made a monster like they are."

"What's honor have to do with this?" she growled at him

"I get it; they hurt you. Thing is they're our prisoners. Honorable people do not murder prisoners."

Elizabeth stared down at the two bound men at her feet through narrowed eyes, then back up at Eric.

"They'll be punished for what they did?"

"They will," Eric told her and she clenched her jaw. Seeing her conflicted expression, he continued, "Liz, we get off this planet, I promise you I will help you get this information back to your people. Just drop the weapon and come sit back down, okay?"

"Fine," she sighed and threw the shard into the fire. Eric lowered his rifle, putting it on safe as she tugged her blanket back around her. She hovered in front of the fire, emotions raging across her face.

"Liz," Eric began just before she burst into tears and nearly collapsed to the floor. He stayed where he sat, confused and fighting the urge to comfort her. *Just met her, this could be a ploy.* Eric opened his mouth to comfort her, but a series of resounding clacks echoing from the floors below interrupted him. He shot to his feet, rifle up. *The fuck?*

Elizabeth's voice cracked as she asked, "What was that?"

"I'm not sure. Sounded like, like, fuck, I don't know," Eric mumbled as he flipped down his monocle and switched it on. First one and then many lights flickered below them. Brow knit furiously, Eric edged into the darkness and moved toward the diamond patterned grating around the elevator. Leaning over the edge of the concrete, Eric saw what might be more banks of lights flickering to life below.

Flummoxed, he hollered, "Hadrian?"

"What's up?" Hadrian's reply echoed up from below.

"That's you, right? The lights?"

"Yeah. I'm resetting breakers."

"Uh, is that a good idea? What about the drones?"

"The reactor's been online the whole time. If they haven't bombed this place since the EMP, they won't now if we don't give them a reason to. Besides which, the feed for the top floor is fucked so it's staying off," Hadrian yelled back.

Eric stepped back from the edge and looked back towards the camp fire.

"Reactor?" a bewildered Elizabeth asked.

"Don't ask me. I'm just as lost as you are," Eric replied as more lights flickered below them. He retreated back to the shadows amongst the crate maze with Elizabeth, staying near the entry way while she returned to the fire. He decided to keep his monocle on, just in case the power failed. *Will have to change batteries soon.*

Several minutes later, his skin started crawling again. He turned just as Hadrian came to a halt behind him.

"Elizabeth's asleep," the man commented flatly with a nonplussed expression.

"What's wrong?"

"I found Alan and his crew downstairs outside the power shed."

"Alan?"

"Turing's grandfather. Turing's father, Nathan, told me when the fleet EMPed the valley, Alan was down here in the bunker. He assumed the worst when they couldn't get the door open. He wasn't wrong."

"That sounds unpleasant."

Hadrian nodded. "It looks like it was. Alan was supervising a few of his people moving stuff in the lower levels. Based off the mess in the shed, something in the grid up here picked up the EMP and reflected it into the junctions downstairs. When the grid tripped, it knocked all the security systems offline, everything failed closed."

"Oh, damn."

"They were a bit more resourceful than the crew up here and actually managed to bypass the lock to the stairwell."

"Didn't do them any good, did it?"

"No. They couldn't get into the power shed. Even if they did, I'm not sure any of them knew enough to fix the damage and get the bunker hatch open. There's enough spare material they might've rigged it if they had access to the power room."

"Shit. So, trapped in the dark and suffocated?"

"No," Hadrian sighed and pulled rolled notebook out of a pouch. "They had flashlights and enough time to write their good-byes in this. It looked like they passed Alan's pistol around. He had one bullet left in the magazine at the end. Based off the mess, I think they waited a few days."

Eric looked away, staring at his feet for several seconds before his brain snagged on a detail in the story. "Wait, you said they couldn't bypass the locks. How did you?"

Hadrian opened his palm to reveal a set of keys.

"Nathan gave them to me when he asked me to be head of security. Blamed himself for his father's death."

"It wasn't his fault."

"No, it wasn't," Hadrian said softly.

"I guess that didn't really matter though, did it?" Eric asked just as somber.

"Not to him. If what I saw when he was alive was any indication, Nathan spent his entire life trying to be perfect. He demanded a lot out of himself, out of all of us, really. His son's just like him that way. Nathan would have been a good sergeant. Hell, a good officer. Look, it's late, and we're both beat. Go get some shut-eye. I'll keep an eye on the place."

"I might be tired, but you're beat to fuck and back. You sure you got this?" Eric asked, looking Hadrian in the eye.

"Yeah," Hadrian replied. "Go get some sleep."

"Alright," Eric said with a nod. He took one last look over his shoulder at the entryway before wandering back to the fire.

Together

DAY 14

"Meat, time to wake up."

Eric jerked awake and swung his rifle stock up into Frost's face. Except it wasn't Frost groping at his face with blood streaming between his fingers Eric saw.

"Oh shit, Leah, I'm--"

"What the fuck?" Leah blurted and scrabbled away from him.

Wait. Where the hell did she come from? Where am I? Eric glanced around the cleared area. *Okay, I remember this.* The fire had been out long enough it he could barely smell the smoke. Bleary-eyed, Eric stumbled to his feet. A shadow hung by one of the crates near the path to the entryway. The shadow moved.

"You okay?" Hadrian asked.

"Er, sure?" Eric answered.

"What just happened?"

Eric muttered, "Nothing."

Hadrian shook his head. "That wasn't nothing."

"I," Eric started. He sighed and sat against the nearest crate, deflated.

"Don't know what the hell just happened?" Hadrian finished.

Mortified, Eric rubbed his eyes and nodded.

"One second I was sleeping, then Frost was grabbing me."

"Frost? Oh, Frost. Shit. No, this is my fault."

"How do you figure? I'm pretty sure I'm the one who fucked up here."

"Well, you did, but I didn't see it coming. Look, I'm not a professional counselor but I've seen my share of shit. I've had the kind of mornings where the ghosts of your past jump out at you and you just react. Everyone in my line of work does."

"How do you deal with it?"

"Come to terms with your past, Eric."

"Or?"

"Or it eats you alive and shits out a sad, shattered shell of a man more liability than anything else."

Eric chewed on his lip for several seconds and asked, "How? How do I come to terms then?"

"Everyone's path is different, lad. The rocks I stumbled over you might not. I never hit the rock that's tripping you up, so I'm not the best person to ask for that one. I can tell you this, though. When I was a lot younger, back when I'd first got my jump wings, I was part of a pacification campaign on Seraphim Prime. We killed a lot of folks. Men mostly, but women and children, too. I'm not saying I'm proud of that last part, but there wasn't any way around it. When an eight year old child comes running at you strapped with two kilos of homemade simpex screaming, 'death to heretics,' you don't have much choice if you want to live." Eric considered Hadrian's words somberly. "And when some asshole loads up the back of his van with explosives and puts a kid in every seat in front of it, you don't have much of a choice either. No matter how much you wished to God you did."

"Holy shit, Hadrian."

"We knew the guy was building something to hit our patrol base, we got intel the day before. Team showed up a few hours later and he was gone along with the vehicle bomb. I was up in the tower when he came barreling toward the gate, swerving around the barriers. I hit him with a three hundred kilowatt pulse laser. He hit the last safety barrier with a gaping hole in the front end, smoke and fire streaming out everywhere. I still see the burning kids rolling out of that slagged hulk, right before the ANFO went up. I woke up in the evac bird. Four of my buddies didn't."

"I-There's nothing I can really say, Hadrian."

"You don't need to. Nothing I haven't said to myself in the twenty years since then."

"How did you deal with that?"

"Poorly. I drank at first. Got busted down, twice, before I pulled my shit together. I'm not going to tell you I found God. I can't see how God would want anything to do with me after what I've done. But I did find peace, in a fashion. After that many drunken fist fights, disciplinary boards, and nearly losing my wife, I had to. In the end, I did what I had to do, Eric. Not just so I could come home, but so my buddies could come home. Later, so my men could come home. People like to shit on mercenaries, but we were no less human because someone hired us. I found peace because we were doing the right thing most of the time."

"And when you weren't?"

"And the thankful few times when I wasn't, I did my duty to Caledon. Duty is a hard thing, Eric, but without it a man has no purpose. Without purpose, idle hands only destroy. I guess when the time comes, you need to know what your duty is."

Eric regarded the man standing across from him. Gone was the giant Eric had marched up the mountain behind, replaced with a gaunt shadow that echoed only pain.

"Live with honor," Eric whispered.

"Protect the weak," Hadrian said, a hint of a smile under his beard.

"Punish the wicked," Eric finished. At Hadrian's sudden frown, Eric asked, "What?"

"Where'd ya hear that, lad?"

"That's the last thing my father told me when I was a kid, why?"

"The first two are part of the oath to Caledon," Hadrian told him, his gaze serious for a moment before evaporating. "Two oaths out of three ain't bad for an orphaned pirate, I guess. We'll make a proper Caledonian out of you yet. Tell you what, you keep your shit together for us a bit longer, and maybe we'll have a drink or three for memories past when we get home." Hadrian snorted. "Home. To think I call that place home now, I'm surrounded by former Protectorate elite, and I have to see them safe. The Creator has an awful sense of humor, I tell you." Eric nodded and opened his mouth, but realized the old commando had merely paused in thought. "I miss home, lad. Real home. I miss my wife, my three kids. I should've filed my retirement papers when I thought to and not taken one last assignment," Hadrian sighed.

Uncomfortable, Eric stepped forward and laid his hand on Hadrian's shoulder.

"I'll see you there, Hadrian. Until then, duty calls."

Hadrian blinked and looked around as if he'd just woken up. The commando squinted at him for several long seconds before replying, "Aye. Duty calls."

Eric could hear voices downstairs as the pair walked over to the open grating.

Hadrian saw Eric's questioning glance and commented, "The relief crew got here a bit over an hour ago. They're doing a quick inventory to see what's here. Turing's probably going to use that to prioritize what we pull out of here. By the sounds of it, there's some terribly useful stuff in the crates down there."

"Like what?" Eric asked. The pair came to a stop near the inoperable elevator.

"Terry was saying he found a half dozen machining mills."

"Why would Turing's grandfather have mills here?"

Hadrian shrugged. "Beats me. Turing was pretty surprised to hear it, too. I'd imagine he's probably asking the same questions, assuming he hasn't figured it out yet."

"He probably has," Byron said, joining them. "I have."

"Then?" Hadrian asked.

"He was smuggling," Byron told them.

"Say what?" Eric blurted.

"Call it a feeling. Layout of the place, the type and quantity of what we've found. Top floor has weapons, ammunition, rations, medical supplies, a little bit of everything. Things get more ordered

266

as you go down. More specialized and expensive, too. Casual observer or someone who has never worked a warehouse would miss the fact that every crate, every pallet up here is sorted into discrete but subtle groups."

Eric eyed the crates behind him, tuning out Hadrian's follow-up.

"Yeah," Eric interrupted. "You're right, Byron. I can see it now that you say it. Shit, why didn't I see that?"

"Oh, you saw that," Byron said. "You just didn't put it together. Like I was telling Hadrian, there are crates of shit downstairs that would not have been available to anyone who couldn't drop six or seven figures to grease palms. Some of them? Add a few digits to that. Goods made in the Confederacy, primarily. Now, Eric, the stuff here, how valuable would it be back home? Wherever the *Fortune* called home, specifically."

Eric dredged through his memory. "Quite a bit, actually. Especially the machine tooling. Equipment was constantly breaking down and replacement parts were a bitch to find, if there were any. Making your own parts would be priceless. How can you be sure he was smuggling? They ran the largest shipping company in the Protectorate, right? I mean, they were wealthy enough to terraform this planet for a vacation home. Couldn't he have just bought the stuff?"

"Anywhere else and you'd have a point, Eric. Consider this, Turing's family was Inner Party, but that only gets you so much leeway. Other Inner Party members are always looking for an advantage. Money can buy a lot of things, except when it can't. How Turing's family got here demonstrates that point amply. I would imagine some amount of smuggling was done using his ships, but one can only move so much without getting noticed. Bribing a few local officials isn't hard, nor is paying your people a little better, but the more illicit goods you move, the more noticeable it gets. As your operation gets more notice, the illicit costs stack exponentially. At least until you run into someone who can't be bought, or has been bought by someone else already.

"So, we have a bunker stacked to the brim with crates filled with things not found in vacation and retirement homes, much less in the nonsensical quantities they're present in. Either Turing's parents were irrational or they had good reason. Their position in the Protectorate hierarchy makes irrational implausible, so what was their reason? What better reason than money? Who knows, maybe they were dealing with pirates to skirt customs inspections, maybe not. Could be they suspected what might be coming and were preparing to move?"

Someone coughed behind them.

"Both, actually," Turing said, joining them. A dozen conflicting thoughts and questions bubbled through Eric's head in the moments before Turing continued, "Hadrian, the manifests back at the house were not up to date. I've a preliminary inventory. It's rough, but still useful."

"What'd they take?" Hadrian asked.

"Sixteen crates of weapons, handguns to rifles, six crew served weapons, possibly heavier weapons. Still a few unopened crates in that area. In addition to that, somewhere around a hundred thousand cartridges, total."

Byron whistled.

"Fuck. That's more than what we have in the armory," Hadrian said.

"I am," Turing paused to rub the bridge of his nose, "Not pleased."

"Will you reconsider my request?" Hadrian said.

"I've been reconsidering it for ten minutes. I'm still uncomfortable with the idea. We'll speak later."

"What idea?" Eric asked.

"What heavy weapons do we think they might have gotten their hands on?" Byron asked simultaneously.

"I asked some of the others to spot check the crates and see if the labels were accurate. They're not. Some crates don't match the label, others didn't match the manifests we found, nor the list found on Father. There are some crates that don't exist on any of the lists. What worries me is that they took four crates of 83mm rockets. One would think they took at least one launcher to go with that."

The group shifted uncomfortably.

Byron broke the silence. "Well, shit."

Turing sighed and muttered, "Nothing to be done for it now." He rubbed his chin for a few moments before asking Byron, "What are you about right now?"

"I was coming back in from checking with the sled team, but in light of the weapons theft, I'll need to debrief Hadrian and Eric on last night's operation," Byron replied.

Turing nodded, "Good, if you can come up with a--"

"Excuse me, sorry for interrupting," Pascal said, coming out of the maze of crates. "I'm sorry, I'll be quick. Turing, I just went over the numbers Denise has on what's here. You wanted to know about the ag plan right away, so, with what we have here, I can get you a harvest that will feed everyone. There's one catch."

Turing frowned at Pascal for several seconds before saying, "Your interruption is forgiven, go on."

"Labor. To do it, I'd need every hand we have here working almost constantly on the fields. I heard a bit of what you were saying from below, so I know I'm not going to get that."

"No. No, you probably won't," Turing said as his features darkened ever so slightly. "I'll find a way to get you your labor, Lieutenant. Carry on."

Turing started pacing, staring off into space while Pascal departed.

"Turing?" Eric said. The man startled and looked over at him. "Hadrian said something about groups of people living in some of your outlying cabins. Couldn't we contact them, make some sort of arrangement? Food for labor?"

A slow smile came over Turing. "That might just work. Thank you, Eric. Byron, finish your debriefing, I'll want to speak to you about Eric's idea. I'll be downstairs inspecting the cryogenic tanks." A shadow passed over Turing's features and he quietly added, "We'll see to grandpa later, when the bulk of the work is done. He'd understand."

Eric muttered as Turing departed, "Cryo tanks, huh. Wonder what's in them."

"Embryos mostly," Hadrian told him. "Was with Turing earlier when Pascal told us. No clue if they're useful or not. Turing wasn't sure the backup power had kept the tanks chilled enough." Hadrian grunted and looked over at Byron. "We already had my debriefing."

Byron held up a hand. "This won't take long. I have something to show both of you. Eric, recount what happened after Hadrian was wounded. We'll cover the rest when we have time back at the manor."

Eric talked through the creeping approach and the following gunfight as he followed Byron out of the bunker and toward the house. Trevor waited near the corner the two raiders had relieved themselves on the night before. The man's rifle had left a light pink patch on his snow gear where it hung.

"Nice rifle, Trevor," Eric said.

"Yeah, only moderately used. Brains are surprisingly hard to get out of fabric, did you know that?" Byron quipped.

Trevor's hard stare slowed Eric's step. The man turned and walked away, following the tree line to the south side of the house.

"Careful, Byron. These folks aren't used to seeing this kind of thing," Hadrian said. The wind picked up as the trio pushed into the new clearing.

"They'll get used to it. That, or they'll break. They don't have a choice," Byron replied, deliberately picking his way through the shattered trees.

"True, but--" Hadrian started.

"No buts, Hadrian. I haven't told Turing about this yet, look," Byron said as he stopped by a pair of legs protruding from under a fallen trunk. He pointed to the other side of the trunk. Hadrian glared at Byron before leaning over the trunk. The commando winced.

"Now, tell me we have time to pamper them," Byron grated.

Concerned, Eric stepped forward and peered over the edge at a florid mess of splintered wood, bloody clothing, and broken flesh. *Why-why doesn't it look like a person?*

Eric swallowed back bile and choked out, "Hadrian, what am I looking at?"

"Neck line, where it would've been mostly protected by the coat. Tattoo. And the trophies."

"Trophies?" Eric started to ask but the words lodged in his throat when his brain quit refusing to put it all together and he saw. Revulsion surged through his gut and he staggered to the side fighting back the urge to puke. "Holy shit, Byron. That guy's face is gone."

"Yep. Jaw's gone too, and pretty much everything else that wasn't bone. You fucked him up good, Eric. Found another who didn't even have hands. Good timing on the clacker." Byron's tone conveyed a weary sympathy.

Eric swallowed back bile again. *Those were--*

"Byron, why does he have ears? On a necklace?" Eric managed.

"Trophies."

"The fuck? Who the fuck does that? There's at least a dozen ears!"

"Twenty three. You catch what's left of the tattoo?"

"Looked like something skeletal in some kinda squarish outline? Hard to tell, there's not a lot left."

"Skull in a hexagon."

Hadrian spat into the snow and said, "Sixth penal legion. Death's Head. They're the only ones that match. Well, guess we know how they trim down their numbers now."

"Complicates things, doesn't it?" Byron asked Hadrian with a grim smile.

"Yeah, yeah it does. Fuck. I have to tell Turing about this."

"No, you don't. When I'm done recovering what I can from this clearing, I'll inform Turing myself. Until then, neither of you will say a damn thing about this. Trev's the only other person who knows."

Eric spat to clear the flavor from his mouth.

"Who's this penal legion?" he asked.

"Prisoners given a choice between execution or giving their life for the Protectorate. Shock troops, more or less. Each odd numbered legion is field army strength, the even numbered ones vary by the unit. Some are division strength, some are company," Byron replied.

"The even legions are usually special assignments," Hadrian grimly added. "The penal equivalent of maximum security."

"If you armed your inmates and let them police themselves," Byron added.

Eric's gaze drifted back to the legs jutting from underneath the fallen trunk.

"So rabid animals?"

"Rabid?" Byron contemplated. "Possibly. Probably. Depends on who leads them. But they're here somewhere relatively nearby. Their numbers are unknown but they're at least as well armed as we are. So long as they live, we are in danger."

"What are we going to do about it?" Eric asked numbly.

"We?" Byron asked with a clipped laugh. "Trev saw this but doesn't know the significance. We'll keep this amongst us until I tell Turing. As for last night, it sounds like you were incredibly lucky. One of us will go over it in a bit finer detail with you at the house to see what lessons you need to learn. Until then, unless Hadrian has any objections, you should probably go help the sled teams load up."

Eric glanced to Hadrian who nodded.

"That works. I know Turing was wanting the first group out of here in less than an hour," the commando said.

Eric nodded and carefully made his way out of the kill zone to find Trevor back at the same corner.

"Trev," Eric began and the man scowled in reply. "Look, sorry, I didn't know. Not that it helps, but I wasn't trying to be an asshole. You know what's up with the sled crews?"

Trevor stared a moment before replying, "Fair enough. Terry was putting the finishing touches on the first batch. Jeff and the rest should be inside prepping stuff to move."

"Ah, that's what the folks near the hole were doing. I'll go see if they need help. Thanks, Trev."

A bit over an hour later, Eric found himself learning against the bunker door sweating profusely despite the chill.

"Jeff, remind me to never ask if you need help moving shit again."

The burly machinist grinned and pulled out his canteen. "There's a reason I didn't tell you we were moving ammunition first. Soft kids tend to disappear when hard work shows up."

"Well, I didn't disappear. Didn't bitch either."

"Nope, you might actually have some work ethic in you," Jeff said as several people emerged from the pit. The first two down the slope to the sleds were last night's prisoners. Hadrian and Byron followed a few steps behind them carrying rifles.

Hadrian waved to Eric.

"What do you need?" Eric asked, hustling over.

"Byron has the rest of your kit. Your rifle's on the last sled. You're going back to the manor with them. Get your shit," Hadrian told him.

Walking back to the group a few minutes later with rifle in hand, Eric found Hadrian addressing the prisoners while Byron fit apparently heavy packs onto their backs.

"So we're clear, right?" he asked. The two prisoners nodded in unison. "Good. But just in case we're not, I have something for the two of you. It makes a fashion statement."

Byron handed Hadrian two braided loops of detcord and Hadrian snugged them around the prisoner's necks.

"Now, I know one of you knows what those are, but for the other's benefit," Hadrian said and pulled a small device from a chest pocket. "This is an RF trigger. So long as it's active, all I need to do is press a button and you stop being a problem. If, at any point of time, those detonators lose contact with the trigger without hearing a disarm code, you cease to be a problem. So, to be clear, if you get outside twenty meters from whoever is carrying this, your body will stop at twenty five meters, your head a few meters further. Got it? Good." Hadrian smiled and handed the device out to Eric. "They're your problem now."

Eric stared at the device in his hand.

"Head out!" Byron yelled at the assembled teams.

"I'm staying here with Turing to oversee the rest of the recovery," Hadrian told Eric. "Other than the prisoners, your primary concern is keeping the folks with the sleds safe. Got it?" Eric nodded. "Good. Remember, stay safe."

"Roger that," Eric muttered as he slipped the detonator gingerly into his vest. He glanced over his shoulder to the two prisoners and snorted. Neither had moved to follow. Eric's step didn't slow as he mused out loud, "You guys might want to keep up. Or not. Your choice, but if you do decide to come along, keep your distance and keep your mouth shut. We don't need the supplies in your rucks that badly."

The next several hours proved trying in ways he hadn't expected. The travel downhill wasn't taxing but his newfound responsibility weighed heavily. The return trip simply did not have the same level of anticipation, the adrenaline induced alertness. Instead, he faced a constant struggle to focus, to fight off boredom and remain alert. People were depending on him.

Eric was mildly surprised when the group stopped for their first break. He wasn't close to tired, but with fatigue evident on every face but his and Byron's, he couldn't help but wonder how soft these people were. The prisoners didn't appear to have even broken a sweat.

Lost watching the falling sun's rays peek randomly through the growing cloud cover, he barely noticed Byron's footsteps before the man spoke.

"Looks like snow soon." Eric nodded silently. "I talked with Turing. He didn't take the legionnaire news well. Still, that's put things in motion. Hadrian has a plan, but it's going to take a bit to implement. This is strictly voluntary."

"What is?"

"Hadrian's idea is a training program. We teach everyone which way to point a rifle, drill them on small unit tactics. Try to get them to where they don't panic under fire. If we're lucky, we'll be able to mount a half-assed defense. Caledon has specialists for this kind of thing, and we're not them. I figure though, between Hadrian and me, we could train a half dozen people at a time, figure two or three months for the basics, but then we'd still be training people a year from now. We don't have time for that. We need a training cadre we can trust to be there when we can't."

Eric frowned. "Isn't that a bit overkill? I mean, there's only twenty of us and some of those can't easily spend two months away from their jobs."

"Think long term, Eric. Do you think we'll always have just twenty-two people here? Right now you have three folks with solid military backgrounds we can depend on, maybe four if you count that woman--"

"Elizabeth."

"Yes, Elizabeth. But she's a pilot, not a grunt. What happens if Hadrian or I buy it? There's plenty of ways to die here, and not all of them are on purpose."

"Well, yeah, I guess you have a point."

"This first group of folks, part of it is proving to everyone else they can learn, too. Part of it is giving me and Hadrian some peace of mind, some hope that if we don't come back one day, our loss won't cripple the rest of you. Are you in?"

"Do I get to almost shoot more cats?"

Byron gave him a flat look for several seconds before he snorted and shook his head. "Sure."

Eric broke into a grin, "Well, if you guys taught me anything so far, if it's don't settle for half an ass. Get the whole thing."

Byron chuckled. "This leads to the next question. When we get back, I'm interrogating these two. I'm going to need someone to help. You interested?" Eric shifted uncomfortably as memories of Doctor Isaacs flickered by. "I wouldn't ask if I didn't think it would help you deal with what happened on the *Shrike*."

"I--"

"Don't tell me you don't have any problems. I know better."

"Well--"

"I'm not asking you to do the difficult stuff. Mostly I just want you to watch, learn, and be another set of eyes and ears. Round the clock interrogation isn't a job for one man."

"Okay, okay. I'll do it."

"Good, now you can apologize to Leah for that broken nose you gave her."

"What?"

"She's walking over here. Have fun!" Byron winked and walked off.

Motherfucker.

"Uh, hi?" Leah said, slowing as she neared. Her face was mostly hidden behind a dark scarf, but what little was exposed to the sun was red and bruised.

Eric took a deep breath and said, "Hi. Look, I'm sorry about earlier. I would've apologized earlier if I'd known you were part of the crew. Hard to tell people apart under the all the jackets, hats, and scarfs."

"It's okay. I should be the one apologizing."

Eric blinked at her before saying, "Huh, why?"

"Well, I've been talking with Elizabeth since Doc looked at my nose. She told me I kind of had it coming."

"Really?"

"Yeah. I didn't want to hear it, but I calmed down and thought about it while we were moving boxes. Ever since we got off the *Shrike* I've been, I dunno, jumpy. Makes sense you would be, too. I didn't think about it that way. Sorry?"

"It's okay, I guess. You okay otherwise?"

Leah nodded.

"I think I like Elizabeth," Leah said. At his quizzical gaze, she continued, "She's been through what I have, but she doesn't act like it bothers her that much. And she listens. She's pretty much everything I'm not."

"What do you mean by that?"

"She's smart. I mean, she's a pilot and a navigator. You'd have to be to get those kinda jobs. Still, she's useful too. She'd actually set my nose before Doc got to me. I- I dunno. She's just better at this than I am, I guess."

"Okay?"

"I dunno," Leah said, suddenly sounding very flustered as she looked away. "I- I'm, I don't know. I'm jealous? Maybe? I just

By Dawn's Early Light

feel broken. But she's not broken at all. I wish I could be like that."

"Leah?" Eric said. She looked back at him without saying a word. "I don't think you're broken. Paint might be a bit scuffed up around the edges, but that adds character. If you were as broken as you think you are, you'd probably have just given up and laid down to die a long time ago."

"You don't understand--"

"I don't understand feeling lost? Feeling that shit just keeps happening and you don't know how much longer you can keep it together? Afraid that people will see through you and realize just what kinda of hot mess you are and abandon you? Like you're hurting and can't make it stop? That the pain won't ever go away?" Leah's gaze dropped to her boots and Eric sighed. He didn't hide the pain in his voice when he continued, "Or maybe I don't understand being worried that nobody gives a damn about you? Like there isn't anything you can do right? Feeling like you're alone? Like you need someone to talk to, but you're afraid to talk at the same time? Maybe because you think the moment you open your mouth, people will see you for the fraud you think you are?"

Leah's voice trembled, "Yeah, that. I'm just crazy."

Eric smirked. "Crazy? No, you're hurting, Leah. There's a difference. I don't know if I look like I have my shit together or what, but trust me, I'm thinking all the same things you are."

"I'm still useless," she muttered and plopped onto the rock outcropping, defeated.

"How do you figure?"

"Turing pulled me off that project the moment your friend showed up. I didn't even have a chance to really start working on it. That, and think about it, anyone on these teams here, whatever we were doing obviously wasn't important."

Looking askance at her, Eric asked, "Leah, do you know what was in that bunker?"

"Heavy shit. Jeff had us moving boxes almost the moment we got here. Everyone else was too busy to really talk. I tried waking you up on my only real break."

Eric glanced about at the rest of the work crew to make sure none were close enough to overhear and squatted next to her.

"I don't know how much of this we're supposed to talk about, Leah, so don't repeat any of this. You understand?" he whispered. She slowly nodded. "We- I killed maybe a dozen men to take that place back. I don't know if or how much of that you knew, but they were not good men."

"Of course not, they," Leah paused with a shudder, "They used Elizabeth."

"Yeah, they did. They were also stealing crates out of there, taking them back to wherever they came from. Weapons, ammunition. Lots of ammunition."

Eric saw recognition and concern blossom in her eyes.

"That's bad!" she said, horrified.

"Yeah, very bad. That's why we're pulling out what we can as fast as we can so they don't get more. But more than that, there's equipment down there. Tons, probably enough to make a really small colony work."

"A really small colony? Like ours?" she wondered.

"Exactly. They're still inventorying the lower levels as far as I know, but I did hear something about milling machines, and crates of long-term food. Turing said something about cryogenics tubes. I'm not sure if Turing or anyone else has let on how low we've been on supplies, but getting the rest out too might be the difference between starving to death this coming winter or not. What you're doing here is tremendously important to all of us. Who knows, maybe there's stuff in there that's more your specialty than the mills are Jeff's. Just be patient, Leah. There's reason to have hope, you know."

The clouds of worry in her eyes began to evaporate.

"Maybe, but I'm afraid to hope, Eric. I- every time I start to hope, I remember Fro- the *Shrike*," she said.

"Be patient with yourself. Hurt takes time to heal and forcing it only makes it hurt more," Eric told her. *This is probably not a good idea, but fuck it.* He cautiously looped an arm around her shoulders. "I'm here for you if you need someone to talk to, Leah. We both have scars from the *Shrike*."

Chewing on her lip, Leah looked away. "I don't know, Eric. I don't know I'll ever want to talk about what happened. Talking about it makes it--"

"Real," Eric finished her sentence when she paused for a word. "It's okay, Leah. You're at least trying to get better. Don't rush yourself. Forcing it might only break things worse."

Leah jumped when Byron barked, "Alright, finish whatever you're doing. We're heading out in five."

Eric squeezed Leah's hand. "Things will get better, just keep doing what you're doing."

He caught her weak smile in reply as he stood. The old commando nodded at him as he trudged through the snow back to the main group.

Sometime later when the two were marching ahead of the column together, Eric glanced over at the old man beside him. The clouds had long since obscured the sun and a sharp chill rode the air. The chill had descended hard within minutes of the sun's disappearance. Every inch of even slightly exposed skin burnt from the cold. He kept having to readjust the wrap covering his face. The cloth kept freezing.

"Byron? This training program of Hadrian's, you figure they haven't found the manor yet, don't you? Hoping we can make ourselves look like a lot harder target than we really are? Maybe convince them it's not worth the effort?"

Byron's eyes flicked over to him and the man regarded him quietly a few seconds before giving a nigh imperceptible nod.

"Correct me if I'm wrong, they had quite a few folks at that site, all of them military trained. Nobody would leave that many men out somewhere if they didn't have more back home, unless it was an emergency. So either we got them all, or we're outnumbered. Handily," Eric said and waited.

Byron kept plodding alongside him, silent.

"I don't think we're that lucky, so what if looking bigger than we are doesn't work? If they're armed as well as we are, and I'm pretty sure that's a fair bet, what do we do?" Eric asked as he spotted the stone wall through the recent mist.

"You're a smart kid, Eric. You know what the answer to that is. We can't let them take the bunker or Turing's place. There's nowhere else to go."

"How badly do you think it'd go?"

"Well, standard military doctrine states that to take a nominally prepared position you must have at least three times as many fighters as the enemy. Depending on how well trained and prepared the defenders are, in reality, that can vary from one to one or as high as ten to one."

Eric grunted, processing Byron's words. They followed the wall another hundred meters before Eric asked, "So we're worth what, maybe a dozen of them right now?"

"A dozen? No, figure a bit more than that," Byron answered, fishing a key from his pocket to unlock the gate ahead. "I'm probably worth four. Hadrian five. Julien the same. You might get two, same with Elizabeth. The rest of you though, not something I want to think about. But six months from now? We can triple that number at the minimum."

Pushing the gate open, Byron chuckled, "Though to be fair, we let Julien loose with all the explosives we just recovered, we can probably quadruple the number by the end of the week off that alone."

Eric stepped to one side to allow the rest of the group through

"He's good with those?"

Byron snorted. "To hear Hadrian talk about it, the man could probably get packed snow to deflagrate."

One of the prisoners turned his head at Byron's comment.

"Eyes front, specialist," Eric ordered.

"Lance Corporal," the prisoner sighed. "Sounds like your buddy's my kind of man."

"Mind your own business, Corporal," Eric growled at the man. Byron stepped forward and shoved the prisoner onward.

Anne met them at the front door. Eric didn't miss the pistol holstered at her side.

"I've got water on the stove for you boys," she told Byron while they knocked the snow from their clothes.

"Good," Byron replied. "We've got two new guests. I need someplace quiet to keep them. Downstairs preferably, away from anything they could get their hands on. Julien about?"

Anne nodded.

"He's been pacing the halls since you left with that ridiculous machinegun of his," Anne replied as she eyed the two prisoners. "I think I know just the place for them, give me a few minutes. I'll get Julien for you while I'm at it."

"Take fifteen, everybody," Byron told the others as Anne went inside. "We need to get the sleds unloaded before it starts snowing, so don't wander far."

Byron motivated the prisoners to follow the team inside with a few jerks of his rifle. Eric closed the door behind them, but stayed close enough to the doorway to an eye on the sleds through the windows. By the time Anne returned a few minutes later, a sparse flurry had begun to fall.

Eric trailed the prisoners as they followed Byron and Anne through the halls. A short time later, Anne led them down a set of stairs Eric had missed in the back of the kitchen. The boxes cluttering the cold concrete halls and side rooms in the new area reminded him of the bunker until he noticed most of them were empty or nearly so.

Pausing at a doorway, Anne asked Byron, "Will this do?"

"Looks like it," the old soldier replied, glancing inside. "Eric, I'll watch these two. Go sack out. I'll wake you in a few hours with a plan."

––––––––––

Only a few paces behind Anne on the way up, Eric asked, "Anne? What's this space? An extension of the pantry?"

She smiled, "Cellar, dear."

"Pretty empty down here."

Anne quietly laughed, but Eric heard little humor.

"Yeah, it's pretty bare now. We've run through quite a bit of everything originally down here. Makes me happy I grew up where I did. We learned tricks to get through the lean times when I was younger. I've had to use them all here and learn more."

Eric frowned as his eyes jumped from one empty box to another.

"What's on your mind?" she asked as they reached the stairs up.

"I dunno. I guess I figured things were pretty set here? You know, based off what I've seen?"

"Oh," Anne sighed with a shake of her head, "No. I've been doing everything I can to keep life here close to the way it was before. Sometimes I'm a bit more successful at fooling than others. The last few years, any time we got a new group of people in Turing would have me splurge a bit on the food. Your group is the last we could afford to do that with unless your friend manages a miracle. Even if he does, the list of what we won't have after spring is way too long."

"Like?" Eric asked, pausing at the door to the main hall.

"Don't worry about what you can't change, dear," Anne gave a wistful smile. "On your way, now."

"What's this about prisoners?" Julien asked from behind him. "I don't remember the plan including taking prisoners."

"Wasn't planned. It just turned out that way."

"Eh, that happens I suppose. I'll have to ask Hadrian about how he took them."

"You'll have to wait. He's still at the bunker. Wasn't in much shape for the walk back."

"What happened?"

"Got shot before we made it inside. He's lucky he was wearing one of those gel inserts. I ended up having to clear the bunker on my own."

"Oh, I see," Julien said, but Eric heard, "Bullshit."

"I won't lie, I was lucky as shit. They didn't see me, I flanked them. They panicked."

Julien's eyes narrowed. Doubt still clouded the man's eyes.

"Anyway, I'm going to help the sled folks unload and then get some sleep. I'm supposed to help Byron interrogate our new friends later."

"Ah. Luck to you then and good night."

———

"So," Byron said as he stared across the table at the man. "Lance Corporal?"

"Taylor."

"Got a first name, Corporal?" Eric asked and sipped his coffee. The interrogation room was quite small, formerly a storeroom in the basement. Byron and Eric had spent a few hours removing anything that wasn't the ceiling lighting, the lone desk Lance Corporal Taylor sat at, and the metal folding chairs everyone had.

"Chris. Christopher."

"Well, Chris," Byron said as he wrote in his notebook, "You have a problem."

"I do? Well, yeah, I do."

"Yes, you do," Byron said and tilted his notebook toward Eric revealing a simple message in large lettering. *Play along.*

"See, my job is to fix problems," Byron told Corporal Taylor. "Right now, I've got a lot of people who want me to fix yours in a very abrupt fashion. Final even. Seems you might have pissed off a few of them, to include my boss.

"But I'm a reasonable man, Chris. My friend here can be, too. Usually. But seeing as your friends tried to shoot him and you were setting to blow him up, I'm not thinking he's feeling too charitable right about now. Eric?"

Eric scowled at the prisoner as he slowly shook his head.

Byron finished with, "So, seeing as I'm the only one in this building that doesn't want to use your carcass for fertilizer, we have a lot of work to do if I'm going to help you."

"Help me?" Chris said.

"Well, you do want help, don't you? Most people tend to not care for getting executed."

"You got me. Not a big fan of executions, especially my own."

"Good. So, help me help you. You can start by telling us what exactly you were doing at the bunker complex."

"Well, we found it a few months back."

"Who's we?" Eric interrupted.

"Me and twenty some-odd other guys. Major Gore was in charge."

"So you found the bunker. Who came up with the idea of getting into it?" Byron prodded.

"Idea? We found it that way. I figured the tree came down a few days earlier. It'd been raining for a week straight, like the clouds were trying to drown us."

"And then?"

"The major spent a few days sorting through what we'd found. First time I'd eaten that well since I got here. He sent back a group with as much as they could carry. Started getting cold a week after that."

"I'm having a hard time believing a dozen men carried out all that's missing," Byron said flatly.

"Because they didn't. Colonel Gliar sent a detachment back with the first group to help recover what we could. They left right before the real snows came in. Figure it was about sixty people."

Byron scribbled notes and asked, "So, how exactly did you get here?"

"Well, it's kind of a long story."

"Good, we'll come back to that. This Gliar guy, he's a marine like you?"

Taylor's complexion darkened and the man looked stuck between angry and ill.

"Hardly. He's legion scum."

"Oh really?" Byron replied with raised eyebrows. "How exactly does a Marine come to take orders from a legionnaire?"

Chris grit his teeth. "When he has no other choice."

"So for all the talk about how honorable and competent a Marine has to be, you're going to hide behind that? No choice?"

Chris clenched his jaw. "Look, buddy. I knew something was fishy when they sent me along as a technical adviser to a bunch of legion types. Orders are orders right? So I help them do the job and the next thing I know we're all getting dropped on this shitball. We wander around for part of a day and get spotted by a hunting party that turns out to be legion as well. It's not like they gave me a choice. Work with them or die."

"Let me get this straight," Byron said. "You were detached from your regular unit?"

Chris nodded.

"You performed some mission attached to a legion group?"

Another nod.

"And instead of returning to your unit, the fleet dropped you and the folks you were attached to on this planet?"

"Exactly."

"And you were forcibly conscripted by legion types already on planet?"

"You're tracking."

"Were the legionnaires here from the same unit as the ones you were working with?"

"Some of them. They're not all from the same legion."

Curiosity got the best of him and Eric asked, "Are there others like you? Folks who aren't legion?"

"Damn few."

"Why's that?" Byron followed up

"Easy. If you don't have a legion tattoo or have someone with one to vouch for you, you're prey. Hell, even if you do have someone to vouch for you, you're still not completely safe."

Byron's lip twitched. "Define 'prey', Corporal."

"Exactly what it sounds like. You're not even human to them. If you have something they want, they'll take it. If they have a use for you, they'll force you to do it. Slavery, whoring, those are starts. I haven't seen it, but I've heard stories that last winter when they ran low on food, the unmarked were on the menu."

Eric blinked and asked, "On the menu? Your group ate people?"

"Woah, 'your group' is awfully personal. They're their own group. I just happened to have the bad luck to get stuck with them and just enough good luck to not end up dead. I didn't eat anyone. I didn't kill anyone unless they were trying to kill me and I sure as hell didn't rape anyone either."

"Eric," Byron said, sitting his pen down. "How about you go get us some more coffee and have Anne start another pot. This might take a while. Oh, and take this note to Turing."

Day 21

Solid blows rattled his bedroom door in its frame. Eric startled out of deep sleep to find his pistol already in his hand. *Hard knocking, not someone trying to kick the door in. Relax.*

"What?" he groaned, exhausted. The last five days had taken its toll. Six on, six off had been his least favorite shift schedule on the *Fortune*. The change of venue planetside did little to alter his opinion. It sucked no matter where you were. Six hours off meant four hours of sleep at best. After a certain point, creeping exhaustion always won, but in the end with Eric's help Byron had won as well. Corporal Taylor had cooperated freely, but the legion prisoner had not. Eric shivered slightly, knowing that he'd only seen a small portion of what Byron had put the man through to break him.

"Turing's getting everyone together out back in fifteen minutes," Hadrian said through the door.

"What for?" Eric growled.

"He needs witnesses."

"What? No, fuck it, I'll find out when I get there."

So tired he felt three steps behind his physical body, Eric fumbled on a set of clothes and made his way to the back door with a short detour through the bathroom. Still rubbing his eyes, he emerged onto the back porch to find Hadrian and Byron standing to either side of the prisoners a short walk from the porch.

Turing stood a few meters in front of the group in his long leather coat. The quiet officiousness from Turing's dress and demeanor clicked home with cold realization.

Oh.

A small crowd had gathered around the edge of the porch.

"What's this about?" someone muttered.

Leah sidled up to him and asked quietly, "Any idea what's going on?"

Eric nodded grimly as old memories flashed through his head. The tang of freshly polished boots and recently polished brass toyed with him. *Captain's mast is being held in the wardroom. Please remain quiet in the vicinity of the wardroom.*

"Good morning, everyone," Turing began. "I am sorry for pulling some of you away from important work, but I regret its necessity. The charges facing these two men are as severe as they are many. For the sake of unity, you have been called to stand witness to these men's crimes."

As Captain of this ship, it lies on my shoulders to enforce discipline. Your actions have dishonored us and stained the Fortune's name. For the crimes you have committed against your victims and the shame you have brought upon us, you are sentenced to death. Bosun, show the man the airlock.

"Gregor Zeitchev, Sergeant of the Sixth Penal Legion, you stand before us to face the following charges: theft of military supplies during a time of crisis, one count; vandalism of vital facilities during a time of crisis, one count; attempted murder, four counts; aggravated robbery, twelve counts; murder in the first degree, ten counts; aggravated rape, eight counts; treason, one count. How do you plead?"

"I've seen enough of your precious Protectorate justice already," the ranking prisoner snarled and spat on the grass.

"Very well. Let it be known by the witnesses that Sergeant Zeitchev led a small unit that raided my father's house and its attached bunker. Amongst the supplies pilfered were food, water, explosives, machineguns, miscellaneous heavy weapons, and a plethora of ammunition for the same. This account is confirmed by the direct evidence, the accused own admission during interrogation, and collaborated by his comrade-in-arms.

"During his occupation of the structure, the accused led multiple patrols in which they intercepted exile groups dropped from orbit. These groups were held at gun-point, robbed, and summarily executed. This account is confirmed by the accused's own admission during interrogation and collaborated by his comrade in arms. This account is also confirmed by witnesses, one Lieutenant Pascal, formerly of the independent privateer *Fortune*, and one Lieutenant Commander Grace of the Pershing Navy, both of whom belonged to groups waylaid by the Sergeant's men.

"Let it be known that under the Sergeant's direction female exiles were taken into captivity where they were forced to service the sergeant's men until such a time they were deemed to have lost their value and then summarily executed. This account is confirmed by direct evidence, collaboration by his comrade-in-arms, and testimony of the witnesses.

"Finally, let it be known that as this planet's sole legitimate authority, engaging in hostilities, direct or otherwise, against myself or agents of the same constitutes treason. Sergeant Zeitchev and his men mounted a spirited defense against our attempts to reclaim property justly ours. In doing so, they destroyed and defaced property belonging to myself and injured one of my agents with intent to kill. This account is confirmed by direct evidence and witness statements from both Hadrian MacGregor and Eric Friedrich.

"Under Protectorate law, the penalty for these charges is death."

Turing's pronouncement silenced the crowd.

"Are there any objections?" Turing asked no one in particular. "Seeing none, the sentence is to be carried out forthwith. I do understand that a request has been made in accordance with Pershing custom and law. Barring objections, Lieutenant Commander Grace is now recognized as the executing authority. Commander?"

Snow crunched under Elizabeth's boots as she stepped from the porch and joined Turing. Hadrian pulled Lance Corporal Taylor to the side as Turing handed Elizabeth the weapon. She turned toward the prisoner and stepped forward, stopping just outside of arm's reach.

"As required by Protectorate law, an appeal has been filed on your behalf," Turing informed the condemned. "Commander?"

Byron stepped back as the pistol came up to knee level. Two shots rang out and the accused grunted and fell to his side.

"Appeal denied," she rasped. A third shot interrupted faint echoes from the first two returning from the mountains around them. Blood welled up from the wounds to the man's stomach and knees, staining the snow.

Elizabeth stood mute, the pistol hovering in the man's direction. After a half dozen heartbeats, she looked over her shoulder and asked Turing, "This is supposed to be quick, relatively speaking?"

Turing nodded.

The pistol barked. A sizable hole appeared in Zeitchev's throat with a small burst of gore.

Ignoring the gurgling prisoner, Turing cleared his throat.

"Christopher Taylor, Lance Corporal of the Protectorate Marine Corps, you stand before us to face the following charges: theft of military supplies during a time of crisis, one count; vandalism of vital facilities during a time of crisis, one count; attempted murder, two counts; aggravated robbery, six counts; murder in the first degree, one count; treason, one count. How do you plead?"

The prisoner crisply replied, "Not guilty."

Turing raised an eyebrow. "Your defense?"

"Admiralty code stipulates that Protectorate combatants cut off from support in hostile territory may engage in any and all activities deemed necessary to their unit's continued survival at their commanding officer's discretion. The code also stipulates that responsibility for such acts falls on the commanding officer's shoulders, not his men. Appropriation of supplies, defense of self, accosting non-uniformed locals to acquire supplies, all are allowed. It appears you've adequately punished the person immediately responsible just now. For the murder bit, it was defense of a comrade. The exile, as you put it, had disarmed one of the men I was with and was preparing to fire on us. As for the count of treason, I do believe the Admiralty code stipulates that only actions knowingly committed qualify for the charge. Considering we had no idea this was a Protectorate planet, how could I consciously commit treason? If you are, in fact, the only legitimate authority here, then that makes my chain of command quite a bit clearer. Much shorter, too. Considering I'm the last from my platoon, that makes you my new CO."

Eric snorted at Turing's lingering silence.

"What's so funny?" Leah whispered.

"Barracks lawyers and berthing barristers," Eric muttered. "Turing doesn't seem the type to get stopped cold like this."

Turing waved Hadrian over and the pair whispered for a few minutes before Turing stepped back. Hadrian stalked off as Turing spoke.

"On the grounds of your cooperation and witness testimony from Commander Grace, I am inclined to grant some measure of leniency. The sentence of death is suspended pending further review. You are to be remanded to the custody of the head of security where you will engage in such duties and responsibilities as he sees fit until such a time that further legal review can ascertain the validity of your defense. Be aware that any acts deemed a threat to our security will result in reinstatement of the punishment immediately and without appeal. Do you understand, Lance Corporal?"

"Yes, sir."

A slow murmur went through the onlookers.

I'll be damned.

Byron waved Eric over as the crowd began to disperse. Eric looked over his shoulder at Leah.

"Work to do. See you around," she said.

"Go back to bed," the old commando told Eric when he got near. "We're leaving day after tomorrow."

"We heading out to the cabins like I suggested?"

Byron nodded.

"You think we could get Doc to come with us?"

"Why would we do that?" Byron asked, giving him sly grin, a look Eric had seen more than a few times since they arrived. Byron knew why it was a good idea, but he was testing him.

"Well, anyone out there isn't likely to have a doctor. If we're trying to get people on our side, scaring them with stories about the legion might work, but then they'd only be on our side out of fear. Fear only makes allies until the threat is gone. Good will can make much better allies.

"That, and I don't know about you, but having another set of eyes to watch my back wouldn't hurt."

Byron smiled. "I already asked Turing if they could spare him for the week we're gone."

"And?"

"Turing agreed," Byron replied. As the old man walked away he added, "Go to bed."

Despite Byron's instructions, Eric found himself leaning on the porch railing staring at the cooling corpse, lost in thought. *How much shit have I seen in the last month? Three? Is that how this is going to end for me? Stuck here until someone pulls the trigger?*

Snow crunching drug him out of his reverie. He glanced over to see Elizabeth at the foot of the porch steps with a haunted look on her face.

"You okay?"

She jerked and looked up at him with wide eyes as if he'd appeared out of thin air.

"Woah, relax," Eric stammered, suddenly happy she'd given the pistol back at the end of the court martial. "Just making sure you're okay, Elizabeth. You look a bit frazzled, that's all."

She stared at him for several long seconds before asking, "Did you wait up for me?"

"Honestly? I think we were both doing the same thing, lost in our thoughts," Eric said.

"Oh," she said softly, climbing the stairs to stand next to him. "What were you thinking about?"

"A lot of things really. Life's been a bit chaotic the last few months," Eric said and snorted. "I'm being stupid. It's been chaotic for everyone."

He trailed off, his eyes returning to the corpse. She followed his gaze.

"Tell me?" she said to him.

"I can't help but wonder that, well, I don't know. What the hell am I doing here? I mean, what do I have to look forward to? How does this all end? For me? For us? Like that? I don't know. Just feeling kinda hopeless."

"Alone."

"Yeah, that too. I want off this damn rock, but that's not going to happen. Stuck here with only a mountain between me and a bunch of legion assholes that, if we're lucky, just want us dead. I guess seeing how it ended for him makes me wonder how it's going to be when it's my time. What were you thinking about?"

The pair stared at the corpse for several heartbeats.

"That it's a lot easier to train to kill someone than it is to actually do it."

Eric cocked his head slightly.

She explained, "Every person I've killed has been a readout or flash on a monitor. Doing it yourself is a hell of a lot different. Even with that scumbag. He had it coming. I don't regret what I did. It just, it takes something out of you."

"Yeah, it does," Eric started sagely, but a smirk peeked through. Mortified, he added, "Sorry. It hit me that I'm not some kind of expert on this like Hadrian or Byron. I'm a newbie compared to you and them. Seems funny for me to be saying it, but I've been where you're at, and you're right. So far, I'd say it doesn't get easy, it just bothers you less."

"New at this? The way you handled things at the bunker, weren't you trained to do this?"

Eric snorted. "Me? Hadrian and Byron have been trying to get me up to speed, but I'm a pirate, or at least I was. Never even been on a boarding crew. I killed my first man a month before I got here. I'm evidently just good at picking things up fast. And lucky. But like I said, I have an idea where you're at right now. It sucks."

Elizabeth looked out over the snow for several moments before asking, "What happened to the sharp young man I met a few days ago who told me he'd help get word back to Pershing?"

"That's what I've been wondering, Liz. I don't want to give up, but I think Turing's right. There's no way off this rock and we're fools to hope for more. The promise still stands, I just don't think it's going to happen."

Eric could see the gears turning behind her eyes as she regarded him.

"That's bullshit, Eric. Sometimes hope is all you have left. I don't care how smart Turing is; you can't live without hope."

Eric shrugged.

"I never claimed to be a genius. This six on, six off schedule has me dead on my feet and in the skull."

Elizabeth grimaced and she asked, "That's the schedule they've had you working since we got back?"

Eric nodded and replied, "Helped Byron interrogate those two."

"Oh, well that explains why I haven't seen you around."

"Well, I'm going to go rack out. You going to be alright?"

She replied with a nod and Eric went inside.

He was half asleep with the lights off when he thought he heard his door open. Something made out of cloth fell on the floor. He stirred, half sitting up.

"I don't really want to be alone with my thoughts anymore. Do you mind?" Elizabeth asked in the dark.

Eric moved over what little he could and she slid in beside him.

"Thanks," she said. She draped his arm over her as she scooted her back into him.

Day 33

"You ready?" Byron asked.

Eric wiped the fresh snowflakes off his tablet and stashed it in his pack. He grabbed his rifle as he stood and nodded.

"What were you reading?" Doc asked as he rubbed his gloved hands together.

"Been skipping around, there's quite a bit of interesting stuff on there. Working on a piece called the Art of War right now. Seemed appropriate." *And trying not to think about Liz.*

Doc shook his head as the trio set off up slope to the last cabin.

"We'd all be a lot better off without that kind of thinking. Look what it's got us so far," Doc grumbled.

"True, but until no one intends to kill you, it's pretty helpful to be better at it than they are," Byron piped up.

"One of Sun Tzu's teachings is that it is best to win without fighting," Eric added.

Doc grumbled and remained quiet until they spotted the last cabin in their multi-week trek an hour later. Approaching from the south, Eric saw little moving around the cabin besides the trees in the wind. The woodpile built up against the south wall had been half knocked over since the last snow. Discarded clothing littered the area in front of the cabin's east wall.

Doc asked, "Do you figure these folks will actually be useful?"

"Well, these folks can't be worse than the last group. I will admit though," Byron said with a pause. "These folks look like they could use a few lessons on how to take care of things. I can't say that leaving trash sitting about is a good sign."

Eric squinted and used his hand to shield his eyes from the glare off the snow. His selector clicked as he thumbed it to 'fire.'

"That's not trash."

Byron's rifle came up and he muttered, "Best let us have a look about, Doc."

The wind died as the pair crept forward, leaving only eerie silence broken by the soft crunch of snow under their boots.

Leading the way, Byron held a hand up for Eric to hold back. A hint of pink beneath the snow ahead confirmed his suspicion moments before he recognized a finger poking from a torn glove in the snow by the wood pile. *Still nothing moving.* Byron paused at the corner and waved him on.

"Door's messed up real bad from what I could see," Byron whispered, nodding his head up the east wall. "I don't think we're alone here. Cover me, I'm going to swing wide."

Eric crouched by the corner while Bryon cautiously stepped out into the open, trying to figure out how to get his rifle around the corner without exposing himself. *Bad time to be left handed. Real bad time.* He shifted the rifle to his other shoulder so he could peek around the edge without exposing himself completely.

Eric glanced over to Byron who had covered ten or so meters and then jerked to a halt. *What are you doing, Byron?*

Byron was staring towards the door, completely motionless. Eric turned his gaze to the front door in time to see a massive furry grey muzzle poke out where the door should have been.

Oh fuck.

The highland wolverine ambled out of the doorway a short distance and began dragging a body out of a mound of snow towards the ruined doorway.

Fucking great. Byron? What are we doing here?

"What's going on?" Doc yelled from far behind them.

Motherfucker.

The wolverine flinched and dropped the corpse. Its head came up.

"Guys?"

The wolverine's head snapped about. It snarled at him.

Shit. Shit. Shit.

Eric pulled the trigger as the beast launched into a lumbering gallop that propelled it entirely too fast for something its size. Heart pounding in his ears, Eric squeezed the trigger as fast as he could manage while trying to keep his red dot centered on the creature's chin. A fog of fear boiled up, attempting to wrest away control of his hands as the wolverine drew closer. He squeezed the trigger again. Nothing happened.

Fuuu--

He tried to backpedal, but his boots slipped in the snow. Falling backwards, he lost his grip on the rifle. The creature crashed into the snow and slid toward him, stopping just outside of arms reach. He lay there barely able to breathe and stared at the wolverine as it whined pitifully. Eric heard a faint pop. The beast grunted and went still.

Eric pulled his eyes from the creature to find Byron standing a short distance away, lowering his rifle.

"Well, guess we're not going to make a rug out of this one,"

Byron groused. The commando scratched his chin and glanced over at Eric. "You okay?"

Eric tried to reply calmly, but his mouth acted on its own accord. "Holy shit, no, I'm not okay. What the fuck?"

"Well, you started shooting. I plugged it in the shoulder until it stopped moving. Looks like you opened its throat up pretty good."

Eric "Throat? I was aiming at its chin."

"We zeroed for a hundred meters. Closer than that and your point of impact is lower than point of aim. Oh, and put your pig-sticker away."

"What?" Eric said and looked down. Somewhere in his panicked fall, he'd drawn his boot knife. With some deliberate effort he loosened his white-knuckle grip on the blade.

"Got to hand it to you. Most folks freeze up when they run into a wolverine face to face like that. Says something about you that you went to the knife when you emptied the magazine instead of just giving up."

Not giving up? Fuck, I didn't have time to figure out what I was doing.

Confused, Eric grabbed his rifle and found the bolt locked back on an empty magazine.

"But, but it jammed. I got like, six shots off?" Eric said, befuddled.

Byron snorted. "You burned through that mag like that rifle was automatic. Adrenaline is a motherfucker, Eric. Tell you what, swap mags and take a few minutes to get yourself back together. Bet you're happy we stopped to take a dump a half hour ago. I'll go check the house."

"What was that," Doc said, huffing as jogged over. "Oh. Wow."

Suddenly exhausted, Eric weakly shook his head and sighed, "Yeah, it didn't notice us until you yelled."

Doc managed to look embarrassed for once.

"Sorry? Where'd Byron go?"

"He's checking the house.

"Find anything?" Eric asked Byron when the man emerged a few minutes later.

Byron shook his head. "Most of the place is ruined. Big guy over here got into the cabinets and crushed most of the cans, too. Floor collapsed in one spot and he got into the stores under the place, too. This place is a total loss.

Eric sighed.

"On the plus side, it's a four hour hump back home with warm beds waiting for us," Byron finished.

"Are we going to salvage any of the meat off him?"

"Oh, no," Byron chuckled. "Wolverine is not for the faint of stomach. It's tough, oily, and particularly horrid. I knew some folks back home who claimed to like it, but I'm pretty sure they were either lying or they hated themselves. Hadrian will probably have someone come back out here once spring hits and clean this place up. Bury what they can, burn the rest."

"You ready to get back home?" Byron asked and offered his hand.

Eric pulled himself up and replied, "Sure."

The post-rush adrenaline drain dragged at him the entire walk back. He was fighting to keep his eyes open when they made it to the front door.

"Hey," Byron said as they stripped out of their cold weather gear. "Do you mind giving Turing a heads up on how the trip went? I'm going to talk with Hadrian about our visitor and prep an actual report."

"Sure," Eric grunted, trying to keep any hint of disappointment out of his voice. *Sleep would be nice.*

"We really need a dedicated locker room or something. Can't say I care for changing in the foyer," Byron muttered to himself before adding, "Oh, and when you're done, Eric, hit your rack. I'd be surprised if you didn't sleepwalk half the way here. You look like reheated hell leftovers."

Eric gave a guilty grin on the way down the hall. He rapped on the door to Turing's study twice and opened the door to find the man sitting at his desk surrounded by open books.

"How'd our diplomatic mission go?" Turing asked.

"As my old XO would say, it was a qualified success."

"What are the caveats?"

"Well, we managed to make it to all twelve cabins. All of them were occupied. Five of them agreed without hearing much more than we would pay them in food. Four wanted to barter over how much. Two of them weren't interested. For now," Eric said, easing himself into one of the chairs before Turing's desk. *Oh thank God for soft chairs.*

"That's eleven."

"No survivors at the last cabin," Eric said as he looked over Turing's desk. Turing nodded, his expression neutral and Eric could see he was retreating back to whatever he'd been working on. "Literally no survivors. They were dead." That got Turing's attention. "At least five people were killed by a highland wolverine. It using the place as a den. We killed it."

"Oh, well done. You killing it, that is. Their loss is unfortunate. How many people do we expect for planting and harvest?"

"Better part of fifty. Bringing Doc turned out to be a good idea. I'm pretty sure he's the main reason most were agreeable."

"Fifty? Good. Pascal will be pleased, no doubt. With the two groups Hadrian brought in while you were away, that brings us to eighty mostly able bodies. With luck, that will be enough for us to spare people for Hadrian's project. Depending on how the spring goes and if this acceleration in drop-offs continues, we might be able to break a hundred and fifty before next winter if nothing untoward happens. Thank you, Eric."

Eric stood and began to leave when he caught sight of something metallic mostly concealed under a stack of papers. The object connected with an old memory from the *Fortune*.

"Where'd you get that?" Eric asked.

Turing looked at him and then glanced at the desk. "Get what?"

"The drive bay from a Sentec data array. From the bunker, I presume."

"Oh," Turing said and sighed. "I was rather hoping you wouldn't notice that."

Taken aback, Eric asked, "Why?"

"Expectations. I don't want people expecting a miracle when none will come of it. I've already cracked the security on them. The device encryption was embarrassingly easy to bypass. Still, how did you know what brand they were? There weren't any labels."

"One of our last jobs before we found the American warship, we hit a freighter carrying a ridiculous amount of computer equipment. Captain Fox decided it was time to upgrade our processing and storage capability, so I spent a few weeks with the folks doing the installs. The Sentecs were a real pain in the ass."

Turing snorted. "That they are."

"So what's on the drives, really?"

"Nothing major. I'm making copies of the planetary maps for Hadrian, but it's mostly old family history. Journals, old business ledgers, photos. Goes back nearly to the start of the Protectorate. Nothing useful for anyone other than me. I did find a fairly large encrypted file I haven't been able to crack yet, but it's only a matter of time. Reading over what I have already is going to take a while, I'm already too busy as it is."

"Oh, well hopefully you find some entertaining stuff to read over."

"Speaking of reading," Turing commented, "How has your education been going?"

"Byron and Hadrian have been teaching me a lot. Infantry stuff, mostly. I did get around to checking out what was on the tablet, too."

"Oh? I kept a copy of most of it, but haven't had the time yet."

"Yeah, Captain Morneault's library is extensive. I'm skimming something called *The Art of War* right now."

"Sun Tzu, good."

"You've read it?"

Turing grinned. "Read it? Several times. It was one of the first books Father gave me before I set off to the University. I also have a late twentieth century Earth copy on the shelf over there. If there's anything by Carl von Clausewitz on your tablet, that's worth your time too. Do me a favor if you don't mind and let me know if you find anything relating to a Colonel John Boyd. I've seen several references to some ideas of his, but never a complete work by him."

"Sure."

"Any advancement on honest academics? I believe I have a few modern math and physics books you could borrow. Once you get into differentials and partials I'm thinking of asking Commander Grace to tutor you on the navigation equations. Should keep you both busy."

"Navigation equations? In system or between systems?"

"Yes," Turing said with a smile before he went back to reading.

Eric showed himself out and made his way to his room.

"Oh, Eric?" he heard Elizabeth say behind him. He glanced back to find her leaving the communal bathroom in a towel.

"Yes?"

"Got a minute?"

"I guess. Sorry, I'm beat. Just got back."

She looked about, obviously checking to see who might overhear.

"Look," she said quietly, "I just wanted to apologize."

"Why?"

"Well, I don't know how things worked where you came from. On Pershing, women tend to be pretty forward about things, but that's Pershing. Not every culture's women are that way."

Eric opened his mouth to speak but Elizabeth nodded at his open door. She followed him inside and closed it behind them.

"Look, I'm not saying you did anything wrong," she told him. "You're very much too young for me. I wasn't thinking straight after the trial."

Eric frowned. "And the next morning?"

Elizabeth gave him a weak shrug with a guilty smile. "Couldn't resist temptation?"

Eric returned the smile and said, "Neither could I."

"So yeah, I just wanted to make sure you understood. I'm not looking for a relationship. I guess if anything I wanted to feel like I was in control of myself, if that makes sense."

He nodded. "It does. I know how that feels."

"Yeah, well, sorry. I can't say you have anything to be sorry about though. You've made more than a few girls happy, I'm sure."

Eric blushed at her sudden mischievous grin.

"What?" she asked and then blood drained from her face. "Wait, you were a virgin? Shit."

"Technically?" Scratching his head, Eric looked away.

"I'm not sure I follow. Virginity is like pregnancy. You either are or you aren't."

"You're not the only rape survivor in the room, Liz. Protectorate prison, remember?"

Liz's jaw dropped and her face burned. Almost as an afterthought, she covered her mouth with a hand. "Oh my god. How did I forget that? You told me at the bunker."

"It's okay, Liz. I'm not upset. It's something that happened to me, nothing more," Eric told her.

"But, but," she sputtered.

"You're okay, Liz," Eric said and sat on his rack. "Honestly, after everything that's happened in the last few months, a relationship is the last thing I need. If it helps any, I was pretty happy with the whole thing. I slept a lot better. Still, I need to crash out. You can stay if you want, I'd appreciate the company. Up to you."

Eric watched emotion play across Elizabeth's face for several seconds before she shrugged and let the towel drop.

Day 45

The forest around Eric stirred with constant motion. Intermittent morning spring breezes pushed at new leaves and young foliage while the birds pranced and sang their springtime melodies. Eric frowned at the squirrel barking at him in the tree across from his stand. *Shut up, will you, buddy? I'd shoot you, but you're not worth the ammo. Well that, and I'd scare off what I'm actually out here for.* Some distance behind him, he heard Hadrian make another one of his random deer calls. *Two hours and nothing. At least I enjoy being out here.*

Eric sat back and stretched.

"Thank God, it's finally warm enough I don't need a coat," he whispered to himself and froze. Something out of sight was moving through the woods. *Better not be another goddamn squirrel.*

He caught his breath as a deer entered the clearing's far side. It was small, and at this range he couldn't tell if it was a doe or a young buck. *Hadrian insisted bucks only.* His pulse picked up a moment before he breathed as deep as he could quietly and willed himself to stillness. *The forest is your camouflage. Only movement will give you away.* Eric shouldered his rifle with languid ease. *Shit. Doe.* As he sighed a second deer, a much larger buck, meandered in followed by several other smaller deer. Eric didn't bother with the others, he was fixated on the buck. The nubs on its head were obvious without the scope from where he sat.

Few centimeters back from the armpit. He caught himself as he began to squeeze the trigger. *Dumbass, this isn't the range. Use the chevron, not the 100m dot.* He swallowed, trying to wet his mouth, took one more breath and squeezed the trigger. His rifle kicked against his shoulder. The buck jumped and reared about to bolt, but instead of disappearing off into the brush, it stumbled when it came down and drunkenly staggered a handful of steps before collapsing to the ground.

Eric slung his rifle and began climbing down. Half way down Eric heard the tuk-tuk-tuk call of what Hadrian had told him was a Highland Tanager. He replied to Hadrian's query with what he hoped was a halfway decent Caledonian Cardinal. By the time Hadrian had caught up to him, the deer had stopped pawing at the air and its labored breathing had ceased.

"Nice shot," Hadrian commented, dropping his backpack and kneeling to pull his boot knife. He looked up at Eric a moment and said, "Something on your mind, Eric?"

"Nah."

"Spit it out."

"Eh. Just thought it was odd that watching it die bothered me more than the shit at the bunker did."

Hadrian regarded him for several silent moments.

"It just struck me as confused, like it couldn't understand what was going on. Just bothered me a bit. I'll be fine."

Hadrian nodded as he stood and held out the knife. "Third lesson of the day. Field dressing."

A number of long minutes later, while cutting as he'd been shown Eric asked, "So how do you think our training is coming along? The cadre?"

"Too early to tell, really, but it'll have to do."

"Oh?"

"Watch what you're doing. Puncture the gall bladder and, well, you won't make that mistake again. Turing told me before we set out that a number of our outlying guests approached him about my militia idea. Seems they like the idea of being stuck out here with the Legion even less than we do. Which is odd. Most pommie civilians never hear about the legions. Makes me wonder what their backgrounds are, but I'll find that out when we get home."

"Yeah, they were supposed to show up today, right?"

Hadrian nodded. "Okay, so--"

Eric looked up a moment of silence later to see Hadrian staring off into the woods. He opened his mouth just as he heard what Hadrian had. Something was moving and it definitely wasn't deer. Hurriedly, Eric wiped off Hadrian's knife and held it out. Hadrian took it without a word and sheathed it. As the commando shuffled over to kneel behind some nearby greenery, Eric drifted over to the stout oak and brought his rifle up to his shoulder as he took cover behind it.

Long moments passed as whoever it was got closer. Eric spotted movement and settled his chevron on the chest of one of the approaching disheveled men.

"Halt!" Hadrian barked a heartbeat later.

The group, all six of them froze almost instantly, gaunt hands going to the sky. Eric let his eyes play across the group. To a man, they were all clearly starving, all their clothing was unwashed and torn.

"Where do you lads think you're going? You do know you're trespassing, yes?" Hadrian said casually.

"N-no, sir," the closest one managed. "We did not."

"Well, I'd suggest turning about and going back the way you came."

"Please, please don't send us back," one of the men in the back groaned.

"Back? Back to where?"

"Back to the legionnaires," the second man replied.

"Speak," Hadrian ordered.

"They came back with a load of loot early in the winter. Talk was how they found a bunker out this way over the winter and that there were other people living out this way."

"And?"

"We waited until it looked warm enough we could get across the pass, overpowered our guards, and made a break for it."

"This all of you?"

"What's left. We started with a dozen."

"Your name?"

"Elias Lainz. Doctor Elias Lainz."

Hadrian glanced over to Eric and ordered, "Check them for tattoos."

Eric slung his rifle and drew his sidearm as he recalled the discussion he'd had with Hadrian and Byron on how the Legion conducted business.

Stepping forward cautiously, he stated, "All of you will bare your necks and show me your wrists and forearms." Nearly gagging on the smell of unwashed humanity a few moments later, he added, "And if I can't see skin, rub the grime off for fuck's sake."

Despite wanting desperately to step away from the cloud of human funk, Eric went over each person thoroughly. Inspection complete, Eric stepped back and called over his shoulder, "This last guy has some sort of scarring on the neck in the right spot, Hadrian. Looks like a burn or branding."

"The rest?" Hadrian asked.

"They're clear."

Eric jerked as Hadrian's rifle barked. The man fell to the earth followed a few seconds later by the pattering of most of the upper portion of his skull as it did the same.

"Now that we understand each other when it comes to the Legion," Hadrian said, "if you're willing to help us carry back our kill, you're welcome to come back with us. Can't promise you can stay, but you'll get a meal at least. There's a stream a few minutes' walk to your right. It'll be cold, but I really would appreciate it if you lads washed before handling anything."

"We got five new foundlings," Eric said when Turing glanced up from the new computer he'd set up in his study. New being relative. It was still in the original packing when they'd pulled it out of the bunker.

"Drop-offs? Bit late for that I'd think."

"Nah, escapees from the Legion."

Turing's eyebrows rose. "Do tell."

"They say that they were part of a larger group who heard stories passed around that there were survivors on this side of the mountains. Rumors from the crew that hit the bunker, evidently. The group waited until they thought the Spring thaw had started and made a break from the Legion camps on the west side of the mountains. They guessed wrong. There were originally a dozen. Only six made it across the mountains. One of them had a Legion mark branded over. Hadrian took care of him." Turing nodded and Eric continued, "Their story matches what Lance Corporal Taylor had to say about conditions. Migratory camps of two to three dozen Legion each, all of which answer to this Colonel Gliar. Non-Legion and the Legion criminals are subject to a chattel system."

"Any idea of their actual numbers?" Turing asked.

"Only order of magnitude, hundreds."

"Bother."

Eric nodded in agreement before saying, "That does complicate things."

"Did Hadrian have anything to say?"

"Nothing he was willing to talk about in front of them, no."

"I suppose that's probably best. Do you think we can trust

them?"

Eric chewed his lip in thought a moment before answering, "Honestly, Turing? I think I might be spending too much time around Byron and Hadrian."

Turing chuckled and said, "Oh, trust no one, eh?"

"Pretty much. I mean, they were pretty forthcoming on anything Hadrian asked about, but." Eric paused in thought.

"But there's a little voice in the back of your head that prefers to remain cautious?"

"Pretty much. Probably just being paranoid."

Turing snorted.

"Eric," he said, "Paranoia is your subconscious's way of keeping you alive. It's an instinct that has been bred into each of us over thousands of generations. Listening to that instinct saved my life on more than one occasion."

Smiling, Eric said, "I guess it's not paranoia if they're actually out to get you then."

"Certainly not. Like anything, the key is moderation. I suppose Hadrian is seeing that they're being fed?"

"He is."

"Good. Go enjoy lunch, I'll interview them afterwards. Let Hadrian know I wish to speak with him."

Day 51

"Eric."

Still breathing hard from helping fit the last of several logs into place for what would hopefully be their lumber mill, Eric looked up from his dirty shoes at Byron.

"Turing wants to speak with you."

"Oh?" Eric asked as he stumbled to his feet. "He say why?"

"Meeting of the minds. Militia business."

"Militia, eh? Didn't know we had one of those," Eric replied with a weak grin as they set off.

"We don't. Yet."

Fifteen minutes of walking found Eric in Turing's study. Hadrian and Elizabeth were already present and Julian showed himself in a few minutes later.

"Everybody," Turing said as he entered shortly after Julian. "Thanks for joining me. Hadrian, update them."

Hadrian sighed before beginning, "We've all heard about the newcomers, yes?"

Everyone nodded.

"Thanks to them, we now have a much better idea as to the number of Legionnaires we're facing. Conservative estimates number roughly three hundred, upper limit is closer to five."

Elizabeth glanced at Eric in concern as Turing typed away.

"Going over our new set of maps with details from their stories, we've tentative locations for at least some of their camps, chief of which is located on the shore of Lake Ainne," Hadrian said. Moments later one of the devices on Turing's desk hummed and an image, a topography map of the valley appeared projected over the closed curtains in the back of the room. Red circles appeared in several places, the largest of which appeared next to a kilometer wide lake at least a week march from the bunker.

"No less than a hundred Legionnaires are present at their base camp. Likely to ensure superiority in numbers by Gliar should one or more of the scattered camps decide they don't care for the Colonel anymore."

"Makes sense," Elizabeth said.

Good, she's focusing on details instead of her shock.

"How are they supporting these numbers?" she asked.

Hadrian answered, "The camps are migratory in nature and are required to send back a large portion of their hunt to support the base camp. Primary food source is hunting, foraging, and fishing. This supplemented by very basic agriculture."

Byron nodded and asked, "What are their defensive capabilities?"

"Per one of our newcomers, the lakefront camp is surrounded by a palisade wall. Gliar has kept to military discipline. Patrols, OPs, and the like. Most likely to keep his men sharp, but also probably to keep the occupied. Discipline had frayed significantly until the news of how we dealt with the bunker raiders got back to them. Evidently we missed one, Eric."

"Shit," Eric managed.

"Is what it is," Hadrian said. "At any rate, our new guests reported overhearing discussions concerning our existence. One of Gliar's officers was reported as quashing talks on returning to the bunker in force. It seems they're being just as cautious as we are. They don't know our numbers and they suspect, rightly so, that we're far better armed than they are. Thankfully, they also have no idea how woefully undertrained we are."

"What was this officer's name?" Byron inquired.

"Unfortunately, he was only referred to by his nickname, Redcap."

Byron's lips quirked up into a smirk that vanished almost as sudden as it appeared.

"Interesting," Bryon commented. "I would expect them to be scouting this place soon, if they aren't already."

"That was my conclusion as well. We unfortunately do not have the manpower or the facilities to properly watch even a small part of the wall, much less the bunker," Hadrian said quietly.

"Speaking of which," Turing interjected. "What is the status on training the cadre?"

"They're coming along," Hadrian said with a nod. "Another two weeks and I should have them about where I want them."

"Good. I want you to get ten volunteers for the first class and have them started within the week cadre is finished. We still have a lot of manual labor that needs done, so their, eh, PT I think you called it? Their PT should largely be helping out with that if at all possible. The next round of drop offs will be in three or four months. I'd like to have multiple teams capable of recovering those drop-offs before the Legion gets to them. We need more people under arms, Hadrian. Make that happen. I don't care if you cut corners, so long as it doesn't affect the quality of the soldiers you're training."

Hadrian cleared his throat. "Soldiers, Turing? Militia at best."

"Be that as it may. Once you get beyond, what was that name? A dozen men?"

"Squad?" Eric asked.

"Yes, once you get above squad strength, we'll need some sort of formal chain of command. Look into it. Pick officers as you see fit, just ensure they're both trustworthy and capable."

Hadrian nodded.

"Are we not planning on scouting them back?" Eric asked.

Turing nodded in agreement and his eyes went to Hadrian.

"We've done what we can with what we have," Hadrian replied. "There are plans to do more, but the same problems apply."

"Have we considered assassinating Gliar?" Elizabeth asked.

All eyes turned to her.

"No," Hadrian said.

"Why not?" she asked.

"Specifically, we have and decided it was a bad idea," Byron said. "We're not in a position to pick a fight with the Legion. Sending a sniper out to bag Gliar would be doing precisely that. Besides which, you have only two trained snipers here, neither of which are expendable."

Hadrian nodded.

"So what are we doing about this?" she asked.

"As it stands, we've given Julien free reign over the bunker. That's where he's been a bit over the last week. Anyone goes in there now and we'll hear it from here. As for other efforts, Byron and I have been hiking about since the bunker. We've identified two usable passages over the mountains that don't require dedicated climbing gear. Byron's already prepped an OP overlooking one. I did the other. Neither had signs of recent passage, but depending on the Legionnaire, I wouldn't necessarily expect to see clear signs.

"Once we have enough people, I'd like to rotate people through both OPs. If we end up with enough people, I'd like to select the folks who are most comfortable out in the woods and set up a handful of stalker teams."

"Stalkers?" Eric asked.

Byron looked over and said, "Spiders. Their job is to stay out in the woods, quiet and unseen. If they spot the enemy, they are to cautiously follow and engage if necessary."

"Spiders. Gotcha," Eric said. "So that's it? Sit and wait?"

"As unsatisfying as it is," Hadrian began, "we have little choice. Right now, we attack, we die. They attack, we die. This time next year might be a different story. So we sit tight and try to make it look like we're more trouble than they're willing to tackle. This means stepping up the training programs and more infrastructure work. Clearing trees for clear fields of fire, building watch towers, basic fortifications at the gates, whatever else we can manage."

"Jeff's managed to get a decent machine shop and basic forge up and running. We're lacking ability in terms of smelting and casting new materials, but he's working on that. If we repurpose explosives we already have or if we get to the point where we can make our own explosives and we'll be able to make our own land mines. As it is with the metal we have on hand, we can make replacement parts for most of the weapons we have given a bit of time."

"Good," Turing commented. "Anything else?"

"Byron and I had already discussed the chain of command issue, Turing. If I may?" Hadrian said.

"By all means."

"Byron and myself will be our first captains. I'll oversee imme-diate operations. Byron will take special projects. Commander Grace will be my lieutenant. Sorry for the demotion, Liz. Julien will temporarily be Byron's lieutenant. As we grow in size, I would recommend shuffling everyone up a rank and drawing from promising candidates for the new lieutenants. Eric, for example, is already competent enough to be a butter bar. By that point he'll be seasoned enough to be reliable and we can give him to Byron."

After a few moments of consideration Turing said, "This seems acceptable. If there are no objections, then this is likely what we'll do."

I wonder how much good this will all be in the end. Hopefully it will be enough, right?

Birds-eye View

"As requested," Eric said as he dropped a stack of handwritten papers on Turing's desk. The man didn't bother to look up. Eric turned and as he walked away he mumbled, "I don't know why we're bothering, though."

"Excuse me?"

The sudden anger and disappointment in Turing's words hitched Eric's step. He looked back and repeated himself.

Turing sighed. "Sit."

"I'm supposed to go help Byron with--"

"I don't care what you might have been about to do. You are instead going to sit. Now."

Eric awkwardly made his way back as Turing shuffled through the papers Eric had left.

"Now, what is it you don't understand? Why do you think this is a waste?" Turing asked.

Memories of every stern lecture Fox had given him flickered by. *Every time I'd disappointed him.* Eric flushed.

"I don't know why you can't see it. Why have me learn all this math? Why drill me on physics? Like you said, we're stuck here. We're not getting off this rock. You said you wanted Liz to teach me stellar nav. How does it help us survive if I can do navigation plots by hand? Even if we were off this rock, that's all done by computers."

Turing leaned back in his chair and gave Eric a long considering stare.

"Eric, what use is a battery that can only hold half its rated charge?"

What? What's the got to do with anything? Eric waited for Turing to give him the answer. Seconds ticked by.

"What's the use of a one liter cup that only holds a quarter of a liter? Sure, it's still a cup and, sure, you can still carry a quarter liter in it, but is it as useful as a full liter cup? No?"

Eric slowly shook his head.

"Do you know where I'd be now if I'd learned only half as much as I had?"

"No?"

"Dead. I never would have made it far enough to see this planet. Hell, if I'd been nine-tenths as educated, we'd all be dead," Turing said. At Eric's look of confusion he continued, "Because if I'd been nine-tenths as educated, I would know just enough to think I know everything, Eric. I probably would have made it here and then killed us all with my arrogance by now. You would have shown up to an empty house populated only the whispers of the dead.

"So, can you explain to me how much harder your life would be if you only knew half of what you did then, at any given point in time?"

"Well, uh, no? I mean, it'd be harder, for sure."

"Exactly. Do you enjoy a hard life?"

"Not particularly?"

"So at what point is it acceptable to not live up to your potential?"

Eric blinked. "Well, when you put it that way, it isn't."

"Precisely. Now, this might be my conceit, and if it is I beg you grant me it, but I've kept tabs on your progress. Commander Grace tells me you're a very capable student, which is good. Intellect will get you far if you hone it. You've pushed through harder math than many will bother to even try to learn in far shorter a time than it takes the determined average student to grasp. She also tells me you are far more mature than your years might indicate. Both are excellent. I will not lie to you by omission, I do see some of myself at that age in you. That is why I push you to learn, because learning is why I am still here."

Oh.

"So letting me go on without this education, you see that as," Eric stalled, trying to think of the right words. "You see that as failing yourself? Your younger self, that is."

Turing nodded and said quietly, "And so you begin to see. Now, do you know what is it that Byron and Hadrian are teaching you?"

"Oh, military stuff, er, science. Infantry tactics, shooting, and the like?"

"No."

Has to be something more complex or esoteric then; some deeper meaning he's getting at. Eric scrambled for the correct answer. "Threat analysis?"

Turing shook his head. "No. They are teaching you to be a dangerous man."

"That makes sense," Eric said.

"Do you know what I am teaching you?"

"So far? Math. Lots of math. And also physics," Eric replied, adding a hint of faux disappointment on the topics.

Turing broke a smile.

"No, Eric. I am teaching you the same thing. I am teaching you to be a dangerous man. Oh, not in the same way, I'll admit. Think of it this way, Byron and Hadrian are teaching you to be a dangerous person in a very physical, personal manner. I am teaching you to be dangerous in an intellectual one."

"I guess that makes sense. I guess?"

"Let me clarify. Do you know how I am making you dangerous? The ability to think. Now, I'm not saying Byron and Hadrian can't think. They most assuredly can, otherwise they'd be useless to me, little better than trained attack dogs.

"Many places, the Protectorate included, make the mistake of confusing what an education is supposed to be about with what they want it to accomplish. They want conformity far more than utility. Just as mindlessly repeating facts by rote is not intelligence, neither is mindlessly repeating the words of others an education. As such, they teach what to think, not how. Their students' ability to be useful is a happy accident, provided they repeat what they're told. But you? No, you will be dangerous because you will be taught how to see things for what they are, not for what you or someone else wants them to be.

"History is filled with great men, Eric. People who have illuminated the darkness around them despite the efforts to get them to conform. All of those men, those women, were dangerous people in their own ways. Some, take the soldiers for example, were literally dangerous, but the scientists, the philosophers, the artists? They held ideas dangerous to the accepted order of their times in some fashion. All had influence that reached out through time long past their deaths. Do you know what the difference between a great man and a dangerous one is?"

"Not the slightest."

"A dangerous man understands how the system works and how they can exploit it. A great man knows when to work within the system and when he should subvert it. Intellect isn't sufficient, Eric, without the will to use it and the wisdom to know both when to use it and what your limits are. I will be satisfied if you become a dangerous man, but I strive for the better alternative. That said, is there a particular reason for this apparent bout of negative thinking?

Eric shrugged.

"We have been pushing you along rather strenuously, I suppose. Perhaps some time off in the near future would help. At any rate, off to Byron," Turing said. "After I double check these figures to see that you've mastered this, we'll move on to other topics. Chemistry was another favorite of mine."

Day 152

Eric grunted, straining to stand under the weight of his pack.

"No matter how many times I do this, this shit never feels any lighter," he muttered as he turned to his companion.

Corporal Taylor snorted. Taylor had been helping out around the compound since his capture. He seldom had to be asked to do anything. By time someone came up with the idea of having Chris do something, he was already there helping.

"It's forty, fifty kilos at most."

"It's damn heavy is what it is, Chris."

"Not saying it isn't heavy, but some of the loadouts I've had to carry for the Corps were heavier."

"The hell were you carrying?"

"My gear, the other guy's gear, the squad's gear. I'm pretty sure I was humping shit for folks who weren't even enlisted yet, much less out with us then."

Eric rolled his eyes and the pair started through the woods homeward.

"Actually in that case, I was lugging mortar rounds on top of my normal load. Was attached to a mortar company for a bit before I went explosives. Mortars, plates, their ammo, none of it is light," Chris said and chuckled. "Hell, even light infantry isn't light. Unless you're the officer in charge anyway."

"Sounds like I dodged a bullet getting raised on the *Fortune*. Heaviest work I did was helping move cargo onboard. We had lifts for most of it, though."

"Pirates. I'd call you guys pussies, but I've seen boarding action footage, some of it was pretty brutal. You know what? I don't think I ever expected there'd be a day I'd call a pirate friend."

Eric grinned. "You're surprised? Before I ended up here, every pommie bastard I met tried to kill me. This place makes for strange friends. Good thing though, you've taught me a lot. Where'd you learn to hunt?"

"Back home. Grew up with a rifle in my hands. My parents lived out on the outskirts of Twyland. We were ranchers. You make decent money, but it's not always dependable so when you're twelve hours from any reasonable sized town, you learn to live off the land."

"Guess that makes sense. Still, happy I asked if you wanted to come. I wouldn't have gone for the elk by myself."

"Shit, I'm just happy to be out of that house and out here. All that busy work was driving me nuts. You sure Hadrian isn't going to lose his shit over you letting me shoot?"

"Nah, I talked to him before I asked you. You're good. He made it sound like they were going to release you from the whole prisoner bit here soon."

"Sweet. Tired of feeling like a second class citizen because of shit I have no control over. I mean, don't get me wrong, I get it. Security first, feelings whenever. Just gets old after a while. What do you think they'll want me to do around here?"

"Well, if I have any say in it, you'll be hunting or scouting with us. We'd be idiots not to use your skills."

The duo continued through the woods in silence for a while before Eric asked, "So what all did you do in the Corps? You talked about mortars earlier."

"A little bit of this, a little bit of that. Spent most of my first two years in that mortar platoon. My LT wanted me to try out for sniper, but I liked explosives better. Figured I liked hunting too much to hunt people. Didn't want to ruin my hobby. Blowing shit up is a lot more fun than the stories I heard from the snipers anyway. Who wants to spend three weeks in a ditch pissing on yourself waiting for some dumb unlucky bastard when you could light off three thousand kilos of expiring advex? So EOD it was. You?"

"I'm not really sure how to translate it. Life on the boat was different for me than you guys. Based off what Hadrian and Elizabeth have said, I was something of a mix between midshipman and a private. So yeah, I did a little bit of everything. But I wasn't a full member of the crew up until right before the *Fortune* was lost because of my age, so they wouldn't let me do lot of the directly dangerous stuff. I trained for repelling boarding parties and the like, but that was pretty much it. Supervised stuff here and there, but it was all small shit none of the officers wanted to do."

Chris held out a small jar. "Here, take a sip of this, tell me what you think."

"What's this?" Eric asked suspiciously as he took the proffered jar and sniffed the clear liquid inside. *Definitely alcohol.*

"Joint project. Something I convinced Byron to work with me on. Go ahead, try it."

Eric peered at the container a moment, took a sip, and immediately stumbled to his knees in a coughing fit from the surge of fire through his mouth and sinuses.

"Hey, don't spill it!"

"I--didn't spill it," Eric gasped. Still coughing, he weakly offered the container to the laughing marine.

It was almost a minute later before the burning faded and he finally found his voice.

"What is that shit? Rocket fuel?" Eric croaked.

"First pull from the Taylor distillery. Should be about ninety-five percent alcohol by volume. How's it taste?"

"Other than liquid sun and hand sanitizer?"

"We're still working on the recipe."

"I'll have to apologize to Turing," Eric said as he lurched to his feet. "I know what regret tastes like now."

"Hey, I said we're still working on it."

Day 160

"Good morning," Eric said to the group assembled before him on the open field outside Turing's manor. This round of drop-offs so far had turned out to be far larger than expected. Turing's plans figured on adding another twenty people to his guest list over the course of the summer. They'd added that on the first day. They'd recovered sixty so far, and many of them had volunteered.

Eric subconsciously rubbed at the new rank insignia pinned on his collar as he resumed, "Thank you for volunteering for the Solitude Militia. I am Lieutenant Friedrich. In the coming weeks, myself or other cadre will be putting you through some strenuous training. It will not be easy, nor will it be fun. It is, however, necessary. No doubt, you've all heard about the Legion. They are not a scary story we tell people to keep them in line. They are a reality that cannot be ignored. A reality we must prepare against.

"By the time this group finishes training, you will be minimally qualified in small arms training, small unit tactics, and have a modicum of physical conditioning. Those of you who show promise will be asked to stay for additional training and reassignment to active duty. The rest will be counted as militia in the event of an attack on the Manor. While continuing your conditioning and expanding your knowledge after the end of phase one is largely your responsibility, I cannot stress enough that every ounce of sweat you sweat now is likely several pints of blood you don't bleed later. The same applies after phase one. Are we ready to begin?"

The group looked about at each other. A few nodded.

"I'm sorry, I didn't hear a response," Eric said.

"Uh, sure?" one of them timidly managed.

"Sound off," Eric barked. "Sound off like you have a pair!"

"YES, SIR!"

"Better. Still not good enough, but it's something I can work with at least. Jamis, Perkins, why are you here?"

Jamis blinked and said, "Sir?"

"It's a simple question. Why are you here? Both of you have already dealt enough with the Legion."

Jamis swallowed. "Sir," he said, "They owe me a few pints of blood."

Eric nodded and glanced over to Perkins.

"They nearly worked me to death last year. Never again, sir."

Day 183

"So, where are you fuckers?" Eric whispered as he adjusted his binoculars, a matching pair for the set Turing had given him months ago.

He scanned the pass before him three times. Once on visual light, once on thermal, and once again with ultraviolet. Visually, the pass was empty. Thermal said otherwise. A group of mountain goats had been grousing over a section of short grass, mostly hidden behind taller growth. *Probably getting ready to bed down for the night.* Two hundred meters below them, a highland wolverine lay in a collection of fallen trees. Several birds of prey dotted the sky behind clouds, their calls interrupting the incessant wind periodically. Ultraviolet failed to be any more informative, but Byron was insistent that it be checked, just in case the legionnaires had tech of their own.

"I understand you said I'd know it when I saw it, if I saw it, but, shit, UV is a waste of time."

Normally Eric avoided talking to himself, but he hardly noticed it now.

For the last week he'd traveled no further than a dozen meters from where he lay, alone on a rock ledge overlooking the pass Chris said the legionnaires had used to cross over. Eight days had crawled by since Byron left him here to watch the pass.

Check complete, he rolled his head slowly to one side to minimize movement and pressed the transmit toggle on his throat mic.

"Mountain home, Eagle Two. Nothing to report."

Several seconds passed. Eric's skin crawled and he scanned the sky for drones. Byron had reassured him multiple times that the laser relay he'd set up on arrival would minimize any chance of attracting drones. Eric still worried about Byron's choice of wording. *Minimize.*

"Eagle Two, Mountain Home. Acknowledged. Eagle One en route with package. ETA one hour," came the reply. Julien's voice was a welcome reprieve from his own.

Numbed by the monotony of the last week, Eric almost reflexively started to reach for his packaged food when a glint of sunlight from the top of the pass caught his eye.

"Standby, Mountain Home," Eric whispered as he brought his binoculars up. "Mountain Home, how copy?"

"Go ahead, Eagle Two."

"I have twelve foot mobiles carrying small arms under observation in the pass. Unaware of my presence, over."

"Copy. Standby."

A bead of sweat dribbled down his cheek as he lased the group. *Rear is seven hundred forty three meters, front is six hundred twelve.* Deliberate and slow, Eric shifted over to his rifle. With a quick glance at the range card to verify the number of clicks for distance and angle, he adjusted the elevation knob on his scope for the farthest target and mentally noted the change in point of aim on the nearest from the new setting. Patiently he eyed the foliage around the legionnaires below. *Minimal movement, no change in windage.* The legionnaires were strung out in a staggered line almost a hundred meters long. Most of the group wore torn camouflage or ratty clothing. *Probably taken from their victims.* Eric blinked the sweat out of his eyes and placed his crosshair center mass of the rearmost legionnaire.

"Mountain Home, Eagle Two. Please advise."

"Eagle Two, Mountain Home. Cleared to engage. Eagle One has been advised of your situation. ETA unknown."

The rifle bucked against his shoulder, its bark muffled significantly but not silenced by the suppressor. One and a half seconds later, Eric's crosshair was settling on the next man in line when the legion rear guard staggered and grabbed at his throat in the background. *Shit. Aim lower.* Eric's rifle bucked again just as his new target paused and started to turn around. Moments later a puff of pink mist appeared in the center of the second target's chest.

Next target.

Seconds later, the formation's point man made an ungraceful pirouette and fell to the ground as the rest of the group scattered for cover that simply wasn't there. Eric's crosshair settled on another target trying to get behind a patch of stubby bushes. *Concealment is not cover.* His rifle chuffed again. Rock spattered inches away from his target's head. *Shit.* He sent another round down range. The man was not as lucky the second time. Neither were the next two targets.

Eric was searching for his seventh target when he saw the muzzle flash of the first burst of return fire. *Aiming the wrong direction dumbass. Look up.* Eric's reply put a round through the man's arm and into his chest. *Seven down, five to go.*

Going by feel, Eric snagged a fresh magazine from his pack beside him with his off hand while searching for target eight through the scope.

Another muzzle flash got his attention. A bullet buzzed by moments later like an angry hornet. Shards from the rock face above fell around him as Eric put a bullet into that assailant's shoulder. He followed up with another center mass. *Four.*

A hooded figure broke from cover, attempting to sprint back up the pass in a zig-zag fashion. Eric squeezed the trigger. *Miss.* He squeezed again. *Shit.* Another. *Goddamnit, stand still asshole.* Again. *Motherfucker, seriously? Pull.* His target jerked and toppled bonelessly. *About goddamn time.* The fall forward bounced the target's head off a rock, yanking back the hood of his jacket. Long black hair spilled out. *Wait, that's a wo--no. Not going there. Not even. Finish the mission.*

Eric forced down the sudden acrid taste in his mouth looking for number ten. He caught the tenth man trying to crawl into a shallow depression that would have been better cover. A bullet ended that attempt. Only a few rounds left, Eric loaded his fresh magazine and went back to scanning.

Fuck. Number nine was dragging herself across the stony ground, legs trailing limply behind her. Her faint wailing needled his ears. Eric grit his teeth and kept looking for the other two.

Eleven had slid behind a pair of rocks. Eric's first shot missed cleanly. Shards of rock sprayed from his second miss and the dust concealed his target. *Shit.* Writhing in pain from the spalling, number eleven rolled back far enough to expose himself for a third shot a few seconds later. Neither of the targets hands gripping his face slowed the bullet.

Where are you twelve? Where'd you go? Damnit nine, shut the fuck up. Eric scanned the area but found nothing. *Shit.* Forcing his breathing to slow, Eric deliberately inspected the area around each of his targets again. *Wait a second.* His crosshairs returned to number five. Twelve was using five as cover. *You sneaky bastard.*

Eric pulled the trigger just as the target disappeared behind a muzzle flash. Something pinged in front of his face and his head snapped back. Stars filled his vision. *Ow, fuck.* Panicked, he scooted back, and an acrid taste surged into his mouth while he tried to drag the rifle with him. He violently lost what little food he'd eaten in the last few hours as the world wobbled and spun about him.

He wretched again and lay panting. Above the ringing in his ears, nine's now hoarse wailing slackened. *Shit. What do I do? Pop out again? No, he's got my number.* Eric's hand brushed the binoculars as he made to roll over. *Wait.* He cautiously scooted forward, held the binoculars just far enough to see over the rock face he'd been using as cover and pressed the photo button. Nausea didn't make zooming in any easier, but the motion-blurred image told the rest of the story: he'd hit his target squarely in the head. *Got them all.*

Eric swallowed back another set of dry heaves when he noticed something warm dripping down his face. He brushed at it and found his gloved hand glistening with blood. Eric realized a notch was missing out of the top of his scope at the front. He reached up, feeling the helmet under his ghillie hood. Low profile helmets weren't intended to stop bullets. Technically, his didn't stop this one, it had only deflected it a little further, cracking along the groove the bullet left. Eric groaned and pressed his transmit key.

"Mountain Home, Eagle Two. Targets down. Need medical assistance, I don't think I'm getting down from here without help."

"Say again, over?"

Someone knocked on his door. Eric jerked awake. The sheets were wrapped around him, smothering him. His cheeks burned. *Ugh, so hot.* Half trying to get up to answer the door, half just wanting the suffocating heat to go away, he tugged at the sheets. *Fuck, when did someone stitch me into bed? When did I get home?*

The door to his room opened a crack.

"Eric?" Elizabeth poked her head inside.

Eric tried to speak but found he could only manage a tired grunt.

"Doc wanted me to check on you. Leah had to go help at the fields," she said, closing the door behind her. Eric saw the worry hiding in her eyes behind the cautious smile.

"Water," Eric managed to finally croak. "Burning up."

Elizabeth grabbed a pitcher from the nightstand and came to sit at the stool by his bed. Longing screamed through him as the glass filled with crystal clear water. She leaned forward and held the glass to his lips.

"Careful, don't drink too fast. You'll choke, silly," she warned. He didn't listen and paid the price.

"When did I get back here?" he gasped once the coughing fit sputtered out.

"Four days ago," Elizabeth said as she pressed a wet washrag against his head. "You've been through a lot, Eric."

"Four days?" Eric started and nausea swept over him.

"Hadrian found you on the ledge barely conscious about an hour after your last radio call. Do you remember that?"

Eric tried to remember, but only found fog and emptiness. He shook his head slowly.

"Doc said this would be likely. You lost a decent amount of blood, had hypothermia. We had to wake you up every hour the first two days because of the head wound. You picked up an infection, too. Doc treated it the best he could, but it's been touch and go."

"Got infected, huh. How did he treat that?"

"One of the shipments in the bunker had veterinary supplies. Doc gambled that the expired antibiotics would help. You're still breathing and not deaf, so that's a start right?" she said with a nervous laugh.

Even his attempted smile hurt. He realized someone had bandaged his head.

"And this cocoon?" he asked.

"Doc wasn't sure if the meds would help or make things worse. He didn't want you to hurt yourself if you started having convulsions."

"Great, well, can I at least get the sheets off me? I'm broiling to death in here."

It took several minutes of untucking and rolling him over to get him out. He felt better almost immediately.

"You're a lucky guy," Elizabeth said, dabbing his forehead with the rag again.

"Yeah, I remember that much now. Bullet hit my scope first. If it weren't for that," he said trailing off.

Elizabeth shook her head with a faintly concealed grin.

"Well, yes, but that's not what I meant. Leah's watched over you since the moment they put you in that bed."

At a loss for words, Eric blinked a few times with his mouth open.

"You know, I've spent the last, what, four or five months trying to help that girl through her problems? It's obvious she cares about you, Eric. Even if she's too scared to admit it to anyone yet."

Eric smiled as memories of Leah's easy smile over the last few months came to him.

"Yeah, I suppose she's calmed down quite a bit. I think it's been two months since she's snapped at me."

Elizabeth's amiable tone shifted to serious as she asked, "Question is, what do you plan to do about it? Are you actually looking for something?"

"I-I don't know, Liz. Been caught up in all the training, all the stuff to do. I hadn't really had a chance to think about it."

"Well, don't let me hold you back. Don't get me wrong, I'll miss our visits, but from what I've gathered, she's not the kind to simply not get attached. If you're going to tell her no, you need to, soon."

Eric chewed on his lip.

"She's a good girl and has her heart in the right place," Elizabeth said. "You two might be good for each other. Look, have some more water and try to go back to sleep. When Doc said you'd have to be on light duty for at least a week if you pulled through, Turing said he wanted me to teach you actual interstellar navigation next, not just orbital mechanics and orbit changes. He's got a list of practice problems he wants you to be able to solve by the time you're good to get back on your feet."

Eric took the proffered glass of water and emptied it. The sound of the door closing barely registered.

"You awake?"

Leah.

Eric grunted and stretched out. "I guess? How long have I been out?" Eric asked and rolled to face Leah as she sat on the stool. Her clothes were torn and dirty, her hair mussed from the cloth wrap she held in her hands, but Eric's saw little else but the twinkle in her eye and the dimples made by her smile.

"Liz stopped in about four hours ago. She said you were feeling better. You lying to her again?"

Eric couldn't help but return the smile. "Lying? No. 'Better' is a relative term."

She grinned and said, "Well there is that. I just got back in from helping Blaise and his crew. We did a lot of weeding and picking pests. You should see the plants, Eric. I almost want to pull out the carrots right now and eat them."

"Oh?"

"Yeah! They look great. Pascal says we'll be harvesting them along with what's ready from the garlic, onions, and a few others next week. That should help Anne's cooking a bit."

"Oh, right. Didn't you get the garlic and the onions started in those herb boxes you were asking about when we first got here?"

Leah beamed. "Yeah. Turns out I had the right idea. There's no way I could've done what Pascal's been able to do with things, but I did get that right anyway. He's trying to get me more materials so we can have even more ready for next spring.

"I know you've been busy with Hadrian and Byron, but you should see the rest of the fields, Eric. There's so much food, so many beautiful plants. We're going to make it, Eric. I know we are," she said, bubbling with enthusiasm.

I've got to look like a fool, laying here smiling at her like this. Can't help it, that smile's contagious.

"You think so?" he asked.

"Yeah, I talked with Pascal last week. That's actually what I came here to talk to you about when you first got back. Before I found out you were hurt, that is."

"What's that?"

"He wanted to double check his math, so he and I walked the fields last week. If the yields are anything like he expects, we'll have more than enough seed for next year and food to spare, even if the next batch of newcomers is bigger than expected."

"That's great, Leah. You wanted me to come see it?" Eric asked. Something in her tone had suggested something weightier.

"Actually, no. I wanted to tell you I was volunteering. For Hadrian's project. For the militia."

"Woah, hold on."

"What? You don't think I can do it?" Leah asked, an undercurrent of disappointment and hurt nipping at the edges of her words.

"No, no, it's just unexpected. That's all, Leah. Unexpected. I'm sure you can do it. Can I ask what made you decide to volunteer?"

"Well, after talking with Pascal, I realized there will always work to be done, but we've got enough hands to get everything done. He's been reassigning folks to other departments the last few days. Did you know Jorge was a licensed chemist?"

"Jorge? No. Sorry, haven't met him. I'm assuming he was one of the last group that came in?"

Leah nodded. "Him and Jeff have been talking. Terry, too. Now that they got the rest of the machinery from the bunker set up, they think they might be able to do all sorts of things. And," she trailed off.

"And?"

"And well, everyone with a useful skill is off doing more useful stuff than digging in the dirt. Jeff was complaining about needing oils or lubricants or something for everything. Hadrian's been grousing about wanting to make new ammunition from all the brass they've been saving. Jorge said he should be able to set up a lab by the old mill once the construction folks are done rebuilding it. They got the mill mostly working again while you were out, too. I know you haven't met Felix, but he used to be an artist. Worked with glass, he wants to make windows!"

Leah sat there, smiling at him for a few seconds. Eric scratched his chin

"So, not trying to kick you here, but I take it you're afraid you're going to feel useless again?"

Her features wilted a little as she shrugged.

"Yeah, kinda. That's not all of it though. I realized what you do is important, Eric. Just as important as feeding everyone and, well, Hadrian hasn't let on much but I know they're not telling us the worst of it. Just enough to make sure everyone knows the legion people are a threat, and, well, I want to feel like I'm helping more than just making plants grow. I want to feel like I'm in control of myself again. I want to feel alive again, not trapped in my head."

Eric cut to the heart of what he thought she was saying.

"Defenseless."

Her eyes fell to the floor and she shrugged.

"Yeah."

Eric held out his hand. Leah looked at it like it was a wild animal.

"Hon, I'll stand by you if you'll stand by me when the time comes," Eric told her earnestly. Her eyes slowly rose to meet his before she took his hand in hers.

"You barely know who I am. Why would you say that?"

"Barely know you? We spent weeks vacationing together on the *Shrike* and then this sunny planet, how can you say that? You wound me so."

Leah's smile illuminated her face.

"There's the Leah I know. The real you, not the one you're afraid of being."

She grinned wider. "Oh yeah? Who am I then, since you know me so well?"

"Well, I do know you were a lawyer before all this. I was kinda hoping you'd fill me in on the rest. You've been stingy on the details.

I know you're brave and intelligent. Kind. Stronger than you think you are. Beautiful, too."

Leah giggled. "Well I guess I have been a bit tight lipped. What do you want to know?"

Day 189

Eric glanced over to the pile of note paper on the desk beside him. He grumbled, leaning back in his chair. *What the hell am I doing? Why did I agree to this? I am way out of my league here.* The door into the study opened behind him as he sighed.

He looked up from his tablet to find Leah closing the door behind her.

"You look a bit worn out," Eric commented.

"Yeah, I've been up since dawn. We ran a few kilometers and hiked the rest of the day with extra PT thrown in during breaks. For fun, they said."

"Fun?" Eric asked with a smirk.

"That's what they said."

"Doesn't sound like any kind of fun I'm familiar with."

"Me neither. This is the fourth day we've done it this week. I'm about to fall over," Leah told him. She dropped into a nearby chair. "What are you up to?"

"Oh, Turing has me working on orbital mechanics. Liz is helping but some of the math is… unpleasant? Accounting for interstellar drag, nonlinear planet shape and density creating non-linear gravity fields."

"Ick, I was a lawyer, not a physicist. I only took intro to calculus on a dare. Save me the agony, please."

"What? You're plenty bright, Leah. You could handle some of what I'm doing."

"I highly doubt that. I saw your notes. It looked like someone vomited numbers and random letters from several different alphabets all over the page. No thanks." Eric snorted. "Besides which, you were reading your tablet when I came in. Looking stuff up?"

"Nah," Eric replied. "Taking a break from that actually. Was reading some of the old stuff on the tablet."

"Like?"

"It's political theory stuff, mostly."

Leah tilted her head. "Why?"

"What do you mean why?"

"Well, it's not like there's anything you can do with it, not here anyway."

"Oh, well yeah, there is that. It's something different to think about, break up the monotony. Some of this stuff is interesting to think about," Eric said.

"Like what?" Leah asked.

"Well, let's see," Eric glanced down at his tablet and began to read aloud. "The three last numbers of this paper have been dedicated to an enumeration of the dangers to which we should be exposed, in a state of disunion, from the arms and arts of foreign nations. I shall now proceed to delineate dangers of a different and, perhaps, still more alarming kind--those which will in all probability flow from dissensions between the States themselves, and from domestic factions and convulsions. These have been already in some instances slightly anticipated; but they deserve a more particular and more full investigation.

"A man must be far gone in Utopian speculations who can seriously doubt that, if these States should either be wholly disunited, or only united in partial confederacies, the subdivisions into which they might be thrown would have frequent and violent contests with each other. To presume a want of motives for such contests as an argument against their existence, would be to forget that men are ambitious, vindictive, and rapacious. To look for a continuation of harmony between a number of independent, unconnected sovereignties in the same neighborhood, would be to disregard the uniform course of human events, and to set at defiance the accumulated experience of ages."

Leah's brow rumpled and she asked, "Is that even English?"

"It's an acquired taste," Eric told her.

"Sounds like some of the older legal texts I had to read back in law school. Run that by me again." Leah's brow creased further as Eric read the tract again. She held out her hand and asked, "Do you mind?"

Eric smiled and handed her the tablet.

She read in silent concentration for several minutes before looking up at him.

"This is interesting, Eric. I don't know these places they're talking about, but I think I understand what he's getting at."

Eric nodded.

"You don't have a lot of context, either. I spent the last few days reading the history of the era on break just to get context. That paper is one of over eighty published back on old Earth. The country in question had won its independence only a bit over a decade before. Their first attempt at forming a government was a failure at best. Those papers were part of a larger media campaign to sway the public in supporting a change to a new system."

"Did it work?"

"The campaign? Yeah. It worked and they recreated their government. Some of the stuff they talk about in that specific paper though? Yeah, not entirely accurate."

"How so?"

"In the third or fourth paragraph, the author makes a case that the commercial interests would keep the different states from warring with each other. That didn't happen."

"Oh?"

"Yeah, about eighty years later there was a civil war. I suppose I should be fair, it's not that the author was wrong, he just wasn't entirely correct. Same difference as me telling you that if I dropped this apple it'd land on my foot. It would, but it would end up on the floor shortly thereafter. I'd be right in either case, but more correct with the full explanation."

Leah nodded and said, "You see the same thing in law. Word choice is terribly important. Most folks don't seem to ever understand that words mean things."

Eric snickered, "That they do. Though based off of what I've read, it seems that folks are also pretty fond of pretending words mean only what they want them to instead of what they actually mean."

"Truth. Do you think it's possible the author knew there was more to it but didn't say anything? I mean, if it's a media campaign to get folks to sign on, you only have so much time to get people on your side. Why give someone the ten minute explanation for a small part of your argument when you only have twelve to make the whole argument? People only have so big of an attention span and you only have so much time," Leah asked.

"That's entirely possible. Everything else I've seen from these folks has seemed remarkably spot-on. Your theory would make sense."

Leah grinned and handed him the tablet.

"I'll have to borrow that sometime, it sounds interesting. Anyway, I'm going to raid the kitchen for leftovers before I go pass out, want to come with?"

Eric shrugged and stretched as he stood. "Sure."

"Great. I have it on good authority that Anne is hiding some of yesterday's apple pie."

"More apple pie? Why didn't you say that up front? Let's go."

Eric looked up at the opening door as he swallowed the last of the apple pie.

"Oh, hey, Pascal," he said. "If you were after the pie, too late."

Blaise snorted and said, "There was pie? Damn. And here I was, just getting tea."

"Tea? This late?" Leah asked.

"Yeah," Blaise said, "I'm meeting with Turing here in a bit. Me, Denise and Jeff have things to sort out. Figured a little caffeine wouldn't hurt if the meeting ran long. That, and you know Turing. He loves his tea. Might make him a bit more tractable."

"What about?" Eric asked.

"Well, Jeff got the last of the fabricators from the bunker up and running a while ago. I've got some stuff we'll need to get the greenhouse up and running, but I'm pretty sure he doesn't have the raw materials to build some of it. We'll have to brainstorm on how to improvise, if that's even possible. Do some horse trading as it were. I'll have to pony up labor I don't really have to help gather materials, most likely."

"Anything I might be able to help with?"

"What, and have Turing looking over my shoulder the whole time? No thanks."

"Really? I didn't know having me working for you was that bad," Eric groused.

Blaise smirked, "It's not, really. I just know you're doing well with what you're doing. Not saying I couldn't use the help, but I don't want to short-sheet other people if I don't have to. You and the other hunters are making your quotas for the kitchen. As much as my job is to make sure we don't starve in the long term, I'd hate to be the reason we stopped eating as well as we are right now. You remember Fox's bit, morale is damn important and food is morale. We eat worse now, that'll lower productivity across the board, so you helping a few hours or a few days could cost me a lot more than it might gain me."

"How are you doing otherwise?" Eric asked. "Leah's being worked to death by Hadrian. I'm pretty sure she misses your work details already."

Leah rolled her eyes.

"Eh, living the dream, Eric. Living the dream. Well, if by 'the dream' you mean a dream that periodically borders on a nightmare. I always liked everything that came with agronomy. Feel of the dirt under your feet, the smell of--"

"Fresh shit you're spreading as fertilizer?" Eric interrupted.

"Not exactly where I was going with that," Blaise said with a snort. "More like having something you could point at and say you grew it. It's kinda like having kids without having kids. It's rewarding in ways you can't really explain. Always liked being a farmer more than being a pirate, but piracy paid the bills when farming couldn't.

Now? I get to do what I enjoy and possibly end up being a hero for it. Who wouldn't like that?"

Day 302

"There he is," Eric whispered.

"What? Where?" Leah asked just as quietly.

"By the big oak over there," Eric whispered as he slowly pointed. "Now remember, aim a bit back and below from the front shoulder. You want to hit lungs or the heart."

Leah gulped as she brought her rifle to her shoulder.

"Just keep calm. You've shot paper plenty the last three months, you can do this," Eric said. Her suppressed rifle chuffed. The deer jerked its head up and looked about.

"Shit," she groused and went back to her sights.

"Wait," Eric whispered, putting his hand on her shoulder.

The deer took a single step and toppled onto its side.

"Holy shit! I got it! I got it, Eric!" she said, bouncing several times before hugging him with one arm.

"That you did. Square in the gravy pump, I'd say. Good shot, hon. Now I show you how to clean them."

Leah wrinkled her nose at him before grinning even wider and grabbing his hand to drag him onward.

Day 335

Turing looked up from his tablet as Eric entered his study. "I did it. I cracked the file and now I wish I hadn't."

Eric noticed the slur in Turing's words. *Shit, he's been drinking. This is bad.* Eric asked, "Really? When? And why? What'd you find?"

"A few days ago. Been lost in all the data ever since. Humanity's problems haven't changed in the last six hundred years, if not longer. I've only gotten to the early 1800s from modern day and it's depressing, Eric. Everything we know? Lies. All of it. Do you know what history is? History is a bubbling mass of bright spots amid a sea of midnight. Sparks of promise born in an instant and drowned in a sea of turgid idiocy and jealousy before they can illuminate the world. Only a handful survive in any given generation, and their influence is hobbled by limited minds, greed, and weakness.

"Did you know the first nuclear technology tests were accomplished a bit over five hundred years ago? By their calendar, the 1930s? They barely suspected what atoms were less than thirty years before that, but thirty years later they were splitting them. And then what? Fear. Radiation is horrible! Of course it is, cretins, but it's everywhere, what are you going to do, outlaw life? Of course they will. They did, more or less. Tried to anyway. Idiots."

At the confluence of tears and lashing out, Turing's rant ground to a sputtering halt.

"Okay?" Eric asked. "That doesn't make any sense. Why would they do that?"

Turing sighed before continuing in a much quieter tone, "Half of us are too stupid to see reason and lash out like idiot children. At least a quarter are merely masquerading as adults for their own benefit. It's like it isn't that we can't learn, but most choose not to. They choose not to and haven't for hundreds of years. None of this has changed, Eric. Not in five hundred years. From the merest glimmer of understanding to splitting the atom in fifty years. About a decade later, weaponized fusion. And then what? It's too dangerous. Cowards and simpletons. That's why it took you another century to make practical fusion. Too dangerous. And yet those cowards rule us now. They won, Eric. Welcome to the Protectorate. There's no place for 'man' in humanity, only children to be coddled and kept in line while their masters live stolen lives."

Turing picked up the bottle of Irish whiskey next to him and twisted at the top several times before he realized the cap was already off. He shook his head and took a slug straight from the bottle. "History's a wreck, Eric. Our ancestors made it so, but have we managed any better? No? How could they have been such fools? How could we be such fools?"

"Okay, what's this about, Turing? What did you find in that file that's gotten you riled up enough to drink?"

"The key. It's lies. All of it. Fucking lies. Everything I grew up believing was right in the world. All of it. All of it, Eric," Turing growled and then pounded his hand on the desk. "All. Of. It. How can one champion the truth if everything you know is built on lies? How can you be any better than the liars?"

"I got that much, Turing. Care to expand instead of repeating yourself?"

Turing sputtered and then looked mortified. He coughed into his hand a few times.

"The file was filled with more old journals, photos. Stuff that my forebearers refused to delete as ordered but couldn't talk about. I found out how this all started, Eric, the files go back to before the Protectorate was even an idea."

"Now that is interesting. Go on."

"It took me a bit to put it all together. The Protectorate claims to be the only source of good left in this galaxy, but it's simply not true. Sure, we do some good, but our system of government, it's built on lies. Do you know what the Protectorate's official stance on the Confederacy is?"

"Not a clue."

"They're planets the Protectorate couldn't afford to keep. The people too unproductive, too unruly to keep in line. We had no choice but to let the heathens go or they would have dragged us down. The average citizen thinks the Confederacy is populated with backwards, lazy cretins languishing under their own lack of work ethic. The Accorded territories? Same story, but we're told they're better off than the Confederacy, more like us and less like them. You pirates are all savages, scourges of the stars living like jackals off the corpses and refuse of your betters."

"Well, that's mildly insulting."

Turing finally managed a rakish grin.

"Eric, the Accorded territories exist because the Protectorate's last push to take back the Confederacy failed. They spent themselves into oblivion and couldn't prosecute the war any further. They lost billions of lives along with countless ships and dozens of exterminated planets. They ended up suing for peace. That was just over a hundred years ago."

"Okay, I didn't know that."

"No, but your average Confed citizen probably does. Here, only the Inner Party knows. Our government operates with extensive information controls, Eric. Why?"

Eric shrugged and said, "I'm too tired to play intellectual games right now, Turing."

"Because the system would implode the moment people found out they'd been conned, that the entire thing is rigged. I suspected as much when I was younger. My family fell from favor before I was let in on the secret. Now? I have proof. So much proof. All the dirty little secrets."

"The hundred years or so before the Accords, war would sweep across the stars every twenty or thirty years. Protectorate or the Confeds, someone would get impatient and fleets would sail." Turing snorted. "Sorry, I find it funny we still use the term even though a surface naval engagement hasn't been fought in over three hundred years."

Eric nodded. "I can see the humor."

"So, the Protectorate of two hundred years ago was twice the size it is now in number of planets, Eric. The Confederacy three times as many. Populations even larger. Can you imagine? We controlled sixty eight systems to the Confederacy's sixty. And over two hundred years we bombed out seventy four planets. Seventy four. That's not counting moons or orbitals. Think of all those lives snuffed out, gone. Those systems? Where do you think the Reach came from? It's a graveyard, all of it."

Contemplating the scale of the destruction turned Eric's stomach. He found himself dropping into one of the chairs in front of Turing's desk. Turing poured himself a drink and then paused. The man pushed the crystal tumbler of amber fire towards Eric and pulled another tumbler from a drawer.

"Now you start to see it," Turing said, filling the second tumbler. "But I'm not done, this is just the barest outline. That's not why I started drinking. Concerning, yes, but not something to yank the carpet out from under you."

"Okay, so what was, Turing? Not trying to be an ass, but asking the same question over and over again gets tedious."

"Oh, right then. Sorry. What's worse than finding out how heavily edited our histories are? Finding out the motives, the real motives behind why the Inner Party did what they did. It's not just that it was all lies. Anyone should assume the moment a politician's mouth starts moving that he's lying. No, you see, the war against the Confederacy? That was all a distraction."

Eric's whiskey caught in his throat. He beat on his chest as the drink tried to burn its way out.

Eric's eyebrows narrowed and he asked, "From what?"

Turing snorted.

"A distraction for the common people. The Inner Party came up with propaganda to rile them up against the Confederacy."

"To distract them from what?"

"Earth."

Eric sat there, blinking.

"I'm not following."

"You were right, Eric. I was wrong. Earth is dangerous. I-I guess it'd make more sense if I started at the beginning. Context tends to help. The Protectorate of today isn't the original incarnation. Today, we are the Protectorate of Man, the last bastion of civilization amidst the stars bravely fighting against the dying of the light as it were. Before the wars, before the second round of pogroms, mass exterminations, and executions, we had the People's Protectorate of Mankind, breaker of chains, savior of the enslaved, liberator and champion of the oppressed. That's what they claimed anyway. Neither version was better in terms of exterminations. The modern one though? Better focused, I suppose. The People's Protectorate of Mankind became today's Protectorate of Man, not slowly over the course of decades, but in the space of a few short years. And it all started with a single event."

Following Turing's lead Eric poured more whiskey down his throat.

"Before that day, the Protectorate controlled all of space, but keep in mind I say controlled in the loosest sense. What's known as the Confederacy was considered a semi-autonomous territory of sorts then. Systems that were being brought under our wing after being lost to the darkness for so long, if you would. With force when necessary, I'll add. Now, know this, Earth had been under embargo for almost a century when the current Protectorate rose to power." Turing coughed. "I'll get to that in a bit, but Earth was embargoed. The Protectorate fleet swept the system regularly, much like here. Nothing space faring was permitted, landings and communications were closely monitored. And then the fleet monitoring Sol and four populated planets ceased to be such. Populated, in the case of the planets, that is. Multiple fusion devices evaporated major population centers, orbitals vanished in similar flashes of light. The State Security Bureau interrupted the group who'd tried to make Unity planet number five. It seems Earth had sent a message."

Horrified, Eric knocked back what remained in his tumbler and poured himself another as Turing chuckled darkly.

"Still, no one but the Inner Party heard that message. The average citizen heard that extremists in the Confederacy conducted the attack and that meant war. Behind closed doors, the Protectorate conceded Sol to the new masters of Earth and agreed to a treaty forbidding us from the system in exchange for no further attacks."

"But why? That's stupid. They could have just glassed the planet."

"I know. They probably should have, but from what my forebears wrote, the Bureau of State Security couldn't be sure they'd caught them all. The Inner Party wouldn't risk losing more than they already had. And what's sick is that no one outside the Inner Party knew. It was easier for the Party to blame the innocent than it was to own up to their failure. Easier to blame the people of the Confederacy to distract from what really happened. Billions died for their arrogance. Worse yet, the war of false retribution nearly turned into a civil war, and by the end of it, after the denunciations and chaos settled, only a quarter of the Inner Party remained. Billions more were purged, we lost more citizens by our own hands than we did to the Confederacy.

"Today's tradition of being unusually efficient fools must have started then. In all that, they did manage to get around to purging the citizenry of the Earth-based death cult behind the attacks from our systems. Under the cover of night, of course. Well, insomuch as one can do that while murdering twelve billion people. Can't have the average citizen questioning things, can we?"

Stupefied, Eric sputtered and asked, "Twelve billion?"

"Twelve billion. When the dust had settled from the first war, they sent a fleet back to Earth. It was never heard from again. Another planet vanished, another four billion lives. They never tried it again."

"Wait, I thought you said they purged those cultists?" Eric asked.

"I did," Turing replied dryly.

"But how did that planet get bombed?"

"Nobody knows."

"Oh. Well shit."

"It's possible my interpretation of the timelines might be incorrect, some of the writing is fragmented quite badly. Not every file is original, some are recovery attempts from corrupted files."

"That's sick, Turing," Eric said and Turing chuckled. "What?"

"That's not the worst of it. What's truly sick is that none of this had to happen," Turing said.

"Well, of course not."

"No, I don't think you follow. Don't take this like I'm telling you that humanity consisted of only the purest angels before the People's Protectorate came to be, because it wasn't. Far from it, in fact. However, for the people who came to be Inner Party, they had to destroy the old order to build a new one to their liking.

"Before the old Protectorate, all these planets were Earth colonies. Earth didn't have a unified government, it had many different nations with almost as many outlooks on life. An unheard of diversity in thought by our standards, though I suppose it wasn't much different than how the Confederacy operates today. In the Protectorate today though, there is only the party line. Things weren't quite so different in some of the countries then. Some were run nigh identically as we are, but in effect you had dozens, hundreds of party lines globally. Only a handful of them mattered though.

"The major players fell into two major blocs. You had the western nations on one side, the United Kingdom, its client states, and the United States, conveniently a former colony of the UK. On the other, you had the Russian Federation and China, who spent no small effort trying to differentiate between each other, but for all their outward bickering they were close allies."

"I won't bore you with the details, I'll copy you the files sometime so you can read yourself, but suffice it to say those two groups were the only two that mattered in the big picture. The western states prided themselves on the ideals of liberty, even if they weren't near as devout as they were earlier in their history. The Eastern states only cared about control. Does this sound familiar?"

"It sounds like today," Eric commented. Turing gave a quiet clap.

"Point for you. The more things change, the more they stay the same."

"So the Confederacy today is the successor for the Western states?"

"Surprisingly, or maybe not as surprisingly, really. Most of the Confederacy's dominant cultures are descended from those very states or their neighbors. One of them is technically not a descendant if what I've read is true. One of the UK royal family happened to be visiting what we now know as the British Systems when the Protectorate struck."

"Then the Protectorate came from the Eastern states?

"In a manner of speaking. Unity was originally called Novaya Moskva."

"I hear the caveat in your voice. What gives?"

"Well, the Eastern states had locked down on their colonies

fiercely, mostly on information control at first. Trade restrictions followed as the colonies built themselves up and could compete with their native lands. Now, you have to understand that these Eastern states were separate nations with a shared ideology. Both of these Eastern cultures loved the strong man and were infatuated with the State.

"The biggest difference between the two ideological bases, the East and the West, revolves around a very simple concept: who owns you?"

"Well, nobody does."

Turing nodded sagely and sipped his drink.

"Spoken like a Westerner. To the West, the individual was the highest authority and they only answered to whichever deity they worshipped. The State derived its power from the consent of the governed. To the East, the State was the highest authority. The individual lived only to further the interests of the state. No more, no less."

Eric wrinkled his nose and drank from his tumbler.

"Most of the Eastern ideology used the words of a man by the name of Marx as its foundation. For Marx's followers, everything was oppression, everything was struggle even when it wasn't. There was literally no other valid interpretation in their eyes. Much like today, if you challenged the party line, you were branded with whatever labels were necessary to shut you up and then disposed of. Would you be surprised that a non-trivial number in the West worshiped the man's ideas as well? This one of the chief reasons the West had as many issues as it did, that and the Marxists were sadly much better at the propaganda game. Easier and more effective to convince people they were oppressed and someone owed them then to tell a man that his woes were his own making or that the only person who could save him is himself.

"Either way, you can see how control by the Eastern states chafed the citizens of their colonies, yes?

Eric nodded.

"So over the course of time, there came a conspiracy amongst the Eastern colonies. Technically nothing major at first considering they couldn't do anything about their positions but fume. That and their parent states kept a close eye on them. Or thought they did."

"Yeah, I'm not seeing how this turns into the fall of civilization," Eric prompted.

Turing gave a dark smile and quietly said, "Enter my forebearers and Turing Interstellar, the largest shipping and industrial conglomerate in the West. Secret channels were formed, promises made, bribes paid, and one day, as far as a citizen on Earth was concerned, the world ended."

Turing shook his head at Eric's lack of reaction.

"Turing Interstellar had connections to every major industry that existed. You'd have to in order to achieve market dominance the way they had. They also had a supply of massive old, mothballed ships they'd never gotten around to quite scrapping yet. Under the auspices of a holding company, one of their ventures bought old ships, another refitted them. Some of them were legitimately resold, but a large number of them were converted for a variety of uses. In a company that big, even things as big as starships can fall through the cracks. And they did. Purposefully.

"The primary refit the conspirators made to these 'lost' ships essentially created large drone fireships. A fireship's only goal in life is to get close to a target, ramming it if possible, and detonate. Ships like that took out most of the main orbitals in Sol. Shipyards, military docks, vessels. A surprising percentage of Earth's forces were neutralized by an empty hull stripped of everything but the necessary operating components. Financially speaking, it was genius. Hell, from an intelligence standpoint, it was genius. Nobody saw it coming because the number of people involved were kept to a minimum. As for the military side, it must have been a terrible thing to pour fire into an oncoming vessel and it simply kept coming despite the fusillade.

"Eh, I digress. Eventually they needed people. They needed someone to conduct the negotiations. While the orbitals were burning up on reentry, Earth governments were informed that their signed capitulations were to be submitted within the hour. Four nations objected. Care to guess which four?"

"That's fairly obvious."

"True. Most of inhabited China disappeared under orbital bombardment ten minutes after the deadline. A bit over two billion people gone in minutes. The early Protectorate had a thing about quantity. The Americans responded with surface to orbit weaponry. Took out a decent number of ships before they were EMPed and the ten most populous cities vaporized. The Russian Federation submitted five minutes later. The United Kingdom, seven."

"That's--"

"Horrific? Awe inspiring? Either appellation works. So, you see, Turing Interstellar single-handedly waged war on all the governments of Earth. All at once. And we won. We. The others that helped up? They became Inner Party. They supplied manpower, financial backing, but without my forbearers there would be no Protectorate. And for what? They gave us this planet, but was that truly what my forebears wanted? Maybe they wanted to live like kings, perhaps? Does it matter? Did it ever matter? They burnt humanity to ash because they fought for an ideology of poison. Greed and hate. I wonder, did they think that maybe this time their ideals would work? That somehow they could ignore the cumulative experience of Man throughout history like it meant nothing? Were they so arrogant to think that this time, Marx would work because this time they had all the right people and all the right knowledge? Just like every fool before them? And to think we traded liberty for slavery.

"And now you see why I am drinking myself silly today."

"So," Eric began flatly. "You're why we can't have nice things."

Silence strangled the room for several seconds while Turing gaped. *Might've overstepped on that one.* A smirk broke Turing's mask of shock and he broke into dark laughter.

"Point for you. Well played, sir."

Day 350

Sitting on the porch steps lost in thought, the sound of footsteps behind him didn't register.

"Nawgale," Eric muttered to himself.

"What?" Byron asked, peering down at him. "What did you say?"

"Oh, sorry, didn't hear you come up to me. Nawgale huayheh."

Byron shook his head slowly and said, "You mean, ná géill choíche."

"That's what I said."

Byron chuckled, "No, that's what was lodged in your mouth. That's my native tongue you're butchering and I'm highly curious as to where you heard that phrase."

"You remember when Frost put me in medical back on the *Shrike*?"

Byron slowly nodded.

"The ship's doctor told me that before he turned me over to Hettinger. What's it mean?"

"Interesting. Very interesting."

"That doesn't make any sense."

Byron snorted, realizing Eric's mistake. "No, that the doctor would tell you that. Our language has a lot of nuance in pronunciation. Simply put, he told you 'never surrender' or 'give them nothing.'"

"So he was a Caledonian agent?"

"Now you see why I find that interesting."

"I mean, I'm pretty sure that was when I started having issues with my memory. Do you think he's the one who gave me those nanites Turing said I was dosed with?"

"Anything is possible. Some possibilities sure seem convincing, don't they?"

Eric stared at the grinning Caledonian intelligence agent before slowly shaking his head.

"So, what are you up to, Eric?" Byron asked.

"Taking a break from studying. Figured I'd come out here, get some fresh air, and watch Hadrian run the volunteers in circles a bit. You?"

"Oh, the same. You sure you aren't shirking and hoping Leah will come over here once they're done with morning PT?"

Eric grinned. "Anything is possible. Some of the possibilities sure seem convincing, don't they?"

Byron chuckled. "Touché, sir. Touché. I'll leave you to it. Places to go, people to kill, secrets to steal. You know how it goes."

Day 362

"Don't be too terribly hard on yourself," Turing told Eric. "Chemistry is a fair bit easier to study when you have a lab and plenty of reagents."

"I did that badly?" Eric asked and slumped on the stool. His eyes fell to the kitchen floor.

"Not as well compared to the other topics we've covered so far, but quite well by most academic standards. I will have to thank Jorge for his time. It doesn't appear to have been misspent at all," Turing commented as he poured boiling water for his tea.

"So what's next?" Eric asked.

"I'm thinking a few more specialties of math. After that? Maybe economics."

"Economics? That's just more math. Math, math, and more math."

Turing belly-laughed. "Econ is a fair bit more than that, Eric. I don't have an economist on staff, and honestly, I wouldn't let a Protectorate economist teach you. I'll lend you one of our econ books so you have an idea where we went wrong, but there's actually an excellent discussion of economics on your tablet by a man named Thomas Sowell."

Eric nodded. *Some of the stuff I've read--*"Turing, what makes economics so hard for most people?"

"Evidently, when you put a currency symbol in front of the numbers, it makes math harder," Turing replied.

Eric shared a grin and checked his watch.

"Have somewhere to be?" Turing asked.

"Not really? Leah's patrol was supposed to be back six hours ago."

"Understandable thing to worry about. I'm sure she's fine. She's out with Hadrian and the others from this batch of recruits. I'm sure if there were issues, we would have heard about it over the link by now."

Eric jerked in his chair by a thump in the hall. *Was that the door?*

In the hall outside, Hadrian's voice boomed with urgency, "Read, go get Doc."

Doc? Leaping from his stool, Eric's mind went to dark places. He rushed out of the kitchen and nearly collided with one of the recruits in the hall.

"Sorry," the man blurted as he sidestepped him at nearly a run.

Eric blinked. Blood coated the man's coat and had dribbled a trail down the hall. *Oh shit.*

"Leah?" Eric yelled as he ran for the foyer.

Hadrian stepped into the doorway with his hand up, blocking Eric. Amidst the piles of gear and packs behind the man in the foyer, two frightened recruits tended to a prone figure lying on a tarp.

"Hadrian," Eric growled, "Move."

"You don't want to see this," Hadrian said.

Eric's eyes narrowed to slits. "Move or I'll move you myself."

The two exchanged determined glares a moment before Hadrian nodded and stepped back.

Eric rushed to the prone figure and knelt at her side, "Leah?"

Her eyes flittered open.

"Eric?" she asked, her voice little more than a whisper. "Eric?"

He took her dirty hands in his and squeezed them. She reeked of spent gunpowder and blood.

"I'm here, hon. I'm here." Tears welled in his eyes and he wiped them away. "What happened?"

The recruit nearest to him looked away. Eric counted heads.

"Hadrian? Where's Chris?"

"Outside in a tarp."

"Drink," Turing told him and handed Eric another tumbler. "Hadrian, now that Doc has seen to Leah and we know she'll be okay, what exactly happened?"

"We were on our way back when Chris came across some tracks. I looked at them. Tracks from six people. Since we were the only ones out that direction, we followed them. Turned out to be twelve." Hadrian's expression darkened before he finished, "We lost Lance Corporal Taylor in the first few seconds. Leah risked herself to recover his weapon. That grenade launcher is the only reason everyone else walked away. If this were a regular line unit, I'd recommend both of them for medals."

"You're a much better tracker than that," Turing commented flatly through steepled fingers.

"The tracks were for six. The others had to be another group that came in from somewhere else. I'll go back tomorrow and check the tracks though, it wasn't but an hour outside the wall."

Byron frowned and said what everyone was thinking, "They must have found another way here."

Turing brooded while the rest sat in silence.

"I have a few observation units that could be moved," Turing eventually said. Everyone looked at him. "We'll need more laser repeaters set up if we're going to make it work. It will stretch what little processing power is left in the medusa, but we have the topography maps and there's only so many ways into this valley from their direction. We might be able to cover the majority of them if we're creative."

Eric rocked back in his chair and said, "A medusa? That's how you've been monitoring the pass?"

Both Turing and Byron nodded back, but Turing spoke, "It was the only way. I'd hoped to have some level of overlap off the sensors so more of the processing could be kept on the local devices, but this is too much area to cover, especially with only one blade in the chassis. The other wouldn't boot up. Ideally, you'd want a cluster and five times as many optical sensors."

"You know a whole lot about how they're used," Eric groused with no small amount of suspicion.

"I would. I knew the man who designed the prototype. We went to the University together; it was his thesis project. I might have helped refine the initial designs a smidge. Everyone, you can go. Hadrian, stay. We need to discuss expanding your project again. It appears we need to teach the Legion to stay on their side of the mountain."

"And so today we lay to rest our cherished friend and valued comrade. Lance Corporal Chris Taylor gave his life so that others may live. Greater love hath no man than this, that a man lay down his life for his friends. Major, render honors."

Eric bowed his head as Turing continued and the words washed over him. Leah shifted in uncomfortable silence next to him as she clenched her one good hand. Eric laid his hand on hers as Hadrian barked orders to the honor guard when Turing finished.

"Ready! Aim! Fire!"

They both jerked when the honor guard fired the first volley. She clutched his hands like a vice at the second. Eric felt her tremble at the third.

"Present, arms!"

Both Eric and Leah snapped a final salute as the coffin descended into the hole.

When the ceremony had finished and the crowd began to drift away, Eric stood riveted to the spot. Leah squeezed his hand and he looked up at the mound of fresh earth. After a final salute, Eric turned to help Leah stand.

Peace in Our Time

DAY 365

"So, I've been thinking," Leah said, handing him his tablet.

"What about?"

"Well, I've read a few of the political theory bits. I found Algernon Sydney and the Bastiat pieces fascinating, but I'm pretty sure I need to be more up to speed on the history. Maybe I'm blind, I just didn't find them, but all the talk on how government should work and all that. Well, like I was saying, I was thinking and, well, why have government at all?"

"I'm not following?"

"Well, the Protectorate's government is supposed to protect its people, right?"

"Ostensibly, sure. It's easy to say one thing and do the other. That and, no offense, you Protectorate types have an awfully odd idea of what protecting people means."

"Hmm, well, what I was thinking was if we can't trust politicians to do the right thing, why not just do away with all of them? We don't have any politicians here and shit works, right?"

"Not exactly," Eric said, pausing to consider his next words carefully.

"Okay?" Leah asked a few moments later when he didn't continue.

"Well, first off, we do have a politician. Just one. Turing. Primarily, it works because we're small scale and Turing isn't so big of an ass we can't stand him. Not having any other viable alternatives other than starvation doesn't hurt, either. That said, anarchy isn't a thing, really."

"How so?"

"Well, I get the impression from what I've read that society is self-assembling. You simply can't have no government, it builds itself whether you want it to or not. What that ends up as comes in only a few flavors. You have rule by one, rule by few, rule by many, rule by law, and rule by none."

"Okay?" Leah prompted when Eric fell silent a few moments to collect his memory.

"If you accept that a single person simply does not and cannot have the time or ability to coordinate everything, rule by one becomes rule by few. Monarchy and the rest are essentially the same thing with prettier words and justifications. Oligarchy. I suppose that's a better word for what we have here now that I think of it. Turing has all his department heads. Rule by many? In a democracy the majority sets the rules. Simple majority and you get your way. Every case I've read about, this system falls apart because the people are, I believe the phrase was ambitious, vindictive, and rapacious. Eventually the strain results in open violence against the various factions which leads to rule by none.

"But rule by none is little more than a way station on the way to somewhere else. People will always have problems they can't fix on their own and they'll turn to someone else to try to fix them. Imagine if you reset society and now nobody was in charge. How long do you think it would be before someone decided they wanted to be in charge? How long after that do you think it'd be before someone rose to the top? When that someone else has enough people turning to them, they might as well be the government, at least insomuch as authority is concerned. And that's despotism and back to oligarchy in almost every case.

"Rule by law boils down to an attempt to restrain the government just as much as it restrains the people. The law dictates what's right, not a single dictator or his cronies. If you do it right, the law is a reflection of the people not the will of well-connected men.

"So really it boils down to oligarchy or the rule of law in a Republic. Neither of which are permanent. I don't know about you, but I'm not a fan of the chosen few dictating to me how to live."

Leah frowned and brushed her hair back but didn't speak.

"As a pirate, I grew up with what most might think of as anarchy. Ship's captains set the rules on their boats. The owners of the various stations set their rules. Everyone has their own little fiefdom where they're king and when you're in another king's territory, you step mighty lightly. Even then, that's not really anarchy, not by definition. It's just a web of oligarchies that may or may not even bother cooperating. Even the pirates can't make anarchy work.

"Hell, the only agreement that connects them is the Compact, but aside from a few choice points, I don't know more about it. It's supposed to dictate how pirates deal with each other out in the black when the normal rules aren't so easily enforced. I'm not sure what would happen if someone attacked the pirates as a whole. Your guess is as good as mine, but I don't really see all those kings cooperating to defend people they don't know and never cared to know. The system would shatter.

"So yeah, if I had to pick, I'd live in a Republic as long as we could keep it. Though, keep in mind, I'm still reading the history and the like so I might not have a good picture, but that's my uninformed opinion."

Leah looked at the floor a few moments before commenting, "Maybe you're right. You've read a lot more on this than I have yet."

Eric laid his hand on her shoulder.

"Sorry, I'm not trying to be a dick about it. It's just, reading all this history, I get frustrated with how people have handled things. That's not your fault, I'm sorry."

"It's okay, I guess. I just don't like not knowing what you're talking about sometimes."

"Well, it's not like there's a rush, hon. We've got pretty much all the time in the world and it's not like we need to hammer out a new government tomorrow. You'll be caught up in no time. Are you feeling okay?"

"About as well as can be expected, I guess."

"Eh, I got wrapped up talking about history and it occurred to me that you're still dealing with Chris's loss on top of all this."

"I'm fine, Eric. Or as fine as anyone has a right to be. Chris died. Nothing I can do will change that. Like Byron told me, I just need to make sure I live up to his sacrifice."

Eric nodded as he squeezed her hand. He said, "Speaking of having time, did you find the media cache on this thing?"

"Media cache?"

"Oh, you'll love this. Here, let me find the one I watched last week. It was ancient long before this tablet was made."

"What's it called?"

"Full Metal Jacket."

Day 391

"Captain Friedrich?" an unfamiliar voice called out behind him. Eric smirked at the irony of his new militia rank as he had nearly every time someone called him by it. *Leave it to the pirate to be a captain, but not a Captain.*

"Ceasefire on the firing line," Eric called out and turned around to find an unfamiliar young man jogging toward him, huffing.

"Sir, Major MacGregor told me to come get you. Something big is going on."

Damn, that can't be good.

Eric turned and growled at the newest batch of recruits, "Everybody take five. Sergeant, we might be done with this exercise for the day. See that they start on cleaning their weapons when break's over."

"Yes, sir," Leah said with a grin. As he stalked off toward the manor house, her best drill instructor voice carried over the sound of the running saws at the mill down the way. "All right, maggots, you heard the captain, range session is over."

Eric was still smirking at just how incongruous that voice was to her normal demeanor when he stepped onto the porch. *Watching all those old war movies on Mournealt's tablet while she recovered may have been a bad idea.*

Julien opened the back door.

"They're waiting for you in Turing's study," the Orleanian said. Eric noted the sour tone, but thanked the man anyway before making his way down the hall.

"And you think we can trust them?" Byron was asking as Eric entered the study.

"Not in the slightest, but what choice do we have?" Turing said.

"Perkins can put one in the guy's head and we can go on like we were, for one," Hadrian snarled.

"Woah, hey, someone mind catching me up here?" Eric asked the assembled militia leadership.

Byron sighed and shook his head before saying, "Our esteemed Colonel Gliar made contact ten minutes ago."

"What? I thought we were still shooting them on sight?" Eric asked.

"We are. Perkins couldn't pull the trigger," Hadrian spat. "Single guy showed up in the pass waving a white flag. Perk had one of the sweeper teams go up to check it out."

"You're shitting me?"

"No," Byron said. "The guy claims to be one of Gliar's majors here as a diplomatic gesture. Julien told them he had to get leadership together before making any commitments and not to expect an answer in less than a half hour."

Eric nodded. "Great, so they know we have radio that works and doesn't get us smoked by the drones. That could be good or bad."

"Or both," Byron muttered.

"Or both," Eric said. "Surveillance?"

"None of the monitors show any identifiable human movement beyond the one intruder," Byron stated.

"So what does this Major say they want?" Eric asked.

"Nothing, really," Turing said.

"Nothing? Well, we can afford that, right?" Eric said, grinning.

"Not nothing," Hadrian said. "According to this guy, Colonel Gliar apologizes for encroaching on our territory and would like to negotiate some form of non-aggression pact so he stops losing people to our snipers."

"You're serious?" Eric snorted and looked at the others, "He's serious?"

"Like a shot to the gut," Hadrian replied.

"Well, shit," Eric stalled and rubbed the bridge of his nose. "Hadrian, you're obviously against. Turing, you're for. Byron?"

"Leaning against. Not enough information, but the legion has never been known to be honorable in any setting. I can't imagine that would change now," the old commando said. "At best, we might save some ammunition in the short term, but we'd risk waking up with our throats slit." Byron shrugged at Turing's scowl over that comment and added, "It's what I'd do."

Eric turned to Turing, "Well, unless you overrule us, then it's settled. No negotiating. If they want to stop losing men, then they avoid the valley and any pass entering it."

Turing sighed and looked up from his desk, "Fine. Major, relay the terms to Perkins."

"Roger that, Colonel," Hadrian said sourly and left the room.

Seriously? We finally start getting our shit together and now all this drama? Kids today.

Day 411

Eric glanced over to Leah and squeezed her hand. The two shared a short private smile as Turing stood and tapped his glass with his fork.

"Normally we spend the winter solstice celebrating our accomplishments for the year, but this year we have something special,"

Turing said from the head of the table. "Of course, not to minimize what we have accomplished. We've seen the best year here that I'm aware of. We've had the best harvest I've ever seen thanks to Mister Pascal. Thanks to the efforts of Ms. Carter and her people, we've rebuilt the mill, started on a greenhouse, and so much more. Seeing as I'm not fond of long speeches, please allow me to introduce our newest couple, Mister and Misses Friedrich."

Leah blushed as the room filled with applause and cheers.

"Thanks," Eric told the well-wishers.

"Back home, there'd be forms to fill out, licenses and all that, but it seems we're a bit short on bureaucracy here on Solitude, so as the presiding government official, I can only wish you well and hope that you enjoy the evening's festivities," Turing told the pair.

As the man returned to his seat, the improvised band began to play. They weren't much, but on the shortest, coldest day of the year, not much was required. As time ticked on, Eric wasn't sure if they were actually playing better or if it was just the drink getting to him.

"You know, I never would have guessed that Byron knew anything about distillation or brewing," Leah told him sometime later that night. She nearly had to shout to be heard over the crowd.

"Yeah. The beer and ale isn't bad, but some of this stuff still tastes like jet fuel," Eric leaned in and replied. "I think he said it was something he learned from his son."

Leah's eyes widened and she glanced over at the door where Byron and Julien were talking.

"Wait, the old goat has family?"

Eric grinned and nodded.

"Didn't think he had it in him. Or her, in this case, whoever she is."

"Was," Eric added.

"Oh, that's sad."

Eric nodded. "He hasn't said much beyond what I just told you. Doesn't talk about life back home at all, really."

"I can understand that," Leah said.

A sudden look of consternation made him ask, "What is it, hon?"

"I was just thinking, Eric. I realized that I've been happier the last three months than I think I ever was back on Celion. Is that bad?"

Head cocked to the side, Eric asked, "Why would that be bad?"

"Well, I had everything going for me. I'd just made junior partner in the law firm I was working at. I finally stopped worrying about being able to pay the bills. I guess, looking back, everything was just dropping into place. I was set. Here though? It's so totally different. I was sure we were all going to starve or freeze to death by now for the longest time. And now, I don't think I'd trade places with the old me, even if it meant I could avoid how I got here, too. I'd have to give you up to do that."

Eric blushed and said, "Aww, well, I love you, too."

They sat back and watched the crowd together. More than once he caught his wife absentmindedly smiling and rubbing the ring on her finger he'd made her with Jeff's help.

The fourth time, he asked her, "You like the ring?"

She blushed, realizing what she'd been doing.

"Of course I do, silly. I told you when you gave it to me. I still can't believe you made us both rings."

"Well, you can thank Jeff for them looking like rings instead of globs of metal shit."

Leah shook her head at him, grinning.

Eric kissed his wife and told her, "I'm going to find Turing and thank him for all this. When I get back, maybe we can head back to our room?"

Leah grinned back at him. "You do that. I think saw him over at a table there in the far corner."

Eric made his way over and found Turing lounging in the corner with a tumbler in his hand looking rather pleased with himself.

"Turing," Eric said with a nod.

"Eric," Turing said, replying with a nod of his own. "Enjoying yourself?"

"It's been a great evening. Anne's cooked up another master-piece. Happy to see she's got a new assistant, too. You?"

"Just happy to see everyone enjoying themselves. I don't think this house has seen a night like tonight in a very long time. I know I haven't."

"I heard the last group had a programmer in it," Eric said.

"Oh? Wesley? He's okay, I guess. He'd be better if his ego would get out of the way."

"Sounds like one of our new volunteers. He's a good kid, I guess. Hadrian's had me riding his ass the last two weeks trying to get him to wake up and see what's going on."

Turing's smile weakened momentarily. "Good luck with that. This last batch of drop-offs is proving decidedly less useful than expected. Something has changed upstairs and I'm not sure what. We might have to go back to being selective on who we let in again if this doesn't change."

Eric nodded. "That's possible. Anyway, I wanted to let you know my bride and I are retiring for the night."

Turing wobbled to his feet. He shook Eric's hand with a conspir-atorial smile and said, "Enjoy the rest of your evening, Eric."

Day 607

Eric flopped the latest exam on Turing's desk and said, "Turing, if you're going to keep running me through math, could you give my brain a little time to congeal first? It's a bit melty right now."

Turing snorted.

"I figured we'd spend a bit, a week at least, recapping what you've covered so far to make sure you're actually retaining all this. The economics won't phase you at this point, but I do have some engineering textbooks and adequate teachers we can use to mix things up a bit."

Eric sighed and Turing regarded him with mock disappointment.

"Eric, you do realize we're only teaching you at the rate you're soaking up the information, correct? Honestly, I'm surprised you've made it this far at the pace you've set yourself. My professors would be scandalized."

"Huh?"

"You, a pirate, capable of outpacing most of those I knew at the University? And across this many subjects? Most people tend to only absorb a narrow field. I'd bet even the old sciences dean would be forced to grudgingly admit your accomplishments so far are impressive. You're easily in the ninetieth to ninety-fifth percentile, perhaps higher."

"I'm pretty sure that's good, right?"

Turing grinned and shook his head. "Oh, of course. It is quite good. Percentiles and quartiles are covered in stats, but we haven't gone over that in detail yet. The ninetieth percentile places you in the top ten percent. Though, to be honest, once you get so far up the measure ceases to have much meaning beyond extremely bright."

"So, pacing, huh? The University teaches at a self-paced speed as well?"

"Depends on the class level. The lowest tier classes not so much. So many students, not enough professors. Students are also encouraged to take a wide variety of classes. This is partially on the belief in a well-rounded education and partially to help people find what they're truly interested in."

"That seems like a waste of time. I mean, it's inefficient, isn't it? If you're expected to pay for your time there, why waste money on classes you'll never use?"

"True, which is why the University is set up the way it is. The introductory level classes are very low cost. Of course, the University is entrusted to develop the brightest minds in the Protectorate so it's very easy for the exceptionally bright to obtain tuition waivers, partial or otherwise."

"So how long is the average stay?"

"That depends. Students are allowed to stay so long as they are progressing at a satisfactory rate for the level they're at. When whichever party decides the student has had enough, they tally the amount of credits and assign the applicable degrees. That's how I managed to get mine in the ten years I attended."

"Ten years? How's that work? You're thirty-five, right? Five years here, five on the run. If that started when you graduated, you were twenty-five."

Turing smiled. "The University does not care about a student's age, only their academic accomplishments and potential. My family being who they were probably didn't hurt, either."

"Yeah, I'd imagine that whole Inner Party thing didn't hurt at all."

Turing smirked. "Neither does founding the school and providing over half the annual operating budget. Oh, while it is on my mind, we haven't heard a peep from the Legion in a while. Hadrian is toying with the idea of sending a scouting party over to their side of the mountain if this keeps up."

"Joy. Maybe if we're lucky, they hunted out their food supply and either starved off or moved farther away."

"We're never that lucky."

Day 815

"This just keeps getting better," Eric said to himself as he peeled back the lid off the tin. *Not a fan of pickled fish. Muffin would be going nuts for this shit though.* He shivered from the cold, wishing he could make a fire. *Not yet, they could still find me.* He popped the sardines into his mouth one after another, hoping if he ate them fast enough he wouldn't taste them. *God I hate these. Better than starving. Though not by much.*

He washed the sour taste from his mouth with the remainder of the flavored water he'd made with the drink mix packets he'd found in the Cerberus supply crate in the pine needles next to his feet.

Eric eyed the crate again, looking for any sign of its age. There weren't any dates on it, but the few he'd recovered before were weathered about the same.

"Are you new?" he absent-mindedly asked the crate. "Or have you been sitting here for a year since the last drop we've found?"

The pines around him whispered louder as the wind picked up. Eric leaned over, peering between the branches of the tree he was under. Dark clouds choked the horizon to the west.

"Well, that's not good," he mumbled to himself. "Okay, supplies, say goodbye to your crate. I need to get back on the right side of the mountain before those clouds catch up. I'm not getting caught up here in that. Not a fan of mountain thunderstorms or blizzards."

Two hours later, Eric found himself ducking into a cave just short of the saddle he'd used to cross over two weeks earlier. *Only so far you can push yourself in these altitudes without extra oxygen. Wish I'd had space for one of those old masks.*

"Fuck my life," he muttered as the clouds unleashed a torrent of blinding snow. Periodically the blinding swarm would flash brilliantly followed several short seconds later by muted thunder. *It's a thunderstorm and it's also snow. Thundersnow?* He stood watching, hoping for some sign he could be on his way soon. *Nah, I'm going to be stuck here a while.* Something skittered across the rocks behind him.

Eric spun, rifle up and squeezed the trigger pad on his foregrip. Bathed in brilliant light, the cave's front chamber clearly empty. A crevice leading further into the cave twisted out of view.

"Oh, don't be shy now," he told the cave as he cautiously advanced. "I already know you're there. Come on out."

Hearing nothing, Eric crept forward. *You know, I think this is high enough that nothing really totally thaws out.* Eric froze as a barely perceptible musk wafted by. *Aww shit, I know what that is.* As he tugged aside the retaining strap of one of his spare magazines a reflection head caught his eye. Just inside the second chamber some twenty meters further down the bend Eric found a mass of matted fur and bones. Several seconds passed before he recognized the mostly skeletal remains of a wolverine. An ice axe hung from a hole in the side of its skull. Long scratches in the bone near the hole made it clear that more than one blow had been required to seat the blade.

"You don't see that every day," Eric said to himself after several moments of consideration.

Another set of bones and tattered material, this one human, lay a handful of meters away from the wolverine. *Scavengers.* Eric spat and glanced bout to find the missing leg half hidden in the wolverine remains. *That's a shitty way to go. Well, you got him, too, buddy.*

Eric found another set of human remains, this one intact, on the far side of the chamber. This person had died bent over a rock but had no immediately obvious cause of death. The discoloration of what remained of the skin threw him for a second. He realized her cold weather pants had been around her ankles when she died. *The shit is this?*

He looked at the body from several angles, but the details refused to fit together. He began to turn when he noticed the tattered clothing, had lettering on it. *PMV Relentless? Wait.* Eric looked closer at the discoloration of the hood and pulled it back. The remains of long dark hair spilled out and Eric found the killing blow. Someone had driven an ice axe into the back of her head.

"Oh, you've got to be fucking kidding me," Eric blurted. "What kind of sick fuck does--no, this is not what it looks like. I've been stuck on this goddamn planet forever, but I will not believe that."

Eric glanced between the human corpses. *One ice axe, a rope, and, there on the rock, a compass.* The ghost of an old memory stirred. *No. Not only no, but hell no.* Eric left the macabre scene behind, refusing to contemplate it any further. *This fucking planet has gone too far.*

He walked to the mouth of the cave and sat, studiously removing every memory of what lie behind him. He turned his eyes to the snow outside with purpose. Entranced by the whirling chaos outside, Eric lost the passage of time until a faint buzzing reached his ears through the white haze. Curiosity piqued, he straightened up and then lurched to his feet. The whine proceeded to get progressively louder.

"That's a--no, it's, shit. It's a drone," Eric muttered to himself and started scooting farther back into the cave. *Those things have optics that can see in this shit.* The snow outside strobed. A second later, muffled thunder reached him. A muted pop followed moments later.

Several more pops split the air a heartbeat after the first and the droning roar shot into a throaty whine.

Eric stood and curiously peeked out into the whiteout. *Whatever that is, it's heading this*—The snowstorm lit up with a deafening roar and the ground shook.

Holy shit. Eric rubbed his eyes furiously while debris fell from the cave ceiling. He blinked away the afterimage and spotted a rapidly fading glow in the distance.

"I don't think anyone's seen a drone that close. Or what's left of one," Eric muttered, watching the flickering glow of the crash site. He paused in his steps. "No, it can wait. As hot as that is, finding it once the snow's let up will be easy. Don't want to get lost in this shit, that's death."

Back under the lip of the cave, Eric sighed.

"No, if I were in charge up there, I'd send someone the moment I found out my drone crashed. This place is going to be flooded with troops soon. That or they'll hit it with something big to keep anyone from recovering it. Well shit."

Eric grabbed his pack and his rifle and stepped out into the snow.

The things I put up with here.

Though the glow guttered and eventually vanished before he arrived, Eric found little trouble in following the trail of smoldering wreckage. First he found a small section he figured was a tail fin, then a long trail of skewed shards punctuating the snow. An obvious control surface lead him to believe that had been part of a wing. The creaking and popping of rapidly cooling metal lead him onward to the steaming remains of the battered and blackened hull amid a small lake of semi-frozen mud. A thin layer of snow was just beginning to stick on the surface.

"Damn," Eric muttered as he fished out his tablet and took hurried photos as he circled the wreck looking for anything that appeared useful. Several minutes of slogging around the shattered drone produced nothing. Eric sighed with resignation. *Nothing. Dammit. Hey, is that an access panel?* Seeing lettering next to the hatch, he wiped off the soot and grime to find a simple label: avionics access.

"What have we here?" Eric mumbled. He frowned a few seconds later as prying at the panel with his boot knife only bent the edges and caused bits of the fractured coating to flake off. The shorn spar he retrieved from the drone's shattered wing provided enough leverage to pop the crumpled panel clear off. *Cheater bar always wins.* Eric stared at the mangled electronics behind the panel. *Shit, oh well--heh, bingo.*

A metal box sat nestled in the back, half hidden by loose cabling and broken, half-melted circuit boards. He gingerly reached into the mess and carefully tugged out it out of its retainers. High bandwidth data connectors plastered the back end of the case. With a slow grin, he turned the case over and popped the latches.

"Bingo. Turing will find this interesting. Now to get the hell out of here."

Eric had barely made it a kilometer when he heard the arrival of the first drone and ducked into a copse of pines. Not long after, echoes from a series of explosions rippled through the mountainside. The pattern repeated three more times in the next hour. Still as a mouse and freezing, Eric waited another four hours before he emerged and made off for home.

Day 817

"Good to see you," Turing said as Eric pushed open the door to the man's study. "I was worried the bombing indicated we were wrong about the relays. Did you find Gliar's men?"

"Find them? Yes, but this might be a little more important," Eric said and dropped his pack. He fished the case out and tossed it to Turing.

"What is--no, where did you get this?" Turing said breathlessly.

"Those explosions weren't random. One of their drones came down in the snow storm."

"And you recovered this from the crash site?"

"And they pounded it with everything a few minutes after I'd left."

"Speak of this to no one. Not even Byron and Hadrian until we speak again on this."

"But--"

"No buts, Eric. You never came back with this. I'll get what data I can off of these drives, but I can't promise anything useful."

"You've heard the grumblings, Turing. Folks need a morale boost."

"Oh, they do. Trust me, I know. That morale boost will be temporary at best when this comes back to be nothing. With the discontent as of late, it might even hurt morale more than it helps. There's already a sizable faction of these newcomers questioning our judgement. If this gets out and nothing comes of it, that discontent will spread. What about your original mission?"

Eric sighed. *No use in rehashing that argument.*

"Well, you'll be happy to know that Chris's intelligence was right. Gliar's people are spread out over a wide area on the other side. Temporary camps. It looks like they move every few months, probably to keep from hunting out an area."

"Probably," Turing concurred.

"The whole time I was out, I didn't hear a gunshot. The hunters I did find were using spears and bows, but they did have firearms on them so they're not out of ammunition. It would make sense if they were conserving that ammunition for something more important, I think. Probably us."

"That is likely."

"Either way, I have photos and video. It could've been a lot worse. I was worried I'd find just empty camps."

Turing nodded. "I'd worried something similar. Not a peep from them this year had me on edge. This narrows things down a bit. Actually, find Hadrian and Byron and let them know I want to see them this evening at their earliest convenience, would you? I need to streamline the chain of command a bit. How do you feel about additional responsibility?"

"About the same as I've felt with all the other responsibilities you've given me. No extra pay, no extra vacation time. Why are you smiling?"

Day 830

Eric looked up at the door to his new office.

"Enter," he said. "Oh, Elias. Please, have a seat," Eric followed up, hurriedly finishing signing off on another project Denise was asking about. He closed his email and sat back. "What can I do for you, Doctor?"

"Well, first I'd like to congratulate you on your promotion," the doctor said.

Eric tried not to roll his eyes at what he saw as blatant manipulation. He had an email chain going back several months between him, Byron, and a few others about problem children showing up to bitch about how things were being done, about how things would be so much better if the decisions being made were done more fairly. Per Byron, every one of these people were either closely associated with Doctor Lainz or were close friends with someone who was. Lainz had been helpful when he'd first arrived, but as far as anyone could prove, somewhere along the way, the man became a veritable font of discontent with how Turing had been running things, almost overnight.

"Thanks. Is this a social visit or do you need me for something in particular?" Eric asked.

"A little of both, I suppose. Other than the congratulations, I was hoping that with our mutual past, I'd be able to convince you to review some of Turing's policies now that you're the one calling the shots."

Eric sat back in his chair, making a show of thinking about it before commenting, "Well, then I'm sorry to disappoint you, Doctor Lainz. I didn't take over Turing's position of authority, I'm merely a caretaker for that authority while he's indisposed. Besides which, he and I are of much the same mind on things."

"Are you sure I can't appeal to your sense of fairness?" Doctor Lainz asked plaintively.

"Doctor, things are about as fair as they can be while ensuring all of our mutual survivals. If folks find how we run things is that intolerable, we do have a number of empty cabins throughout the valley that we can make available."

"None of which have your protection from the Legion."

"Odd how that works, Elias. I'm sure you remember where the door is. Do please find the other side of it and let me know what it looks like when I see you next."

Day 922

"So what have you been up to? Other than work?" Leah asked as she passed Eric the salt.

"Still getting used to Turing making me his factor. Thankfully not much has gone on today, so I've mostly been reading. "

"Careful, people might think you've gone soft, Eric," Leah giggled.

"Gone soft? Well, if you hear that, you'll just have to tell them I'm as hard as ever. If anyone would know, it'd be you," Eric told her with a wry grin. Leah responded with a faux scandalized glare and rolled her eyes.

"If they're cute, maybe you could invite them upstairs," Eric said. He trailed off on seeing a particularly disheveled Turing shuffle into the dining room.

"My, you're up early," Leah said.

"Or up late?" Eric added.

Turing's red-rimmed eyes jerked up from the floor.

"Oh. Sorry, but what time is it?" the man asked.

"Seven?" Leah replied.

Turing's brow knit with thought.

"PM," Eric told him. When that didn't change Turing's affectation he followed up with, "Friday."

"Oh, well, that explains that," Turing said.

"Explains what?" Leah asked.

"Why I'm so tired. I came down to get some coffee."

"Don't you normally drink tea?" she asked.

"I haven't been sleeping well. I'm all right. It's just insomnia," Turing said as he shuffled into the kitchen behind them.

A glance to his wife told Eric she'd also heard Turing's verbal lag between sleeping and well. *Haven't been sleeping is more likely, looking like that.*

"Is he alright?" she whispered to him. Eric glanced back at the partially open kitchen door.

"I'm not sure. I've had six people ask me the same question in the last week."

"Well, he did tell everyone that he wasn't to be needlessly bothered and to go through you."

"Yeah," Eric whispered back and sipped his milk. "He's been acting particularly off. Jeff was telling me Turing put in a request for two dozen metal hooks with pad eyes drilled into them."

"Metal hooks with pad eyes?"

Eric nodded.

"Each one's about the size of your hand. Jeff showed me the sketches, holes are big enough to run decent sized rope through."

"What for?"

"Fucked if I know," Eric said with a shrug. He speared a chunk of potato as Turing shuffled back into the room.

"Do you think he's finally lost it?" Leah whispered.

"Mind if I join you?" Turing asked before Eric could answer.

"Go ahead. This is your house after all," Eric said and the man sat.

Turing's eyes closed as he lifted his cup to his mouth. "This is how I know God loves us," he said with a weary smile.

"I didn't think you were particularly religious," Leah said.

"I'm not, but if there were a loving God, coffee would be His gift to mankind."

Leah smiled and nodded.

The three sat in silence for a short time before she asked, "Are you sure you're okay? You're not working on some super secret project?"

"Hardly. I get bouts of insomnia all the time. They're almost never this bad, though," he said, lowering his head. His narrowing eyes stayed fixed to Eric's. The two men shared a long, knowing look that ended when Eric shook his head almost imperceptibly. Turing answered with a similar nigh imperceptible nod.

"Oh," Leah commented. "So what have you been teaching Eric? He's always got his face in a book or that tablet lately."

"Teaching? Suggesting reading material is more like it. What have you been learning, Eric?"

"That the Protectorate method of running a government is a travesty and their economic concepts are so nonsensical they approach wronger than wrong. Or maybe 'not even wrong,' I forget the proper usage," Eric said. He didn't miss his wife's shocked glance.

"Interesting. Why is that?" Turing asked.

"Legitimate power comes from the consent of the governed. The Protectorate gains that consent only by concealing the truth. Your rant that night a while ago, Turing? You were right, it's all lies. The Protectorate is little more than a cartel. What was the term? A plutocracy?"

"As I've said before, everyone should expect politicians to lie, Eric," Turing commented. "What's particularly egregious in this case to give rise to travesty instead of embarrassment?"

"A government's purpose is to protect the rights of its populace, not to arbitrarily dictate them in a fashion that benefits only those in power. A proper government doesn't use the farcical ruse that they're protecting its citizens while instead it's actively preying on them."

"My, that's an interesting concept," Turing said through a cat's grin and asked conspiratorially, "Can you defend it?"

"Defend it? Which part? That the Protectorate lies about everything or what the purpose of government is? One is obvious to anyone who pays attention, the other is so nearly self-evident I'm confused why you'd ask about it."

"Pretend I'm one of our newly acquired residents," Turing told him with a wry grin.

"Well, then I'd have to apologize for everything you think you know being unfit for even a compost pile," Eric started. "There's so much wrong I barely know where to begin."

"Try starting with the necessities of what you consider proper governance then," Turing prompted.

"Necessities, huh? Well, a functioning government needs several things to function properly. An educated citizenry is one, a means to transmit information amongst the populace is another.

"Now, the Protectorate makes a big deal about how free everyone is and the media goes along with it. But the joke? From what little you've said about those documents you recovered, Turing, the Inner Party doesn't just control the media, they are effectively the media. Your freedom of the press? It's a giant stage play, a hall of smoke and mirrors. The media tells people what the Inner Party wants them to hear and every now and then, they make a calculated disclosure of truth. When the censors slap them, it's all been planned out and calculated to perpetuate the system. Thanks to you, Turing, I've seen some of the University textbooks on how they do this. There's a degree path for it. It's called Social Engineering."

"They do. I found the courses distasteful, even then," Turing agreed with a sour grimace. "Continue."

"A properly functioning government needs an efficient system of creating and maintaining its body of law," Eric said. He snorted, "What you guys have? You have two chambers of legislature that meet and accomplish nothing but what they're told. The Inner Party effectively dictates what the laws are to a very large degree. What they can't dictate, they still steer because they control the means of communication. Your media is complicit and so are your elected officials.

"Your justice system is a joke. At best, it's a legal system. A properly functioning system of justice does not care who you are, who your parents were, or what affiliations you have. Yet almost every law has some sort of escape clause written into it. The Inner Party influences who gets punished and to what extent. Reality seldom asserts itself in the courtroom because if the judges aren't Inner Party, they want to be. In fact, the only thing that the Protectorate seems to be good at is maintaining the military and police.

"All of this made possible, no, condoned by the populace because they believe that you can trust a self-appointed group of people with total control of their civilization. Of course, they're so much smarter, just better people as the arguments I've read go, right? From what I've read, Turing, you're an outlier. The average Inner Party member is not much smarter than the average citizen, just better connected. I would be repeating myself indirectly to point out they're also far less honest and far more ruthless."

"Honey," Leah interrupted, "The Inner Party gets used as a boogeyman all the time. They're not as bad as you're making them out to be."

Eric snorted and then mentally cringed at the hurt in Leah's eyes.

"Leah, the Inner party does not care one iota about anything but itself and the accumulation of power. They're not just used as a boogeyman, they are the boogeymen," he told her. Blood drained from Leah's face as he summarized parts of the history of the Protectorate that Turing revealed to him so many nights before.

"Turing, this is true? Your family--" Leah asked.

"Did all that? Helped this happen? Yes, all of it," Turing said quietly and continued more confidently with, "Well, you've done a decent job trashing our way of life, Eric. What is your alternative?"

"Liberty," Eric replied.

Someone sighed behind him and said, "Freedom? That's it?"

Eric turned in his chair to find a half dozen people standing in the kitchen door. *How long have you guys been standing there?*

"Well, Doctor Lainz, Turing asked what the alternative was. Freedom is the simplest, most concise answer. Granted, as you're a University taught sociologist, I don't expect you to understand that."

Doctor Lainz's face flushed while he sputtered.

Go ahead, Doctor, get angry. I'm tired of having someone come complaining to me about how unfair shit is here only to find you're the one who put the bug in their ear about it. We'd been better off if they'd shown you the airlock and not the shuttle down.

"Mister Friedrich," the young man standing next to Lainz exclaimed.

Eric cut him off, "Shut up, Wesley. You're even less of an expert on this topic than he is, though that hasn't stopped you yet."

While Wesley sputtered, Eric pushed on, "What Doctor Lainz is about to say is that my alternative is akin to anarchy. That I would have everyone living like animals, like the pirates or mucking about in their own refuse like the Confeds. He wants you to believe that the freedom I'm talking about is dangerous. Am I right, Doctor? Is that a yes? Silence is consent."

Doctor Lainz regarded him coldly but remained silent.

"I've done nothing but read history and policy documents in what little free time I've had the last few months. Presenting freedom as dangerous and akin to anarchy is part of the current prescription by the Inner Party's social engineers. Isn't it, Doc? I'd advise you not to incriminate yourself with that one, Doctor Lainz. People tend to be rather nonplussed when they find out their trusted friends and leader types have been manipulating them.

"Look, make no mistake, freedom is dangerous. When you are truly free, you are not just free to decide, you are also free to make mistakes. You are free to fail, and as any astronautics guy will tell you, not all failure modes are survivable.

"The most concise way I can tell any of you why freedom is the only answer, why it is and will always be better than the Protectorate approach is simple. Information can only move so quickly, only so much data can be compared at one time. One person or a group of people can only oversee so much. Economies are too large, societies are too large for that kind of central planning. No matter if you have one person or a group of planners, they are always too far away from the data to ensure it's all current and even then they can't see the whole picture. Every transaction ruled only by the people involved in the transaction works best. Admittedly, they need accurate price information to be informed of the bigger picture, but my alternative has far better long term results. Capitalism is the worst economic system after all the others."

"It's been shown that state-driven central planning works, Eric," Doctor Lainz insisted. "If it didn't, the Protectorate would have failed a long time ago.

"Sure, economically speaking, Marx's philosophy works in small groups, but as you scale the number of people up, self-interest begins to play a larger and larger part until eventually there isn't enough collective buy-in, a sense of personal responsibility to the group to keep the machine running smoothly. People see others getting the same benefit for less work, so they adjust their output accordingly. Everything slowly starts to grind to a halt."

Doctor Lainz began to open his mouth just as Eric added, "Before you say it though, you're right, the Protectorate does not practice Marxism or old school Communism anymore. Even you guys were bright enough to figure out most aspects of his work were more or less intellectually fraudulent. Here's the thing though, the Protectorate did fail. You just don't know about it."

"Excuse me?" Doctor Lainz said.

Eric had gotten his attention with that. More than a few others as well, Leah included.

"Control the communications, remember? That goes for communicating history, too. I can't blame you for not knowing, no one here was ever taught it happened. But it did. The Protectorate of Man? Originally the People's Protectorate of Mankind and, when it failed, what came out the other side was your Protectorate. The Confederacy, too, by the way."

"Be that as it may," Doctor Lainz said, "Nothing you said supports what you've said or counters what I said."

"I'm getting there, Doctor Lainz. Patience. See, the original Protectorate construct actually was Marxist. It lasted almost a hundred years, almost as long as the biggest example of state Marxism before that did the first time it was tried. And just like that first example, per Turing's documentation, it survived mostly by extracting wealth from its productive systems to smooth things over for the least productive ones. Redistribution of wealth on an interstellar scale. There were forced labor camps, criminal work camps, massive taxation, forced unionization, dictated price restrictions, dictated wages. That being the natural end state of Marxism right before it all falls apart as I was talking about earlier. Directly, your argument only stands with the data you had access to, but that data was incomplete."

Lainz pulled a chair out and sat down, brow furrowed the entire time.

"If that's the case, then how did it change? Why?" Lainz asked. The wind had been taken out of his sails.

Maybe there's still hope for this guy.

"For the record," Turing interjected, "It ended rather suddenly."

Turing coughed into his hand before continuing, "The records were rather incomplete on specifics, but it resulted in a civil war between, essentially, the Marxist true believer hold-outs and those that would make the Protectorate what it is today."

So that's how you're going to spin that? Eric mentally chuckled and then said, "Which is what you'd expect when the breadbasket you've been raiding starts to object to being handled roughly. The political reality in the remnants changed though, Doctor Lainz."

"From what to what?" Wesley asked.

"From blind faith in the State's ability to miraculously fix any problem to one more concerned with the realities of actually fixing any problem," Eric looked to Turing to confirm he wasn't stepping on how Turing wanted to spin the unfortunate details. At Turing's nod he continued, "As a Protectorate sociologist, you're familiar with the concepts of Marxism, communism, and socialism, yes?"

"Of course," Doctor Lainz.

"How about fascism?" Eric asked. Lainz nodded. "In short, the People's Protectorate was a socialist construct with strong communist features. The new Protectorate on the other hand knew the lies in Marxism. They had no other choice but to acknowledge them, but they had help. Not every person who was Inner Party from the beginning was a Marxist. More than a few held beliefs that eventually lead to strongly nationalistic fervor. When the dust had settled, the shadow civil war Turing was politely circling around, that cabal had grabbed the reigns of the new Protectorate. They spun a nice socialist illusion far and wide, but the fascists stay in the shadows most of the time. That allows people to believe the illusion most believe in today. Luckily, your fascists were smart enough to realize that they needed a working form of economics. State control still exists, but it's far looser and less blindingly obvious than direct dictation. Less Soviet era Russia, more communist China or Nazi Germany."

Doctor Lainz sat, scratching his chin, so Eric continued, "I touched on the idea of how advocates of liberty in the Protectorate are labeled anarchists, give me a few minutes to clarify. While anarchists have hotly disputed this assertion throughout the centuries, government is a necessary evil. There are no valid alternatives, as all the alternatives end in violence over a startlingly immediate timeframe compared to the presence of a government. Disputes will arise, we are human after all. How can those disputes be easily, effectively, and quickly resolved without an agreed-upon third party to mediate? What if outside forces threaten the whole? How else can you form an effective defense composed of a disparate but ideologically aligned people in a short time, much less maintain it for any period? A room full of self-made kings, and that's what each anarchist styles themselves as, is just as effective at banding together as a room full of politicians are at running a government. As pro is the opposite of con, I leave it to your imagination what Congress or any other legislature is the opposite of. That said, governments do fund militaries and while their legislative types might fiddle as things burn, the military tends to react far quicker and with far more force than anything the self-styled kings could put together. As for anarchists with a capitalist bent, money may buy many things, but it does not buy the kind of love necessary for a man to lay his life down for another.

"Despite anarchist protests, there are legitimate sovereign powers, just as there are responsibilities. In the end, such a government is only as good as its founding documents, provided its populace is well-educated, supports those principles, and endeavors to actually follow them, not subvert them.

"So when I said freedom, there's a lot more to it than just that one word."

"Like what? Give us something concrete," Turing asked. "What makes your freedom different from what the Protectorate offers?"

"Negative rights, for one."

"Negative rights?" Turing inquired.

Oh, you bastard. I know that hint of a smile.

"Things that the government cannot do or force you to do. The current ruling document for the Protectorate includes positive rights like a right to housing. If you have a right to a house, then someone has to provide it to you. If they're providing something you can't pay for, who is going to pay for it? The government? Government gets their funding via taxation, so it isn't the government paying, but everyone else. This doesn't touch on related issues like what happens when the government gets to decide just how much they'll pay or how taxation beyond need is essentially legalized theft, morally speaking. I have a hard time calling a system that forces third parties to pay a bill they never agreed to a just system, much less one that tells the seller they have to sell it at a fraction of what it's worth. If the government refuses to pay at all? Last I checked, demanding someone's work without compensation is slavery. Positive rights do little more than put a nice face on the fact that the government is authorized to swindle, cheat, steal, and enslave its own citizens in order to bribe other citizens into supporting those in charge.

"That's why property rights are arguably the most important tenet of a functioning, free government. You own yourself, your income, and whatever you purchase with it. Nobody can take it away without your consent."

"Oh, so what if someone decides they don't want to pay taxes? After the fact?" Doctor Lainz asked.

Eric faltered a moment before stating, "Simple. Don't provide them the services those taxes would normally pay for. They're also free to leave. Nobody is forced to stay."

"That seems fairly arbitrary," Turing commented.

"To a degree it is, but this assumes that the populace as a whole has already consented and passed this as law. I'm not saying this is a perfect system, but it's the best one I've seen in any of my studies."

"If they choose to leave, what about their property? Unmovable property they can't just take with them. Land for example," Turing asked.

"What about it?"

Leah asked, "If they leave, what happens to the land?"

"Well, if it's abandoned, I'd assume it would be recovered and resold at some point."

"So your objectors would be left penniless? That's rather harsh. Oppressive even," Doctor Lainz scoffed.

"Hardly. They have the option to sell available to them as well."

"That's a remarkably poor consolation prize," Turing noted.

"There aren't any valid alternatives. If you allow them to remain without paying, they'll soak up services without paying for them. That's not sustainable. It's also morally equivalent to theft. If you kowtow to them, you're subverting legitimate government authority to unelected kleptocrats. Selling the keys to the castle cheaply, I suppose. Authority, I might add, that's been granted to the government by every other citizen. The idea is to avoid anarchy, not encourage it."

"So, what about this taking property without your consent you mentioned?" Doctor Lainz asked.

"What about it? I can't necessarily enumerate all of the cases where such a thing might be valid, but it's fair to say they might exist. With just compensation, of course. Let the electorate vote on those conditions. They're then bound by their own decision."

"And this process is incorruptible? Nobody could do something like say, buy the election?" Turing prompted.

"No, I never asserted that. Anything made by man can be unmade by man."

"So if anything can be corrupted, how is your system any better?" Doctor Lainz asked.

"By that standard, how is anything better than anything else? That line of criticism goes nowhere. It's null. Power corrupts, that much is true, but the corrupt seldom tend to have the same aims.

One could slow the spread of corruption by setting up a strict dispersal of powers across different levels of government. Set things up so that corruption plays off against corruption as it were. That method wouldn't stop the corruption, but it would limit its influence and spread, provided it's not systemic to the whole anyway."

"As interesting a concept as you've made it sound," Doctor Lainz said, "I fail to see how your proposed government is any more morally or ethically superior to ours."

Eric blinked a few times before saying, "Other than the whole you've been lied to since the day you were born bit by your government and the system it created to keep itself in power? How do you think your outlook is better than mine, Doctor Lainz?"

"Equally simple," Doctor Lainz said with a smile. "The Protectorate strives for equality in all things, to quash discrimination, and we have a duty to help the poor. I haven't heard a single word about any of those topics."

"There's a good reason for that. None of those topics is the responsibility of the government," Eric stated flatly.

"So much for your case's moral superiority," Wesley snarked.

"Shut up, Wesley," Eric growled. "Look, you wouldn't use a screwdriver as a hammer unless you absolutely had to, right? So why use the government to set social policy when that's not what governments are supposed to do? Society sets its own rules. Having the government enforce them is a bad precedent. Suppose for a moment that you were a member of a certain group. A government believing they had the authority to impose social policy on the populace, were they opposed to what your group stood for, would find it perfectly acceptable to, quote unquote, do something about your beliefs. You say you're against discrimination, but down that path lies madness. Down that path lies the police antagonizing the targeted group I just mentioned, possibly even rounding them up for incarceration or maybe even just shooting them in the street. How's that equality or non-discrimination? All because you belonged to some arbitrary group. The point is that no government should be able to simply stamp out portions of the populace for having unpopular beliefs. They can't be trusted with that sort of power. The

Protectorate civil war saw billions put in the dirt for not toeing the party line, even when that line shifted underneath them. Your own history, even if you were unaware of it, proves my assertion out. Now, we both believe governments should be fiscally responsible, right?"

Doctor Lainz cautiously nodded.

"Well, if you're hiring people on any basis other than competency, does it not stand to reason that you're not necessarily hiring the best person for the job?"

Doctor Lainz frowned and said, "But all things being equal, the hiring preference should go to the underrepresented person."

"Why?" Eric asked. Turing looked like he had been about to ask the same thing.

"They're underrepresented. Maybe historically discriminated against. Society owes them that much. The workforce and the government should be representative of the population they draw from."

"Point of order," Turing broke in. "Doctor Lainz, we never did discuss in detail why you were exiled to my beautiful, if somewhat inconveniently deadly, planet. You are aware that what you just said is directly contradictory to both established sociological study and Protectorate policy, yes? There are no protected classes in the Protectorate. All are equal. Equally disposable."

"Well aware," Doctor Lainz said dryly. "It isn't my fault my colleagues were short-sighted and eager to see what they wanted to see."

Eric took a deep breath and said, "So you were sent here because someone in power deemed you a--"

"I believe the word you're looking for is throwback," Turing offered when Eric faltered a moment.

"That would be one of the more polite appellations, yes," Doctor Lainz stated flatly.

"Okay," Eric said. "Heresy aside, spell it out for me. How exactly is your system so obviously better than what I supposed? I'm clearly not seeing it."

"And while you're at it, good Doctor, if you would care to highlight how your vision is somehow superior to the Protectorate's current philosophy, I would be greatly interested to hear it."

Doctor Lainz sighed and cast his eyes to Turing before beginning, "The problem with the Protectorate is that it is corrupt, Edward."

"Doctor Turing," Turing corrected icily.

"Doctor Turing then," Lainz said. "We've lost sight of our own humanity. Nobody in power cares about the people. We take care of the poor, but those in power do so only to prevent civil unrest. They calculate down to the hundredth of a credit just how much needs be spent to accomplish that and they spend no more. Billions are stuck in poverty across the entire Protectorate. Billions."

"Be that as it may," Turing commented, "Poverty is man's natural state. You start with nothing and if you don't work to earn more than that, you continue to have nothing."

"I'll point out," Eric interjected, "That the less the government takes from you, the easier it is to actually have something at the end of the day, too."

"That's not the point, Doctor. So many people wouldn't need to be living so poorly if they just had a hand up. They don't have the privilege of coming from wealthier backgrounds like most other citizens. Such as yourself, for example. Those born into positions of power never have to work for it."

"Privilege?" Turing said with a snort. "Every generation of the Turing family moved planets to earn what they had, sometimes literally since we're standing on proof of that. We're also responsible for funding the University. Do I need remind you the student body numbers over two hundred thousand? Do you know how many tens of thousands of scholarships we fund so that the poor you speak of have the chance to reach their potential?"

Lainz's eyes lit up and he asked, "What about the applicants your scholarships don't fund?"

"What about them? Even as rich as we were, we had only so much. We focused on those who would be able to take that opportunity and better themselves. The rest? We'd be shoveling our money into a burning pit," Turing responded.

"And there we have it, Doctor Turing. Your family thought it could buy the moral high ground, just the same as the rest of the rich."

"Okay, okay," Eric butted in. Turing scowled, but did not argue further. "You were supposed to be explaining how your idea was morally superior to either of ours, Doctor Lainz, not starting an irrelevant argument with Turing."

Doctor Lainz closed his eyes and breathed in deeply. Eric noticed for the first time that the room had gotten crowded. At least two dozen people were watching them argue now.

"The Protectorate gets so much right, dear Eric. They just don't go far enough," he said. Several of the newcomers nodded in agreement.

"In what regard? I mean, everything I've seen, they go a hell of a lot further than I'm willing to," Eric commented. More than a few of the crowd seemed to agree. "I mean, how are the poor treated now, exactly?"

"The poor? They beg for scraps, hoping that someone like Turing's family will take notice and lift them up. That's no way to treat a fellow human."

"Damn right it's not," Wesley added.

Eric recognized Perkin's voice when the young man agreed, "He's right, you know."

Turing's lips quirked a moment and before Eric could interrupt he asked, "Doctor Lainz, we've danced around this quite enough. What would you propose we do with the rich then? And what of the truly damaged people our gene clinics cannot help? What about places where prenatal resequencing isn't widely available?"

"I thought you'd never ask," Doctor Lainz said. The grin on his face said Turing had walked into a trap. "First, we must stop pretending that the rich aren't stealing from the poor. We stop giving them legal protection to keep their plunder and we tax it back out of their claws if they won't stop their greed. If they resist, that's what the SSB and the Provost is for. Treat them like they've treated us. Put them against a wall and shoot them or, I suppose, exile them."

Half the crowd, all recent newcomers, smiled or nodded furiously, but Eric saw looks of concern on the faces of the people who'd been on Solitude longer. Then it struck him. Those dubious to Lainz's words, most weren't just old hands here on Solitude. They were the engineers, the scientists, the lawyers, the scholars.

Is it their education or the fact that they'd probably be considered rich by Lainz? Or maybe because they're older than the others? Does a decade really change people that much?

"As for the genetic accidents? We're already resequencing the truly worthless. Those that resequencing didn't help? They're already given opportunities to be something useful already. We'll never stop needing test subjects. No need to change that."

Eric gazed at Doctor Lainz in horror. Similar looks spread through the crowd, but Lainz didn't seem to notice.

"And what of the people who would come to the rich's defense when you start, and I quote, putting them up against the wall?" Turing asked wryly.

"Their toadies can join them, same with anyone who can't understand what needs to be done. Any reasonably intelligent person can easily see this is the only way, but I guess some people just can't be reeducated. Their continued existence only harms society, so we'd have to address that."

"Wow," Eric managed.

Doctor Lainz shook his head and said, "That's why your idea of freedom can't work, Eric. Your so-called free society would fester on the vine because you can't cull the herd. Instead of being run by the properly enlightened, your society would be pegged to the lowest common denominator. Beset on all sides by cretins and greed with no way to combat either. It would be only a matter of time before the brightest amongst you would only be able to do little more than scrawl on the walls in their own feces."

Turing turned to the crowd and said, "And there you have it. All must serve the State. All are equally disposable to the State. Only the properly enlightened will have any say, the rest will be eliminated. Any questions?"

381

The crowd chose instead to begin dispersing in stunned silence. Doctor Lainz seemed unfazed by the revulsion in people's faces.

"Turn your noses up then," he spat.

"Doctor Lainz," Turing said quietly. "Count your blessings I am not the sort of person who subscribes to the Protectorate way of thinking. Or your own. You won't be shot for what you said, but I do expect that you will stop poisoning my guests with your nonsense. We can coexist or not. Your choice."

Doctor Lainz's expression soured even further and he stalked off muttering under his breath.

"You know, based on how he reacted to finding out his idea of history was manufactured, I'd hoped he'd come around," Eric commented.

Turing turned to Eric with a sigh. "When a man erects his idea of himself around a false foundation and spends decades building atop it, Eric, asking them to let go of the lie seldom works, even with proof on your side. They're too invested. Still, I think we've deviated quite a bit from the original discussion. Would you mind picking our discussion back up next week in my study? Say around noon on Friday?"

Eric nodded and then looked down at his plate. He wasn't hungry anymore.

As they left a few minutes later, Leah commented, "I'm not going to say you were right, but, well, Lainz certainly wasn't. Good God, what that man said." Leah shivered. "Look, as a lawyer I saw no end to the special exceptions written into everything. That's why I went contract law and not criminal. I guess I knew things were twisted. I just wouldn't admit it to myself. I-I had no idea they used people as test subjects. How horrible." Leah shrugged after several moments of silence and commented, "What you said fits with what you've had me read. Was there ever a place like that? I mean, where they actually implemented your alternative?"

"Yeah, actually there was. Until the Protectorate bombed most of the United States flat, anyway. Almost everything I've shown you led up to the creation of the United States."

Leah sighed. "Do you think you could put together a reading list for me? I'm tired of not having the bigger picture and not knowing what you're talking about."

Eric squeezed her hand. "Sure."

Day 930

"Eric," Turing said with a broad smile, "You have surpassed even my expectations. You have satisfied any and all tests put before you by every expert in the fields you have tested on. You have mastered every topic put before you as best can be expected given our circumstances and limited resources. While this will not be honored beyond our circle, I confer to you this token of recognition with the concurrence of your peers. Know that in our eyes, this is equivalent to a degree in Mathematics, Physics, and History, in addition to the Political and Military Sciences. I only regret that I cannot give you recognition that would be more widely recognized. May you find your thirst for knowledge never slaked, for the journey to true knowledge seeks an ideal not a destination. Do you have anything to say to your peers?"

"You guys are assholes," Eric said. "If I'd known I was going to show up for a six hour grilling session by everyone, I'd either prepared or gone off to live in a cave by myself. I don't know what else to say other than maybe, 'Thank you'?"

"Doctor," Elizabeth said as she shook his hand.

"What?" Eric blurted.

"Oh," Turing said with a grin, "It's by joint decision. It wouldn't pass a University review board. Hell, it wouldn't pass any collegiate review, but you did stand a thesis defense even if it was highly irregular and wholly unrelated to what we're conferring the title for. Commander Grace, Travis, Trevor, and Terry all agreed that your competence on mathematical matters was sufficient for the title, even if we didn't force you to write a needlessly long dissertation or publish some new pointless theorem for our posterity to forget and rediscover a century from now on their own."

"Translation," Elizabeth laughed, "Don't let it go to your head."

Turing smiled and said, "Precisely. If you'd like to appeal, you can talk to the guy in charge, but I hear he's a bit of an eccentric asshole."

Eric snorted.

"Eat, drink, have fun," Turing told him. "As for me, I'm going to get another drink."

"So what's it like to be a bigshot doctor now?" Leah asked him.

"Same as all the other positions I hold. More responsibility, no additional pay. No pay, actually. I really should talk to Turing about that. I'm pretty sure I get a stipend or something now, right?"

Elizabeth rolled her eyes.

"That only comes with tenure," Turing joked.

Sometime later Eric spotted Turing alone where the bottles had been set up.

"Nice party?" Turing asked.

"Been fun, sure," Eric said as he checked to see if anyone was close enough to overhear. "So, how's your insomnia?"

"It got better."

"So still not in?"

"I didn't say that," Turing said. He sounded almost insulted.

"Well?"

"Like I said, it's mostly boring details. Navigational data, surveillance data. On the plus side, we now know that our wardens have become incredibly lax. They're not actively scanning for laser at all, only monitoring RF and visual. Granted, knowing what the low end of what they consider an RF threat is useful, but overall this is a pile of nothing so far."

"Nothing?" Eric sighed.

Turing nodded. "Trust me, if anything comes out of what little I have left to go through, you'll be the first one down here to know."

"So no ulterior motives for the party, eh?"

"Nope. I needed the distraction to decompress. Happy?"

"For you? Sure. For the rest of us, not so much."

"It'd be poor form to rub it in, but that disappointment is

precisely what I was trying to avoid in everyone else. Have we had any further problems with Doctor Lainz since our little show?"

Eric answered, "None that I can tell. He's been pretty quiet from what Byron's said."

Turing allowed himself a brief smile. "Good. At least that's settled."

Day 1023

Leah rolled off him and curled against his side to nuzzle his chest. The two lay for some time getting their breath back.

"You know, Doc was telling me the prophylactic injections they give prisoners should be wearing off any time now," Eric said.

Leah looked up at him and said, "So?"

"Well, we might want to be a bit more careful about things. Just saying."

"Why? Eric, I've never wanted children before I found you. If we're not getting off this rock, I'll raise them here. They'd grow up free, which is better than I can say for anywhere in the Protectorate."

"Oh, well, are you sure?" Eric asked.

Leah giggled. "Am I sure what? Doc said the same thing to me last week. I'm pretty sure what we just did is proof enough that I'm okay with it. Why, are you afraid of being a dad?"

"Me? A dad? Okay, maybe a little. Our children could be little monsters."

"I'm pretty sure they all are," Leah purred. "It's up to us to make them civilized, isn't that what that piece on your tablet said? Still, if all you're going to do is worry, it's not like we're in danger of having kids. Care for another try?"

Forsaken

DAY 1024

DISTANT RUMBLING DREDGED ERIC FROM A DEAD SLEEP.

"Goddamnit, if that's Julien testing Jorge's new explosives formulas again," he groused.

Leah stirred next to him and mumbled, "Go back to sleep, hon."

On the nightstand next to him, Eric's tablet screen lit up. Buzzing, the tablet flashed red as a second rumble sent shivers through the floor. Eric glanced over at the device. Tired disbelief broke under a cascade of sudden cold realization.

"Honey? Hon, get up!" Eric barked as he rolled out of the bed.

"What? Why?" Leah groaned.

"We're being attacked!" he barked as he raced to get dressed.

"WHAT?"

Long strings of distant gunfire interrupted the silence followed by several loud concussions. Only half into his jeans, Eric nearly tripped as he groped for his tablet. Eric furiously tapped the screen and opened the app for their radio monitor.

"CONTACT! CONTACT WEST GATE!" a terrified young man shouted. "We're taking heavy fire. Rockets and small arms, over. Heavy casualties."

"Copy that, west gate," the reply came moments later.

After a short pause the voice continued, "Break, break. All units on this station, Mountain Home is under attack. I repeat, Mountain Home is under attack. Instructions to follow, standby."

Eric had finally managed to get dressed and was slipping into his rifle plates when the amount of gunfire to west doubled and was joined by more to the north.

The radio squawked, "Contact! Contact! North Gate! Foot mobiles incoming north and northwest."

"Copy that, North Gate. All mountain home units, wolverine actual," Byron's voice burst from the speaker. "Hold your positions, reinforcements are coming. Spiders two, three, and four, guillotine. I say again, spiders two, three, and four, guillotine. Spiders one, five, six, seven, and eight, move to support. All units, acknowledge."

"This is it," Leah gulped as he silenced the tablet. Eric handed Leah her rifle. He fit his earpiece in and pulled on his helmet while she tugged the charging handle on her rifle.

"Sounds like it," Eric told her. He put a reassuring hand her shoulder as he handed Leah her helmet. "Stand by me?"

She nodded earnestly and squeezed his hand before following him out into the hall.

"All Mountain Home units, Mountain Battery. We are online and waiting targets, over."

"Mountain Battery, west gate. At least a hundred foot in the open. Peg whiskey-fifteen-twelve and closing."

"West gate, copy. Fire mission incoming, danger close. One round, whiskey papa." Eric felt the vibration from the concussion through the ceiling in his lungs. "Shot out."

Racing through the chaos clogging the foyer, Eric missed several seconds of radio traffic.

"West gate, copy. Firing for effect."

Every other second, the 120mm mortars on the roof barked.

"How bad is it?" Eric asked a grim-faced Byron as he and Leah made it to Turing's study.

"Bad. Lost half of west gate in the opening barrage. Gate's broken, Gliar's moving to breach," Byron said calmly between the rhythmic thump of the mortars. The men know their orders. They've already set off a few preset explosives. With luck we won't need the fougasse."

"North gate's in contact, but holding," Hadrian said. He winced and spoke into his microphone, "Negative west gate. Hold your position, over."

Byron shot Hadrian a look of concern and spoke into his radio, "West gate, Wolverine Actual. Badger's ETA is two minutes. Hold your position at all costs, over."

Byron growled and threw an old Earth stapler across the room. "Badger, Wolverine Actual. West gate has fallen, move to cover. Mountain battery, correct fire to west gate proper. Load frag, airburst. Fire for effect, how copy?"

"Fallen?" Leah gasped.

Hadrian shook his head. "They're breaking and running."

"But those are our people! They're still alive!" she shouted at the commando.

"Our plans always centered around getting reinforcements to a fallback position before the gate retreated and using the fougasse to turn it into a bloodbath. If they fall back now, we can't stop Gliar from taking the wall. If they get in the walls we're done. This is a house, not a fortress. Those men are already dead and if we don't shell the gate, we will be too."

"Where do you need us?" Eric asked.

Byron opened his mouth to reply when Turing burst through the door.

"Sorry, misplaced my radio," the man gasped. "All the cameras on the south side went dark. I thought it was a glitch but I couldn't find anything wrong on my end."

The first to break the stunned silence, Hadrian told Eric, "Take Leah. Julien and his team will meet you in the south hall."

As he stalked from the room, Eric overheard the reply to Byron's request for status, "Mountain home, south gate. Situation normal. No contact."

Eric grit his teeth while they waited in the hall and cycled through frequencies.

"Mountain battery, wolverine actual. Have one of your troops check South Gate. Report, over."

"Wolverine, battery, copy," came the reply. A few moments later the same voice said, "Wolverine, battery, there's at least a thirty in white passing through the gate."

"You heard that?" Julien asked Eric as they stalked down the hall. Eric nodded grimly.

"Battery, wolverine. Priority tasking as follows. Guns three and four, correct fire to south gate minus fifty. Twenty rounds mixed, how copy?"

"Guns three and four, twenty rounds HE and frag, south gate minus fifty."

"Okay, you guys stick with me," Julien told Eric and Leah. "Edwards, Chambers, Volk, and Lear, second floor, overwatch and keep anything from getting near the house. Oleg, Veer, guard this door like your life depends on it. Everyone else, we'll mop up whatever makes it past the mortars."

Eric followed Julien onto the porch as the mortars fired overhead. Julien held out a set of binoculars. Eric peered through them. At least fifty men in white camouflage were fanning out from the southern gate, sprinting in their direction. He spotted the crew that had been trusted to man the gate milling about to either side of it. Eric swapped to the command frequency and jerked as the group he'd been observing disappeared in a sudden cloud of snow and debris.

"Holy shit," he muttered.

"Behold artillery, the fist of God, king of the battlefield," Julien said with pleased grin and stepped off the porch. "Battery, wolverine three. South gate targets suppressed. Keep it up."

Round after round dropped ahead of them. Some detonated several meters off the ground, the resulting angry balls black smoke filled the air around them with shards of metal. Others tore divots into what had been a field full of corn before winter's arrival.

"Wolverine Actual, Eagle Two," Eric transmitted hoarsely. A heavy machinegun opened up from the second floor sending tracers streaking overhead through the thin line of trees separating him from the field before him.

"Copy Eagle Two, go ahead."

"South gate did not fall."

"Say again."

"South gate did not fall. They let them in."

Eric heard anger and disgust in Byron's reply, "Copy that."

Eric ducked as something buzzed through the air past him.

"Relax. It's only mortar shrapnel," Julien jovially called out over his shoulder. "At this distance they're not lethal."

Eric ran faster.

"Battery, wolverine actual. When active mission for guns three and four complete, correct fire to south gate actual. Four rounds frag, pick your fusing."

"Four rounds, copy. ETA sixty seconds."

"Eric," Julien's voice jumped into his ear over the radio. "Eight guys up ahead, scratch that, two. Nope, one. He making a run for the storage shed. You and Leah take the front. Vic and I will take the back. You flush him and we'll take him when he runs for it. He's panicked, so this should be easy."

The lone man in white ducked into the storage shed Eric had helped build six month ago. Veering to stay out of line of sight, Julien's group trotted up to the shed's north wall two minutes later.

"Don't think he saw us," Eric whispered, out of breath.

Julien shook his head with a smile. Using hand signals Julien directed them to the corners and told them to pause ten seconds before going.

Eric glanced around the corner. Still bodies populated the area towards the gate. The shed's front door was closed. He glanced over his shoulder at Leah. She nodded at the unspoken question. *Of course she's ready.*

He counted and moved to the door.

"I got left," he signaled to his wife.

She gave a quick nod and jerked her head to the right.

She's got right. Eric closed his eyes for a moment and breathed deeply. *Just like we did in training. We got this.*

Eric's brought his boot up as he thumbed his safety off. He planted his foot squarely by the handle and the door crashed open. In the center of the open structure, their quarry spun towards the noise to face him. Eric advanced, rifle coming down. The man's rifle came up as Eric's chevron settled on the man's chest.

Both sides opened fire.

Gliar's man stumbled back a step. Unfazed by the angry buzz of the man's near misses, Eric kept shooting until the enemy fell.

"Got him!" Eric shouted with a smile. The door on the far side of the shed, burst open and Julien leaned into view.

Something bumped into the wood wall behind him and slid against it. Eric jerked around and his rifle fell from nerveless hands. Leah sat slumped against the battered doorframe, her hands around her throat. Blood streamed between her fingers as she stared at him with confused eyes. Her mouth opened and closed but made no sound.

Sinking to his knees at her side, Eric gasped.

"No, no, fuck no," Eric blurted as he franticly dug at his LBE for his first aid kit. "Leah, it'll be okay. You're okay. We got this, we trained for this."

Eric pried back her hands and began wrapping the bandaging material around her throat. She looked at her blood coated hands and panic replaced confusion in her eyes. She gurgled and started to flail.

"Easy, love, easy. You're going to be okay. I'm going to get you to Doc, he can fix this," Eric told her fervently as wrapped tape to hold the bandage in place. He leaned back and, forcing the worry from his face, gave her a hopeful smile. The glassy surface of her eyes clouded over. Eric blinked, unable to process what he just witnessed.

"But, but," he sputtered, unable to pull his eyes from hers. Shaking, he reached out and touched her cheek. "Leah?"

A hand rested on his shoulder. Eric haltingly turned his head towards the hand's owner.

"She's gone, Eric," Julien told him softly.

"But--"

"She's gone," Julien repeated in the same sad tone.

Eric's gaze crept back to his fallen wife. *She's gone? No. No, she can't be. I just-I. No, this has to be a dream. Has to be. I'm going to wake up any minute now.*

"Eric, I know this hurts," Julien said firmly. "Keep it together. Mourn her later, when it's safe. If we don't secure the south gate now, this will be only the beginning."

This, no. A single tear trickled down his face. He started to shake as despair and rage tore through him, mauling each other as much as they mauled him for control. *Keep it together. Keep. It. Together.*

"Secure the south gate. Got it," he muttered numbly seconds later.

Eric found himself standing. His rifle appeared in his hands. He watched himself smoothly, but robotically check the chamber, load a fresh magazine, and follow Julien.

As they approached the torn south gate, Eric spotted several of the Gliar's men still twitching on the ground. One was leaving a long red trail across the snow as he tried to drag himself away. Eric didn't wait for Julien to give any orders. He knew what had to be done and did his duty. The infiltrator no longer moved when Eric moved to catch up to Julien.

His radio hissed and he heard Julien's voice. It sounded distant and tinny.

"South gate retaken. Reinforcements needed, we've taken casualties."

"Copy that. Bear is en route. ETA ten minutes."

Eric heard something move inside the tattered gatehouse he'd helped build. His rifle came up.

"Come out with your hands up," he heard himself bark.

Three men limped out. Eric recognized one immediately. His eyes narrowed.

"Who was behind this?" he asked flatly.

When none of them replied Eric lowered his rifle and hissed, "If you expect any mercy whatsoever, tell me."

The two privates pointed at Specialist Perkins. *The man who wouldn't shoot.* Leah's lifeless face loomed before him. He couldn't hold the gyre of rage back any longer. Mentally he smiled, letting it take him. Eric watched himself raise his rifle, shoot both privates in their startled faces, and then butt stroke Perkins unconscious. The darkness consumed everything.

Day 1025

Eric groaned. His everything hurt.

"Honey, I had the weirdest-" Eric said as he rolled over in bed. His hand found only cold, empty space where Leah should have been. "-Dream."

He grunted as he sat up and looked around their bedroom. He spotted his rifle. His plates weren't where he normally put them, they were lying next to his rifle. *Where's her gear? Maybe she got up before me and decided to do some target practice?*

Every muscle, every joint protested his decision to stand loudly. He shuffled over to their chest of drawers and dressed. *My gear's filthy. Why's my gear filthy? Someone's got to be screwing with me. Not going out there with a dirty rifle. What is that smell? Anne's assistant burnt something in the kitchen again.*

Eric took his rifle to their desk. He pulled out the basket of chemicals from under the desk, broke down the rifle, and cleaned it. He picked up the magazine to reseat it and realized it was almost empty.

"Okay, this shit is getting old," Eric muttered as he looked through their closet. Someone had clearly dug through their storage bins and left their contents strewn across the floor. All forty of their spare magazines were nowhere to be found. Eric seated the mostly empty magazine with a frown and slung his rifle over his shoulder. He stepped out into the hall and froze. *What the?*

Carefully, he picked his way through the slumbering forms that lined the hallway in their twisted masses of worn blankets and sheets.

A half dozen of his recruits sat leaning against sandbags that lined the wall to either side of the front door in full gear. They stood as he reached the bottom of the stairs.

"Sir, nothing to report," their group's officer snapped a salute and told him. Warily Eric returned the salute. Eric did not miss the respect and fear in the man's eyes. *What's this about?*

He shuffled into the kitchen. Bags, boxes, and their contents were strewn about. It looked like someone forgotten they'd left meat to thaw on both the prep tables. Blood pooled on the tops and had dripped to the floor into puddles and blood soaked gauze. Anne sat on a stool in the middle of the disaster, her head in her hands.

"Anne?" Eric asked. "You okay?"

She looked up with bleary, red-rimmed eyes and slowly shook her head before resting it back on her hands. Flickering light from the yard brought his attention to one of the windows. *A bonfire?* As he watched, the two men by the fire turned and bent over the dark pile next to them. They heaved something large up and hefted it into the fire.

"Anne, they're burning--"

"Bodies."

Dark realization needled at him, but memory did not come.

"Anne, why are they burning bodies?"

Anne began to cry. Not knowing what else to do, Eric stepped through the debris and squeezed her shoulder. She bawled and leaned into him. Eventually the crying became sniffles.

"Turing is in his study." she managed and blew her nose. "He'll want to see you."

Turing half stood and raised his pistol toward the door as Eric walked in. Hadrian snored loudly, face down on one of the other desks.

"Oh, you're up," Turing said and sat his pistol down.

Hadrian jerked awake at Turing's words.

"I guess," Eric said with a shrug. "I feel like I got hit by a starship. No, a small moon."

Grim-faced, Hadrian staggered to his feet, holstering the pistol his face had concealed.

"Eric?" the commando asked as he dug something out of a pocket.

"What?" Eric asked, concerned by Hadrian's tone. Horror crept over him as Hadrian's resigned look tugged at his memory. *No, this isn't happening.* Eric stepped back, but Hadrian caught his arm and pressed something small into his hand. Eric looked down. The simple metal band in his palm glinted in the light where flakes of dried blood fallen off.

"Well, you can thank Jeff for them looking like rings instead of globs of metal shit."

Leah shook her head at him, grinning.

Eric gasped and his knees buckled. Hadrian caught him.

Day 1027

Eric shifted, rubbing his toes together in his boots in a vain attempt to keep them warm as the crowd assembled. Turing's lack of sleep had finally caught up with him, leaving him bedridden and forcing Eric to conduct the final pronouncement.

He glanced to the prisoners next to him and scowled. Two days of interrogation had produced a fair amount of information, but with the strain he'd been under, most details slid from his mind like rain off glass. What little he retained lit his heart like a small black sun.

Traitors.

Eric glanced about the crowd again as he pulled out his notepad.

That should be enough.

Eric sneered as he reviewed his notes from the night before and began to speak, "Let it be known that Doctor Lainz was sent here as a plant by Colonel Gliar with the direct goal of fomenting distrust and rebellion in our ranks so as to weaken our defenses. This account is confirmed by direct evidence, collaboration by the other prisoners, and video recorded testimony by witnesses and the defendants."

Eric paused, letting his pronouncement sink in. A low mumble raced through the crowd

"Let it be also known that under the under the influence of Doctor Lainz, Specialist Perkins convinced the members of his squad that a peaceful solution was possible. In so many words, Perkins convinced his squad that Turing's council wrongly refused to negotiate terms with the Legion, that we were using everyone here as slave labor and had no regard for their lives despite more than ample evidence to the contrary. Convinced of these lies, that their leadership were more the enemy than the legionnaires, the members of his squad opened the south gate for the invaders and greeted them as brothers. This account is confirmed by direct evidence, collaboration by other prisoners, and video recorded testimony by the accused.

"Under Protectorate law, the penalty for treason and espionage is death."

Eric's pronouncement hushed the crowd.

"Are there any objections?" Eric asked no one in particular. Without waiting, he continued, "Seeing none, the sentence is to be carried out forthwith. Under lesser circumstances, I would be well within my rights to personally execute each and every one of you."

Eric caressed the butt of the flintlock tucked in his belt.

"However, I will not stain the honor of common criminals by treating these traitors as I would criminals," Eric told the crowd. "Doctor Lainz, Specialist Perkins, you and your co-conspirators are hereby stripped of your ranks and your names struck from the roll. You and the rest of your ilk are sentenced to hang by the neck until dead whereupon your remains will be fed to the animals and your bones, much like your names, will be forgotten. May God have mercy on your souls. You will find none here. Sergeant-at-Arms, you have your instructions."

Day 1028

Eric stared in silent disbelief at the flag-draped coffin before of him. *Turing did say he was going to do something special for her.* Dimly he realized Elizabeth was squeezing his hand as Turing said something. None of it mattered. Not the words, not the condolences. None of it mattered. *My wife is gone.*

Images and half remembered memories floated by. Leah, scared and hiding under a scratchy wool prison blanket. The serious cast on her face as she handed him the knife as he stood over the dying man. A wary hint of a smile from that first spring. *You were still too afraid to smile then.* Leah stood at attention mocking him with skewed helmet and a silly grin under the salute. *I miss that smile, Leah. God, I miss you.* Eric pushed at the last memory, but it came anyway. Leah lying next to him, breathless and flushed. *You laid there giddy about how the contraceptives were wearing off, about how we could start a family soon. That was the night before, before--*

The first volley of fire interrupted that thought and sent his heart racing. More memories tumbled through him as the shots rang out. The angry buzz of bullets passing only centimeters from him. Firing. Firing. *He's shooting at me! Keep firing! Why is he still shooting back? Keep firing!* He gripped Elizabeth's hand until his knuckles ached.

He knew the droning that followed was a recording, but the soft bugle call reached through silent centuries to pull the pain from his heart and the tears from his eyes.

People moved. Words were spoken.

Someone stood before him. Blinking the tears away, he looked up. A watery-eyed Hadrian was handing him a folded flag. The flag of a fallen nation given for the loss of another. The white stars amongst the dark blue burnt holes into his eyes. *You came to love what they stood for, Leah.* Eric wept as we weakly accepted the flag.

Leah, my love. It should have been me. Why couldn't it have been me?

Day 1052

Eric grumbled as slid his feet out of bed and sat up. He leaned forward, rubbing at his eyes. Leah's ring swung on its chain against his chest, its weight tugged memories he no longer wanted to feel. Eric squinted at the bottle on his nightstand. Grabbing it while he stood, Eric lurched over to his desk to sit down. He stared at the bottle in his lap for several long seconds and had started to twist the cap off when someone knocked at the door.

"What?"

"Can I come in?" Elizabeth asked outside.

Eric sighed and sat the bottle on the desk.

"Sure."

He reached for the tumbler he'd used the night before as Elizabeth let herself in.

"Don't you think it's a bit early to be drinking alone?" she asked.

Eric glanced at the sunlight filtering through the heavy curtains and back to her.

"I'm not drinking alone. Muffin's sleeping over there in the clothes pile. That, and you're here, too."

Eric saw a brief flicker of a smile in Elizabeth's face before she shook her head at him.

"You know what I meant," she said and pulled a chair out from the small table.

Leah's chair. Eric tried not to wince as memories of sharing breakfast with Leah at that table spun through him. Every one of Leah's happy smiles cut deeper into him than the last. His eyes slid back to the bottle.

Eric felt concern rolling off Elizabeth in waves. He sighed.

"What did you want?" he asked, trying to keep the hurt out of his voice. He failed.

"Eric, I'm worried about you. We're worried about you."

Eric stared blankly at the bottle in his hands. *When did I pick it up?*

"And?" he asked, casually pouring what was left of the bottle into his tumbler.

"And what?" she said, anger heating her words. "Eric, when

you're not downstairs acting like a robot, you're up here drinking. You're destroying yourself."

Eric glared at her and growled, "Maybe that's what I want. Why do any of you care?"

Liz gaped at him. Her features hardened and she rose to her feet.

"I came up here to talk to you as a friend, Eric, but it's pretty clear to me now I should have come up here as your superior officer."

Eric blinked. She continued before the words had sunk in, "With what little respect I have left for you, Eric, you're Turing's factor and a high ranking militia officer, but you're not acting like either and you haven't for the last month.

"So far, people have understood. Everyone's lost someone they cared for, but how much longer will their understanding last? How much longer will it take before they start losing respect for you? No, I get it, what do you care? Why should you give a thrice-damned piss about what all these people think, right?

"I'll tell you why, Eric. Because these people depend on you. You might not be the keystone holding everything together, but you're damn close to it. What happens to an officer when no one respects them? Orders, even proper, correct ones, don't get followed. Insubordination becomes the norm, morale tanks. Fights start. Do you honestly want to take this place along with you on your path to self-destruction? Because that's exactly what you're doing right now."

"Liz--"

"Don't 'Liz', me, Eric. Do you understand how much of what we've built here depends on you? Do you have an idea, any idea at all?"

Words failed him.

"Eric, when I was a young ensign, I saw all the perks the senior officers got and I kept thinking to myself that with rank comes privilege. I got hung up on the idea that the more important I was, the less the rules applied to me. Thinking like that damn near cost me my commission when I was a lieutenant. Yes, with rank comes privilege, but it also comes with responsibility.

"Doesn't matter if you're officer or enlisted, people depend on you, and the higher up you are, the more important you're supposed to be. Failing to live up to your responsibilities might be fine and dandy in the civilian world, but doing that in the military gets people killed. This isn't just a military setting, Eric, we're stuck here with nothing, with no one else. If we fuck up, everyone dies."

Eric glared at the tumbler on his desk, trying to keep his emotions at bay.

"Liz, I don't think you understand," Eric managed to squeeze out through the building haze of anger.

"What's there to understand? You're an officer. Act like it."

Eric snapped, "Oh, so I'm supposed to just switch off? I'm supposed to pretend nothing happened, that nothing bothers me? How exactly is that supposed to work? I tried that already. The memories don't just go away, Liz. The pain doesn't just disappear. Why the fuck else do you think I've been drinking?"

Liz closed her eyes in frustration and slowly sat down.

"Eric, do you know the hardest lesson to learn when you're a good officer? Good officers give a shit about their people. The problem is that any decision an officer makes can get their men killed. Any one of them. Any number of them. The first death, accident or not, can make any person doubt their ability to lead. That doubt holds you back, which leads to the second death, and so on until you can't see past your nose anymore." She paused. With a sigh she added, "Sometimes it only takes the first one to get you there."

Eric took his eyes off the tumbler in time to see the angry officer in her face dissolve.

He quietly asked, "How do I get past this?"

"You have to learn to compartmentalize. Every leader, from the NCOs up to the officer corps, has a duty to the men and women they lead. No obligation gets changed because you're having a bad day, Eric. Feelings aren't part of the equation in determining what the right thing to do. Duty doesn't care about fairness either. If you want to lead, you need your people to trust you, to respect you. So that means keeping your shit together when you're out there. They'll respect you more for it."

"But how do I handle what I'm locking away? Bottling shit up isn't healthy."

"No, it's not. You still have to deal with it, just not in front of folks you command. You have friends here, Eric. You have peers to talk to. You could have gone to Turing, Hadrian, Byron, or even Julien or Pascal at any point. You could have come to me."

"Come to you? I thought everyone had enough to worry about without dealing with my problems, too."

Elizabeth nodded.

"Eric, we've all been through some shit, but being there for each other is what counts. Doesn't matter what we call it, soldier, sailor, marine; you're always there for your friends. Sharing the pain makes it easier. You and I have been through a lot together. Let me help you."

"But--"

"I just want to help. Talk to me. Talking to another woman isn't cheating on Leah's memory if that's what you're worried about. Hell, as if I could replace her to begin with. That's not how love works. I miss her, too. She was my friend and I'd like to not lose another one."

Bounty

"WHAT DO YOU SEE?" TURING ASKED HIM.

Eric lowered the binoculars.

"Looks like a supply ship," he replied.

Turing nodded. "And about five degrees prograde and retrograde?"

Eric checked the black overhead, taking his time to dial in the advanced optics.

"Prograde looks like a destroyer. Retrograde, I think that's a cruiser. Is that the *Relentless*?"

Turing nodded again. "Yes. The *Relentless* and its escort, the *Silent Hunter*. The supply ship is the *Bounty*."

"So why'd you want me to see this?"

Turing's eyes fell to his feet and he said with sorrow, "This much of the cordon for Solitude in one place only happens once a year."

Eric glanced back and forth between Turing and the sky.

Suspiciously he asked, "Okay?"

"I promised you'd be the first to know."

"Know what, Turing?" Eric asked as the man pulled his tablet from his coat.

"It's easy to get in a rut, Eric. It's easy to lose all hope and believe things will never change. Easy to believe you're responsible for things you're not, or that you're not responsible for things you are. We all do it. We did it this spring, this summer. The naval forces overhead have been in the same rut the last five years."

Realization crept away from him, staying just out of reach.

"I'm not quite following, Turing," Eric said as he looked over at the man.

"Once one is in that rut, one is blind. When things do change suddenly, to borrow a turn of phrase from you, one tends to lose their shit," Turing said. The man looked skyward. As he pressed on his tablet screen Turing whispered, "Q.E.D."

A split second later a dozen searing white blooms flared to life across the sky.

"What the shit, Turing?" Eric gawped. Each bloom sent a streak of angry light towards the same vicinity in the sky, toward Cerberus Station and her escorts. The shiny dots of the *Relentless* and the *Silent Hunter* flared and then began losing form. The binoculars came up. The debris field glittered as it dispersed.

"Remember when I told you the surveillance satellites were also kill vehicles?" Turing said with predatory grin.

"Holy shit!"

"Have Hadrian and Byron meet me in my study. Go, we haven't much time."

Eric's tablet chimed fifteen seconds later.

"I'm getting multiple reports of a disturbance in the sky from our spiders, Eric," Julien's voice echoed.

"I know, Julien. It's a surprise from Turing. Send a runner to Hadrian and Byron, have them meet me in Turing's study. Put everyone else on high alert."

"Acknowledged."

Eric continued onward. He found Hadrian waiting for him in the study.

"I was already here. What's going on?" Hadrian asked.

Eric forestalled Hadrian with a raised hand.

Moments later, Byron burst in the door. "What's going on? Why did I just hear a description of multiple orbital detonations over the radio?"

"It seems our friend has been playing his cards close to his chest," Eric told the two.

The Caledonians glanced at each other and back to him.

"What do you mean? Turing set those off? How?" Byron asked.

"How?" Turing returned the question as he walked in. "Thanks to Eric, it wasn't terribly difficult. The drives he recovered from the drone contained a multitude of data. You already know about the surveillance data and what we managed to do with it.

"But, I didn't tell you about the security data I'd extracted. Using what I found, I infiltrated Cerberus Station's surveillance network. Once I was in unnoticed, it was only a matter of time before I could move laterally. I've been watching them from the inside for the past year, waiting for the right time. That time is now. Rather, the window of opportunity opened a half hour ago when the Bounty docked with Cerberus."

"So those explosions were?"

"The surveillance satellites. Their secondary function was to act as kill vehicles. I activated that function and targeted both escorts. The first pieces should be striking atmosphere in about two hours, give or take twenty minutes or so."

"Those escorts were?" Hadrian asked.

"The *Silent Hunter*, a Tomsk class destroyer, and the *Relentless*, a Pobeda class strike cruiser," Turing replied.

"Good," Hadrian responded, "This supply ship was the *Bounty*? Class?"

"Zelenyy."

Hadrian's eyes lit up. "A Zelenyy? Oh, very good."

Eric looked over at the man. "Why's that good?"

"One of my last missions, we trained to board a Zelenyy, lad. That, and the Zelenyy are fleet support ships. They've got a bit more in the propulsion department than normal supply boats so they can keep up with the fleet."

Turing smiled. "Write down what you can, we'll need it. Your ride arrives in fifteen minutes."

Hadrian's grin lit the room. "My memory might be a bit off, but, give me a second." Hadrian grabbed a sheet of paper and started scribbling.

"His ride?" Eric asked.

"Your ride, too. I trust all of you will tell me if I'm wrong somewhere, but the plan is straightforward. The drone I co-opted will be landing in fifteen minutes in the field by the south gate. I've taken the liberty of ordering it to empty its weapons bays on the western side of the mountain, so they'll be empty when it arrives. I would like you three, plus Commander Grace to stow away on it. The bays aren't pressurized, which is why you'll be riding up in the suits my father was selling the pirates. Trevor has gone over their seals and verified they should all still hold. Once aboard the Cerberus, you will do whatever it is you dirty soldier types do until you can reach the Bounty. Take the ship at all costs. Once that's accomplished, Commander Grace returns here with a heavy lift shuttle. We evacuate everybody we can along with whatever supplies we can manage and depart before the other two escorts in the system can stop our escape. I do believe our numbers are a fair bit larger than the standard crew of a Zelenyy, so we'll need plenty of food and water."

"That sounds remarkably workable," Byron said.

"Also, here is the old layout of Cerberus before they refitted her for her current duties. The drone bay is the old observation deck. Transit time to the station should be twenty-five minutes, which gives us," Turing paused and his face bunched up as he did calculations in his head. "Somewhere around three hours from your arrival to be underway on the Bounty. We'll be able to make two sorties with the shuttle safely, three if we push it."

"Or we could augment with the drones? Stow gear in the bays like we're doing on the way up," Eric offered.

"Oh, yes, I don't know why I hadn't considered that," Turing said.

"Let's get those suits," Hadrian told them. "We'll plan while we get dressed and hash it out on the way up."

"Good. Eric, take this," Turing told him as he handed him a bundle. "It's a weaponized pad. Strap it on your forearm, everything else is pretty straightforward, all the standard plug adapters. Just in case I can't access something from where I'm at."

His heart beat in his ears as momentum pushed him into the loading clamps he'd spent the last twenty minutes nestled against.

"Crystal clear," Turing's voice came over the radio, "That's the last major course change. You're on final approach. It looks like they fixed the 'damaged' sensors I gave them in the reactor space. I'm seeing traffic that tells me they're trying to figure out why none of the transmitters are working. You've got maybe ten minutes before someone gets bright enough to poke around in places they'll find me in. They don't have time to actually fix what I've done completely, but figure another five or ten minutes after that for them to start shutting it all down. Catch them before they catch me, otherwise you'll be on your own until you can bring the grid back up. If you can bring the grid back up.

"By the way, the *Bounty* just tried to undock. I've put the clamps in a diagnostic loop. That should stall them for at least twenty minutes before someone realizes what's going on and can cut the power."

"Well, shit," Eric sighed.

"The only easy day was yesterday," Byron said.

"How's this change the plan?" Elizabeth asked.

"We'll split up," Hadrian said. "Eric, you and Byron secure Cerberus proper. There's only a dozen crew, mostly eggheads. Elizabeth and I will board the *Bounty* and head to the bridge. So six kills for each the two of you, and two dozen or so between me and Liz. Sorry, looks like we're going to win by points."

"Leave it to the operational detachments to steal all the glory," Byron snorted.

"Steal it?" Hadrian jibed. "Old man, you've been off the teams at least a decade now, if not two. I'm just looking out for you. I did give you some decent backup."

Eric felt Bryon's helmet shift by his feet.

"There is that. He's passable, I guess. Think we should keep him?" Byron asked.

"He's a better shooter than he is a scholar. We'd be doing academia a favor," Hadrian replied.

"Hey!" Eric protested.

"Alright, cut the chatter," Hadrian told them all. "Do whatever you do before all hell breaks loose. Five minutes to showtime."

Eric closed his eyes and focused on his breathing. Every heart beat pushed his chest against the chain sandwiched between it and the suit. *Leah.*

"However rigorous the task that awaits me," Elizabeth's whisper filtered over the radio. "May I fulfill my duty with courage. If death should overtake me, grant that I die in the state of grace. Forgive me all my sins, those I have forgotten and those I recall now: grant me the grace of perfect contrition."

"Amen," Byron whispered and the drone shook.

A grinding whine filled his ears and then ceased with a jolt. Eric fell against the straps holding him in the bay.

He activated the video link to the drone's external sensors as Hadrian announced, "Showtime."

The display flickered in the corner of his visor for several moments before showing a sizable open bay lined with smaller chambers, each containing a drone. The control arm that had guided the drone inside the bay detached as a man in a vac suit approached. The man's mouth moved. Eric started to frown.

Block lettering appeared at the bottom of the feed:

<Technician Phelps: "What do you mean it's damaged? There's not a scratch on her. I don't care what the CTA is telling you, it's wrong. Something's fucked up with the computer.">

A second man joined the technician as he walked to drone's port side. *Our side.*

Eric tapped Byron's helmet with his boot.

"On three," Byron said.

"One."

Eric shifted, drawing his sidearm.

"Two."

With his offhand, he grabbed the hooks, Turing's specially made hooks, securing the cargo netting to the loading clamps.

"Three."

Eric tugged the first hook free as Byron disengaged the magnetic clamps for the weapon's bay. Gravity pulled his torso down, freeing his arm for the rest of the draw. He fired three shots the moment his hand reached full extension, echoed by another pistol near his feet.

Two bodies dropped before him. Byron and Eric freed themselves from the rest of the webbing and dropped to the floor.

"Mountain home, fox one. We are in the henhouse and are oscar mike," Hadrian announced over the radio.

Eric swapped a fresh magazine into his pistol and holstered it. Bringing up his rifle, he made his way to the primary hangar access hatch. Byron came up behind him and swiped the fallen technician's badge by the reader. The light flashed green. The airlock cycled open and the team stepped in.

Ten seconds later, they passed into the secondary lock.

"They still haven't found me," Turing told them. "Just a heads up, starting the lightshow. Disregard any and all alarms you don't cause yourself. Oh, cutting their internal comms, too."

The inner hatch opened and immediately the lights died. Moments later, a series of yellow lights dropped from ceiling while a loudspeaker made a looped announcement, "Fire, fire, fire. Class delta fire in the drone bay. Fire, fire, fire."

"That'll get their attention," Eric muttered as the team bounced the length of the access passage in pairs. *Metal fires are no joke.*

"We'll take this access-way," Hadrian said, tugging open a small hatch near the end of the passage. "It'll put us a few frames short of the docking clamps and keep us out of sight."

"Good hunting," Byron told Hadrian as he climbed through the scuttle.

"You, too," Hadrian replied. Byron shut the scuttle behind Elizabeth.

"Company should be here any second," Byron said. He hefted his rifle and nodded toward the central elevator.

Eric took a knee as the elevator display lit up. The number

began counting down. At one, the doors dinged and opened. Between Eric and Byron, the pair dumped an entire magazine into the four surprised occupants.

"Fox One, Fox Three. Fifty papa. Oscar mike. Primary ETA thirty seconds," Byron called out as the pair stepped into the elevator.

"Fox Three, Fox One. Oscar mike. Docking bay ETA three minutes."

Byron punched the button labeled bridge. The backlighting on the button cycled red.

Eric's radio chirped and Turing said, "I've got that."

The backlight went green and the doors cycled closed.

"Huh," Byron said. His grin was audible. "Looks like putting up with him was worth it after all."

"I heard that," Turing said.

"Good," Byron said with a grin.

The elevator announced their arrival with a cheerful ding. The doors slid open to reveal an open layout filled with displays, workstations, four bridge crew in their emergency breathers, and three armored Protectorate marines. *Oh shit.*

The station's captain and one of the marine's looked over at the opening doors.

"Oh, sorry, wrong floor," Byron's suit speakers crackled. Byron opened fire while Eric dove behind the nearest workstation for cover.

Moments later Eric came up firing to give Byron time to find cover.

"These rifles aren't doing shit with that armor!"

"Of course they aren't. Focus on the bridge crew, the marines aren't armed."

Pivoting between the crew, Eric put lead on target. The three stunned marines slowly held their hands up.

"Now let's not get any funny ideas," Byron told them. "We've got you outnumbered two to three."

"What? We out number you and your guns are useless against us," the marine on the left said.

"Oh, look Eric, a marine that can do math. They must've upped their standards while we were exiled," Byron joked as he pulled a long knife from the belt sheath behind his back. "No, the guns won't hurt you, but this knife knows every seam in that armor. Surrender."

The marine on the right bolted towards them. Byron calmly sidestepped and helped the man fall to the floor. Eric had seen that move countless times during the last two years on Solitude. The knife sawing through the throat was a different ending than he was used to, however.

"Now we outnumber you two to two. Still confused?" Byron said.

Both marines shook their heads.

"Good, sit down over there. Eric, find something to restrain them with," Byron said.

"While you're at it," Turing broke in, "Look for a door near the elevator. Should be a networking closet. You should find zip ties in there. I need you to crosspatch a set of ports for me when you're done."

"Fox One, Fox Three. Bridge secure. Four crew and a target of opportunity down, two prisoners."

"Fox Three, Fox One," Hadrian replied and immediately broke protocol, "Two prisoners? Really?"

"They're Marines. In armor, Hadrian."

"Oh. Well shit, that complicates things. Anyway, we popped two of your targets at the dock, proceeding with a bit more caution onto the Bounty."

"So where's your overpowered flashlights?" Byron asked the prisoners while Eric punched the door key for the network closet.

The counting marine mumbled, "Cerberus wouldn't let us onto the station with them."

The closet's button flashed red while Byron snorted.

"Don't you guy's love protocol?" the old commando asked the marines. He glanced to the station captain's corpse and commented, "Bet you're regretting that one now, eh?"

"Can't help you with that," Turing told Eric. "It's not responding."

"I got a problem, Byron. Door's locked," Eric said.

"Open it, you've got Turing's pad, don't you?"

"Duh," Eric said and peeled back the flap on his forearm. The tablet instantly lit up.

<CONNECTING TO WIRELESS.>

<WIRELESS CONNECTION REFUSED – SELECTING INVASIVE TECHNIQUE.>

Eric frowned and tapped cancel. *No, I need you to open this door, not hack some wireless network. Dammit, I wish I had training on this thing.* Eric pulled his knife out and popped the panel off. He dug through the pad's various connectors until he found a set that matched the slots inside.

<DEVICE DETECTED ON /dev/UPB-C.>

<CONNECTING TO DEVICE USC502 via /dev/UPB-C.>

<PROTOCOL ERROR: TARGET DEVICE RESPONSE INVALID.>

Shit.

<FORCING HARD RESET.>

Eric jumped as a brilliant flash illuminated the mass of electronics and blue smoke puffed out. *Well, that's one way to do it, I guess.*

<BYPASS COMPLETE.>

The door slid open.

"I'm in," Eric announced to both Turing and Byron as he pulled his adapter from the smoking controller's jack. "Found some beefy zip-ties. What am I looking for while I'm in here, Turing?"

"There should be spare cable there somewhere. If they're following the standard wiring protocols, plug one end of the spare into the switch with all the green cables running to it and the other end into the switch with all the yellow cables."

"That's it?" Eric said as he grabbed a cable off a shelf.

"That's it."

"What's this do?" Eric asked as he plugged the cable in as requested.

"Violates the airgap between their normal networks and their security grid. Hold on, I have to bypass port security. Give me a few minutes to run my network scan once this is done. I'll have total access to the station shortly after if the other side is as secure as everything else. Maybe even the *Bounty* if they haven't cut their feeds yet. Oh, the joys of trust relationships."

Eric shook his head. *Eggheads.* He grabbed the zip-ties. *Wait, I'm an egghead.* He rolled his eyes and turned to go secure their prisoners.

A minute later Eric gave Byron a thumbs up.

"They're not going anywhere anytime soon."

"Huh, you know, I might know some people back home who'd pay pretty well for that kinda thing," Byron said before cutting over to the radio. "Fox One, Fox Three. Prisoners secured, we're heading your direction."

"Fox Three, Fox Four, we're kinda busy." The unmistakable pulse of a Protectorate energy rifle in the background sent chills down Eric's spine. "Our rifles aren't slowing them down. They're trying to take us prisoner, I think, but their stun setting isn't getting past the insulation in these suits. They're herding us."

"Fox Three, Fox One," Hadrian followed up a few moments later. "What Liz said. We got the drop on a few crew though. Maybe a dozen. Can't do shit about these guys though."

"Sit tight, boys," Byron told the two marines calmly and waved at Eric. "Someone will be by to pick you up. Be nice, okay? Fox One, Fox Three. We're oscar mike."

The pair stepped into the elevator and Byron punched the button for the docking bay.

"Turing, you mind doing some computer magic and making sure those guys stay out of trouble?" Byron asked as the elevator started to move.

"No problem, already done."

"You into the security system yet?" Eric asked.

"Not entirely. Someone actually changed passwords on a few systems. Accident, probably. Won't take long. Feeds are still live to the *Bounty* though. What do you need?"

"Do you have some sort of video of what's going on there? A map?" Byron asked.

"No, sorry. That's one of the systems I'm breaching still. Based off the alarms I'm seeing in their life support grid, I'd say they're on the third deck heading forward though. Ozone spikes."

The elevator dinged and the pair emerged into the docking area to strobing white emergency lighting and the speakers looping, "Danger. Radiation spike in the vicinity of clamp A. Ten Sieverts and climbing. Danger."

Eric stumbled to a halt, remembering fried crewmen from an accident on the *Fortune*.

"It's one of Turing's alarms," Byron called out as he trotted onward.

Eric raced to catch up, joining Byron as they reached the umbilical to the *Bounty*.

"Fox One, Fox Three, we are crossing onto the quarterdeck now."

No response.

Shit.

Byron came up short on the far side and pointed at a doorway off to the side. "Eric, work that black magic on this door. Now."

Eric used the butt of his rifle to smash the casing open. He fumbled for the correct adapter.

<DEVICE DETECTED ON /dev/UPB-C.>

<CONNECTING TO DEVICE USC552 via /dev/UPB-C.>

<HANDSHAKE COMPLETE.>

The door jerked on its pressure hinges and hissed open.

<BYPASS COMPLETE.>

Eric's eyes grew wide and he glanced to the nameplate above the door. *Secondary Armory.* Byron tossed his rifle to the floor.

"Regular or extra crispy?" the man asked as he pulled an energy rifle from the rack.

"Extra crispy."

"Oh, good, I love plasma weapons," Byron chuckled. "Just don't point this at me or a thin external bulkhead."

"Oh," Eric replied, taking the hefty device. It vaguely resembled one of Julien's heavy machineguns in size and mass. Byron smashed the lock off a set of restraints for a shelf full of heavy boxlike devices and then shoved one of those boxes in the weapon's side.

The power pack clicked and the weapon came to life with a cheerful hum.

"Which, by the way, is all of them by that thing's standards, so be a bit careful. Fox One, Fox Three. We've got flashlights. Oscar mike."

No response.

"Guys, I'm in," Turing broke in. "Hadrian and Commander Grace are on deck four now just aft of the bridge and, and hurry. Just hurry. I'll slow down their pursuers."

All the lighting died, replaced by flickering emergency lighting.

"All hands prepare to abandon ship!" the automated system announced. "Thermal anomaly detected in fusion core two. Destabilization event imminent. All hands prepare to abandon ship!"

"The slider by your trigger finger determines the power setting. I'd suggest the lowest setting or a bit above," Byron said while they jogged down the passage way and hopped over bullet riddled corpses. "Just remember, higher the setting, longer the charge time between shots and the shorter the lifespan of that pack. Anything higher than twenty-five percent is considered anti-vehicle."

"Got it," Eric said.

The pair ducked into a stairwell and started up. As they approached the hatch to the fourth deck it opened. A marine stumbled through it, groping at the knife protruding from his throat. Behind him the darkness strobed with brilliant light as several energy rifles discharged rapidly.

Shit.

Out of breath, Eric hefted the massive weapon and followed Byron into the scene beyond. Several marines lay with their limbs at odd angles in pools of blood. Two were attempting to regain their feet. Quick shots from Byron to the sides of their helmets sent them back to the floor minus a fair amount of skull.

Eric spotted a marine wrestling someone up off the floor. He leveled his weapon, thumbed the power up and pulled the trigger. The muzzle glowed angry violet scant moments before the device belched forth a blinding amethyst bolt which traveled the short distance to the target in the blink of an eye. The bolt seared a fist sized hole through the marine's helmet and, having met no serious resistance, a non-trivial portion of the bolt bathed the hall in its brief, baleful glow as it sailed onward. The bolt disappeared through the far wall with a flash leaving behind a cloud of vaporized metal. Smoke and steaming fluids spat from both sides of the marine's helmet as the corpse toppled to the floor. *Holy shit!*

Eric's eyes bulged and he glanced down. *45%. Oops.*

"Uh, guys? What was that?" Turing asked. "Oh, never mind. Plasma discharge. Whoever just shot that might want to tone it down. You just set fire to the next three compartments. Nothing major, mind you, but let's not wreck the ship just yet?"

Eric scanned for targets while Byron put the last two marines down. He paused by the last corpse and swapped his plasma cannon for an energy rifle.

"I think this might be a bit safer for everyone concerned," he said with a guilty smile.

Byron cracked a smile before keying his radio.

"Fox One, Fox Three. How copy, over? Fox One, do you read?"

No response.

Elizabeth shoved the dead marine with the hole punched through his head off her. Smoke drifted off the top of her helmet as she staggered to her feet. Blackened flakes fell from her helmet as she pulled it off.

"Those fucking assholes," she raged.

"What happened?" Byron asked her.

"They herded us into a dead end corner a few frames back. Radio went out. Hadrian rushed them, told me to run the other direction. I don't know where he went. I heard shooting and then someone grabbed me. I just starting stabbing people."

Eric slowly turned back towards the dead marine in the stairwell. He followed the path of blood back in the direction Elizabeth had come from. Half buried under a pile of dead marines, Eric spotted Hadrian's boots.

"Byron, over here!"

The pair dug through the pile to find Hadrian still clutching a broken knife in his hand. His suit had been burnt through in a half dozen places and his visor cracked.

"Did we make it?" Hadrian asked through clenched teeth as Eric pried off his helmet. "We can still get off this rock?"

Eric nodded earnestly.

"Good," the man replied and laid his head back on the deck.

Eric looked up to Byron. Byron shook his head slowly.

Hadrian convulsed on the floor, wracked with a sudden coughing fit.

"It was worth it," Hadrian sighed. He stared vacantly at the ceiling for a moment and then muttered, "I'll tell Leah you made it, kid."

Byron knelt over the stricken commando and whispered, "Rest now, son of Caledon."

Hadrian coughed and shivered violently.

With his last breath he sighed, "Duty calls."

Eric stepped back as Byron closed Hadrian's eyes and turned to find a grim-faced Elizabeth with an energy rifle in her hands.

"Turing?" she asked. "How many left?"

"You got everyone on Cerberus other than those two prisoners. I'm seeing only four left on the *Bounty*. All of them on the bridge. They were trying to initiate the self-destruct sequence, but I've null routed all the consoles up there, so they're not getting anywhere with that. I'm fairly certain there's a manual override somewhere though."

They'd made it a handful of meters down the passageway when Turing came over the radio again.

"Yeah, they're going for the manual. Two people running for engineering. They've got sidearms. On the plus side, they're all crew, not marines."

"Eric," Byron said. "Secure the bridge. Elizabeth and I will handle the guys going for Engineering. Turing, give me the fastest path to Engineering from here."

Eric didn't hear the reply, he knew where he was going from Hadrian's briefing and was already racing up the nearby ladderwell two steps at a time. He came to the armored bridge bulkhead a short time later and found the hatch sealed.

"Turing?"

"It's logically isolated. You'll have to override it on-site. Though, how exactly I'm not sure. Those hatches are supposed to be impregnable by anything man portable and not accessible from the outside. Something about mutinies and boarding actions."

Eric looked for an access panel or a controller of some sort. *Where the hell is it?* He leaned against the wall by the doorway, panting.

The tablet on his arm flickered to life.

<DEVICE DETECTED ON /dev/NFC1.>

<CONNECTING TO DEVICE USC602 via /dev/NFC1.>

<HANDSHAKE COMPLETE.>

The solid metal plate hummed and slid to the side. *No shit?*

<BYPASS COMPLETE.>

The two very startled naval officers behind the hatch attempted to draw their weapons. Both were dead long before their sidearms posed a threat.

"Fox Three, Fox Two, over," Eric said as he walked onto the bridge.

"Go ahead, Fox Two."

Eric dropped into the captain's chair. He propped his feet up on the console and smiled bitterly.

"Bridge secured."

"Congratulations, Captain. We just got the last of the runners. I'm sending Elizabeth down to the launch bay now. Turing, you heard?"

"Yeah, I heard. We've got most everyone here ready. The spider teams won't be back in time, but I figure the second shuttle can pick them up, provided we can jam enough people on the first."

"Well, if it's alright with everyone else, I think I'm going to decompress for a bit. I don't think there's anything else useful for me to do. I have no idea what most of these consoles do or how they do it. That and, as Turing said, they're null routed," Eric sighed as he stared into the starry void on the main display.

"Understood," Byron said.

"I'll fix that, but I'll let you know if we need anything," Turing said.

Eric set his radio to external speakers and twisted off his helmet. He let it drop to the floor next to his feet and sat listening to the white noise from the fans running in the various computers. *I'm free. Well, most likely free.*

"Fuck," he whispered to himself to break the silence. Suddenly tired, Eric yawned. He leaned forward, and tapped the captain's screen. The screen flickered and came on. *Connection restored? Now this is interesting. Hmm.* He started typing.

"Eric?" Turing asked over the radio a short time later. "What are you doing?"

"Uh, nothing much? Captain left himself logged in," Eric replied, hoping he kept the guilty mirth from his voice. "Why?'

"Well, the first shuttle is five minutes out and they're telling me they see drones leaving the station."

"And?"

"There's evidently quite a few of them."

"They must be seeing things?"

Turing snorted. "I checked the CTA. CPU usage on the medusa array is nearly pegged and the only active login is from a terminal on the *Bounty's* bridge."

"Oh, well, maybe they're not seeing things?"

"Eric." Turing didn't sound pleased.

"Well, I got to thinking, Turing. You only had those dozen or so hooks and nets made, right? Well, without more of those, loading the weapons bays with stuff is going to be less efficient. I figured I'd send more empty bays down."

"And I suppose the reports I'm getting from Spider 3 of explosions on the far side of the mountain are mere coincidence?"

"Sure, sure. Mere coincidence. A happy one, but coincidence."

"Right, right. So, if you did program the drones to bomb Gliar's men, and I'm not saying you did, but if you decided to do so," Turing paused. "What instructions might you have been tempted to use?"

"Well, if I were so inclined, and I'm not saying I was, I may or may not have instructed the AI to select for every identifiable human visual and IR signature on the western side of the mountain and upped their targeting priority and tasking from surveil to priority hostile. I might've considered bumping priorities for humans already in its ID catalog, specifically the legionnaires."

"Well, since you didn't do that, I'd suggest doing that. Would save me the time, I'm supervising the next load."

"Oh, and I may or may not have asked it to task a drone for Gliar himself and that package, in all its eight thousand kilos of glory, may or may not be getting delivered as we speak."

"Eight thousand kilos?" Byron broke in. "That's--"

"Just enough for a man of his stature?" Eric asked.

Byron snorted. "Well, intel did say he got a bit on the heavy side, so I suppose."

"You know, they do have drone portable physics packages up here,"

"No," Turing cut in and the humor evaporated. "We will not be atomizing a single square millimeter of my planet. Not even for Gliar. It may take decades, but I will be coming back."

"Oh, well, okay. I've got a few ideas, but I'll just queue them up as awaiting confirmation so you can review them when you get here, Turing."

"Sleeping? Really?" Turing asked as he walked onto the bridge.

Eric sat up and groused, "What? First rule of the infantry: sleep where you can when you can."

Behind Turing, Byron nodded and said, "You can't say I never taught him anything, Turing."

One of the bridge speakers cracked, "Turing, Trevor here."

Turing walked over to the speaker and pulled down a hand set.

"What is it Trevor?" Turing asked.

"Engineering's spun up already. Reactor is nominal. Life support terminal here reports all systems green except three log entries about a fire suppression system being used?"

"Good, don't worry about the log entries. We'll be spooling up here in a few minutes. Keep an eye on things," Turing replied.

"Will do."

"Make yourself useful and go to the navigation console," Turing said as he tossed a large binder into Eric's lap.

Eric shrugged, walked over to sit in the navigator's chair, and gave Turing a questioning look.

"Power cycle the box. While it's booting hold down the control, alt, and escape keys."

"Okay?" Eric said while he did as told.

"Ships in the Protectorate are tightly controlled. While this is a fleet vessel, it's run by contractors so it's treated like a civilian ship. Civilian routes are preprogrammed and the system won't let you get around that without hefty authorization. We don't have time nor the equipment to crack the authentication routines so you're booting the system into its debug mode. No security checks at all. No corrections or sanity checks either."

"Oh, well, that's different," Eric said several seconds later as he clicked on things. "Uh, Turing? There's no routes for me to select."

"Of course not, that's what the binder's for."

Eric opened the binder to find page upon page of handwritten notes. Notes written in his own handwriting.

"You've got to be shitting me," Eric snorted.

"Better hope you were right," Turing said with a smile. "Based off our fuel levels, I'd say Celion is our best bet. Unless something's happened, I have contacts there. Input navigational route C-3."

Eric flipped through his stellar navigation homework. He chewed on his lip while he figured out which sections from his notes fit in what input boxes while Turing looked on.

"That looks about right," Turing said. "Byron, have you found our friends yet?"

Byron's head popped up over the row of monitors on the other side.

"If I'm reading this right, we've got less than a half hour left in our departure window. The spinward destroyer is going for a gravity assist off the sun. The other is burning fuel like a madman. They'll be first to fire."

"Good," Turing told him and pulled down another handset. "Commander Grace, status?"

The radio crackled, "Just set the last shuttle down. She's spinning down, so I'll be up front in about five."

"This all looks like it's been put in correct," Elizabeth said. "And it looks like out of the options we've got available for fuel, you picked the only one with a transfer window that doesn't keep us here too long. Impressive, Turing. I'm starting the EM drives now. We'll start burning mass in six minutes."

"I'm going to go rack out," Eric said from the hatchway. "I'm taking the captain's cabin if no one objects."

"Oh, Eric, I'm sorry, I've been so busy I forgot. I made sure we got all your personal stuff on the last trip. Muffin was scared senseless the whole way up. I think Anne has her in a crate."

Eric smiled. "That means a lot to me. That furball is one of the few reasons I haven't done anything terminally stupid not in this room. Thanks, Liz."

"Sleep well," Liz told him and turned back to her console. Byron and Turing waved.

"This just isn't right," Eric sighed as he shucked off various piece of his suit. He laid back on the bed and Muffin jumped onto his chest, purring. He sighed again, trying to forget the sorrow eating at his heart by petting the insistent cat. *I should have just come straight here and gone to sleep. I didn't need to waste a half hour on the way back the observation deck watching us leave.*

Fuck it.

Muffin hopped off his chest as Eric rolled over and dug out his tablet. He powered it on and pulled up his image gallery while the cat curled up on one of his pillows.

A large photo splashed across the screen. *Your first deer, hon. You were so proud.* Next. *You were so happy at our wedding. There's Turing in the background. That sneaky bastard.* Next. *See, I told you that wedding dress looked better on the floor. You never thought you were pretty, hon. I never figured out why.* Next. *You always looked funny in full battle rattle. Helmet too big and a vest that didn't quite work with your boobs.* Next. *Hadrian didn't appreciate that joke as much as we did. I hope you have better luck explaining it to him than I did.*

One of the videos he'd dug out of Captain Morneault's old files popped up and started playing. *Oh, no, I'm not going to watch this.* Try as he might, he couldn't muster the strength to pause the video. *You loved the version with the violin. You said it was our song.*

Tears dropped onto the screen.

God dammit.

"Couldn't sleep?" Elizabeth asked from the navigator's station as Eric stumbled onto the bridge.

"No," he grumbled.

"As of an hour ago," Turing announced, "Unless the *Maelstrom* gets a lucky shot in, they can't stop us from reaching the gravity horizon. Commander Grace's course variance makes that terribly unlikely. We might not be home free until we're out of Protectorate space, but we're a damn sight closer, Eric."

Eric gave Turing a weak smile as he slumped into the vacant captain's chair.

"We were talking about what we plan to do once we make it to Accorded space," Turing said.

"Accorded space?" Eric scoffed. "Hope your plans started at getting black bagged and ended at execution."

Turing stared at him.

"Admittedly, Commander Grace did have an issue like that, I don't see what other option we have."

"Easy, get Blaise up here. He should know enough of the charts to get us to one of the *Fortune*'s old haunts, provided we have the fuel. We sell off every last thing on this boat when we get there, maybe sell the boat, too. You can buy anything for the right price in the Reach. Passage to Confed space is cheap if you ask the right captain. Shavely's has my money, too." Eric paused a moment and then noticed the looks being directed at him. "Eh, sorry, I'm being an asshole. What was everyone else planning, long-term?"

"Well, I have to return to Pershing or get in touch with our military at the very least. They'll want to debrief me. Beyond that, I haven't the slightest idea. Honestly, if I could afford it, I'd take the military pension they'll owe me for this shit and go retire someplace quiet," Elizabeth said. "I've had enough."

Byron nodded as he said, "Caledon would find what we've learned terribly interesting as well. They'd want to know what happened to Hadrian and his unit. I don't know what they'll want with me after that, but I'm too old for this kind of shit."

Eric looked at Turing and asked, "You? I seem to remember something about paying back family debts."

Turing's teeth glinted as he smiled.

"I've been considering my options. I'm still not sure which direction I'll go. Too many unknowns as of yet and that won't change until we make Celion and I get network access. Overall, you're right. I always pay my debts. What about you, Eric?"

"Honestly, I haven't the slightest idea. Who would hire an unexperienced crewman, a former pirate with a raft of unrecognized degrees and no recognizable job experience? Everything I ever wanted to keep we just left behind and I don't have anywhere to go."

Eric looked away from Elizabeth's soft eyes.

"Well, that does sound bleak," Turing said. "But what if I knew someone who'd take you on?"

"Who?" Eric asked.

"Me. You did well as my factor and you do seem to have a certain set of skills that I'll likely find very useful in the near future. There's one snag."

"Which is?"

"I'm bloody sick of being in charge of everything. I'd be lying if I said I wasn't tempted to take what I have and go slink off somewhere quiet. Inconveniently, I can't do that. So, say you and I collaborate?"

"I'm a bit fond of conspiracy," Eric said with a grin.

"Ah, yes, conspiracy. So, tell me Eric, if you had a sizeable sum of money, what would you have our conspiracy do with it?"

Eric leaned back in the captain's chair and took in the view of the bridge while he thought.

After some consideration he said, "It seems your former associates have an excess amount of credits in their accounts. I say we rectify that. If some of those happen to find their way into our pockets, so much the better. Without more detail to work on, I'd say our main strengths seem to be piracy and business, so why not do both? But respectably?"

"Respectably? How does one do piracy respectably?" Turing asked.

Eric flashed a grin as he told him, "By using a different word, Turing. I vaguely remember reading that the systems of the Confederacy still issue letters of marque. We won't be pirates, we'll be privateers. We'll still be breaking people's shit and setting it on fire, but with a letter of marque, someone will pay us to do what we were going to do anyway."

Turing slowly clapped. "Brilliant."

Eric glanced at Byron and Elizabeth.

"Provided I can," Elizabeth said with an unknowing shrug.

"Assume you can," Eric said.

"In that case, why the hell not? Would be nice to be on the giving end for once."

"Byron? Same assumption."

"Privateers are still bad guys," Byron said in a noncommittal tone. Eric caught the twinkle in the man's eyes.

"Well, yes," Eric said. "They'd be awfully useless if they weren't. Think bad guys for a good cause."

"Oh. Put that way, how can I say no? I've spent my whole life being a bad guy for a good cause. This is something I'm good at. Sounds like it pays better, too."

"I can't promise it will, Byron. It might just earn us all an early grave for all I know. Well, early for some of us anyway. Speaking of which, we need to have some sort of service for Hadrian. It wouldn't be right to just keep going like nothing's changed after what he did for us."

Everyone nodded solemnly.

"What do you intend to do with the body?" Byron asked. "Spacer's funeral?"

"Leave him here? Fuck that. I'm not leaving one of my best friends in orbit around a Protectorate sun if I can help it. No, we'll put him in cold storage. If I have any say in the matter, he's going back home to Caledon."

Byron nodded appreciatively.

"So we're all in?" Eric asked as he looked each of his friends, his new crew in the eyes. They nodded in return.

Eric leaned back in his chair and propped his feet up.

"Then let's be bad guys."

About the Author

Jason currently resides in a non-descript Midwestern town where he is working toward an applied math/physics dual major. As a former member of the armed forces, he is fluent in multiple languages including sarcasm, profanity, and, thanks to the US Navy, acronyms. Along with his wife, he is owned by two cats who declined interview. When not writing or toying with powers reserved for the Elder Gods, he enjoys a wide variety of gaming, both in pen/pencil format and electronic. He may also be infrequently found punching holes in paper via applied ballistics depending on the market price of ammunition, which is, like the rent, always too damn high.

Made in the USA
Columbia, SC
01 May 2019